BIRTH
OF THE
KINGDOM

THE CRUSADES TRILOGY

The Road to Jerusalem
The Templar Knight
Birth of the Kingdom

BIRTH OF THE KINGDOM

BOOK THREE OF THE
Crusades Trilogy

JAN GUILLOU

TRANSLATED FROM THE SWEDISH
BY STEVEN T. MURRAY

HARPER

An Imprint of HarperCollins*Publishers*
www.harpercollins.com

HarperCollins books may be purchased for educational, business, or sales promotional use. For information, please write: Special Markets Department, HarperCollins Publishers, 10 East 53rd Street, New York, NY 10022.

FIRST EDITION

Library of Congress Cataloging-in-Publication Data has been applied for.

ISBN: 978-0-06-168863-8 (Hardcover)
ISBN: 978-0-06-208279-4 (International Edition)

11 12 13 14 15 DIX/RRD 10 9 8 7 6 5 4 3 2 1

We who are strong are obliged to help the weak
with their burdens, and should not think of ourselves.
Each of us must think of his neighbor,
of what is good and edifying.

Romans 15:1–2

Principal Characters

THE FOLKUNG CLAN

Magnus Folkesson, Arn's father

Erika Joarsdotter, his wife and Arn's stepmother

Sir Arn Magnusson

Cecilia Algotsdotter (Cecilia Rosa), betrothed and then wife of Arn

Magnus Månesköld, Arn and Cecilia's son

Ingrid Ylva, his wife

Birger Magnusson, their son, Arn's grandson, who becomes Birger jarl, King of Sverige, the new Sweden

Alde Arnsdotter, Arn and Cecilia's daughter

Eskil Magnusson, Arn's brother

Torgils, Eskil's son

Birger Brosa, Arn's uncle

Sune Folkesson

THE ERIK CLAN

Knut Eriksson, King of the Swedes and the Goths

Cecilia Blanca, his wife and close friend of Cecilia Rosa

Erik jarl, their son, later King Erik

Sverre, King of Norway

Harald Øysteinsson, leader of the Norwegian forces

THE SVERKER CLAN

King Sverker Karlsson

Helena Sverkersdotter, his daughter, who marries Sune Folkesson

Archbishop Petrus

Archbishop Absalon

Archbishop Valerius

Father Guillaume

Brother Guilbert

Brother Joseph d'Anjou

BIRTH
OF THE
KINGDOM

Chapter 1

In the year of Grace 1192 just before the mass of Saint Eskil, when the nights turned white and the work of sowing the turnips would soon begin, a mighty storm came over Western Götaland. The storm lasted for three days and three nights, and it transformed the bright, promising season into autumn.

On the third night after the midnight mass, most of the monks at Varnhem cloister were still sleeping soundly, convinced that their prayers were resisting the powers of darkness and that the storm would soon die down. It was then that Brother Pietro out in the receptorium at first thought that he'd been wakened from his sleep by something in his imagination. He awoke and sat up in bed without knowing what he had heard. Outside the walls and the heavy oak door of the receptorium was only the howling of the storm and the lashing of the rain on the roof tiles and the leafy crowns of the tall ash trees.

Then he heard it again. It sounded like an iron fist pounding on the door.

In terror he tumbled out of bed, grabbed his rosary, and started muttering a prayer that he didn't quite remember but that was supposed to ward off evil spirits. Then he went out to the vaulted entry and listened in the dark. Three heavy blows came again, and Brother Pietro could do nothing but shout through the oaken door for the stranger to make himself known. He shouted in Latin, because that language had the most power against the dark forces and because he was too groggy to say anything in the oddly singing vernacular that was spoken outside those walls.

"Who comes this night to the Lord's steps?" he called, with his mouth close to the door's lock.

"A servant of the Lord with pure intentions and a worthy mission," replied the stranger in perfect Latin.

This calmed Brother Pietro's fears, and he struggled with the heavy door handle of black cast-iron before he managed to open the door a crack.

Outside stood a stranger in an ankle-length leather cape with a hood to protect him from the rain. He shoved open the door at once with a strength that Brother Pietro could never have resisted and entered the shelter of the entryway as he pushed the monk before him.

"God's peace, a very long journey is now at an end. But let's not talk in the dark. Fetch your lamp from the receptorium, my unknown brother," said the stranger.

Brother Pietro did as he was told, already reassured by the fact that the stranger spoke the language of the church and knew that there was a lamp in the receptorium. The monk fumbled for a moment with the last embers in the heating pan before he managed to light a wick and insert it into an oil lamp. When he returned to the vaulted entry outside the receptorium, both he and the stranger became bathed in the light reflecting off the white-washed walls. The stranger swept off his leather cape and shook the rain from it. Brother Pietro involuntarily caught his breath when he saw the white surcoat with the red cross. From his time in Rome he knew quite well what that meant. A Templar knight had come to Varnhem.

"My name is Arn de Gothia and you have nothing to fear from me, brother, for I was raised here in Varnhem, and from here I once rode forth to the Holy Land. But I don't know you; what is your name, brother?"

"I am Brother Pietro de Siena, and I have been here only two years."

"So you're new here. That's why you have to guard the door when no one else wishes to do so. But tell me first, is Father Henri still alive?"

"No, he died four years ago."

"Let us pray for his eternal bliss," said the Templar knight, crossing himself and bowing his head for a moment.

"Is Brother Guilbert alive?" the knight asked when he looked up.

"Yes, brother, he's an old man but he still has much vigor."

"That doesn't surprise me. What is our new abbot called?"

"His name is Father Guillaume de Bourges, and he came to us three years ago."

"Almost two hours remain before matins, but would you please wake him and say that Arn de Gothia has come to Varnhem?" said the knight, with what looked almost like a jocular gleam in his eyes.

"I'd rather not, brother. Father Guillaume maintains that sleep is a gift from God which we are duty-bound to administer well," replied Brother Pietro uneasily, squirming with displeasure at the thought of waking Father Guillaume for a matter that might not be of sufficient urgency.

"I understand. Go instead and wake Brother Guilbert and tell him that his apprentice Arn de Gothia is waiting in the receptorium," the knight said kindly, although it was still an order.

"Brother Guilbert might also be cross . . . I cannot leave my post in the receptorium in the middle of this evil night," said Brother Pietro, attempting to wriggle out of obeying the command.

"Ah!" said the knight with a laugh. "First of all, you may confidently leave the watch to a Templar knight of the Lord; you could have no stronger replacement. Second, I swear that you will be waking that old bear Guilbert with good news. So, go now. I'll wait here and assume your watch as best I can, I promise you."

The Templar knight had stated his command in a way that could not be refuted. Brother Pietro nodded and scurried down the arcade toward the little courtyard that was the last open space before entering the monastery proper through another oaken door.

It was not long before the door from the monastery to the receptorium courtyard was thrown open with a bang and a familiar voice echoed down the white arcade. Brother Guilbert came striding down the hallway, holding a tar torch in his hand. He did not seem as huge as before; no longer a giant. When he spied the stranger by the door, he raised his torch to see better. Then he handed the torch to Brother Pietro and went over to embrace the stranger. Neither of them uttered a word for a long time.

"I thought you had fallen at the battle of Tiberias, my dear Arn," Brother Guilbert finally said in Frankish. "Father Henri thought so too, and we've said many unnecessary prayers for your soul."

"Those prayers were not unnecessary, seeing as I can now thank you for them in *this* life, brother," Arn de Gothia said.

Then neither of them seemed able to say anything more, and they both had to wrestle for control so as not to express unseemly emotions. It occurred to Brother Pietro that the two men must have been very close.

"Have you come to pray at the grave of your mother, Fru Sigrid?" Brother Guilbert asked at last, in a tone he would use with an ordinary traveler.

"Yes, of course I want to do that," replied the knight in the same tone of voice. "But I also have a great many other things to do here at home in Varnhem, and I must first ask your help with a number of small matters that are best done before taking on the larger tasks."

"You know that I'll help you with anything. Just say the word and we'll get started."

"I have twenty men and ten wagons out there in the rain. Many of the men are of an ilk that cannot so easily set foot within these walls. I also have ten heavily loaded wagons, and the first three of them would be best brought into the courtyard." The knight spoke rapidly, as if he were talking of commonplace things, although the wagons must be very important if they had to be protected within the cloister walls.

Without a word Brother Guilbert grabbed the torch from the younger monk's hand and stepped into the rain outside the door of the receptorium. There was indeed a line of ten muddy wagons out there, and they must have had a difficult journey. Hunched over the reins of the oxen sat surly men who did not look to have the heart for any more traveling.

Brother Guilbert laughed when he saw them, shaking his head with a smile. Then he called to Brother Pietro and began barking orders as though he himself were a Templar knight and not a Cistercian monk.

It took less than an hour to arrange accommodations for the visitors. One of the many rules at Varnhem said that anyone who came traveling by night should be accorded the same hospitality as the Lord Himself. It was a rule that Brother Guilbert kept repeating to himself, first half in jest but with ever greater amusement when he heard from the Templar knight that perhaps smoked hams were not the best sort of delicacy to serve the men in welcome. The joke about the unsuitability of smoked hams, however, went straight over Brother Pietro's head.

But Varnhem's entire hospitium outside the walls was empty and dark, since few travelers had arrived during the storms of the past few days. Soon the guests were both housed and fed.

Then Brother Guilbert and Arn de Gothia pulled open the heavy gates to the cloister so that the three wagons that required protection could be driven into the courtyard next to the workshops. There the oxen were unharnessed and settled in stalls for the night.

When the work was done the rain began to taper off, and bright light was clearly visible coming through rents in the black clouds. The weather was about to change. It was still about an hour until matins.

Brother Guilbert led his guest to the church and unlocked the door. They entered without a word.

In silence Arn stopped at the baptismal font just inside the doors. He removed his wide leather cloak and placed it on the floor, then pointed with an inquiring look at the water in the font, which had no cover. He received an affirmative nod from the old monk. Arn drew his sword, dipped his fingers in the water of the font, and stroked three fingers over the flat of his sword before he slipped it back into its sheath. With more of the holy water he touched his brow, both shoulders, and his heart. Then they walked side by side up the aisle toward the altar to the spot that Brother Guilbert indicated. There they knelt and prayed in silence until they heard the monks filing in for matins. Neither of them spoke. Arn knew the monastery's rules about the silent hours of the day as well as any monk.

By the time they began gathering for song, the storm had abated and the chirping of birds could be heard in the first light of dawn.

Father Guillaume de Bourges was first in the procession of

monks coming down the side aisle. The two men who had been praying stood up and bowed silently. He bowed in return. But then he caught sight of the knight's sword and raised his eyebrows. Brother Guilbert pointed to Arn's red cross signifying a Templar knight, and then at the font by the church door. Father Guillaume nodded, looking reassured and smiling that he had understood.

When the singing began, Brother Guilbert explained to his traveling friend in the monastery's secret sign language that the new abbot was strict about the rule of silence.

During the hymn, in which Arn de Gothia took part with all the rest, since he was familiar with the Psalms, he glanced from one monk to the other. Now the light was streaming into the sanctuary more brightly, and they could make out one another's faces. A third of the brothers recognized the knight and cautiously acknowledged his nods of greeting. But most were unknown to him.

When the hymn was over and the monks began their procession back to the monastery, Father Guillaume came over and signed to Brother Guilbert that he wanted to speak with both of them in the parlatorium after breakfast. They bowed in acknowledgment.

Arn and Brother Guilbert left the church through the main door, still in silence, walked past the courtyard with the workshops, and went down to the horse stables. The morning sun was already crimson and bright, and the song of birds could be heard in every direction. At least they would have one more lovely summer day.

When they reached the horses they headed straight for the stable area where the stallions were kept. The Templar knight took hold of the top rail of the fence with both hands and vaulted over it easily. He signed with exaggerated politeness for Brother Guilbert to do the same. But the latter shook his head with a smile and slowly climbed over the way people usually did. At the other end of the stable ten stallions were standing together, as if they had not yet decided what to think about the man in white.

"So, my dear Arn," said Brother Guilbert, abruptly breaking the rule of silence that was supposed to last until after breakfast, "have you finally learned the language of the horses?"

Arn gave him a long, searching look before he nodded with a meaningful expression. Then he whistled to get the attention of the stallions at the other end. He called to them softly, in the language of horses.

"In the name of Allah the Merciful, the Compassionate, you who are the sons of the wind, come to your brother and protector!"

The horses were instantly alert, with their ears standing straight up. Then a powerful dappled gray began to approach, and soon the others followed. When the first gray raised his tail and broke into a trot, they all moved faster and then came galloping so fast that the ground shook.

"By the Prophet, peace be unto him, you have indeed learned the language of horses down there in Outremer," Brother Guilbert whispered in Arabic.

"Quite true," replied Arn in the same language, opening his white coat wide to stop the onrushing stallions, "and you seem still to recall the language that I once thought was the language of horses and not that of the unbelievers."

They each mounted a stallion, although Brother Guilbert had to lead his to the fence to get enough support to climb onto the steed's back. Then they rode around in the corral bareback with only their left hands lightly gripping the horses' manes.

Arn asked whether things were still so wretched that the West Goths continued to be the last men in the world who failed to understand the value of these horses. Brother Guilbert confirmed this with a sigh. In most other places in the Cistercian world, horses were their best business. But not up here in the North. The art of mounted warfare had not yet reached these parts. So these particular horses were worth not more but less than native West Gothic horses.

Arn was astonished, and he asked whether his kinsmen still believed that one could not use cavalry in war. With a sigh Brother Guilbert said that this was true. Nordic men rode to their battles, dismounted from their horses and secured their reins. Then they rushed at one another, hacking and slashing, on the closest field.

But now Brother Guilbert could no longer hold back all the questions he had been wanting to ask since the first moment he saw this man, whom he believed to be a prodigal son standing in the receptorium, dripping with rain and muddy from his long journey. Arn began recounting his lengthy story.

✠

The young, innocent Arn Magnusson, who once set out from Varnhem to serve in the Holy War until death or until twenty years had passed, which was usually the same thing, no longer existed. It was no untainted knight Perceval who had come back from the war.

Brother Guilbert understood this almost at once when the conversation with Father Guillaume commenced out in the cloister. It had turned into a radiantly beautiful morning with not a cloud in the sky and no wind, so Father Guillaume had taken his unusual guest and Brother Guilbert out to the conversation area by the stone benches in the cloister garden instead of summoning them to the parlatorium. There they now sat with their feet practically on top of Father Henri's grave, because he and his broken seal had been laid to rest right here, just as he had instructed on his deathbed. They had begun their meeting by praying for Father Henri's eternal bliss.

Brother Guilbert watched carefully as Arn began presenting his business to Father Guillaume. The latter listened attentively and kindly, and as usual with a rather patronizing expression, as if in the presence of someone who knew less than he did. Father Guillaume was a talented theologian, that was indisputable, but he was not very good at seeing through a Templar knight, thought Brother Guilbert as he soon realized what Arn was getting at.

There were obvious indications on Arn's face that he had not been one of those monks who served the Lord by copying manuscripts or keeping accounts. He must have spent the greater part of his time in the Holy Land in the saddle with sword and lance. Only now did Brother Guilbert notice the black border at the bottom of Arn's mantle that showed he held the rank of a fortress master in the Knights Templar and thus was in command of both war and trade. Arn would probably be able to convince the younger and less experienced Father Guillaume to go along with whatever he wished, without the latter realizing what he was doing.

As his first response to the question of why he had returned to Varnhem, Arn had said that he had come to deliver a donation of no less than ten marks in gold. Varnhem, after all, had been the place where the brothers had raised him, with the help of God, and ten marks in gold was truly no small sum to express his gratitude. In addition, he wanted his future resting place to be next to his mother, inside the church under the center aisle.

Confronted with such good and Christian proposals, young Father Guillaume became just as accommodating as Brother Guilbert imagined that Arn must have intended. Arn made an even better impression when he excused himself, went over to the ox-carts in the courtyard, and returned with a heavy, clinking leather sack, which he handed to Father Guillaume with the utmost respect and a deep bow.

Father Guillaume clearly had a hard time resisting the temptation to open the leather purse and begin counting the gold.

Then Arn made his next move. He spoke for a moment about Varnhem's beautiful horses, about what a shame it was that his kinsmen in this northern land did not understand the true value of these animals. He also mentioned the great and commendable work that his old friend Brother Guilbert had done without recompense to care for and improve the breeding of the horses for so many years. He added that many diligent workers in the vineyards of the Lord received their wages long after their work was done, while others who may have come late to the work received their wages more promptly. Father Guillaume solemnly pondered this familiar example of how the human view of justice so often seemed to deviate from God's intention. Then Arn suggested that he buy all of Varnhem's horses, and for a very good price. In this way, he was quick to add before Father Guillaume could recover from his astonishment, Varnhem would finally receive payment for its arduous labor. The cloister would also be quit of a business that produced no income up here in the North, all with a single decision.

Arn then fell silent and waited to continue until Father Guillaume had collected himself enough to utter words of gratitude.

There might be a small catch to such a large settlement, Arn was quick to add. Because for the care of the horses the buyer would need a skilled man; that person was here in Varnhem and was none other than Brother Guilbert. On the other hand, if Brother Guilbert's most important work vanished with the horses . . . ?

Father Guillaume then suggested that Brother Guilbert's services be included in the purchase to assist the buyer, at least for a time . . . no, for as long as necessary. Arn nodded gratefully as if acknowledging a very wise decision. Brother Guilbert, who was now observing his face closely, could see not a single sign to reveal whether this had been Arn's intention all along. He looked as though upon reflection he was agreeing with the wisdom of Father Guillaume's proposal. Then he suggested that they see to having the donation documents drawn up, signed, and sealed that very day, since both parties happened to be present.

When Father Guillaume immediately agreed to this as well, Arn spread out his hands in a gesture of gratitude and relief. Then he asked both monks to share with him information of the type that only men of the cloth might know, about how things really stood in his homeland.

As he was swift to point out, down at the marketplace in Lödöse he had already learned who was king, jarl, and queen. He also knew that there had been peace in the country for a long time. But the answer to the question of whether this peace between the Goth lands and the Swedes to the north would last in years to come could only be learned from the men of the church, for only they were privy to the deeper truths.

Father Guillaume looked pleased at this thought, and he nodded in agreement and approval, but he still seemed unsure of what Arn wanted to know. Arn helped him out by asking a concise but very difficult question which he presented in a low voice with no change in expression.

"Will there be war in our land again, and if so, why and when?"

The two monks frowned for a moment in contemplation. Brother Guilbert answered first, with Father Guillaume's assent, by saying that as long as King Knut Eriksson and his jarl Birger Brosa held power, there was no danger of war. The question was, what would happen after King Knut's demise.

"Then the risk of a new war would be great," sighed Father Guillaume.

He recounted how at the previous year's church convocation in Linköping the new Archbishop Petrus had clearly demonstrated

to the men of the church where he stood. He was a supporter of
the Sverker dynasty, and he had received his pallium from the
Danish Archbishop Absalon in Lund. This same Absalon had
plotted against the Erik dynasty and wanted to restore the royal
crown of the Goths and Swedes to the Sverkers. There was also
a means for achieving that goal, though King Knut Eriksson undoubtedly knew as little about it as he knew that his new archbishop was a man of the Danes and Sverkers. Bishop Absalon in
Lund possessed a letter from the blessed Abbess Rikissa which
she had dictated on her deathbed. In this letter she recounted
how King Knut's queen Cecilia Blanca, during the time she had
spent among the novices at Gudhem convent, had taken vows
of chastity and pledged to remain forever a handmaiden of the
Lord. Since King Knut later brought Cecilia Blanca from Gudhem and made her his queen, and she later bore him four sons
and two daughters . . .

It could therefore be claimed that the king's children were illegitimate and had no right to the crown, Arn quickly summed up.
Had the Holy Father in Rome given his opinion on this matter?

No, since a new Pope had just been elected, taking the name
Celestinus III, they still knew nothing about what opinion the
Holy See might have regarding legitimate or illegitimate royal
progeny in Götaland. Surely there were greater problems demanding the immediate attention of the one who had been elevated to the Holy See.

"But if none of King Knut's sons could succeed him," Arn
said, and it sounded more like a statement than a question, "then
might not Archbishop Petrus and possibly other bishops propose
a Sverker kinsman as the new king? It would not be entirely unexpected."

The two monks nodded in gloomy affirmation. Arn sat in
thought for a moment before he stood up with an expression
that showed he had already dismissed these minor concerns. He

thanked the monks for the valuable information, and suggested that they proceed immediately to the scriptorium to weigh the gold accurately and to have the donation documents drawn up and stamped with the proper seal.

Father Guillaume, who for a moment had thought that the conversation had taken a quite base and uninteresting turn, accepted this suggestion at once.

✠

The odd caravan of heavily laden ox-carts escorted by light and fast Saracen horses left Varnhem cloister the next morning on the way to Skara, the market town and bishop's see in the middle of Western Götaland, eight miles due west of Varnhem. Brother Guilbert was part of all the newly purchased goods—that was his ironic view of the sudden change in his life. Arn had bought him as easily as he had bought his gravesite, the horses, and almost all the saddle tack and bridles that were made at Varnhem. Brother Guilbert could not have had it any other way even if he had protested, since Father Guillaume seemed dazzled by the payments in gold from Arn. Instead of quietly awaiting the end of his life in Varnhem, Brother Guilbert was now riding with strangers toward an unknown destination, and he found that to be an exceedingly good situation. He had no idea what sort of plans Arn might have, but he didn't believe that all these horses had been bought merely to please the eye.

The Saracen knights who were in the lead—and it was no secret to Brother Guilbert that they were Saracens—seemed childishly enchanted at being able to continue their long journey on horseback. This was easy to understand, especially since they were allowed to ride such magnificent steeds. It occurred to Brother Guilbert that now Saint Bernard in his Heaven must be teasing his monk who once had despaired that anyone would ever want to buy Varnhem's horses, and in his powerlessness had shrieked that he would settle for Saracen buyers at the very least. Now these unexpected Saracens rode along, joking loudly and talking all around him. At the oxen-reins sat men who spoke other languages. Brother Guilbert had still not figured them out—who they were or where they had come from.

But there was one big problem. What Arn had done was a type of deception which the young and naïve Father Guillaume hadn't had the wit to see through, blinded as he was by all that gold. Yet a Templar knight was allowed to own no more than a monk in Varnhem cloister. Any Templar knight who was discovered with a single gold coin would immediately have to relinquish his white mantle and leave the Templar order in disgrace.

Brother Guilbert decided that the unpleasant matter should be broached sooner rather than later, which was how every Templar knight had learned to think. He urged on his dapple gray, rode up alongside Arn at the head of the column, and asked him the question straight out.

But Arn did not seem to take offense at the troublesome query. He merely smiled and turned his exquisite stallion—which was from Outremer but of a type that Brother Guilbert did not know—and galloped back to one of the last carts in the column. He leaped onto it and began searching for something among the loaded goods.

He remounted his horse and was back at once with a water-tight leather roll which he handed without a word to Brother Guilbert, who opened it with as much trepidation as curiosity.

It was a document in three languages, signed by the Grand Master of the Knights Templar, Gérard de Ridefort. It said that Arn de Gothia, after twenty years of service as a provisional brother, had now left his position in the Order of the Knights Templar, released from his obligations by the Grand Master himself. But because of all the services he had rendered to the Order, whenever he desired and at his own discretion he had the right to wear the white mantle with the same status he'd enjoyed before he left the Order.

"So you see, my dear Brother Guilbert," Arn said, taking the document, rolling it up and inserting it carefully back into the leather sheath, "I am a Templar knight and yet not. And to be honest, I can't see there is any great harm done if someone who has so long served the crimson cross should occasionally seek protection behind it."

At first it was not quite clear to Brother Guilbert what Arn meant by that. But after they had ridden for a while, Arn began to talk about his homeward journey, and then his words about taking protection behind the bloodred cross made more sense.

Arn had bought, taken captive, or employed in his service the men who now rode with him in the column on the roads all over Outremer, where everyone had become everyone else's foe and where a Saracen who served the Christians was just as much at risk as a Christian who served the Saracens. But putting together a ship's crew and a group of men who would be of good use when traveling the long way back to Western Götaland had not been the hard part.

Brother Guilbert studied his friend's face now and then when he thought Arn wasn't looking. He found nothing in Arn's outward appearance that surprised him. Had someone asked him to guess how Arn might look if, against all logic, he survived twenty years as a Templar knight in Outremer, Brother Guilbert would have guessed at something like this: A blond beard that had not yet begun to gray but had nevertheless lost its luster. All Templar knights wore beards, of course. Short hair as well. White scars on his hands and all over his face, the marks of arrows and swords and perhaps an ax-blow over one eyebrow which made that eye seem a bit stiff. This was more or less the appearance that he would have guessed. The war in Outremer had been no banquet.

But there was an unease inside Arn that could not be as easily discerned with a mere glance. He had already admitted the day before that he considered his service in the Holy War to be finished, and his reasons were good. But now that Arn was riding the last day's march toward home and with great wealth besides—which was truly an unusual way for a Templar knight to return—he should have felt happier, exhilarated and full of eager plans. Instead there was a great sense of unease about him, something resembling fear, if that word could be applied to a Templar knight. There was still much to understand and to question.

"Where did you get such a vast amount of gold?" asked Brother Guilbert resolutely as they rode past Skara without entering the town. He felt that he needed to resume their conversation.

"If I answered that question right now you wouldn't believe me, dear Guilbert," replied Arn, but he looked down at the ground. "Or even worse, you would think that I had committed treason. And were you to believe that, however briefly, it would make both of us sad. You must take my word for it. This wealth was not come by unjustly. And I will tell you everything when we have time, for it is not a story that is easily fathomed."

"I believe you, of course, but don't ever ask me again to believe you without question," Brother Guilbert said bitterly. "You and I never lied to each other inside the walls, and outside the walls I take it for granted that we speak to each other as the Templar knights we both once were."

"That is precisely how I want it to be, and I will never make another request that you take my word for something on faith," Arn almost whispered, still with his eyes cast down.

"Well, then I'll ask you something simpler," said Brother Guilbert more cheerfully and in a louder voice. "We're riding toward Arnäs now, your father's estate, are we not? Well, you're bringing with you baggage that is not insignificant, including horses from

Outremer and a monk you just acquired in Varnhem—no, don't contradict me! I'm also part of your purchase. I admit that I'm not used to such things, but that's the way it is. And you have bought other men, possibly after negotiations more difficult than those you pursued with Father Guillaume, but they are going to be used for something, just as I am. Won't you tell me something about all this? Who are these men in the caravan?"

"Two of the men, those two riding the mares to your left, are physicians from Damascus," replied Arn without hesitation. "The two sitting on the ox-carts at the rear of the column are deserters from the army of King Richard Lionheart, an archer and a crossbowman. The Norwegian Harald Øysteinsson, who wears the coat of a sergeant of the Knights Templar, served with me, but I've already told you that. The two sitting on the ox-carts just behind us are Armenian armorers and craftsmen from Damascus, and most of the rest of the men are builders and sappers from both sides in the war. They are all in my service, except Harald, because in their direst hour I made them an offer they couldn't refuse. Does that answer the question you really wanted to ask?"

"Yes, to a great extent,"replied Brother Guilbert meditatively. "You intend to build something great. Will you tell me what it is you want all of us to build?"

"Peace," said Arn resolutely.

Brother Guilbert was so surprised by the answer that for a long while he could not bring himself to ask anything more.

✠

When on the second day of the journey the caravan neared the church in Forshem, summer had returned in all its glory. It was hard to imagine that the whole village had been rocked by storms and foul weather only a few days earlier. Trees and other debris that had fallen across roads and farms had already been removed. Out in the fields the turnip harvest was in full swing.

Since there had long been peace in the country, no armed guards rode forth along the roads, and no one disturbed the travelers, even though it must have been evident from a great distance that many of them were foreigners. The workers in the fields would straighten up for a moment to watch with curiosity the ox-carts and the knights on the lively horses, but then they went back to their labor.

When the caravan reached Forshem, Arn led his men up the hill to the church and signaled for them to rest. When all had dismounted he went over to the Prophet's people, who usually kept to themselves, and told them there was still plenty of time before the afternoon prayer hour, but that here the Bible's people were going to pray for a while. Then he asked the two Armenian brothers, and Harald and Brother Guilbert, to come with him into the church. But as they approached the door, the priest came hurrying out of his presbytery and called to them not to enter God's house in disarray. He ran over and took up position before the old-fashioned ornamented doors of the wooden church. Trembling, he blocked the way with arms outstretched.

Arn then calmly told him who he was, that he was the son of Herr Magnus of Arnäs, and that all in his party were good Christians. After a long journey they wanted to give thanks at the altar and also leave an offering. They were allowed in at once by the priest, who only now seemed to notice that one of the strangers was a Cistercian in a white cloak, and that two of the men bore big red crosses on their shields. Fumbling and apologizing, he unlocked the big church doors.

But Arn did not go far up the aisle toward the altar before the priest caught up with him and tugged on his sword, saying something in an odd mixture of Latin and Swedish to indicate that swords were an abomination in God's house. Brother Guilbert

then shooed him away like a fly, explaining that the sword at Sir
Arn's side was blessed. It was the sword of a Templar knight, even
if it was the only one that had ever been inside Forshem church.

At the altar the Christians fell to their knees, lighted some candles from the one that burned at the altar, and said their prayers.
They also placed silver on the altar, which instantly calmed the
agitated priest standing behind them.

After a while Arn asked to be left alone with his God, and
everyone complied with no objections. They all went outside,
closing the church doors behind them.

Arn prayed a long time for support and guidance, as he had
done so often before. But never had he felt anything stir within
him or seen any sign that Our Lady had answered him.

In spite of this constant lack of an answer he had never been
stricken with doubt. People filled the earth, just as God had prescribed. At any one moment God and the saints had to listen to
thousands of people offering up prayers, and if they had to take
time to answer every one of them it would lead to great confusion. How many foolish prayers did people voice every moment,
asking for luck in the hunt, success in trade, the birth of a son, or
to be allowed to continue their earthly lives?

And how many thousands of times had Arn asked Our Lady
for protection for Cecilia and their child? How many times had
he prayed for success in war? Before every attack in the Holy
War, clad in their white mantles, they all sat their horses knee
to knee, about to dash headlong toward death or toward victory,
and Our Lady had to listen to their prayers. Almost all prayers
had selfish intent.

But this time Arn prayed to Our Lady that she might guide him
and advise him in what he could and should do with all the power
he had brought home; that he might not succumb and become a
covetous man, that he might not be tempted by the knowledge
that he was a warrior who knew more than his kinsmen did, that

all the gold and all the knowledge he now had in his possession might not fall on infertile ground.

And then, for the first time ever, Our Lady answered the praying Arn so that he could hear her clear voice inside him and see her in the dazzling light that had just struck his face from one of the high windows in the little wooden church. It was not a miracle, because many people could testify to receiving an answer to prayer. But for Arn it was the first time, and he now knew with certainty what he had to do, because Our Lady herself had revealed it to him.

It was only two days' journey from Forshem church to the fortress of Arnäs. At the halfway point they stopped for a short rest, because it was the prayer hour for the Prophet's people. The Christians took the opportunity to have a nap.

But Arn went out to a clearing in the forest and let God's light filter down through the delicate light-green foliage of the beeches onto his scarred face. For the first time in this long journey he felt at peace, because he had finally understood God's intent in sparing his life all these years.

That was the important thing, the most crucial. At this particular moment he would not allow himself to be concerned with anything secondary.

✠

For some time a strange rumor had been circulating in Western Götaland. A mighty foreign ship had been sighted, first near Lödöse in the Göta River, and then all the way up by the Troll's Rapids. Foreigners had tried to drag the ship up the rapids using many oxen and hired draymen. But finally they had been forced to give up and go back down the river to the marketplace near Lödöse.

No one could understand the point of trying to drag such a

ship up into Lake Vänern. Some of the Norwegian guards at Arnäs fortress thought that the ship must have business on the Norwegian side of Vänern. King Sverre of Norway had more than once attempted the strangest military advances by arriving by ship where no one expected him. But right now there was not much in the way of war in Norway, although it was not entirely peaceful either.

And no one could say for sure that it was a warship, for according to the rumor the ship's big lateen sail bore a red cross which was so large that the cross was visible before anything else. No ship in the North bore such a mark, that much was certain.

For a few days extra vigilance was taken to keep watch over the calm summer waters of Lake Vänern from the high tower at Arnäs, at least until those three days of storm arrived. But when no ship appeared, and since it was a time of peace in Western Götaland, soon all went back to their normal tasks and the delayed turnip sowing.

One man never tired of sitting up in the tower and straining his watery old man's eyes by gazing out across the water glittering in the sun. He was the lord of Arnäs, and he would remain that for as long as he lived. His name was Magnus Folkesson. Three winters ago he'd had a stroke, and since then he could not speak clearly and was paralyzed on his left side from head to toe. He kept to himself up there in the tower with a couple of house thralls, as if ashamed to show himself in public. Or perhaps it was because his eldest son Eskil did not like to see his father mocked behind his back. Yet now the old man sat up there each day in plain view of everyone in Arnäs. The wind tore at his tangled white hair, but his patience seemed without limit. Many jokes were told about what the old man must imagine he could see from up there.

Yet every jester would come to rue his scorn. Herr Magnus had sensed an omen, although it turned out that he was waiting for a miracle sent by Our Lady. And he was the one, with his wide view of the surrounding countryside, who first saw what happened.

Three young thralls came running along the still wet and muddy road from Forshem to Arnäs. They were shouting and waving their arms, and all three were racing to be the first to arrive, since sometimes a poor wretch who brought important news would be given a silver coin.

When they ran out onto the long, swaying wooden causeway that led across the marsh to the fortress itself, the thrall who was somewhat bigger and stronger overtook first one and then the other, so that he arrived first, gasping and red-faced, with the others hobbling far behind.

They had been spotted even before they reached the causeway, and someone called for Svein, who was in charge of the lifeguards. He staunchly confronted the first runner at the gate of the fortress, grabbing the young thrall by the neck just as he tried to run past and forcing him to his knees in a puddle of water. He held the boy in a strong grip with his iron glove and asked to hear the news. It was not easy to understand, since his grip caused so much pain that the boy mostly whimpered, but also the other two thralls had now caught up with him and of their own accord fell to their knees, jabbering at the same time as they tried to tell what they had seen.

Svein, the captain of the guards, then gave them all a box on the ears and questioned the boys one by one. At last some sense was made of what they had witnessed. A caravan with many warriors and heavy ox-carts was approaching Arnäs on the road from Forshem. They were not Sverkers or any associated clan, nor were they Folkungs or Eriks. They were from a foreign land.

There was the sound of horns being blown and guards went running for the stables, where thralls had already begun saddling the horses. People were sent to wake Herr Eskil, who at this time of day was sleeping his lordly sleep, and others were sent to the drawbridge down by the causeway to hoist it up, so that the foreigners would not be able to enter Arnäs before it was determined whether they were friend or foe.

Before long Herr Eskil was sitting on his horse, accompanied by ten guards near the drawn-up bridge to Arnäs and tensely watching the other side of the marsh where the foreigners would soon appear. It was late in the afternoon, so the men outside Arnäs had the sun in their eyes, since the opposite end of the bridge lay to the south. When the strangers appeared on the other side it was hard to see them in the bright sunlight. Some said they saw monks, others said that they were foreign warriors. The strangers seemed confused for a moment when they discovered the closed drawbridge and men in full armor on the other side. But then a knight in a white mantle and white surcoat emblazoned with a red cross slowly rode alone out onto the causeway toward the drawbridge.

Herr Eskil and his men waited in tense silence as the bearded, bare-headed knight approached. Someone whispered that the stranger was riding an oddly pitiful horse. Two of the guards dismounted to draw their bows.

Then something happened that some people would later call a miracle. Old Herr Magnus called out from up in the high tower, and later there were some who would swear that Herr Magnus clearly uttered the words "The Lord be praised," because the Prodigal Son had come back from the Holy Land.

Eskil was of another mind. As he later explained, he understood everything as soon as he heard one of the guards mention the wretched horse, since he had both good and painful memories from his youth about what sort of wenches' horses were called pitiful, and what sort of men rode such horses.

Speaking in a voice which some described as quavering and weak, Herr Eskil ordered the drawbridge lowered for the unknown knight. He had to give the order twice before he was obeyed.

Then Herr Eskil got down from his horse and fell to his knees in prayer before the creaking drawbridge, now lowered so that the sun's glare was in everyone's eyes. The horse belonging to the white-clad knight appeared to have danced across the drawbridge long before it had been lowered all the way to its supports. The knight jumped down from his horse with a motion that no one had ever seen before and was quickly on his knees before Herr Eskil. The two embraced, and there were tears in Herr Eskil's eyes.

Whether it was a double or single miracle was a subject of debate long afterward. No one knew for certain whether it was at that moment that old Herr Magnus up in the tower regained his senses. But it was clear that Arn Magnusson, the warrior known only from the sagas in those days, had now come home after many years in the Holy Land.

⠀⠀⠀⠀⠀⠀⠀⠀⠀⠀⠀⠀✠

There was great noise and commotion that day at Arnäs. When the mistress of the manor, Erika Joarsdotter, came out to greet the guests with a welcome ale and saw Arn and Eskil walking across the courtyard with their arms around each other's shoulders, she dropped everything she was carrying and ran forward with her arms spread wide. Arn, who had let go of his brother Eskil, fell to his knees to greet his stepmother courteously; he was almost knocked to the ground when she threw her arms around his neck and kissed him as shamelessly as only a mother can do. Everyone could see that the returning warrior was unused to such practices.

Wagons were pulled creaking and rattling into the courtyard of the fortress. Heavy crates and a multitude of weapons were unloaded and carried into the armory in the tower. Outside the walls a tent camp fashioned from ships' sails and exotic carpets was quickly raised, and many willing hands helped to set up gates and fencing for all of Sir Arn's horses. Calves were taken to be slaughtered and the spit-turners lit their fires. All around Arnäs a promising aroma soon spread of the evening to come.

When Arn greeted the guards, some of whom were unwilling to kneel before him, he abruptly asked after his father with a tense expression, as if preparing himself for sad news. Eskil replied gruffly that their father was no longer in his right mind and had retreated to the tower. Arn strode at once toward the tower, his white mantle with the red cross billowing like a sail around him so that all those in his path quickly moved aside.

Up on the highest parapet he found his father in a miserable state but with a happy expression on his face. His father was standing next to the wall with a house thrall supporting his lame side. In his healthy hand he held a rough walking-stick. Arn quickly bowed his head and kissed his father's good hand and then gathered him in his arms. His father felt as frail as a child, his good arm was as thin as his lame one, and he exuded a rank odor. Arn stood there unable to think of what to say, when his father with great effort, his head trembling, leaned toward him and whispered something.

"The angels of the Lord . . . shall rejoice . . . and the fatted calf . . . shall be slain."

Arn heard the words quite clearly, and they were judiciously chosen, as they so clearly referred to the story in the Holy Scriptures of the return of the Prodigal Son. All the talk of his father's lost reason was simply nonsense. With relief Arn picked the old man up in his arms and began to walk around the parapet to see how he had been living up here. When he saw the dark tower room it was worse than he had feared. He frowned at the strong odor of piss and rotting food. He spun around and headed for the stairs, speaking to his father as to a man of reason like any other, the way no one had spoken to him in many years. Arn said that the lord of Arnäs would no longer have to live in a pigsty.

On the narrow, winding tower staircase he met Eskil slowly ascending, since the stairs were not designed for sizable men with a paunch. Grumbling, Eskil now had to turn around and go back down, with Arn close behind him, carrying their father like a bundle over one shoulder as he barked orders about everything that needed to be done.

Out in the courtyard Arn set his father down, since it would be disgraceful to carry him any further like a sheaf of rye. Eskil ordered the house thralls to bring tables and feather-beds and the dragon-carved seat to one of the cookhouses by the south wall that were used only for large feasts. Arn bellowed that his father's tower room was to be scoured from floor to ceiling, and many pairs of astonished eyes watched as the three men proceeded across the courtyard of the fortress.

The seat with the carved dragon coils was delivered at once to the cookhouse, and there Arn tenderly deposited his father. He dropped to his knees, took his father's face in his hands, looked him in the eyes, and said that he was well aware that he was speaking to a father who understood everything just as well as he had before. Eskil stood in silence behind him and said not a word.

But old Herr Magnus now seemed so overwhelmed and was breathing so hard that there might be a risk he would suffer another stroke. Arn took his hands from his father's face, stood up, and strode past his bewildered older brother out to the courtyard, giving an order in a language nobody could understand.

At once two men from the many foreigners in Arn's entourage came forward. They were both dressed in dark cloaks and had blue cloth wound around their heads; one was young and the other old, and their eyes were as black as those of ravens.

"These two men," said Arn, addressing his brother, but also his father, "are named . . . Abraham and Joseph. They are both my friends from the Holy Land. And they are masters of the healing arts."

He explained something in an unintelligible language to the two raven-eyed men, who nodded that they understood. They began to examine Herr Magnus carefully, but without undue deference. They studied the whites of his eyes, listened to his breathing and his heart, struck his right knee with a little club so that his foot kicked straight out, then did the same several times with his left knee, which moved only slightly. They seemed particularly interested in that. Then they raised and lowered his weak left arm as they whispered to each other.

Eskil, who stood behind Arn, felt left out and at a loss, seeing two foreigners handling the lord of Arnäs as if inspecting some thrall child. But Arn signaled to him that all was as it should be, and then he had a brief whispered conversation in the foreign language, whereupon the two physicians retreated, bowing deeply to Eskil.

"Abraham and Joseph have good news," said Arn when he and Eskil were alone. "Our father is too tired right now, but tomorrow the healing work will begin. With God's help our father will be able to walk and speak once again."

Eskil said nothing. It was as if his first joy at seeing Arn had already been clouded, and he felt a little ashamed at appearing to be the one who had not taken care of his father. Arn gave his brother a searching look and seemed to understand these hidden feelings. He threw his arms wide and they fell into each other's embrace. They stood that way a long time without saying a word. Eskil, who seemed more bothered by the silence than Arn, finally muttered that it was a scrawny little brother who had come to the feast.

Amused, Arn replied that it appeared Eskil had managed well

enough to keep the wolf from the door at Arnäs, and that he had certainly not been diminished by continuing the legacy of their ancestor, jarl Folke the Fat. Then Eskil burst out laughing and shook his younger brother back and forth with feigned indignation, and Arn let himself be shaken as he joined in the laughter.

When their merriment subsided, Arn led his brother over to their father, who was sitting quite still in his beloved chair with the dragon carvings. His left arm hung limp at his side. Arn fell to his knees and pulled Eskil down with him so that their heads were close together. Then he spoke in a kindly tone and not as if to a man who had lost his wits.

"I know that you can hear and understand everything just as before, dear Father. You don't have to answer me now, because if you strain yourself too much it will only get worse. But tomorrow the healing will begin, and starting tomorrow I will sit with you and tell you everything that happened in the Holy Land. But now Eskil and I will take our leave, so that he can tell me what has happened here at home. There is much that I'm impatient to know."

With that the two sons got to their feet and bowed to their father as before. They thought they could see a little smile on his lopsided face, like the glow from a fire that was far from extinguished.

When they left the cookhouse Eskil grabbed a passing house thrall and told him that Herr Magnus was to have his bed, water, and pisspot brought to him there in the cookhouse, and that the floor should be covered with birch boughs.

In the courtyard of the fortress people and house thralls were rushing about on all sorts of errands to prepare for the unexpected welcome feast, which now had to be readied in haste and with greater grandeur than an ordinary banquet at Arnäs. But those who came near the two Folkung brothers, now walking arm in arm toward the gate, shrank back almost as if in terror.

Herr Eskil was said to be the richest man in all of Western Göta-land, and everyone knew enough to fear the power that resided in silver and gold, although Herr Eskil himself often invited more ridicule than fear. But next to him now walked his brother, the long-absent warrior Arn, whom the sagas had made much taller and broader than he was in truth. Yet everyone could see by his stride, by his scarred face, and by the way he wore his sword and chain-mail as though they were his normal attire, that now the other power had indeed come to Arnäs—the power of the sword, which most sensible people feared far more than the power of silver.

Eskil and Arn went out through the gate and down to the tent encampment, which was being made ready by all the foreigners in Arn's retinue. Arn explained that they needed only to greet the freemen, and not his thralls. First he asked Harald Øysteins-son to step forward and told Eskil that the two of them had been comrades in arms for almost fifteen years. When Eskil heard the Norwegian name he frowned as if searching his memory for something. Then he asked whether Harald might possibly have a relative in Norway with the same name. When Harald confirmed this and said that the man was his grandfather, and that his father was named Øystein Møyla, Eskil nodded pensively. He hastened to invite Harald to the feast that evening in the longhouse, and he also pointed out that there would be no lack of Nordic ale in suf-ficient quantities; something he probably thought would cheer a kinsman who had come such a long way. Harald's face lit up and he uttered words so warm, almost like blessings, that Eskil was soon distracted from the subject of his forefathers.

Next they greeted the old monk Brother Guilbert, whose fringe of hair was completely white and whose shiny pate showed that he no longer needed to bother with shaving his tonsure. Arn briefly recounted how while they were in Varnhem Father Guil-laume had granted Brother Guilbert a leave of absence as long as he worked for Arnäs. When he shook hands with the monk, Eskil was surprised to feel a rough grip, like a smith's and with a smith's strength.

There were no other men in Arn's entourage who spoke Norse, and Eskil had a hard time understanding the foreign names that Arn rattled off as they stood before men who bowed politely. To Eskil's ears the language sometimes sounded like Frankish and sometimes like some utterly different tongue.

Arn especially wanted to introduce two brothers who were dark-skinned, but both wore a gold cross around their necks. Their names were Marcus and Jacob Wachtian, Arn explained, and he added that they would be of great use in building anything large or small as well as in conducting business.

The thought of good tradesmen cheered up Eskil, but otherwise he had begun to feel uncomfortable among these foreigners, whose language he could not understand but whose expressions he suspected he could read all too well. He imagined that they were saying things that were not very respectful about his mighty paunch.

Arn also seemed to notice Eskil's embarrassment, so he dismissed all the men around them and led his brother back toward the fortress courtyard. After they passed through the gate he suddenly turned serious and asked his brother to meet with him alone in the tower's accounting chamber for a talk that was to be for their ears only. But first he had a simple matter to take care of, something that would be awkward if he forgot about it before the banquet. Eskil nodded, looking a bit puzzled, and headed for the tower.

Arn strode toward the big brick cookhouses that still stood where as a boy he had helped to build them; with pleasure he noted that they had been repaired and fortified in places and showed no sign of decay.

Inside he found, as expected, Erika Joarsdotter wearing a long leather apron over a simple brown linen shift. Like a cavalry officer she was fully occupied in commanding female house thralls and servants. When she noticed Arn she quickly set down a large pot of steaming root vegetables and threw her arms around his neck for the second time. This time he let it happen without feeling embarrassed, since there were only women inside.

"Do you know, my dearest Arn," said Erika in her somewhat difficult to understand speech that came through her nose as much as through her mouth and which Arn had not heard in years, "that when you first came here I thanked Our Lady for sending an angel to Arnäs. And here you are once again, in a white mantle and surcoat emblazoned with the sign of Our Lord. You are in truth like a warrior angel of God!"

"What a human being sees and what God sees is not always one and the same," Arn muttered self-consciously. "We have much to talk about, you and I, and we shall, be sure of that. But right now my brother awaits, and I want only to ask you a small favor for this evening."

Erika threw out her arms in delight and said something about a favor on any evening, speaking in a suggestive manner that Arn did not fully understand. But the other women broke out in ill-concealed giggles in the midst of the bustle of the cookhouse. Arn pretended not to notice, even though he only half perceived the joke. He quickly hastened to request that the smaller feast served out by the tents contain lamb, veal, and venison, but no meat from swine—either wild or the fatter, tame variety. Since his wishes at first seemed difficult to understand, he hurried to add that in the Holy Land, where the guests came from, there was no pork, and that everyone would much prefer lamb. He also asked that besides ale, they also serve plenty of fresh water with the meal.

It was clear that Erika found this request odd. She stood deep in thought for a moment, her cheeks flushed from the cookhouse heat and breathless from all the rushing about, making her bosom heave. But then she promised to take care of everything just as Arn had asked, and hurried off to arrange for more slaughtering and more spit-turners.

Arn hurried to the tower. The lower port was now being watched by two guards who stared as if petrified at his white mantle and surcoat as he approached. But this expression, which many men assumed upon seeing a Templar knight coming toward them, was something that Arn had years ago learned to ignore.

He found his rather impatient brother up in the accounting chamber. Without explanation Arn unhooked his white mantle, pulled off his surcoat, and folded both garments carefully in the manner prescribed by the Holy Rule. He placed them carefully on a stool, sat down, and motioned for Eskil also to take a seat.

"You have become a man who is used to being in command," Eskil muttered with a mixture of levity and petulance.

"Yes, I have been a commander in war for many years, and it takes time to become accustomed to peace," replied Arn, crossing himself. He seemed to murmur a brief prayer to himself before he went on. "You are my beloved older brother. I am your beloved younger brother. Our friendship was never broken, and the longing of both of us has been great. I have not come home to command; I have come home to serve."

"You still sound like a Dane when you speak, or rather a man of the Danish church, perhaps. I don't think we should overstate the part about service, because you are my brother," Eskil jested, making an exaggerated gesture of welcome across the table.

"Now the time has come that I feared most when I longed so for my homecoming," Arn continued with unabated gravity, as if to show that he had no interest in the levity that had been offered.

Eskil collected himself at once.

"I know that our childhood friend Knut is now king," Arn

went on. "I know that our father's brother Birger Brosa is jarl, I know that for many years there has been peace in the realm. So now to everything I do not know . . ."

"You already know the most important things, but how did you obtain this knowledge on your long journey?" Eskil interrupted his brother, seemingly out of genuine curiosity.

"I come from Varnhem," Arn resolutely continued. "We first intended to sail all the way to the wharves outside Arnäs, but we could not make our way past the Troll's Rapids, since our ship was too big."

"So it was *your* ship with the cross on the sail!"

"Yes, a Templar ship that can carry a large cargo. It will surely be of great use. But let's speak of that later. We were forced to take the land route from Lödöse, and I found it wise to stop at Varnhem. It was there that I obtained the information, along with my friend Brother Guilbert and the horses you saw out in the pasture. Now to my question. Is Cecilia Algotsdotter still alive?"

Eskil stared in astonishment at his younger brother, who seemed to be suffering as he waited for the answer. Arn gripped the tabletop hard with his scarred hands as if preparing himself for the blow of a whip. When Eskil recovered from his surprise at this unexpected question, which came at a time when there were so many important things to discuss, he at first broke out in laughter. But Arn's burning gaze made him quickly cover his mouth with his hand, clear his throat, and turn serious again.

"The first thing you ask about is Cecilia Algotsdotter?"

"I have other questions that are equally important to me, but first this one."

"Ah well," sighed Eskil, hesitating with his reply and smiling in a way that made Arn think of his childhood memories of Birger Brosa. "Ah well, yes, Cecilia Algotsdotter is alive."

"Is she unmarried, has she taken vows at a convent?"

"She is unmarried and is the yconoma at Riseberga convent; she does the bookkeeping."

"So she has not taken vows, yet she manages the convent's affairs. Where is this Riseberga?"

"Three days' journey from here, but you should not ride there," Eskil teased him.

"Why not? Are there enemies there?"

"No, by no means. But Queen Blanca has been there for some time and she is now on her way to Näs, which is the king's fortress . . ."

"Remember, I've been there!"

"Ah yes, that's true. When Knut killed Karl Sverkersson; it's such things one should not forget, although it would be preferable to do so. But now Queen Blanca is on her way to Näs, and I'm sure that Cecilia is with her. Those two are as hard to separate as clay and straw. No, calm yourself, and don't stare at me like that!"

"I am calm! Completely calm."

"Yes, I can see that. So listen calmly to this. In two days' time I'm going to ride to the council meeting at Näs to meet with the king, the jarl, and a bunch of bishops. I think that everyone at Näs would probably be pleased if you came with me."

Arn had fallen to his knees and clasped his hands in prayer. Eskil found no reason to interrupt him, even though he felt ill at ease with this continuous kneeling. Instead he stood up thoughtfully as if testing an idea. Then he nodded to himself and quietly sneaked out to the stairs leading down to the armory. What he intended to fetch he might as well do now rather than later; he had already made up his mind.

When he came huffing back upstairs, without disturbing Arn, he sat down again to wait until he thought the rambling prayer had gone on long enough. Then he cleared his throat.

Arn stood up at once with a glint of joy in his eyes that seemed to Eskil too childish for words. He also thought that Arn's sheep-ish expression was inconsistent with a man clad in expensive chain mail from his head down to his steel-reinforced shoes with spurs of gold.

"Look here!" said Eskil, shoving a surcoat over to Arn. "If you must wear warrior clothes, you should probably be honoring these colors from now on."

Arn unfolded the surcoat without a word and briefly regarded the Folkung lion rampant above three streams. He nodded as if to confirm something to himself before he swiftly donned the gar-ment. Eskil stood up with a blue mantle in his hands and walked around the table. He gave Arn a brief and solemn look before he draped the Folkung mantle over his brother's shoulders.

"Welcome for a second time. Not only to Arnäs but also to our colors," he said.

When Eskil now attempted to embrace his brother, whom he had so readily readmitted to the family and to the right of inheri-tance, Arn once again sank to his knees in prayer. Eskil sighed but saw how Arn with a practiced gesture swept aside the mantle on the left side so that his sword would not get tangled in it. It was as if he were ready at any moment to rise up with his sword drawn.

This time Arn did not remain lost in prayer for long. When he stood up it was he who embraced Eskil.

"I remember the law about pilgrims and penitents, and I un-derstand what you have done. I swear the oath of a Templar knight that I shall always honor these colors," said Arn.

"For my part you may gladly take your oath as a Folkung, and always as a Folkung," replied Eskil.

"And now I can undoubtedly do so!" laughed Arn, opening the Folkung mantle wide with both arms as if imitating a bird of prey. Both of them laughed at this.

"And now it must be high time, by the Devil, for the first ale in too many years between brothers in blue!" shouted Eskil, but rued it at once when he saw how Arn flinched at his blasphemous language. In order to cover his embarrassment, he stood up and went over to an arrow loop in the embrasure facing the courtyard and bellowed something that Arn did not grasp, but he assumed it had something to do with ale.

"Now to my next question. Pardon my selfishness when something else may be of more importance for both our country and Arnäs, yet this is my next query," said Arn. "When I set off on my penitential journey, Cecilia Algotsdotter was expecting my child . . ."

It was as though Arn did not dare complete the question. Eskil, who knew that he had one more piece of good news to relate, delayed his answer and said that he was much too parched in the throat to speak of this until he had some ale. Then he got up impatiently and again went over to the arrow loop and roared something that Arn now definitely knew had to do with ale. He need not have done this. Already bare feet were heard hurrying up the spiral tower staircase. Soon two large foaming wooden tankards were set before the brothers, and the thrall girl who brought them vanished like a ghost.

The brothers raised their tankards to each other. Eskil drank much longer and more manfully than Arn, which was no surprise to either of them.

"Now I shall tell you how it stands with regard to this matter," said Eskil and moved closer to the table, drawing up one knee and resting the ale tankard on it. "Well, it was about your son, I believe—"

"My son!" Arn shouted.

"Yes. Your son. His name is Magnus. He grew up with his grandfather's brother Birger Brosa. He did not take your name, nor did he take the name Birgersson. He calls himself Magnus Månesköld and bears a moon on his shield next to our lion. He is a hereditary member at the *ting* and thereby a genuine Folkung. He knows that he is your son, and he has practiced to become the mightiest archer in all of Eastern Götaland since he heard of your attested skills. What else do you want to know about him?"

"How can he know anything about my archery? Does he also know who his mother is?" asked Arn, as troubled as he was excited.

"Songs have been sung about you, dear brother, and sagas have been told. Some originated from the *ting* of all Goths, that time you won the duel against . . . what was his name?"

"Emund Ulvbane."

"Yes, that's right. And the monks probably told him of one thing and another, such as the time you led twenty thousand Templar knights to a glorious victory at the Mountain of Pigs, where a hundred thousand infidels fell to your swords, not to mention—"

"The Mountain of Pigs? In the Holy Land?"

Arn broke into a fit of laughter that he could not stop. He repeated to himself the words "Mountain of Pigs" and then laughed even more, as he raised his ale tankard to Eskil, and tried to drink like a man, but he immediately began to cough. When he wiped his mouth a thought occurred to him and his face lit up.

"Mont Gisard," he said. "The battle was at Mont Gisard and there were four hundred Templar knights against five thousand Saracens."

"Well, that wasn't so bad either," Eskil said with a smile. "It was true then, and it's no surprise that the truth takes on a bit more luster in songs and sagas. But where were we? Oh yes, Magnus knows from the sagas who you are, and that's why he keeps practicing with the bow. That's one thing. The other is that he knows his mother Cecilia, and they get along well."

"Where does he live?"

"At Bjälbo with Birger Brosa. He was raised by Birger and

Brigida. Oh, that's right, you don't know Brigida. She's King Harald Gille's daughter and still talks like a Norwegian, the way you talk like a Dane. Well, for many years Magnus lived at Bjälbo as their son, and he believed nothing different. Now he is reckoned as a foster brother to Birger, and that's why he bears that moon on his shield instead of Birger's lily. What more would you like to know?"

"I sense that you think I ought to have begun asking questions at the other end. But I hope you'll forgive me. First I saw you, then our father Magnus, and I had no need to ask about what was both closest and most obvious. But during all the wars I prayed before every battle for Cecilia and the child I did not know. During the long journey across the seas there was almost nothing else to think about. Now tell me about you and yours, and about Father and Erika Joarsdotter."

"Well spoken, my dear brother," said Eskil, smacking his lips in jest as he took his mouth from his tankard as if it held the sweetest wine. "You choose your words well, and perhaps you will find use for that gift when you have to wheedle the bunch of bishops in the king's council. But keep in mind that I am your brother and that we always stood close to each other, and God grant that we may remain so. With me you need never wheedle, but speak as only you can to the one who is your brother!"

Arn raised his tankard in assent.

Eskil then gave a brief account, explaining that so much still remained to be said after so many years that if they did it properly it would take all night. But after the evening's banquet was over they would not be so pressed for time.

Eskil related that he had only one son, Torgils, who was seventeen years old and now rode as a young apprentice in the king's guards. He also had two daughters, Beata and Sigrid, who both had married well in Svealand into Queen Blanca's family but had not yet borne any sons. Eskil himself had no reason to complain.

God had stood by him. He sat on the king's council and was responsible for all trade abroad. He could speak the language of Lübeck, and he had sailed there twice to conclude agreements with Henrik the Lion of Saxony. From the land of the Swedes and Goths they sailed with iron, wool, hides, and butter, but above all with dried fish that was caught and prepared in Norway. From Lübeck the ship took on cargo of steel, spices, and fabrics, as well as spun thread of gold and silver, and silver coins which were payment for the dried fish. It was no small treasure that was imported into the country through this trade, and Eskil's share was significant, since he was the sole trader of this dried fish between Norway, both Eastern and Western Götaland, Svealand, and Lübeck. Now Arnäs was surely more than twice as rich as when Arn had left.

Eskil grew excited when he talked about his business affairs. He was used to his listeners tiring quickly, wanting to change the subject. But now that he was allowed to boast longer than usual without interruption, he was both glad and amazed that his brother seemed so interested, as if he understood all about trade. He was almost suspicious of Arn's attentiveness, so he asked some questions to see whether his brother was really following along and not just sitting and daydreaming about something else while he expertly feigned an interest.

But Arn remembered how one time—when they had ridden to the *ting* of all Goths that ended so unhappily for the champion of the Sverkers' side but so happily for the Folkungs—they had spoken about this very idea of exporting the dried fish from the Lofoten Islands in Norway in large quantities. And now it had become a reality.

Arn thought this was very good news. Just as he considered it very wise to take payment for the dried fish in pure silver and not in things that only had value for the vain. But he asked himself how good a trade it was to transport iron to Lübeck and steel the other direction, instead of making steel out of the iron they had in their possession.

Eskil was pleased by his brother's unexpected good sense, which he had not displayed back when he set off for the Holy Land, even though they both had inherited their wits from their mother Sigrid. But now Eskil's ale was gone, and once again he went over to the arrow loop to yell for more, while behind his back Arn poured half of his own ale into the tankard of his thirstier brother.

This time a house thrall had been waiting down by the door to the tower with fresh ale, so two new tankards arrived as swiftly as the wind.

When they resumed their drinking, Eskil's half-full tankard had been replaced without him noticing, and Arn felt youthfully pleased at having avoided discovery. By then they had lost the thread of everything that was left to tell. Each saw the other's predicament and both tried to get in the first word.

"Our father and Erika Joarsdotter—" said Eskil.

"You are well aware that I intend to celebrate a bridal ale with Cecilia," said Arn at the same time.

"That's not for you to decide!" snapped Eskil, but regretted it at once and threw out his hand as if trying to wipe away his words.

"Why not?" Arn asked softly.

Eskil sighed. There was no way to avoid his brother's question, no matter how much he wanted to postpone it along with much else until the following day.

"When you came home—and may God bless your homecoming which is of immeasurable joy to us all—the game board was changed completely," replied Eskil quickly and more gently, as if he were speaking about the trading of dried fish. "The clan *ting* will decide, but if I know our Birger Brosa rightly, he will say that you must go to the bridal bed with Ingrid Ylva. She's the daughter of Sune Sik and so has Karl Sverkersson as her grandfather—King Karl, that is."

"Am I supposed to drink the bridal ale with a woman whose uncle I helped to murder?" Arn exclaimed.

"That is indeed a good thought. Wounds and feuds must be healed for the sake of peace, and it is better done with the bridal bed than with the sword. That is our thinking. In peacetime a man's vow is stronger than his sword. So it must be Ingrid Ylva."

"And if in that case I should prefer a man's sword?"

"I don't think anyone wants to exchange blows with you, and I don't think you wish to come to blows either. Your son Magnus is also old enough to marry, just as Ingrid is. It must be one of you, but it also depends on how much silver is required. No, don't worry about that matter, my brother; the 'morning gift' will be taken care of by us from Arnäs."

"I can take care of the morning gift myself. I had not intended anything immoderate, only the Forsvik estate, as was once agreed at the betrothal feast for Cecilia and myself. One must honor one's agreements," said Arn quickly and in a low voice, but without revealing what he felt, although his brother would surely understand.

"If you ask me for Forsvik, I can hardly say no. On a first evening like this, I cannot say no to anything you may want from me," Eskil continued in the same tone of voice, as if they were two businessmen talking. "But I still want to ask you to wait with such a request until after our first day and evening together after so many years."

Arn did not answer, but seemed to be pondering the matter. Then he got up and took out three keys which he carried on a leather thong around his neck. He went over to the three very heavy chests that were the first to be carried into the tower from his caravan. When he unlocked them one by one, a bright golden glow spread through the room, although the rays of the sun were visible only at the bottom of the western arrow loop.

Eskil stood up slowly and went around the table with his ale tankard in his hand. To Arn's pleasure and surprise he did not look covetous when he gazed at the gold.

"Do you know how much there is?" asked Eskil, as if he were still talking about dried fish.

"No, not in our mode of reckoning," said Arn. "It's about thirty thousand besants, or gold dinars, calculated in the Frankish manner. It might be three thousand marks in our currency."

"And it was not ill-gotten?"

"No, it was not."

"You could buy all of Denmark."

"That's not my intention. I have better things to buy."

Arn slowly closed the three chests, locked them, and tossed the three keys across the table so that they slid to a stop just in front of Eskil's place. Then he went slowly back to his stool and gestured for his brother to sit down again. Eskil did so in meditative silence.

"I have three chests and three thoughts," said Arn when they had raised their tankards high. "My three thoughts are simple. As with everything else, I will tell you more about it when we have more time. But first I want to build a church of stone in Forshem, and with the most beautiful images that can be worked in stone in all of Western Götaland. Then, or rather at the same time, since all the stone must come from the same place, I want to build Arnäs so strong that no one here in the North can vanquish it. To fortify it in such a manner is something that I and the men who came here with me know how to do. We know much about building methods not yet known this far north. And the remaining third chest I will gladly share with my brother . . . after having purchased Forsvik, of course."

"For such a rich man Cecilia Algotsdotter's kinsmen will have a hard time offering a proper dowry. Her father is dead, by the way, he ate himself lame and blind at last year's Christmas ale."

"Peace be unto his soul. But all Cecilia needs is a dowry that is equal in value to Forsvik."

"She cannot afford even that," replied Eskil, but now with a little smile, which showed that he had not yet weighed every coin in this bargain.

"I'm quite certain that she can. For Forsvik she need not pay more than four or five marks in gold, and I know as well as you do where she can get such a small sum," Arn shot back.

Now Eskil could restrain himself no longer; he bellowed with laughter so the ale splashed out of his tankard.

"My brother! My brother, in truth you are my brother!" he snorted, and downed more of his ale before he went on. "I thought that a warrior had come to Arnäs, but you are a man of affairs who is my equal. We must drink to that!"

"I am your equal, since I am your brother," said Arn when he lowered his tankard after only pretending to drink. "But I am also a Templar knight. We Knights Templar conduct many trades in which the most peculiar goods change hands, and we can strike these bargains with the Devil himself and even with Norwegians!"

Laughing, Eskil agreed to everything. It seemed that he needed more ale, but he changed his mind when he looked out through the arrow loop to the west and saw the fading light.

"It probably wouldn't be much of a banquet without us," he muttered.

Arn nodded and said that he would like some time in the bath-house first, and that he ought to fetch one of his men who was best at handling a razor. A man who wore a Folkung mantle was not allowed to stink as he might in the garb of a Templar knight.

Because now a new life had begun, and it had certainly not begun badly.

✠

For the brothers Marcus and Jacob Wachtian the arrival at Arnäs was distressing. A more wretched fortress they had never seen. Marcus, who was the more jovial of the two, said that a man like Count Raymond of Tripoli would have taken a fortress like that in less time than it took to rest soldiers and horses during a hard march. Without a smile Jacob said that a man like Saladin would probably have ridden straight past it, since he wouldn't even have noticed that it was a fortress. If the big, important task Sir Arn had talked about was to make a decent fortress out of this nest for crows, it would surely be harder work for the body than for the mind.

It was true, of course, that they hadn't had many choices when Sir Arn rescued them from trouble after the fall of Jerusalem. A wave of euphoria following the victory had swept over Damascus, but it had soon made the city intolerable for Christians, no matter how skilled they were as craftsmen or businessmen. And during the flight toward Saint Jean d'Acre the brothers had too often encountered Christians who knew that they had been in the service of the unbelievers. Marcus and Jacob had also been robbed of all the belongings they carried with them. Even if they had managed to reach the last Christian city in the Kingdom of Jerusalem, it would not have been long before someone recognized them again. In the worst case they might have ended up on the gallows or burned at the stake. And in those days their homeland of Armenia had been laid waste by savage Turks, so that the journey there would have been even riskier than the one to Saint Jean d'Acre.

When they had stopped in despair by the wayside to say their last prayers to the Mother of God and Saint Sebastian, begging for a miraculous salvation, they had sincerely believed that none would come.

In their hour of despair Sir Arn had found them. He came riding with a small band from Damascus, strangely unafraid despite the fact that the region was teeming with Saracen brigands, as if the white mantle of the Knights Templar would guard against any sort of evil. Sir Arn had instantly recognized them from their businesses and workshops in Damascus. At the time it seemed beyond belief, since no Templar knight should have escaped Damascus alive. But he had at once offered the brothers his protection if they would enter his service for a period of no less than five years and would also accompany him to his homeland in the North.

The brothers hadn't had much choice. And Sir Arn had promised nothing more than a hard and dangerous journey, and hard work upon their arrival—in the beginning, even filthy work. And yet what they had now managed to see of the misery in this godforsaken land in the North was worse than they could have imagined even in their darkest and most seasick hour.

At the moment, however, they had no possibility of breaking their agreement. A hard, dark, and filthy four years awaited them, if the year the journey had already taken was to be subtracted. In that respect their contract was unclear.

They had put things somewhat in order in their tent encampment outside the low, crumbling wall. To make things simpler, the camp had been divided into two parts so that the Muslims had one section to themselves and the Christians the other. Naturally they had all managed to get along on a cramped ship for more than a year, but since their hours of prayer were different there had been much stumbling about at night when the Muslims had to get up to pray and the Christians were sleeping, and vice versa.

From the fortress young girls had come down carrying huge piles of sheepskins, which the foreign guests at first received with great joy, since they had already learned that in the North the nights were cold. But some of them soon discovered that the warm, inviting sheepskins were infested with lice. Laughing at one another's ungodly language and ungrateful jokes, both believers and infidels had stood for a long time side by side, beating the lice out of the skin rugs.

It was strange how the young women, some of whom were quite pretty, thought nothing of approaching strange men unabashed, with their hair uncovered and their arms bare. One of the English archers had half in jest pinched the bottom of a young woman with red hair, and she was not frightened at all. She merely turned and nimbly as a gazelle darted away from the rough hands that were again reaching for her.

After that the two infidel physicians had scolded the archer in a language that he did not understand. The Wachtian brothers gladly translated and concurred with what was said, and everyone in the camp soon agreed that in such a foreign and peculiar land they ought to proceed cautiously at first, especially with womenfolk, until they learned what was good and bad or lawful and unlawful. If there actually were any laws here among these savage folk.

In the evening just before prayer hour Sir Arn came alone to the tent camp. At first no one recognized him, since he seemed so much smaller. He had taken off his Templar mantle and surcoat and now wore instead some faded blue garments that hung loosely around his body. He had also shaved off his beard so that his face was now leather-brown in the middle and pale around the edges. He looked like both a man and a boy, although the scars of war on his face could now be seen more distinctly than when he wore a beard.

But Sir Arn gathered all the men with the same self-confidence he had displayed during the entire journey, and they soon stood in silence around him. As usual he spoke first in the language of the Saracens, and most of the Christians understood very little.

"In the name of the Merciful One, dear brothers," he began, "you are all my guests, both believer and infidel, and you have traveled a long way with me to build peace and happiness, that which did not exist in Outremer. You are now in a foreign land with many customs that might offend your honor. For this reason we will have this evening after the hour of prayer two welcome feasts, one here among the tents and one up at the house. Up there many things will be served of which the Prophet, peace be unto him, expressed his condemnation. Down here in the tents you have my word as an emir that nothing unclean will be placed on a plate. When the food is brought out to you, you must bless it in His name Who sees all and hears all, and you shall enjoy it in good faith."

As he was wont to do, Sir Arn repeated almost the same thing in Frankish, but with the proper words for God and without naming any prophet. Marcus and Jacob, who spoke Arabic as well as four or five other languages, exchanged meaningful smiles when they heard a somewhat different version, as usual, in Frankish.

Then Sir Arn asked to have a wine cask rolled out. He called over the Christians, and then everyone bowed to one another before they separated, and each and every one went to the proper feast.

The Christian guests walked in procession up toward the big longhouse. Halfway there they were met by a group of six armed men who closed ranks in an honor guard around them.

By the portal of the dark, imposing blockhouse with the grass-covered roof waited a woman in a shiny red dress who could easily have come from Outremer. She wore a thick gold sash adorned with blue stones and a blue cloak over her shoulders of the same type that Arn had now draped around himself. On her head she wore a small cap, but it in no way hid her long hair, which hung in a heavy braid down her back.

Now she raised a loaf of bread in her hands and called forth a serving woman with a bowl, the contents of which no one could see. Then she pronounced a blessing.

Sir Arn turned around and translated that they were all welcome in God's name, and that anyone entering had to touch the bread first with his right hand and then dip a right-hand finger into the bowl of salt.

For Harald Øysteinsson, who went first among the Christian guests, still wearing his Templar surcoat and black sergeant's mantle, this custom was not foreign. Marcus and Jacob followed their friend "Aral d'Austin," or so they pronounced his name in jest in Frankish and he did not take offense. They obeyed the same ritual but they turned to whisper in feigned seriousness toward the back of the queue that the salt burned like fire and was perhaps bewitched. So those who followed dipped one finger very quickly and cautiously into the salt.

But when they entered the long hall the Wachtian brothers were indeed struck by a feeling that they were in the presence of sorcery. There were hardly any windows, and it would have been completely dark if not for the huge log fire at the far end of the room, the tar torches burning in iron sconces along the walls, and the wax candles on the longtable against one wall. Their nostrils were filled with the odors of smoke and tar, and the strong smell of roasting meat.

Sir Arn placed his Christian guests in the middle of the long-table and then went around to the other side and sat down far to the right in what looked like a heathen throne with dragons' heads and weird curling patterns that resembled snakes. The woman who had offered the welcome salt now sat down next to him, and on her other side was the man who looked like a barrel who was Sir Arn's older brother; he was a man with whom they should never trifle nor make their enemy.

When the Christian guests and their hosts were seated, twelve men wearing the same blue surcoats as Sir Arn and his brother came in. They sat down on either side of the longtable below the high seat and guests. The upper half of the table was left empty; it was obvious that more than twice as many guests could be accommodated.

Sir Arn said grace in Latin so that only the corpulent old monk could mutter along, while all the others sat with chastely bowed heads and folded hands. Then Sir Arn and the monk sang a brief two-part blessing from the Psalter, and the woman between the two brothers stood up and clapped her hands loudly three times.

Now the double doors at the end of the hall were opened and a strange procession entered. First came a column of maidens with flowing hair and white linen shifts that showed rather than hid their charms, and all carried burning tapers in their hands. Then men and women mixed together came in; they too wore white clothing, and they carried heavy burdens of ale and big steaming pots of meat, fish, and vegetables, many of which the guests could recognize but also some they did not know.

Sir Arn passed out big glass goblets which were more ungainly in form than glasses in Outremer. From long experience he knew who should have what to drink. Brother Guilbert received a wineglass, along with the brothers Wachtian and the seaman Tanguy. Sir Arn himself took a glass which he placed before him with an exaggerated gesture as he joked in Frankish that this was protection against the witchcraft in the Nordic ale. Then the Norwegian protested loudly and pretended to be angry, greedily grabbing the tankard that stood foaming before him, but was stopped by a signal from Sir Arn. It was clear that no one should begin to eat or drink yet, although the food had been blessed with both prayer and song.

What everyone was waiting for now appeared, and there was a great roar from all the warriors at the lower end of the table. A repulsive cow horn covered with silver was borne in, and this object was also filled with ale. The cow horn was brought to Sir Arn's corpulent brother, who held it high while he said something that made the warriors in the hall start banging their fists on the table, making the ale tankards jump.

Then he passed the cow horn with a slow and ceremonious gesture to Sir Arn, who now, seemingly embarrassed, accepted the horn and said something that made everyone in the hall who understood Norse burst into laughter. Then he tried to swallow the entire contents of the horn but he was obviously cheating, since most of the ale ran down his surcoat. When he took the horn from his mouth he pretended to stagger and supported himself on the edge of the table as with a shaking hand he passed the drinking horn back to his brother. For this prank he was met by thundering salvos of laughter from the Nordic warriors at the table.

The ceremony was still not over, since nobody made a move to start eating. Once again a servant filled the drinking horn and handed it to Sir Arn's brother, who raised it above his head, saying something that was no doubt noble and pithy, since it was met by an approving murmur. Then he gulped down all the ale without spilling a drop, as easily as a drunkard gulps down a glass of wine. The jubilation in the hall rose anew, and all the men with ale mugs in front of them raised them high, uttered a blessing, and began drinking like brutes. Harald Øysteinsson was the first to thump down his wooden tankard on the table. He stood up and made a short speech in a singing, rhythmic manner that met with great approval.

Sir Arn poured wine for those he wanted to save from the horrors of ale, as he said not entirely in jest, and translated for the wine drinkers what his friend Harald had said in verse. In Frankish it became something like:

Seldom smacked spuming ale so well
as to the warrior who has lacked it long.
Long was the journey.
Longer was the wait.
Now shall we drink with kinsmen no worse than Thor.

Sir Arn explained that Thor was a god who, according to the sagas, began drinking up the whole ocean when he wanted to impress the giants. Unfortunately, this was only the first of many declaimed verses, and Sir Arn did not think he could translate all of them, since it grew harder both to hear and to understand what was said.

More ale was brought in by young women scampering lightly on bare feet, and the platters of meat, fish, bread, and vegetables were piled up like an enemy army on the huge longtable. The Wachtian brothers each fell at once upon a suckling pig, the big monk and the seaman Tanguy took pieces from one of the steaming salmon that were carried in on planks. The English archers loaded up huge pieces of calf shank, while Sir Arn took a modest piece of salmon. With his long sharp dagger he also sliced a chunk out of the cheek of one of the pig heads that was suddenly plopped down before the eyes of the Wachtian brothers.

At first they both stared at the pig head in horror; it was pointing its snout straight at them. Jacob shrank back involuntarily, but Marcus leaned forward on his elbows and began to converse with the pig, so that everyone nearby who understood Frankish was soon convulsed in laughter.

He said that he presumed Sir Swine belonged in this country, not in Outremer, which seemed hardly conceivable. But it was in truth better to end up with Armenian brothers than it would have been out in the tents, where the danger was great that Sir Swine would not have been met with the greatest courtesy.

At the thought of what would have happened if this pig head

had been borne out to the Muslims, Marcus and Jacob doubled over laughing. Soon the Frankish speakers laughed all the harder when the call to prayer was heard coming from the direction of the tents, since the sun went down very late in this strange land. Sir Arn also smiled a bit at the thought of a pig head being served in the midst of the Muslim evening prayers, but he simply gave a dismissive wave of the hand when his brother asked what was so funny.

"God is grea-ea-eat," snorted Marcus in Arabic and raised his wineglass to Sir Arn, but a new fit of laughter caught in his throat and he spurted wine all over his host, who calmly poured him some more.

It was not long before Sir Arn and the woman next to him carefully pushed away their plates, wiped off their daggers, and stuck them in their belts. Sir Arn's brother ate a couple of more huge pieces of meat before he did the same. Then all three in the high seat devoted themselves to drinking; two of them did so quietly while the third drank like the warriors, the Norwegian, and the two English archers John Strongbow and Athelsten Crossbow, who both showed they could drink ale at the same pace as the barbarians.

The clamor rose higher and higher. The Englishmen and the Norwegian were not too proud to move from their places to join the Nordic warriors, and there a mighty battle of honor commenced, to see who could empty an entire tankard of ale the fastest without removing it from his lips. It appeared that the Norwegian and the Englishmen acquitted themselves well in this Nordic contest. Arn leaned over to his four remaining Frankish-speaking guests and explained that it was good for their honor that at least some of the men from Outremer could do well in this strange competition. As he explained, Nordic men esteemed the ability to drink themselves rapidly senseless almost as much as the ability to handle sword and shield. Why this was so, he could not explain, but merely shrugged his shoulders as if at some mystery that was impossible to comprehend.

When the first man tumbled to the floor, vomiting, the hostess got up with a smile and without exaggerated haste. She took her leave of Sir Arn, whom she kissed on the forehead to his obvious embarrassment, and that of his brother and the Frankish-speaking guests, who by this time were the only ones except for the host and hostess who were in any condition to reply when spoken to.

Sir Arn then poured more wine for the Frankish speakers and explained that they had to remain seated for a while longer, so that it could not be said that those who drank wine had been drunk under the table by those who drank ale. However, after a glance down the longtable he opined that it would all be over within an hour, about the time that the first morning light appeared outside.

✠

As the sun rose over Arnäs and the redwing fell silent, Arn stood alone up in the high tower, daydreaming about the landscape of his childhood. He recalled how he had hunted deer and boar up on Kinnekulle with thralls whose names he now had difficulty remembering. He thought about how he had come riding on a noble stallion named Shimal from Outremer, though the steed was never as close to him as was Khamsiin, and how his father and brother had laughed at the wretched horse that in their eyes was good for nothing.

But most of all he daydreamed about Cecilia. He recalled how the two of them had ridden up Kinnekulle one spring; she had worn a green cloak. It was on that occasion that he intended to declare his love but found himself unable to say anything before

Our Lady sent him orders out of the Song of Songs, the words that he had carried in his memory during all the years of war.

Our Lady had in truth listened to his prayers and had taken mercy on his faithfulness; he had never lost hope. Now there was less than a week left of this longing. In two days' time he would set off on the journey to Näs, where Cecilia might already have arrived, although without knowing he was so near.

He shuddered as if in terror at the thought. His waking dream seemed to have grown too immense, as if he no longer could control it.

Down below him the courtyard was quiet and almost entirely deserted. A few house thralls went about mucking away the vomit. With fir branches they swept up the piss down by the door of the longhouse. Some men came out, puffing and swearing, as they dragged a limp guard whom they would have thought dead but for the fact that he had attended a good feast at Arnäs.

The sun now climbed above the horizon in the east, and naturally the call to prayer came from down in the tent camp.

At first Arn did not react at all, since the call to prayer had so long been a daily sound in his ears that he really did not hear it. But when he looked up toward Kinnekulle and Husaby church, he realized that this must be the first sunrise over Arnäs ever to be greeted in such a manner. He tried to remember where in the Holy Koran the exceptions to the call to prayer were prescribed. Perhaps if one was in a hostile land, if one was at war and the enemy would discern the position of the faithful by the call to prayer?

The situation was somewhat similar now. When everyone moved to Forsvik they could call to prayer whenever they pleased. But if this went on for long at Arnäs it was going to be difficult to give evasive answers or to explain that in the Holy Land the love of God found many inscrutable paths into the human soul.

It might also not suffice to say that these men were thralls and therefore could not be counted as enemies, any more than horses and goats.

As soon as the prayers were done, it was time to begin the day's work. Arn felt his head pounding slightly as he descended the narrow spiral staircase in the tower.

Down in the camp, Arn was not surprised to see that all who had rested for the night in the tents of the faithful were up already, while in the Christians' tents everyone was still asleep. Some were snoring so thunderously that it was hard to comprehend how their comrades could stand the noise.

All the faithful had rolled up their prayer rugs, and water had been set over the fire to cook the morning's mocha. The two physicians were the first to see Arn approach, and they stood up at once to wish him God's peace.

"God's peace unto you, Ibrahim Abd al-Malik and Ibrahim Yussuf, you who here in the land of the infidel must be called Abraham and Joseph." Arn greeted them with a bow. "I hope the food from my home was to your liking."

"The lamb was fat and delicious, and the water very cold and fresh," replied the older of the two.

"I'm glad to hear it," said Arn. "Now it is time to work. Gather the brethren!"

Soon a strange procession of foreign men began walking around the walls of Arnäs, pointing and gesticulating and arguing. They agreed on some things, but other matters had to be investigated further before they could reach a consensus. Accuracy was required to build a fortress that could not be taken by storm by an enemy. The soil around the walls had to be examined with test digs. Much had to be measured and calculated, and the many waterways around Arnäs also had to be measured and inspected closely so that the men could determine the course of the new moats around the walls. The marsh that divided the fortress out on the point from the mainland was a big advantage, and it was important not to drain the area or unintentionally dam it with dikes. Considering the present condition of the soil, it would be impossible to roll up siege towers or catapults to the fortress. All such heavy equipment would sink helplessly into the waterlogged ground. So an important part of the fortress's defense was provided by nature itself, as He who sees all and hears all had created it.

When Arn thought that he had explained his thoughts and desires sufficiently as to what the master builders would need to test and calculate, he took the two physicians over to his father's little cookhouse. On the way he stressed to them that here in the North their names were to be Joseph and Abraham and nothing else. They were the same names in both the Bible and in the Holy Koran; only the pronunciation was different. The two physicians nodded that they understood, or at least were resigned to this decision.

As Arn expected, his father was already awake when they entered his chamber. Herr Magnus tried to prop himself up on his healthy elbow, but it was stiff, and Arn hurried over to help him.

"Take out those foreigners for a minute, I have to piss," Herr Magnus said to him in greeting. Arn was so filled with joy at hearing his father speak clearly that he was not bothered by this brusque way of saying good morning. He asked the two physicians to leave the room for a minute, and then found the pisspot and clumsily helped his father attend to his needs.

When it was done he lifted his father over into the chair with the dragon coils and asked the physicians to come back inside. They repeated their examination from the day before and whispered occasionally to Arn. He translated what was said, although he skipped most of the circumlocutions and drawn-out courtesies that were so characteristic of the Arabic language.

What had befallen Herr Magnus came as a result of blood

that was too thick becoming caught in the brain. When this complaint did not lead to immediate death, which sometimes happened, then there was good reason to hope. Some people healed completely, others almost completely, and others so well that only a few signs of illness remained. However, this had nothing at all to do with the old man's wits; only ignorant people believed such a thing.

What was needed now, besides certain restorative herbs that first had to be prepared and brewed together, were fortifying prayers and exercise. The paralyzed muscles had to be put into motion one by one, but great patience was required. As for his speech, there was only one exercise, and that was to speak, which was surely the easiest demand.

On the other hand, he must never creep away to shame and darkness and stop speaking or moving. That would just make matters worse.

Yussuf, the younger of the two medical men, went outside for a moment. He came back with a round stone the size of half a fist and gave it to Arn. Then he explained that within a week, Sir Al-Ghouti's honored father had to learn to lift the stone with his weak left hand over his lap and place it in his healthy right hand. Each time he failed he had to pick up the stone with his good hand, place it back in the sick one, and start over. He must not give up. With determination and prayer much could be accomplished. In a week the next exercise would begin. Most important were practice and a strong will; the restorative herbs were secondary.

That was all. The two physicians bowed first to Arn and then to his father and left without another word.

Arn put the stone in his father's left hand and explained the exercise again. Herr Magnus tried but dropped the stone at once. Arn then put it back in his hand. And his father dropped it again and angrily hissed something. Arn heard only the words "foreign men."

"Don't speak that way to me, Father. Say it again in clear words. I know that you can, just as I know that you understand everything I say," said Arn, looking him sternly in the eye.

"It's no use . . . listening to . . . foreign men," his father said then, with such an effort that his head trembled a bit.

"You're wrong about that, Father. You proved it yourself just now. They said that you would get your speech back. And you spoke, so now we know that they were right. In medicine these men are among the best I encountered in the Holy Land. They have both been in service with the Knights Templar, and that's why they are here with me now."

Herr Magnus did not reply, but he nodded to show that he agreed that for the first time in three years he was wrong.

Arn put the stone back in his father's left hand and said almost as a command that now he must practice, as the physicians had told him to do. Herr Magnus made a halfhearted attempt but then grabbed the stone with his right hand, raised it straight out over the floor, and dropped it. Arn picked it up with a laugh and put it back in his father's lap.

"Tell me what you want to know about the Holy Land and I will tell you, Father." Arn knelt down before Herr Magnus so that their faces were close together.

"Can't sit . . . long . . . like that," said Herr Magnus with difficulty, though he tried to smile. His smile was crooked because one corner of his mouth drooped.

"My knees are more tempered by prayer than you will ever know, Father. In the Holy Land a warrior of God also has to do a great deal of praying for help. But tell me now what you want to know about, and I will tell you."

"Why did we lose . . . Jerusalem?" asked Herr Magnus, at the same time moving the stone halfway to his good hand before he dropped it.

Arn carefully placed the stone back in his weak hand and said that he would tell him how Jerusalem was lost. But only on the condition that his father practiced with the stone while he listened.

It was not difficult for Arn to begin his story. When it came to the Lord's inscrutable ways there was nothing he had brooded over as much as the question of why the Christians had been punished with the loss of Jerusalem and the Holy Sepulcher.

It was because of their sins. That answer now seemed clear to him. And then he gave a detailed account of those sins. He told the story about a patriarch of the Holy City of Jerusalem who had poisoned two bishops to death, about a whoring queen mother who had installled first one and then the other of her newly arrived lovers from Paris as supreme commander of the Christian army, about greedy men who were said to fight for God's cause but merely grabbed things for themselves; they stole, murdered, and burned, only to return home as soon as their purses were stuffed, and with what they thought was forgiveness for their sins.

As Arn described the Christians' sins, citing the worst examples he could think of, he would now and then pick up the stone and put it once again in his father's left hand.

But when the catalog of sins seemed to repeat itself, his father waved his good hand to put a stop to the list of miseries. Then he took a deep breath and gathered his forces for a new question.

"Where were you . . . my son . . . when Jerusalem was lost?"

Arn was taken aback by the question, since he had grown agitated at the thought of evil men such as the patriarch Heraclius, men who sent others to their deaths at a whim or for the sake of their vanity, like the Grand Master of the Knights Templar,

Gérard de Ridefort, or scoundrels like the whoremonger commander, Guy de Lusignan.

Then Arn replied, truth be told, that he had been in Damascus,
a captive of the enemy. Jerusalem was lost not after a brave stand
at the walls of the city; Jerusalem was lost in a foolish battle at
Tiberias, when the entire Christian army was led to its death by
fools and whoremongers who knew nothing of war. Few prisoners had survived; of the Knights Templar there were only two.

"You . . . came home . . . rich?" Herr Magnus put in.

"Yes, that's true, Father. I came home and I am rich, richer
than Eskil. But it's because I was a friend of the Saracens' king."
Arn had answered truthfully but soon regretted it when he saw
anger flare up in his father's eyes.

Herr Magnus lifted the stone in a single motion from his left
to his right hand and then returned it to his sick hand, so that he
could raise his good hand in a gesture cursing this son who was a
traitor and had thereby grown rich.

"No, no, that was not how it happened at all," Arn lied hastily to calm his father. "I just wanted to see if you could move
the stone from one hand to the other. Your anger gave you unexpected strength. Forgive me this little trick!"

Herr Magnus relaxd at once. He looked down in surprise
at the stone, which was already back in his sick hand. Then he
smiled and nodded.

Chapter 2

Eskil was evidently not in a very good mood, even though he was doing his best not to show it. Not only would he have to ride up to the stone quarry and back, which would take this whole hot summer day and a good bit of the evening, but he no longer felt like the lord of his own house, as he had grown accustomed to being for so many years.

The scaffolding had already been erected along the wall at Arnäs, and more lumber was being brought from the woods by people who'd been set to work without asking his permission. Arn seemed to have become a stranger in many ways. He apparently didn't understand that a younger brother could not usurp the place of his older brother, or why a Folkung in the king's council had to travel with a sizable armed guard even though there was peace in the kingdom.

Behind them rode ten men fully armed, wearing as Arn did unbearably hot chain mail under their surcoats. Eskil himself had dressed as if riding to hunt or to a banquet, with a short surcoat and a hat with a feather. The old monk rode in his monk's habit of thick white wool, which must have made the journey hard to bear, though his face revealed no sign of it. But he didn't look happy, since he'd had to roll his habit up to his knees so that his bare calves were visible. Like Arn he was riding one of the smaller, foreign horses that were so restless.

On the lower slopes of Kinnekulle they reached pleasant shade as they rode in under the tall beech trees. This put Eskil instantly into a better mood, and he thought that now was the time to start discussing the good sense or lack thereof in all the construction going on. In his many years in business he'd learned that it was unwise to dispute even trifles when one was too hot or too thirsty or in a bad mood. Things would go better in the cool shade of the trees.

He urged on his horse to come up alongside Arn, who seemed to be riding with his thoughts far away, surely farther off than any stone quarry.

"You must have ridden during hotter summer days than this, I suppose?" Eskil began innocently.

"Yes," Arn replied, obviously tearing himself away from quite different thoughts. "In the Holy Land the heat in summer was sometimes so great that no man could set his bare foot on the ground without burning himself badly. Riding in the shade like this is like riding in the pastures of Paradise in comparison."

"Yet you insist on dressing in chain mail, as if you were still riding out to battle."

"It's been my custom for more than twenty years; I might even feel cold if I rode dressed like you, my brother," said Arn.

"Yes, that might be so," said Eskil, now that he had turned the conversation onto the desired track. "I suppose you've seen nothing but war ever since you left us as a youth."

"That's true," said Arn pensively. "It's almost like a miracle to ride in such a beautiful country, in such coolness, without refugees and burned houses along the roads, and without peering continually into the woods or glancing to the rear for enemy horsemen. It's hard enough just to describe to you how that feels."

"Just as it's hard for me to describe to you how it feels after fifteen years of peace. When Knut became king and Birger Brosa his jarl, peace came to our land, and there has been peace ever since. You ought to keep that in mind."

"Indeed?" said Arn, casting a glance at his brother, because he sensed that this conversation was about more than sunshine and heat.

"You're imposing great expenses on us now with all your construction," Eskil clarified. "I mean, it might seem unwise to prepare for war at such cost when peace prevails."

"As far as the expense goes, I brought the payment with me in three coffers of gold," Arn retorted.

"But we're losing great sums on all the stone we're now using for ourselves instead of selling. Why have war expenses when there is peace?" Eskil said patiently.

"You'll have to explain yourself better," said Arn.

"I mean . . . it's true that we own all the quarries. So we don't need to spend silver for the stone you want to use. But in these years of peace, many stone churches are being built all over Western Götaland. And much of the stone that's needed comes from our quarries."

"And if we take stone for our own use we'll lose that profit, you mean?"

"Yes, in business that's how one has to think."

"That's true. But if we didn't own these quarries, I would have paid for the stone in any case. Now we can save that expense. One also has to think like that in business."

"Then the question remains whether it's wise to spend so

much wealth building for war when there is peace," Eskil sighed, displeased that for once he was making no headway with his explanations of how everything in life could be calculated in silver.

"In the first place, we're not building for war but for peace. When there is war one has neither the time nor the money to build."

"But if war *doesn't* come," Eskil argued, "then haven't all these efforts and expenses been to no avail?"

"No," said Arn. "Because in the second place, no one can see into the future."

"Nor can you, no matter how wise you are in all matters concerning war."

"That's quite true. And that's why it's the wisest course to build strong defenses while we have time and peace prevails. If you want peace, prepare for war. Do you know what the greatest success of this construction would be? If a foreign army never pitches camp outside Arnäs. Then we will have built our defenses as we should."

Eskil was not entirely convinced, but a seed of doubt had been sown. If they could truly look into the future and see that the time of war was past, then strengthening their fortifications as Arn planned would not be worth all the effort and silver.

As things now stood in the kingdom, it looked as though the time of war was indeed past. Going back to the very beginning of the sagas there had never been a longer peace than under King Knut.

Eskil realized that he now wanted to exclude war as a means to be used in the struggle for power. He would rather see the sort of power that came from putting the right sons and daughters into the right bridal beds, and he would rather see the wealth created by trade with foreign lands as a protection against war. Who would want to demolish his own business? Silver was mightier than the sword, and men who had married into each other's clans were loath to take up the sword against each other.

This was the wise manner in which they had sought to arrange things during King Knut's reign. But no one could be completely secure, because no one could see into the future.

"How strong can we make the castle at Arnäs?" he asked, emerging from his long reverie.

"Strong enough that no one can take it," replied Arn confidently, as though it were a given. "We can make Arnäs so strong that we could house a thousand Folkungs and servants within the walls for more than a year. Not even the most powerful army could endure such a long siege outside the walls without great suffering. Just think of the cold of winter, the rains of autumn, and the wet snow and mud of spring."

"But what would we eat and drink for so long a time?" Eskil exclaimed with such a terrified expression that Arn had to give him a broad smile.

"I'm afraid that the ale would be gone after a couple of months," said Arn. "And toward the end we might have to live on bread and water like penitents in the cloister. But we'd have a water supply within the walls if we dug a couple of new wells. And the advantage of grain and wheat, the same as dried fish and smoked meat, is that they can be stored for a long time in great quantities. But then we'd have to build new types of barns out of stone, which would keep all moisture out. Storing up such supplies is as important as building strong walls. If you then keep strict accounts of what you have, it's possible that you might even be able to brew new ale."

Eskil felt instant relief at these last words from Arn. His suspicion began to change into admiration, and with increased interest he asked how war was conducted in France and the Holy Land and Saxony, and in other countries that had bigger populations and greater riches than they did up here in the North. Arn's replies took him into a new world, in which the armies consisted mostly of cavalry and in which mighty wooden catapults hurled blocks of stone against walls that were twice as high and twice as thick as the walls of Arnäs. Finally Eskil's queries grew so importunate that they stopped to take a rest. Arn scraped away leaves and twigs from the ground next to a thick beech tree and smoothed out the area with his steel-clad foot. He bade Eskil sit down on one of the tree's thick roots and called to the monk, who bowed and then took a seat next to Eskil.

"My brother is a man of affairs who wants to create peace by using silver. Now we have to tell him how to do the same thing with steel and stone," Arn explained. He drew his dagger and began drawing a fortress in the brown dirt he had smoothed out.

The fortress he drew was called Beaufort and was located in Lebanon, in the northern reaches of the kingdom of Jerusalem. It had been besieged more than twenty times for varying periods, several times by the most feared Saracen commanders. But none had been able to take it, not even the great Nur al-Din, who once made the attempt with ten thousand warriors and kept at it for a year and a half. Both Arn and the monk had visited the fortress of Beaufort and remembered it well. They helped each other recall the tiniest details as Arn sketched in the dirt with his dagger.

They explained everything by turns, starting with the most important facts. The location was crucial, either up on a mountain like Beaufort or out in the water like Arnäs. But no matter how good the position for defensive war, they needed to have water inside the walls, not a spring outside that the enemy could find and cut off.

Equally important as access to water and a good position was the ability to store sufficiently large supplies of food, most importantly grain for bread and fodder for the horses. Only then could they begin to think about the construction of the walls and moats that would prevent the enemy from raising siege towers or bringing up trebuchets to fling stones and offal into the castle. And the next most important thing was the placement of the towers and firing positions so that they could cover all the angles along the walls with as few archers as possible.

Arn drew towers that protruded beyond the walls on every corner, explaining how from such towers they could shoot along the walls and not merely outward. In this way they could minimize the number of archers needed up on the ramparts, which would be a great advantage. Better shooting angles and fewer archers were essential.

Here Eskil interrupted, a bit reluctant to show his ignorance at not understanding the advantage of having fewer archers, which seemed to be a given for Arn and the monk. What did they gain by reducing their forces atop the walls?

Endurance, Arn explained. A siege was not like a three-day banquet. The point was to endure, not to let weariness reduce their vigilance. Those who laid siege to a castle wanted to take it by storm in the end, if not by negotiation. The besiegers could choose any time at all: after a day, a week, or a month; in the morning, at night, or in the broad daylight of the afternoon. Suddenly they would all appear at the walls with siege ladders, coming from every direction simultaneously, and if they had been diligent in hiding their intentions the defenders would be taken completely by surprise.

That was the decisive moment. Then it would be crucial that the defenders positioned up on the walls would have been on duty only a few hours. And that two-thirds of the defending force were rested or sleeping. When the alarm bell rang it should not take many seconds before all those who had rested were at their battle stations. If they practiced this several times, the defensive force of the castle would increase from one-third to full force in the same time it took the attackers to bring forward their siege ladders. So sleep was an important part of their defense. With this arrangement they also saved many sleeping berths, since a third of the defenders were always on the walls. And they also had a spot warmed up when they came down from duty.

But back to the fortress of Beaufort. It was indeed one of the strongest in the world, but it was located in a country where it was important to defend against the mightiest armies in the world. It would take ten years to build such a castle at Arnäs, and it would entail much extra work for no good purpose. Or, as Arn explained with a glance at Eskil, it would involve spending too much silver. A war such as that in the Holy Land, with such armies, would never come to Arnäs.

Arn erased the picture of Beaufort with his foot and began to draw Arnäs as it would one day become, with a wall enclosing more than twice the present area. The entire tip of the point would be fortified, and where the point turned into marshland a new gate would be built, but higher up on the wall. Then they would also have to build an equally high ramp of stone and earth with a moat between the wall and the bridgehead on the other side. In this way no one would be able to bring up battering rams against the gate, which would be much weaker than the stone walls no matter how strongly it was constructed. A gate at ground level, like they had now, was an invitation for the enemy to hold a victory feast.

If all this was done according to plan, Arn assured them that with less than two hundred men inside he would be able to defend Arnäs against any existing Nordic army.

Eskil then asked about the danger of fire, and both the monk and Arn nodded and said it was a good question. Arn started drawing again, describing how the courtyards inside the walls would be paved in stone, and all the sod roofs would be replaced with clay slate. Everything flammable would be replaced with stone, or in the event of siege they would be protected by ox-hides that would constantly be kept wet.

And these were just the "defensive" measures that needed to be taken, Arn continued eagerly now that he saw he had captured Eskil's interest. The other part was to mount an attack themselves. It was best to do that with troops on horseback, and long before the enemy began a siege. It would be an immense and slow undertaking to move an army to lay siege to Arnäs. On the way there the enemy's supply column could be attacked by mounted troops on horses much faster than their own, and this alone would take a toll on the enemy's strength and will to fight.

And after the siege had gone on for a week or so, and the enemy's alertness had diminished, the gates of the castle could be suddenly flung open and out would stream horsemen with full weaponry, able to take many times more lives than they lost. Arn drew strong lines on the ground with his dagger.

Eskil couldn't help feeling confused at how differently war was waged in lands outside the North. He thought that he understood Arn's reasoning; that what was already happening out in the world would sooner or later make its way to Western Götaland. So it would be best if they learned the new techniques and built up their strength before their enemies did. But how would all this be accomplished, in addition to the construction work?

Skills were an essential part of the endeavor, said Arn. And he and many of his foreign guests had mastered those skills.

Silver was the other part. The way war was waged in the world at large, the one with the most silver became the strongest. A mounted army did not live on air or on faith, although both were necessary; the soldiers needed supplies and weapons, all of which had to be bought. War in this new age had more to do with business, rather than the willingness of kinsmen to protect each other's lives and property. Behind every fully armed man in chain mail stood a hundred men who cultivated the grain, drove the ox-carts, burned charcoal for the smithies, forged weapons and armor, transported them across the seas, built the ships and sailed them, shoed the horses and fed them—and behind it all were vast sums of silver.

War was no longer two peasant clans fighting about honor or who would be called king or jarl. It was business—the biggest business in the world.

Whoever managed this business with good sense, plenty of silver, and sufficient skill could buy the victory if war came. Or even better, buy the peace. For he who built a strong enough fortress would never be attacked.

Eskil was struck by this sudden insight that he and his business dealings might be more important for war or peace than all his guards put together; he was speechless. Arn and the monk seemed to misunderstand his waning questions, thinking that he was tiring of the lesson, so they immediately prepared to re-mount their horses.

They visited three quarries that day before Arn and the monk seemed to find what they were looking for in the fourth one, which had only recently begun cutting sandstone. There were few stonecutters, but there was a supply of cut stone blocks that had not yet been sold.

This would save a great deal of time, Arn explained. Sandstone was often too soft, especially if used in walls that were subjected to heavy battering rams. But they didn't have to prepare for that sort of battle at Arnäs, because the ground out on the point rose steeply up to the walls, with no possibility of deploying battering rams. And to the east toward the moat and drawbridge, the ground was far too soft and dropped off too abruptly. So sandstone would serve the purpose well.

Sandstone also had the advantage of being easier to cut and shape than limestone, not to mention granite, and here they already had a supply that could be used in construction without further delay. This was good. Choosing the right type of stone would save more than a year in construction.

Eskil made no objections. Arn thought that his brother seemed unexpectedly amenable when he agreed to every decision regarding the work that would have to be done at the quarry the following week, and where and how new stonecutters would be acquired.

But he did complain about having a serious thirst. He gave Brother Guilbert an odd look when the monk kindly handed him a leather sack full of tepid water.

☨

The next journey they took together was not much longer, only two days from Arnäs to Näs out on the island of Visingsö in Lake Vättern. But for Arn this seemed the longest journey of his life.

Or, as he preferred to think of it, the end of a journey that had lasted most of his life.

He had made a sacred vow to Cecilia that for as long as he breathed and as long as his heart beat, his aim would be to come back to her. He had even sworn on his newly consecrated Templar sword; it was an oath that could never be broken.

Of course he had to laugh when he tried to picture himself back then, seventeen years old and unmarked by war in both soul and body. He had been as foolish as only the ignorant can be. It also brought a smile to his lips and mixed feelings to his heart when he tried to imagine that youth with the burning gaze, a sort of Perceval as Brother Guilbert would have said, vowing to survive twenty years of war in Outremer. And as a Templar knight at that. It had been an impossible dream.

But right now it was about to come true.

Over these twenty years he had prayed every day—well, maybe not every day during certain campaigns or lengthy battles when the sword took precedence over prayer—but almost every day, he had prayed to the Mother of God to hold Her protective hand over Cecilia and his unknown child. And She had done so, with some purpose in mind.

Looking at it that way—and it was the only logical way, he thought—he should now fear nothing in the whole world. It was Her divine will to bring them together again. Now it was about to happen, so what was there to worry about?

A lot, it turned out, when he forced himself to ponder how things might go. He had loved a seventeen-year-old maiden named Cecilia Algotsdotter. Then as now that word, to *love* a person, was unsuitable in the mouth of a Folkung and also close to mockery of the love of God. She in turn had loved a seventeen-year-old youth who was a different Arn Magnusson than the one alive today.

But who were they now? Much had happened to him during more than twenty years of war. Just as much must have happened to her during twenty years of penance in Gudhem cloister under an abbess who people had said was an abominable woman.

Would they even recognize each other?

He tried to compare himself at the present moment with that young man he had been at the age of seventeen. It was obvious that the difference in his body was great. If he had once had a handsome face as a youth, he was definitely not good-looking now. Half of his left eyebrow was missing, and his temple was one big white scar; he had received that in the hour of defeat at the Horns of Hattin, that place of eternal dishonor and tribulation. The rest of his face had at least twenty white scars, most of them from arrows. Wouldn't a woman from the kind and peaceful cloistered world of Our Lady turn away in repugnance at such a face, which attested to what sort of man he had become?

Would he really recognize her? Yes, he was sure that he would. His stepmother Erika Joarsdotter was only a few years older than Cecilia, and he had recognized her at once, just as she had recognized him from far off.

Worst of all his worries was what he would say to her when they met. It was as if his mind shut down when he tried to come up with beautiful words for his initial greeting. For this reason he had to seek out even more solace and advice from God's Mother.

They rowed up the river Tidan, against the current and with eight oarsmen. Arn sat alone at the bow and gazed down into the murky water, where he could catch a blurred image of his lacerated face. In the middle of the flat-bottomed riverboat, which spent its entire lifetime going up and down this river, stood their three horses. Arn had persuaded Eskil that no guards were necessary on this journey, since he and Harald bore full weaponry and had brought along their longbows and plenty of arrows. No Nordic guards would be of any consequence, but would only take up room.

Eskil woke Arn from his reverie by suddenly placing his hand on his brother's shoulder. When Arn flinched at the touch, Eskil had a good laugh at this guard who was supposed to be on the alert in the bow. He held out a smoked ham which Arn declined.

"It's a delight to travel on the river on such a lovely summer day," said Eskil.

"Yes," said Arn, gazing at the willows and alders dangling their branches in the gentle current. "This is something I have dreamt of for a long time, but I never thought I'd see it again."

"Yet now it's time to speak a little about some evil things," said Eskil, sitting down heavily on the thwart next to Arn. "Some of it is truly sad to speak of . . ."

"Better to say it now than later if it has to be told," said Arn, sitting up straight from where he was leaning against the boat's planking.

"You and I had a brother. We have two sisters who are already married off, but our brother named Knut was killed by a Dane when he was eighteen."

"Then let us for the first time pray together for his soul," said Arn at once.

Eskil sighed but acquiesced. They prayed much longer than Eskil found reasonable.

"Who killed him and why?" asked Arn when he looked up. In his face there was less sorrow and anger than Eskil had expected.

"The Dane is named Ebbe Sunesson. It was at a bridegroom's feast when one of our sisters was to go to the bridal bed, and it happened at Arnäs."

"So our sister was married into the Sverkers and Danes?" Arn asked without expression.

"Yes. Kristina is the wife of Konrad Pedersson outside Roskilde."

"But how did it happen? How could a bridegroom's feast end in death?"

"Things can get heated, as you know . . . There was no doubt much ale that night, as at such times, and the young Ebbe Sunesson was bragging about what a great swordsman he was, saying that no one had the courage to trade blows with him. Anyone using such language at the ale cask is more likely fooling himself rather than anyone else. But things were different with this Ebbe; he proved to have a skilled hand with a sword. He now rides with the Danish royal guard."

"And the one who let himself be fooled was our brother Knut?"

"Yes, Knut was no swordsman. He was like me and our father; not like you."

"So, tell me what happened. Usually anyone who encounters someone who handles a sword better in such situations comes away with cuts and bruises. But death?"

"First Ebbe sliced off one of Knut's ears and got a great laugh for that feat. Maybe Knut could have backed out after first blood. But Ebbe taunted him so that the laughter grew even louder. When Knut then attacked in anger . . ."

"So he was killed at once. I can understand how it happened," said Arn with more sorrow than wrath in his voice. "If it be God's will, Ebbe Sunesson shall one day meet Knut's brother with a sword. But I don't intend to seek revenge of my own free will. You didn't seek revenge on the killer either? Then you must have demanded a big penalty."

"No, we refrained from demanding a penalty," replied Eskil with shame. "It was no easy matter, but the alternative would have been worse. Ebbe Sunesson is from the Hvide clan, into which our sister Kristina was supposed to marry the very next day. The Hvide clan is the most powerful in Denmark, next to the king's. Archbishop Absalon in Lund is a Hvide."

"That was no merry wedding celebration," said Arn calmly, as if talking about the weather.

"No, truly it was not," Eskil agreed. "All the Danish guests rode south the next day to conclude the bridal ale at home. We buried Knut in Forshem, and one day later our father suffered a stroke. I think it was grief that caused it."

"Dearly have we paid in dowry to ally ourselves with that Hvide clan," Arn muttered, gazing at the dark river water. "And what other sorrows do you have to relate?"

It was obvious from Eskil's expression that there were more misfortunes to relate. But he hesitated a long time, and Arn had to urge him again to cleanse the evil rather than prolong it.

The next sorrow concerned Katarina Algotsdotter, Cecilia's sister, the wife of Eskil and the mother of two married daughters and their son Torgils, whom they would soon be meeting at the king's castle in Näs. Katarina had been neither a bad wife nor a bad mother. Indeed, she had been better than anyone had expected, since she was known to be wily and full of intrigues.

For the sake of honor more than for dowry and power, Eskil had been forced to go to the bridal bed with Katarina. Algot Pålsson, the father of Cecilia and Katarina, had already arranged a betrothal agreement between Cecilia and Arn. But that agreement had been broken when Arn and Cecilia brought down upon themselves the punishment of the Church and twenty years of penance. Algot then demanded redress, which was also his right.

The honor of the Folkungs had thus been one aspect of the matter. The other was a dowry consisting of a quarry and woods and a long stretch of shore along Lake Vänern. Perhaps Eskil had seen the benefits in this part of the bargain better than most people, for he now controlled trade on the lake for all of Western Götaland.

And the quarry brought in a lot of silver during this period when so many churches were being built all over the country. A lot of silver, that is, as long as he didn't waste stone on his own construction projects, he added in a failed attempt at levity. Arn did not deign to smile.

Rewarding Katarina with a morning gift and keys to his estate after the evil she had done to Arn and Cecilia had been no light matter. Yet it was the best way to clean up after themselves. No one was going to say of the Folkungs that they broke promises and business agreements.

For many years Katarina was a good-tempered housewife who fulfillled her duties in everything that was required. But after fifteen years had passed she commenced the worst of sins.

Eskil spent long periods at Näs or in Östra Aros or even over in Visby on Gotland, as well as down in Lübeck in Germany. During these times as a housewife without a husband, Katarina began devoting herself to amusements of a type that could scarcely be cleansed by penance. She took one of the retainers to bed with her at night.

When Eskil found out about this the first time, he spoke in all seriousness to Katarina and explained that if there was more whispering about such a sin in his house, great misfortune could befall them. The strict language of the law regarding whoredom was only one part of the evil. Worse would be if their children lost their mother.

At first Katarina seemed to have complied. But soon the whispering began anew, and Eskil took notice not only at Arnäs but also when he saw the mortifying looks he received at the king's council. He then did everything that honor demanded, though his decision was not made lightly but with sorrow.

His retainer Svein did as he was ordered. One night when Eskil was away visiting the king at Näs, although alone in his own lodgings and as if haunted by the nightmare, Svein and two other men strode into the cookhouse. Everyone at Arnäs knew that it was there the two sinners met.

They did not kill Katarina but instead the man she was whoring with. The bloody sheets were taken to the *ting* so that the sinner would be condemned in disgrace. Katarina was banished to Gudhem cloister, where she took the vows.

As far as silver was concerned in this matter, that had been the easiest to arrange. Eskil donated as much land as he thought necessary to Gudhem, and Katarina relinquished her property to the Folkung clan when she took her vows. That was the price for being allowed to live.

After this news was recounted, the rest of the journey was marked by gloom for a long while. Harald Øysteinsson sat alone in the stern of the boat with the helmsman; he felt that he ought not to get involved in the brothers' conversation up in the bow. He could clearly see even from that distance that their faces were full of sorrow.

⁜

Situated below the old *ting* site at Askeberga, where the River Tidan made a sharp turn to the south, was the inn. Several boats resembling their own, long with flat bottoms but with heavier loads, had been partially drawn up onto the riverbank, and there was a great commotion among the oarsmen and the inn folk when the Folkung owner Herr Eskil arrived. Guests of lesser stature were thrown out of one longhouse, and women ran to sweep up. The man in charge of the inn, who was named Gurmund and was a freed thrall, brought ale for Herr Eskil.

Arn and Harald Øysteinsson took their bows and quivers, fetched straw from one of the barns, and made a target before they went off to practice. Harald joked that the one exercise they had been able to do during their year at sea demanded enemies at close hand, but that now once again, with God's help, they could prepare themselves better. Arn replied curtly that practice was a duty, since it was blasphemous to believe that Our Lady would continue to help someone who had been an idler. Only he who worked hard at his archery would deserve to shoot well.

Some of the thrall boys had crept after them to watch how the two men, neither of whom they knew, would handle a bow and arrow. But soon they came running back to the inn, breathing hard, to tell anyone who cared to listen that these archers must be the best of all. Some of the freedmen then furtively headed in the direction of the archers, and soon they saw with their own eyes that it was true. Both the Folkung and his retainer in the red Norwegian tunic handled the bow and arrow better than anyone they had ever seen.

When evening fell and the lords were about to eat supper, it soon became clear that the unknown warrior in the Folkung garb was Herr Eskil's brother, and it wasn't long before the rumor spread all around the Askeberga area. A man from the sagas had come back to Western Götaland. Surely the man in the Folkung mantle could be none other than Arn Magnusson, who was the subject of so many ballads. The matter was discussed back and forth in cookhouses and courtyards. But no one could be entirely sure.

Two of the innkeeper's younger sons dashed thoughtlessly into the longhouse, stopped inside the door, and called to Arn that he should say his name. Such boldness could have cost them skin on their backs and on Gurmund's as well. He was seated at the nobles' table inside and got up in anger to chide the louts, at the same time offering apologies to his master Eskil.

But Arn stopped him. He went over to the boys himself, grabbed them in jest by the scruff of their necks, and took them out to the courtyard. There he knelt down on one knee, feigned a stern expression, and asked them to repeat their question if they dared.

"Are you . . . Sir Arn Magnusson?" gasped the bolder of the two, shutting his eyes as if he expected a box on the ear.

"Yes, I am Arn Magnusson," said Arn, now dropping the stern expression. But the boys still looked a bit scared, their eyes flicking from the scars of war on his face to the sword which hung at his side, with the golden cross on both the scabbard and the hilt.

"We want to enter your service!" said the bolder one, when he finally dared believe that neither whip nor curses awaited them from the warrior.

Arn laughed and explained that this was doubtless a matter that would have to wait for some years yet. But if they both practiced diligently with their wooden swords and bows, it might just be possible someday.

The smaller of the two now plucked up his courage and asked if they might see Sir Arn's sword. Arn got to his feet, pausing a moment before he drew the sword swiftly and soundlessly out of its sheath. The two boys gasped as the shining steel glinted in the afternoon sun. Like all boys they could see at once that this was a completely different sort of sword than those wielded by both retainers and lords. It was longer and narrower but without the slightest loop or flame festooning the blade. The dragon coils or secret symbols of glowing gold that were inlaid in the upper end of the blade were also impressive.

Arn took the hand of the older boy and cautiously placed his index finger on the edge of the blade, pressing it down with a feather's touch. At once a drop of blood appeared on his fingertip.

He put the finger in the boy's mouth, sheathed the magic sword in its scabbard, then patted the two of them on the head, and explained that swords just as sharp awaited anyone who went into his service. But there would be hard work too. In five years' time they should seek him out if they still had a mind to it.

Then he bowed to them as if they were already his retainers, turned on his heel, and strode with mantle fluttering back to the evening meal. The two boys stared as if bewitched at the Folkung lion on his back. They didn't dare move a muscle until he had shut the door to the longhouse behind him.

Arn was in such a good mood as he returned to the longhouse that Eskil felt prompted to mutter that he didn't understand how their conversation during the day's boat ride could have caused him such delight. Arn instantly turned serious as he sat down across from Eskil at the table and cast a startled glance at the wooden trencher of porridge, drippings, and bacon before him. He shoved the trencher aside and placed his scarred hand over Eskil's.

"Eskil, my brother. You must understand one thing about me and Harald. We rode for many years with the Reaper at our side. At matins with our dear knight-brothers we never knew who might be gone by evensong. I saw many of my brothers die, also many who were better men than I. I saw the heads of the best stuck on lance-tips below the walls of Beaufort, the castle I told you about yesterday. But I leave my sorrows for the hour of prayer; believe me that I am diligent in my prayers after you are asleep. Don't think that I took lightly what you have told me."

"The war in the Holy Land gave you strange habits," Eskil muttered, but was suddenly filled with curiosity. "Were there many Templar knights who were better than you, my brother?"

"Yes," Arn said gravely. "Harald is my witness. Ask him."

"Well, what do you say to that, Harald?"

"That it is true and yet it is not," replied Harald when he looked up from the plate of porridge swimming in fat and bacon, to which he was devoting much more interest than Arn had done. "When I came to the Holy Land I thought I was a warrior, since I had done nothing but fight from the age of fourteen. I thought I was one of the strongest swordsmen of all. That false belief cost me many wounds. The Templar knights were warriors like none I had ever seen or dreamt of. The Saracens thought that a Templar knight was like five ordinary men. And I would agree with them on that. But it's also true that there were some Templar knights who stood far above all the others, and the one who was called Arn de Gothia, your brother, was among them. In the North there is no swordsman who can compare with Arn, I swear to you by the Mother of God!"

"Do not blaspheme Our Lady!" said Arn sternly. "Remember swordsmen like Guy de Carcasonne, Sergio de Livorne, and above all Ernesto de Navarra."

"Yes, I remember them all," replied Harald. "And you should also remember our agreement, that as soon as we set foot on Nordic soil I would no longer be your sergeant or you my master who could command me, but your Norwegian brother. And to you, Eskil, I can say that the names Arn mentioned were those of the most superior swordsmen. But now they are all dead, and Arn is not."

"It's not a matter of sword, lance, or horse," said Arn, his gaze fixed on the table. "Our Lady holds her protective and benevolent hands over me, for She has a plan."

"Living swordsmen are better than dead ones," said Eskil

curtly and in a tone indicating he considered the topic finished. "But porridge and bacon do not seem to please our swordsman?"

Arn admitted that he was not in the habit of rejecting God's gifts at table, but he did have a problem with liquid pig fat. Although he could also understand that such fare would warm the body well during a Nordic winter.

Eskil took an inexplicable pleasure in the fact that his brother complained about the food even on this day. At once he ordered one of the men sitting at the oarsmen's table on the other side of the long fire in the hall to go to the stores in the riverboat. He was to bring from the rear magazine some hams from Arnäs and a bunch of smoked sausages from Lödöse.

After the meal, when all were sated, Eskil went over to the log-fire and picked up a piece of charcoal. Back at the table he swept aside with his elbow the remnants of the meal and quickly began drawing on the tabletop with the charcoal. It was the route from Lödöse up the Göta River and into Lake Vänern, past Arnäs and up to the mouth of the Tidan where their river journey had begun. Via the Tidan they were now on their way to Forsvik on the shore of Lake Vättern, and on the other side of Vättern they would head for Lake Boren and on to Linköping. From there other routes branched out, leading north into Svealand and south to Visby and Lübeck. This was the backbone of his realm of business, he explained proudly. He controlled all the waterways from Lödöse to Linköping. He owned all the boats, riverboats as well as the larger ships with rounded hulls that sailed across Lakes Vänern and Vättern, as well as the portage chests located at the Troll's Fall on the Göta River. More than five hundred men, most of them freed thralls, sailed his ships on these waters. Only during the most severe and snowy winters was trade sometimes brought to a standstill for a few weeks at a time.

Arn and Harald had quietly and attentively studied the lines that Eskil had drawn on the table with his piece of charcoal, and they nodded in agreement. It was a great thing, they both thought, to be able to connect the North Sea and Norway with the Eastern Sea and Lübeck. In this way they could thumb their noses at Danish power.

Eskil's face clouded over, and all the elated self-confidence drained out of him. What did they mean by that, and what did they know about the Danes?

Arn told him that when they had sailed up along the coast of Jutland they had passed the Limfjord. They had turned in there so that Arn could pray and donate some gold to the cloister of Vitskøl where he had spent almost ten years in his childhood. At Vitskøl they couldn't avoid hearing some things and observing others. Denmark was a great power, united first under King Valdemar and now his son Knut. Danish warriors resembled Frankish and Saxon warriors rather than Nordic ones, and the power that Denmark possessed, so evident to the eye, would not go unused. It would grow, most likely at the expense of the German lands.

From Norway they could sail to Lödöse up the Göta River without being captured or paying tolls to the Danes. But to send trading ships to the south from Lödöse and sail between the Danish islands to Saxony and Lübeck could not be done without paying heavy tolls.

Yet they didn't need to trouble themselves with the tolls, since the strongest side would use war to force through its will. War with the great Danish power was what they had to avoid above all.

Eskil objected that they could always try to marry into the Danish clans to keep them quiet, but both Harald and Arn laughed so rudely at this idea that Eskil was offended, and he moped for a while.

"Harald and I have talked about a way to strengthen your trade that I think should cheer you up right now," Arn then said.

"We heartily support your trade, and we agree that you have arranged everything for the best, so listen to our idea. Our ship is in Lödöse. Harald, being the Norwegian helmsman that he is, can sail that ship in any sea. Our proposal is that Harald sail the ship between Lofoten and Lödöse in return for good compensation in silver. Remember that it's a ship that could hold three horses and two dozen men with all their provisions and all the fodder required, as well as the ten ox-carts with goods that we brought from Lödöse. Now convert that into dried fish from Lofoten and you'll find that two voyages each summer will double your income in dried fish."

"To think that you still remember my idea about the dried fish," said Eskil, somewhat encouraged.

"I still remember that ride we made as young boys to the *ting* of all Goths, from both Western and Eastern Götaland, at Axvalla," replied Arn. "That was when you told me about how you wanted to try to bring cod from Lofoten with the help of our Norwegian kinsmen. I remember that we instantly thought of the forty days of fasting before Easter, and that was when the idea came to me. As a cloister boy I had already eaten plenty of *cabalao*. Dried fish is no less expensive now than it was then. That must be good for your business."

"In truth, we are both sons of mother Sigrid," said Eskil nostalgically with a wave toward the room for more ale. "She was the first who understood what we're talking about now. Our father is an honorable man, but without her he wouldn't have amassed much wealth."

"You're definitely right about that," replied Arn, deflecting the ale toward Harald as it was brought in.

"So, Harald, do you want to go into our service as first mate on the foreign ship? And will you sail around Norway for cod?" asked Eskil gravely after he had guzzled a considerable amount of the fresh ale.

"That's the agreement between Arn and myself," said Harald.

"I see that you've got yourself a new surcoat," said Eskil.

"Among your retainers at Arnäs there are several Norsemen, as you know. In your service they all wear blue and have little use for the clothes they were wearing when they arrived. I bought this Birchleg surcoat from one of them, and in it I feel more at home than in the colors I always wore in the Holy Land," Harald replied with some pride.

"Two crossed arrows in gold on a red field," Eskil muttered pensively.

"It suits me even better, since the bow is my best weapon, and these colors are my birthright," Harald assured him. "The bow and arrow was the Birchlegs' primary weapon in their struggle. In Norway I had no equal with the bow, and I grew no worse in the Holy Land."

"That's undoubtedly true," replied Eskil. "The Birchlegs relied heavily on the power of the bow, and that brought them their victory. You left for the Holy Land in their darkest hour. A year later, Sverre Munnsson came from the Faeroe Islands. Birger Brosa and King Knut backed him with weapons, men, and silver. Now you have won, and Sverre is king. But you know all this, don't you?"

"Yes, and that's why I want to accompany your brother to Näs to thank King Knut and Jarl Birger, who supported us."

"No one shall take that right from you," muttered Eskil. "And you're Øystein Møyla's son, aren't you?"

"Yes, that's right. My father fell at the battle of Re, outside Tønsberg. I was there, a mere boy. I escaped the foes to the Holy Land, and now I shall return in our own colors."

Eskil nodded and took another drink, pondering where to lead the conversation. The other two waited patiently.

"If you are indeed Øystein Møyla's son you can assert your right to the crown of Norway," Eskil said in his business voice.

"You're our friend, just as Sverre is, and that's good. But you have a choice. You can choose to support the rebels and become king or possibly die trying. Or you can sail north to King Sverre, taking a letter from King Knut and the jarl, and swear allegiance to him. That is your choice, and there is nothing in between."

"And if I then become your foe?" Harald asked without pausing to consider what this new revelation might mean.

"There's no chance you would become our enemy," replied Eskil in the same clipped, businesslike tone. "Either you'll die in the battle against King Sverre, in which case you wouldn't be much of a foe to us. Or else you'll win. In that case you would still be our friend."

Harald stood up, holding his ale tankard in both hands, and drained it to the bottom. He slammed it to the table so that the charcoal dust outlining Eskil's business realm sprayed in all directions. Then he gestured toward his head and staggered toward the door, sweeping his red mantle tighter around him. When he opened the door the bright summer night dazzled them all, and a nightingale could be heard singing.

"What ideas have you sown in our friend Harald's head now?" Arn asked with a frown.

"Only what I've learned from you in our brief time together, brother. It's better to say what needs to be said now than wait till later. What do you think he should do?"

"The wisest course for Harald would be to swear an oath of allegiance to King Sverre at once, on his first trip," said Arn. "A king would not treat badly the son of a fallen hero who served the same cause as he did. If Harald makes peace with Sverre it would be best for Norway, for Western Götaland, and for us Folkungs."

"I think so too," said Eskil. "But men who catch the scent of the king's crown don't always act with reason. What if Harald joins up with the rebels?"

"Then Sverre will have a warrior opposing him who is stronger than any other in Norway," Arn said quietly. "But the same is true in the other case. If he joins up with Sverre, the king may then have so much power that the struggle for the crown will wane. I know Harald well after the many years of war he has spent at my side. It's easy to understand that it would make a man's head spin if he suddenly found out that he could be king. The same would have happened to you or me. But tomorrow, once he has thought it over, he'll decide to be our first mate rather than chase after the Norwegian crown through fire and a rain of arrows."

Arn got up, declining Eskil's offer of more ale. He took a few sheepskins, bowed goodnight to his brother, and went out into the bright summer night. He heard the nightingale again, and the cold morning light shone in Eskil's eyes before the door closed and he could reach for more ale.

Arn shut his eyes and took a deep breath as he stepped out into the summer night, the likes of which he remembered from his childhood. There was a strong aroma of alder and birch, and the fog hovered like dancing elves down there by the river. There was no one around.

He wrapped his unlined summer mantle around him, crossed the courtyard, and went into the cow pasture so he could be alone. Out there a black bull appeared out of the mist and began to paw with one front hoof and snort at him. Arn drew his sword and slowly continued across the pasture. Once across he sat down under a big willow tree whose lower branches drooped toward the river. Nightingales were singing all around him. They sounded different up here in the North, as if the cool, clear air gave them a better singing voice.

He prayed for the brother he had never known, Knut, who had died from youthful pride and the desire of a young Danish lord to kill someone in order to feel like a real warrior. He prayed that God might forgive the Danish lord's sins, just as they must be forgiven by the dead man's brothers. And he prayed that he might be spared any feelings of revenge.

He prayed for his father's health, for Eskil and Eskil's daughters and his son Torgils, and for the sisters he didn't know who were already married women.

He prayed for Cecilia's treacherous sister Katarina, that she might come to terms with her sins during her time at Gudhem and seek forgiveness for them.

Finally, he prayed for a long time that the Mother of God would give him clarity in his words at the meeting to come, and that no misfortune would befall Cecilia or their son Magnus before they were all united with the blessing of the Church.

When his prayers were done the glow of the sun appeared above the mist. Then he meditated on the great mercy he had received, that his life had been spared despite the fact that his bones should have long since been bleached white under the merciless sun of the Holy Land.

God's Mother had taken pity on him more often than he deserved. In return She had given him a mission, and he promised not to fail Her. With all his power he would work to fulfill Her will, which he had held close to his heart ever since the moment She had appeared to him in Forshem church.

He wrapped a sheepskin round him and lay down among the roots of the willow tree that enfolded him like an embrace. He had often slept this way out in the field after saying his prayers but with one ear open so as not to be surprised by the enemy.

By old habit he woke up abruptly without knowing why. He drew his sword without a sound and stood up as he silently rubbed his hands and looked all around.

It was a wild boar sow with eight small striped piglets cautiously following her along the riverbank. Arn sat down silently and watched them, careful that the light wouldn't glint off the blade of his sword.

✠

The next morning they got a later start than they'd intended; Eskil's contrary mood and somewhat red eyes had something to do with it. They rowed due south for a few hours, which was harder work for the oarsmen since the river was narrowing and the current increasing. But by midday when they reached the rapids of the River Tidan, where the boat had to be hauled by oxen and draymen to the lake of Braxnbolet, the worst of their toil was over. They had to wait a while because the draymen were hauling a boat from the other direction; both the men and the oxen needed to rest before stepping into harness again.

The party had encountered several small cargo boats on the journey, and there were two in front of them waiting their turn to be taken across the portage. There was some grumbling among the boatmen when their helmsman went ashore and began ordering the two waiting boats to yield their places. The harsh words quickly ebbed away when Eskil himself appeared. They were all his men, and he owned all the boats.

Eskil, Arn, and Harald led their horses ashore and then rode in the lead along the towpath beside the corduroy path for the boats. Arn asked whether Eskil had calculated the cost of digging a canal instead of keeping oxen and men for towing the boats. Eskil thought that it would cost the same, since this location wasn't suitable and they would have to dig the canal further to the south across flatter land. A canal south of there would also increase the travel time beyond what it took to tow the boats. During the winter when all vessels were towed on sleds, this portage was just as passable as the frozen river. Runners were fastened to the bottoms of the smaller boats so they could be towed like sleds the whole length of the river.

At the start of the short ride they met the draymen pulling a heavily laden boat; Eskil thought the cargo was iron from Nordanskog. They reined in their horses and made way for the oxen and ox-drivers, who came first. Several of the draymen let go of the towline with one hand to greet Herr Eskil and ask Our Lady to bless him.

"They're all freedmen," Eskil answered Arn's questioning glance. "Some of them I bought and then released in exchange for their labor; others I pay to work. They all work hard, both with the towing and in the fields on their tenant farms. It's a good business."

"For you or for them?" Arn asked with some mockery in his tone.

"For both," replied Eskil, ignoring his brother's gibe. "The truth is that this enterprise brings me in a lot of silver. But the lives of these men and their progeny would be much worse without this work. Maybe you have to be born a thrall to understand the joy they take in this toil."

"Could be," said Arn. "Do you have other portages like this one?"

"There's another on the other side of Lake Vättern, past Lake Boren. But it's not much when you consider that we sail or row the whole way from Lödöse to Linköping," said Eskil, clearly pleased at how well he'd arranged everything.

They were able to make up for the delay they'd had in the morning once they got out onto Lake Braxnbolet and headed north. The wind was from the southwest, so they could set the sail. The next river they followed downstream to Lake Viken, which made the rowing easy. And out on Viken they sailed once again at a good speed.

They reached Forsvik in the early evening, having proceeded with good tailwinds.

Forsvik lay between Viken and Bottensjön, which was actually a part of Lake Vättern. On one side of Forsvik the rapids were powerful and broad, and on the other the outlet was narrower and deeper. There the currents turned two millwheels. The buildings were laid out in a large square and were mostly small and low, except for the longhouse which stood along the shore of Bottensjön. They were all built of graying timber, and the roofs were covered with sod and grass. A row of stables for the livestock stretched to the north along the shore.

They docked their riverboat at the wharves on the Viken side. A similar boat was already tied up there. It was being loaded by laborers with carts who came from the other direction.

Arn at once wanted to saddle his horse and ride out to take a look around, but Eskil didn't think it was proper to show disregard for the farm's hosts. They were Folkungs, after all. Arn agreed with this, and they led the horses into the courtyard and tied them to a rail by a watering trough. The visitors had already occasioned much commotion at the farm when it was discovered that these were no ordinary guests who had arrived.

The mistress stumbled with eagerness as she came running with the welcome chair. Eskil joked that he'd rather have the ale inside him than spilled over him. He and Harald at once downed a manly draft, while Arn as usual merely tasted the proffered ale.

The mistress stammered an apology, saying that the master was out on the lake tending to the trout nets, and since she had not expected company it would be a while before they would have supper ready for their guests.

Eskil grumbled a bit, but Arn quickly explained that this was even better, since all three of them would like to take a ride around the property at Forsvik. They would be back in a few hours.

The mistress curtseyed in relief, not noticing the displeasure in Eskil's eyes. Reluctantly he went over to his horse and led it around the watering trough, where he could more easily mount by placing one foot on the trough before he heavily hoisted himself into the saddle.

Arn and Harald were ready to go. Without mounting, Arn slapped both of their horses so that they started off at a slow trot past Eskil. When Eskil, puzzled, looked up at the riderless horses, Arn and Harald came running fast from behind and then jumped, each landing with both hands on the hindquarters of his horse before pushing himself forward into the saddle and galloping off, the way all Templar knights did when there was an alarm.

Eskil didn't seem the least amused by the performance.

At first they rode to the south. Outside the farm buildings was a garden where the bright green vines had already climbed up their poles to the height of a man. Then they headed down toward the rapids and bridge, where the blossoms from an apple orchard covered the ground like snow.

Across the bridge the fields of Forsvik stretched before them. The closest field lay fallow, and there they discovered to their surprise four youths practicing on horseback with wooden lances and shields. The boys were so engrossed in their game that they didn't notice the three strangers ride up and stop at the edge of the field. The men watched the boys with amusement for a long while before they were discovered.

"They're of our clan, Folkungs all four," Eskil explained as he raised his hand and waved to the four young riders. The boys rode over to them at a gallop, then sprang from their mounts. Holding on to the reins, they came over and knelt quickly before Eskil.

"What sort of foreign manners are these? I thought you were hoping for a place in the royal guard, or with Birger Brosa or myself?" Eskil greeted them jovially.

"This is the new custom. It's the practice of everyone at King Valdemar's court in Denmark, and I've seen it myself," replied the eldest of the boys, giving Eskil a steady gaze.

"We aim to become knights!" one of the younger boys said cockily, since it may have seemed that Eskil misunderstood.

"Indeed? It's no longer enough to be a retainer?" asked Arn, leaning forward in his saddle with a stern look for the boy who had just spoken to Eskil as if he were an elderly kinsman who understood nothing. "Then tell me, what does a knight do?"

"A knight . . ." began the boy, quickly turning unsure as he noticed the Norwegian retainer's amusement. Harald was vainly trying to hide his mirth with a hand over his brow and eyes.

"Don't mind the northerner, my young kinsman; he doesn't know much," said Arn kindly and without the slightest ridicule. "Illuminate me instead! What does a knight do?"

"A knight rides with lance and shield, protects maidens in distress, slays the forces of evil, or the dragon like Saint Örjan, and most of all is the foremost defender of the land during times of war," said the boy, now quite sure of himself and looking Arn straight in the eye. "And the foremost of all knights are the Knights Templar in the Holy Land," he added, as if wanting to demonstrate that he did know what he was talking about.

"I see," said Arn. "Then may Our Lady hold her protective hands over all of you as you practice for such a good cause, and let us hinder you no longer."

"Our Lady? We pray to Saint Örjan, the patron saint of knights," replied the boy boldly, now even more certain that he was the one who was the expert on this topic.

"Yes, that is true, many pray to Saint Georges," said Arn, turning his horse to the side to continue his survey of Forsvik. "But I mentioned Our Lady because She is the High Protectress of the Knights Templar."

When the three men had ridden off a way, they all had a good laugh. But the boys didn't hear them. With great earnestness and renewed zeal they rode at each other, holding out their short wooden lances as if they were attacking with Saracen swords.

By nightfall as they returned to Forsvik, they had seen what they needed to see. In the north the Tiveden woods began, the forest that according to ancient belief was without end. There was timber and fuel in immeasurable quantities, and close at hand. To the south along the shore of Lake Vättern there were fields with pasture that would feed more than five times the live-stock and horses now at Forsvik. But the fields for grain and tur-nips were meager and sandy, and the living quarters decaying and rank.

Eskil now said bluntly that he had wanted Arn to see Forsvik before they decided. A son of Arnäs ought to own a better farm than this, and Eskil at once proposed either of the farms Hön-säter or Hällekis on the slopes of Kinnekulle facing Lake Vänern. Then they could also live on neighboring farms to their mutual enjoyment.

But Arn stubbornly insisted on Forsvik. He admitted that there was much more to build and improve than he had imag-ined. But such things were only a matter of time and sweat. Forsvik had the advantage of possessing enough water power to drive the forging machines, the bellows, and the mills. And there was one more important thing that had already occurred to Eskil. Forsvik was the heart of Eskil's trade route, and that's why he had placed Folkungs as caretakers and not more lowly folk. Whoever controlled Forsvik held a dagger to the entire route, and no one could be better suited to the task than a brother from Arnäs.

There was a constant stream of loaded ships in both direc-tions between Lödöse and Linköping. If Arn was in charge, great smithies would soon be thundering at Forsvik. If the iron from Nordanskog came by boat from Linköping, steel and forged weapons would continue on to Arnäs and plowshares toward Lödöse. If limestone came from Arnäs and Kinnekulle, the boats could continue toward Linköping or return to Arnäs with mor-tar. And if barrels of unmilled grain came from Linköping, bar-rels of flour would move in the other direction.

Much more could be said, but basically these were Arn's ideas. And he had many foreign craftsmen with him; not all those at Arnäs were fortress-builders. Here at Forsvik they would soon be able to manufacture a great number of new things that would benefit all of them. And which could be sold at a good profit, he added with such emphasis that Eskil burst out laughing.

At supper, as was the custom, the master and mistress of the house sat in the high seat together with the three noble guests Eskil, Harald, and Arn. The four boys with bruises on their faces and knuckles sat at the table farther away. They knew enough of manners and customs to understand that the warrior who had asked the childishly ignorant question about knights was no ordinary ruffian of a retainer, since he sat next to their father in the high seat. They also saw that like Herr Eskil he bore the Folkung lion on the back of his mantle, and no mere retainer was allowed to do that. So who was this highborn lord of their clan who treated Eskil as a close friend?

The master and mistress of the house, Erling and Ellen, who were the parents of three of the boys with dreams of knighthood, made a great fuss about their guests in the high seat. Erling had already raised his tankard of ale twice in a toast to Herr Eskil. Now, the third time, he was red in the face and spoke with a bit of a stammer as he sometimes did, exhorting all to drink to Sir Arn Magnusson.

An uncomfortable feeling began to come over one of the boys, Sune Folkesson, who was a foster brother at Forsvik. He was also the one who had spoken most boldly about what it was like to be a knight and to whom knights should direct their prayers.

And when Herr Eskil kept on saying that they now had to thank Our Lady, because a Templar knight of the Lord had returned after many years in the Holy Land, everyone in the hall fell silent. Young Sune Folkesson wished that the earth would open beneath him and swallow him up. Herr Eskil noticed everyone's disquiet. He took a firm grip on his tankard and raised it to his brother Arn. Everyone drank in silence.

All further talk turned to stone after this toast, and everyone's gaze was directed at Arn, who had no idea how to act and looked down at the table.

Eskil was not slow in exploiting the situation, since he already had adopted Arn's rule that it was better to say what was unpleasant or momentous sooner rather than later. He got to his feet, raised his hand quite unnecessarily for silence, and then spoke briefly.

"Arn, my brother, is the new master of Forsvik and all its lands, all the fishing waters and forests, as well as all servants. But you will not be left bereft, kinsmen Erling and Ellen, because I offer you a chance to move to Hönsäter on Kinnekulle, which is a better place than this one. Your leasehold will thus be the same as it was for Forsvik, although the lands at Hönsäter have a greater yield. In the presence of witnesses I now offer you this sack of soil from Hönsäter."

With that he pulled out two leather pouches, fumbling a bit as he hid one of them and then placed the other in the hands of both Erling and Ellen, first showing them how to hold out four hands to accept a gift meant equally for the two of them.

Erling and Ellen sat there a while, their cheeks red. It was as though a miracle had befallen them. But Erling quickly recovered and had livelier thoughts, calling for more ale.

Young Sune Folkesson now thought he had been sitting long enough with his eyes lowered in an unmanly fashion. If he had stepped in cow dung, the situation would not be improved by sitting and pretending nothing had happened, he reasoned. So he stood up and walked resolutely around the table to the high seat, where he sank to his knees before Sir Arn.

His foster father Erling rose halfway to his feet to shoo him off, but was stopped when Arn raised his hand in warning.

"Well?" Arn said kindly to the youth on his knees. "What do you have to tell me this time, kinsman?"

"That I can do naught but regret my ignorant words to you, sir. But I didn't know who you were; I thought you were a retain—"

There young Sune almost bit off his tongue, when too late he realized that instead of smoothing things over he was now making them worse. Imagine, calling Arn Magnusson a retainer!

"You said nothing ignorant, kinsman," Arn replied gravely. "What you said about knights was not wrong, although possibly somewhat too brief. But remember that you are a Folkung speaking to another Folkung, so stand up and look me in the eye!"

Sune at once did as he was told, and when he saw the scarred face of the warrior at close range he was amazed that Sir Arn's eyes were so gentle.

"You said that you wanted to be a knight. Do you stand by your word?" Arn asked.

"Yes, Sir Arn, that dream is dearer to me than life itself!" said Sune Folkesson with such emotion that Arn had a hard time keeping a straight face.

"Well then," said Arn, passing his hand over his eyes, "in that case I'm afraid that you'll be a knight with much too short a life, and we have little use for such men. But here is my offer to you. Stay here at Forsvik with me as your new foster father and teacher, and I shall turn you into a knight. That offer also applies to your foster brother Sigfrid. I will speak to your father about this. Sleep on it overnight. Pray to Our Lady, or Saint Örjan, for guidance, and give me your answer in the morning."

"I can give you my answer right now, Sir Arn!" young Sune Folkesson declared.

But Arn raised his index finger in warning.

"I told you to answer tomorrow after spending a night in prayer, yet you do not listen. To obey and to pray are the first things someone who wants to be a knight must learn."

Arn gave the youth a look of feigned sternness, and he bowed at once and moved backward, bowing once more before he turned and rushed like an arrow back to his brothers at the end of the table. With a smile Arn saw out of the corner of his eye how they began talking excitedly.

Our Lady was indeed helping him in everything she had told him to do, he thought. He had already recruited his first two disciples.

He prayed that Our Lady would also stand by him at the greatest of all moments, which was now inconceivably near at hand, less than a night and a day away.

✠

In the middle of the king's island of Visingsö, only a stone's throw from the horse path between the castle of Näs in the south and the boat harbors in the north, the loveliest of lilies grew, both blue and yellow, like the colors of the Erik clan. Only Queen Cecilia Blanca was allowed to harvest this gift of God, under strict penalty of whipping or worse for anyone who dared take any for himself.

The queen was now riding there with her dearest friend in life, Cecilia Rosa, as she was always called in the king's castle rather than Cecilia Algotsdotter. At some distance behind them rode two castle maidservants. They needed no retainers with them since there had been peace in the kingdom longer than anyone cared to remember, and there were only the king's people on Visingsö.

But neither of the dear friends was particularly interested in lilies on this summer day. As both of them knew more about the struggle for power than most men in the kingdom did, they had important questions to discuss. What the two of them decided could determine whether there would be war or peace in the kingdom. They had that power, and they both knew it. The next day, when the archbishop arrived with his episcopal retinue to meet with the king's council, the decision would be announced.

The women dismounted next to the road some distance from the field of lilies, tied their horses, and sat down on some flat slabs of stone with heathen runic inscriptions that had been dragged out there to serve as the queen's resting place. Cecilia Blanca waved away the two castle maidens and pointed sternly over toward the lilies.

For the longest time, Cecilia Rosa had held off the jarl's importunate and, in recent years, more and more brusque demands. Birger Brosa wanted her to take her vows and enter his convent at Riseberga to become abbess. The moment she took the vows, he assured her, she would become the one who ruled Riseberga, both in spiritual and business matters.

The bishops would agree, and the new abbé at Varnhem, Father Guillaume, who now held authority over Riseberga, would quickly accede. Father Guillaume was a man who allowed himself to see the will of God if at the same time he saw gold and new green forests.

That was how things now stood. If she took her vows she would become abbess of Riseberga at once. But the jarl's intentions were in truth not of the pious sort. It was a matter of power, and it was a matter of war or peace. With ever greater obstinacy in recent years, Birger Brosa had harped on his idea that an abbess's oath was just as good as another abbess's confession and testament.

The evil Mother Rikissa, who for so many years had tormented both Cecilia Blanca and Cecilia Rosa at Gudhem, had borne false witness on her deathbed. In her confession she had sworn that Cecilia Blanca had taken the vows during one of her last years at Gudhem.

If true, it meant that all of King Knut Eriksson's children had been born illegitimately. His eldest son Erik would be prevented from inheriting the crown if this lie were believed.

If Cecilia Rosa were now promoted to abbess, she could deliver an oath stating that the queen had never taken the vows but had served only as the other lay sisters at Gudhem had done. This would unravel the whole knot. And that was precisely Birger Brosa's idea.

The jarl did not lack good reasons for his demand. Cecilia Rosa had not been able to go to the bridal bed with Arn Magnusson as had been both intended and promised, but instead had effectively been sentenced to twenty years of penance. Yet the jarl had never abandoned her. He had taken her son Magnus, who was born out of wedlock at Gudhem, as his own, first as a son, later as a younger brother. Magnus had been raised at Bjälbo and was also brought into the clan at the *ting*. In addition the jarl had done much to alleviate Cecilia Rosa's torments under Rikissa. He had supported and aided her as if she, like her son, had been accepted into the Folkung clan, although she had been merely a poor penitent. It was now time for her to repay that debt.

It wasn't easy to contradict the wisdom of these ideas; the two Cecilias had always been in agreement on that. Cecilia Rosa had only been able to present one strong objection to the jarl. She believed that since she and Arn had sworn to be faithful to each other, and after their time of penance to fulfill what had been interrupted by slander and strict laws in equal measure, she could not take these cloister vows. That would be to betray her word. It would be the same as trampling on Arn Magnusson's vow.

During the first years after her time of penance had expired, Birger Brosa, although he grumbled, accepted this objection. Many times he had assured her that he too wished and prayed that Arn Magnusson would return home unharmed, for any kingdom would have great need of such a warrior. Indeed, such a man ought to be made marshal at the king's council, particularly since he was a Folkung.

But now more than four years had passed since the time of penance had expired, and they had heard nothing about Arn after the time of his great victories in the Holy Land, of which blessed Father Henri had informed them. Now the Christians had lost Jerusalem, and thousands upon thousands of Christian warriors had fallen in battle without anyone knowing their names.

Yet Cecilia Rosa had never given up hope; every evening she had directed the same prayers to Our Lady for Arn's speedy return.

But there were limits to patience, as there were to hope. How could she go before the council the next day—before the king, the jarl, the marshal, the tax-master, the archbishop, and the other bishops—and say that it was impossible for her to accept the high calling of abbess because her earthly love for a man was greater? No, it was hard to imagine such conduct. It was much easier to imagine what a tumult that would provoke. Love was undoubtedly of little consequence. Greater were the struggle for power and the question of war or peace in the kingdom.

Cecilia Rosa had never before expressed this idea as clearly and as despondently as she did now. Cecilia Blanca took her hand in consolation, and they both sat there, dejected and silent.

"It would have been easier for me to do this," the queen said at last. "I'm not like you; I've never loved any man more than I've loved myself or you. I envy you that, because I'd like to know what it's like. But I don't envy you the choice you now have to make."

"Don't you even love King Knut?" asked Cecilia Rosa, although she knew the answer.

"We have lived a good life for the most part. I've borne him a daughter and four sons that lived and two that died. It was not always easy, and two of the childbeds were terrible, as you know. But I have no right to complain. Keep in mind that you had a chance to experience true love and gave birth to a wonderful son in Magnus. Your life could have been much worse."

"You're right," said Cecilia Rosa. "Just think, if the war with the Sverkers had turned out differently, we both would have been trapped forever at Gudhem. True, it's ungrateful to grumble about our lot. And we'll always have our friendship, even if I soon must wear the veil and a cross around my neck."

"Would you like us to pray one last time to Our Lady for a miraculous salvation?" asked Queen Cecilia Blanca. But Cecilia Rosa just looked down at the ground and mutely shook her head. All her prayers seemed to have vanished.

Three riders approached at a leisurely pace from the wharves to the north, but the two Cecilias paid no attention, since many riders were expected at the council meeting.

Then the two castle maidservants returned from the lily field with their aprons full of the loveliest flowers. Laughing they handed them to the queen and her friend. Both were given more lilies than they could carry. Queen Blanca, as she was usually called, then ordered the maids to fetch the baskets quickly. The lilies would soon wither if they grew too warm in their hands, as if they shrank from the captive embrace of humans. As she spoke she glanced without much interest toward the three horsemen who were now quite close. It was the tax-master Herr Eskil, some Norseman, and a Folkung.

Suddenly she was struck dumb by an odd feeling, which she was later never able to explain. It was like a gust of wind or a portent from Our Lady. With her elbow she cautiously nudged Cecilia Rosa, who stood looking the other way at the maids returning with their flower baskets.

When Cecilia Rosa turned around she first saw Eskil, whom she knew well. In the next instant she saw Arn Magnusson.

He got down from his horse and walked slowly toward her. She dropped all her lilies to the ground and moved aside in confusion so as not to step on the flowers.

She took his hands which he held out to her, but she was unable to say a thing. He too seemed totally at a loss for words. He tried to move his lips but not a sound came out.

They sank to their knees and held each other's hands.

"I prayed to Our Lady for this moment during all these years," he finally said, his voice quavering. "Did you do that too, my beloved Cecilia?"

She nodded as she gazed into his ravaged face and was filled with sympathy for all the hardships he had endured, now evident in these white scars.

"Then let us thank Our Lady for never forsaking us, and because we never gave up hope," whispered Arn.

They bowed their heads in prayer to Our Lady, who so clearly had shown them that hope must never be abandoned and that love was truly stronger than the struggle for power—stronger than anything else.

Chapter 3

That day at the King's Näs would be remembered as the Great Tumult. Seldom had anyone seen Birger Brosa in such a rage. The man who was best known for always speaking in a low voice even in the most difficult negotiations now created a din that was heard throughout the castle.

That was not how things began when Arn Magnusson rode into Näs in the company of his brother Eskil, Queen Blanca, and Cecilia Rosa. At first there had been much embracing and show of emotion. Both the jarl and the king had greeted Arn with tears and words of thanksgiving to Our Lady. White Rhine wine was brought out, and everyone was talking at once. It looked to be a day of true joy.

But all at once everything changed, as soon as Arn let slip a few words concerning his coming bridal ale with Cecilia Rosa Algotsdotter.

At first the jarl behaved as was his custom. He turned cold and quiet and suggested, although it sounded more like a command, that the king should repair to the smaller council chamber for an important matter. He also said that he and Arn, as well as the tax-master Eskil, should accompany the king.

The smaller council chamber was located on the next highest floor of the castle's eastern tower. There stood the king's carved wooden chair with the three crowns, the jarl's chair with the Folkung lions, the archbishop's chair with the cross, and a few small wooden stools upholstered in leather. Nearby stood a big oaken table with seals, wax, parchment, and writing implements. The whitewashed stone walls of the room were completely bare.

The king sat calmly in his big chair beneath one of the open arrow loops so that the light streamed in above his head. The jarl paced around the room looking agitated. Arn and Eskil had taken seats on stools.

The jarl was dressed in foreign clothes in shiny gray and black, and on his feet he wore long crackowes of red and gold leather, but his Folkung mantle with the ermine trim fluttered behind him as if blown by the wind as he paced back and forth to calm his wrath. The king, like the jarl, had put on a great paunch since Arn last saw them so long ago. He sat in apparent calm, waiting. He was almost completely bald now.

"Love?" yelled the jarl suddenly at a volume that indicated he had not managed to calm down at all. "Love is for sluggards and milksops, pipers and minstrels, maidens and thralls! But for men, love is the fruit of the devil, a dream of fools that creates more unhappiness than any other dream. It's like a treacherous reef in the sea or trees falling across a road in the forest. It's the mother of murder and intrigues, the father of betrayal and lies! And for this, Arn Magnusson, you come riding home after all these years? For love? When our very destiny is at stake? When your clan and your king need your support, you turn away. And you explain this shame by saying that like a minstrel you have been struck by this illness of children and fools!"

The jarl fell silent and resumed pacing about the room, gnashing his teeth. Arn sat with his arms crossed, leaning back a bit but with an implacable expression on his face. Eskil was looking out through one of the arrow loops at the bright, peaceful summer day, and King Knut was studying his hands with interest.

"You don't even see fit to answer me, kinsman?" shouted the jarl with renewed force. "Soon the archbishop will be here with his throng of bishops. He is a wily man and a member of the Sverker clan; the cowards around him don't dare say boo or baa. He's a man who wants to lead the Sverker clan to the king's crown once again, and weighing heavily in his favor are letters from both the Holy Father in Rome and that schemer Absalon in Lund. We must act before the stream turns into a whole spring flood. You could help us with this, but you demur because you're raving about love! It's like a reproach to all of us. How much war and how many dead kinsmen, how many burned farms will there be in our land because you rave about love? Now I demand that you answer."

In a rage the jarl tore off his mantle and flung it over his chair before he sat down. His own words seemed to have agitated him even more, and realizing this, he tried to regain his normal composure.

"I have taken a vow," said Arn, deliberately keeping his voice low, the way he remembered that Birger Brosa usually spoke. "I have sworn on my honor and I have sworn on my sword, which is the sword of a Templar knight and consecrated to Our Lady, if I should survive my time of penance, that I would return to Cecilia, and that she and I would fulfill the promise we had made to each other. Such a vow cannot be taken back, no matter how angry you become, my dear uncle, or how unsuitable you may find it for your intrigues. A vow is a vow. A holy vow is even stronger."

"A vow is not a vow!" Birger Brosa shouted, regaining his fury in an instant. "A child swears to pull down the moon from the sky. What is that? Childish prattle that has nothing to do with real life. You were a youth then; now you are a man, and a warrior at that. Just as time heals all wounds, so too it grants us wisdom and turns us into men. And that is most fortunate. Would any of us here in this room answer for all the things we may have promised as foolish and naïve youths? A vow is no vow if life sets impediments in its way. And by God, there are strong impediments confronting you now!"

"I was no child when I swore that oath," replied Arn. "And each day for the duration of a war that lasted so long you could hardly imagine it, I repeated that vow in my prayers to Our Lady. And She has heard my prayers, because here I am."

"And yet you bear a Folkung mantle!" yelled the jarl, red in the face. "A Folkung mantle shall be borne with honor toward the clan! Now that I think of it, how can this be? With what right do you, a penitent of twenty years who lost your inheritance and your place in the clan, wear the Folkung mantle over your shoulders?"

"I am the cause of that," interjected Eskil with some trepidation when it seemed that Arn would refuse to reply to that affront. "In my father's stead I am the head of the clan in Western Götaland. I and no other exchanged Arn's Templar mantle for ours. I took him back into our clan with full rights and privileges."

"What has been done can in any case not be undone," Birger Brosa muttered, getting up to resume his pacing. The others in the room exchanged a cautious glance, and the king shrugged his shoulders. Even he had never seen Birger Brosa behave in this manner.

"All the better that you now bear our mantle!" shouted the jarl, pointing an accusing finger at Arn. "For this mantle entails more than protection from our enemies, the right to bear a sword wherever you please, and the right to ride with a retinue. This mantle means an obligation to do what is best for our clan."

"As long as it does not go against God's will or a holy vow," said Arn calmly. "In all else I shall do my best to honor our colors."

"Then you must obey us, otherwise you may as well put your white mantle back on!"

"I most assuredly have the right to bear the mantle of a Knight Templar," replied Arn, pausing before he went on. "But it would not be advisable. As a Templar knight I answer to no jarl or king in the entire world, no bishop or patriarch, but only the Holy Father himself."

Birger Brosa stopped his furious pacing. He gave Arn a searching look before he went over and sat down with a sigh.

"Let's start over," he said in a low voice as if finally bridling his rage. "Let's look at the situation calmly. Sune Sik's daughter Ingrid Ylva will soon be ripe for the bridal bed. I have spoken with Sune, and like me he considers it wise that Ingrid Ylva become yet another link in the chain we are forging to keep future wars in check. Arn, you are the next eldest son of the chieftain, and also a man about whom songs are sung and sagas told. You are a good match. There are two ways we can prevent the Sverkers and the bishops from finding reasons for another war. One is for Cecilia Algotsdotter, who God knows owes us a great deal, to take on the high calling and become abbess of my cloister at Riseberga. Cecilia knows how things stand because of the insidious Mother Rikissa's confession and testament claiming that Queen Blanca supposedly took the vows during her difficult time at Gudhem. Cecilia says she is prepared to swear that this is not true, and we all believe her. You understand?"

"Yes, but I have objections which I will save until I've heard the second choice."

"The second?" said Birger Brosa.

"Yes. You said there were two ways we could entangle the

Sverkers in the yarn of peace with our cunning snare. One was to make Cecilia abbess, which is more properly a matter for the Church than for us. And the second?"

"That someone with a high position in the clan marry Ingrid Ylva!"

"Then I shall tell you what I think," said Arn. "Here is what will happen if you make Cecilia the abbess of Riseberga, although it is properly a matter for the Church and the Cistercians. Mother Cecilia, the new abbess, will swear an oath before the archbishop, because the rules require that it be done in this manner. Then the archbishop will have a hard knot to unravel. He could do two things. He could demand trial by iron, a proof from God that her words were true, because the red-hot iron would not wound her. Or he could take up the matter in Rome. If he's the wily intriguer you claim he is, he will choose the latter, because one never quite knows how it will go with red-hot iron. And if he takes up the matter in Rome, he will couch his words so that it looks as though the new abbess is swearing falsely. With that he will have no difficulty. The Holy Father will then excommunicate Cecilia at once. In this way we will have won something but lost much."

"You can't be sure it will go so badly," said Birger Brosa.

"No," said Arn. "No one can know that. I simply believe, dear uncle, that I know the paths to the Holy Father better than you do, and that my guess is therefore better than yours. But I can't know for sure, nor can you."

"And if we don't attempt this subterfuge, then neither of us will know."

"True. But there is great danger of making a bad situation even worse. With regard to Ingrid Ylva, I wish you success in your plans for her bridal bed. But I have given my word to go to the bridal bed with Cecilia Algotsdotter."

"Take Ingrid Ylva as your wife and consort as much as you

like with your Cecilia!" Birger Brosa shouted. "We all do the same. We choose one woman to live under the same roof with and to bear our children. But what we do beyond that is for pleasure only, what you with your foolish stubbornness call love, and that's something else entirely. Do you think that Brigida and I loved each other when the agreement was concluded at our bridal ale? Brigida was older than me and ugly as sin, or so I thought then. She was no newly blossomed rose, but the widow of King Magnus. And yet our life has been good, and we have raised many sons, and what you call love comes with time. You have to do as we all do! You may be a great warrior with songs sung about you, even though you are merely one of the many who lost the Holy Land. But now you are home with us, and here you must act like a Folkung."

"And yet I would hardly yield to my uncle's advice to sin with an abbess," replied Arn with a look of disgust. "Cecilia and I have already been punished enough for sins of the flesh, and I find it particularly poor counsel to carry on a secret love affair with an abbess."

Birger Brosa realized that his frivolous advice regarding the abbess was undoubtedly the most foolish thing he had said during any negotiations. He was always used to winning.

"And you, my king and childhood friend Knut?" said Arn, careful to release Birger Brosa from his own predicament. "Once I recall that you promised Cecilia to me if only I accompanied you on a journey that ended with King Karl Sverkersson's death. I see that you still wear around your neck the cross that you took from the murdered king. So, what is your opinion?"

"I don't consider it proper for the king to put in his word either for or against this matter," replied Knut uncertainly. "What you and Birger are discussing with such fervor is something for your clan to decide, and it would be ill-advised for the king to interfere in matters concerning weddings of other clans."

"But you gave me your word," Arn replied coldly.

"How so? I don't remember that," said the king, surprised.

"Do you remember the time when you were trying to persuade me to go to Näs, when we had to sail the little black boat through ice and slush at night?"

"Yes, I do, and you were my friend. You stood by my side in the hour of peril, I will never forget it."

"Then you must also remember that first we agreed to shoot with the bow, and if I vanquished you then I would win Cecilia. I have the word of a king."

King Knut sighed and tugged on his thin, graying beard as he pondered. "I was quite a young man, as were you," he said. "But that isn't the crucial thing. For as I said, the king must take care not to interfere in the internal affairs of another clan. This is a matter for the Folkungs. But one thing you must know. Now I am your king, back then I was not. And now I tell you, go to the bridal bed with Ingrid Ylva and release Cecilia Algotsdotter from her vow and promises, so that that she may become our abbess at Riseberga."

"That's impossible. We took a vow before Our Lady. What else can I do for you?"

"Can you swear your loyalty?" asked the king, as if changing the subject.

"I already did that when we both were young. My word holds fast, even if yours does not," said Arn.

Then the king smiled for the first time during this argument, nodding in acknowledgment that Arn's arrow could still strike home.

"Have my uncle and my brother sworn you their loyalty?" Arn asked, and the other three in the room all nodded.

Arn stood up without further ado, drew his sword, and fell to his knees before King Knut. He set the sword with the point on the stone floor, crossed himself, and grasped it with both hands.

"I, Arn Magnusson, swear that as long as you are king of the Folkungs I shall be true to you, Knut Eriksson, in . . . *auxilium et consilium*," he said, hesitating only when he came to those last words in Latin. Then he stood up, slipped his sword back in its sheath, and went back to his seat and sat down.

"What did you mean by those last foreign words?" asked the king.

"That which a knight must swear, I cannot say in our language, but it is no less worthy in church language," said Arn with a shrug. "*Auxilium* is one thing I swore to you, which means assistance . . . or support . . . or my sword, you might say. And *consilium* is the other thing a knight promises his king. It means that I have sworn always to stand by you and offer true counsel, to the best of my ability."

"Good," said King Knut. "Then give me one piece of advice. Archbishop Petrus talks a great deal about how I must atone for my sin of having killed Karl Sverkersson. I don't know how much of his talk is genuine faith in God and how much is merely his desire to vex me. Now he wants me to send a crusade to the Holy Land as atonement. You must have an opinion on this, having fought there for more than twenty years?"

"Yes, I certainly do. Build a cloister, donate gold and forests, build a church, buy relics from Rome for the archbishop's cathedral. Do any of these things, or in the worst case all of them, rather than mount a crusade. If you send Folkungs and Eriks to the Holy Land they will all be slaughtered like sheep and for no reason, other than to cause more grief."

"And you say that you are sure of this?" asked the king. "Is the courage in our breast not sufficient, our faith not strong enough, our swords not good enough?"

"No, they are not!" said Arn.

A despondent silence fell over the council chamber.

✠

While the worst of the noise was issuing from the council chamber in the east tower, Queen Blanca and Cecilia Rosa climbed up to the battlement so they would be free of prying eyes. But the two Cecilias had no difficulty understanding Birger Brosa's fury. It was because Arn Magnusson was defying him. Arn insisted on honoring his vow, while Birger Brosa thought he should rescind the oath so that Cecilia Rosa could go to Riseberga convent, be promoted to abbess, and then repay the debts she owed.

That was what was going on inside the council chamber; it was clear as water.

They tried to listen but could only hear clearly when Birger Brosa was holding forth, as he did time after time, shouting with contempt about love.

Cecilia Rosa felt paralyzed; she could hardly think. Arn was inside, less than an arrow-shot away. It was true and yet inconceivable. Her thoughts ran in circles. as if holding her captive.

But Queen Blanca was thinking more sharply. She knew that it was high time to make a decision. "Come!" she said to Cecilia Rosa, taking her by the hand. "We'll go downstairs, drink some white wine, and decide what to do. It's no use standing here listening to the noise of the menfolk."

"Look!" said Cecilia Rosa, pointing over the battlement as if she were only half awake. "Here comes the archbishop and his retinue."

Up on the road from the north boat harbor they could see the archbishop's cross flashing silver, carried by an outrider in the vanguard of the procession. Behind the outrider with the cross they could see the colors of many bishop's capes, but also the colors of all the retainers, mostly in red mantles, since the archbishop was a Sverker, after all.

"Yes," said Cecilia Blanca, "I saw them coming and suddenly I understood how we must arrange everything before the men even know what's happening. Come on!"

She dragged Cecilia Rosa down one floor to the king's chamber, called for wine, and shoved her friend onto a pile of pillows and cushions from Lübeck and France on one of the beds. They made themselves comfortable without saying a word. Cecilia Rosa still seemed more lost in a dream than awake.

"Now you must pull yourself together, my friend, both of us must," said the queen resolutely. "We have to think, we have to make a decision, and above all we have to act."

"How can the jarl defy the will of Our Lady? I simply don't understand it," Cecilia Rosa murmured.

"That's how it is with men," snorted the queen. "If they find that the plans of God and His Saints agree with their own, then everything is fine. If their own thoughts of power lead in a different direction, they probably think that God will come strolling along behind. That's the way they are. But we don't have much time now, and you have to think clearly!"

Cecilia Rosa took a deep breath and closed her eyes. "I'll try, really I will, I promise. But you must understand that this is not easy for me. After all these years, at the very moment that I succumbed to doubt for the first time, Our Lady brought Arn back to me. What did She mean by that? Isn't it strange?"

"Yes, it's more than strange," Cecilia Blanca was quick to admit. "When we were sitting out there next to the lily field, we were contemplating your unhappiness and my joy. You would have to give up your dream for my sake. I was sad but not surprised that you would accept your unhappiness for the sake of our friendship."

"You would have done the same for me," Cecilia Rosa murmured.

"Wake up now, dear friend!" the queen insisted. "It's happening now, right now. Just as Our Lady showed us; now I must do the same for you. You shall not take the veil and the cross, you shall go to Arn Magnusson's bridal bed, and the sooner the better!"

"But what will we do when the men rage against it?" Cecilia Rosa wondered hopelessly.

"Where is your resolve? This isn't like you. Pull yourself together, dearest Cecilia," said the queen impatiently. "Right now we must think and act; this is no time for dreaming. Do you remember back at Gudhem when we used confession as a weapon?"

"Yes," said Cecilia Rosa. "Those arrows struck home better than we could have hoped."

"Exactly," said the queen, encouraged by the sight of Cecilia Rosa finally waking up. "And today we're going to do the same thing. The archbishop will soon be sitting out there in his tent, hobnobbing with the people before the council meeting. He's showing his love for the lowliest sheep in God's flock, that hypocrite. And anyone at all can come and kiss the bishop's ring and confess. That also applies to a queen and an yconoma from Riseberga . . ."

"What sort of message are we going to send in our confession this time?" Cecilia Rosa asked eagerly, her eyes glittering and with new color in her cheeks.

"I will say how anguished I am at the thought of sending my dearest friend into the convent merely for my own gain, for my children's right of inheritance to the crown. And then it will be your turn—"

"No, don't say a word! Let me think first. All right, I'll confess that I saw the miracle of Our Lady, when she listened to Arn's and my prayers for more than twenty years and sent him home unharmed. And that his holy vow is now about to be fulfillled. In this way Our Lady is showing us how great love can be, how we should never give up hope . . . and how I feel anguish because they are asking me to fulfill earthly obligations by going to the convent instead of accepting the gift of Our Lady. All this is true. Do you think those words will suffice?"

"Undoubtedly," said the queen. "I think that our esteemed archbishop will quickly remember God's words about the miracle of love. He will become a strong advocate for the love between you and Arn, which must not be desecrated, because—"

"Because we would all become implicated in a great sin by denying the obvious and clearly demonstrated will of Our Lady!" Cecilia Rosa said with a laugh.

They were now utterly exhilarated and bursting with ideas. Cecilia Blanca even came up with new plans for how they could eat supper in such a way that there would no longer be any going back to the convent. Cecilia Rosa was astonished, blushing when she heard about these stratagems. But they finally realized that they had no time to lose; they took each other's hand and ran like young girls down the spiral tower staircase, eager to deliver the true confessions that would turn all the men's plans into ashes and ruins. When they came out into the courtyard they forced themselves to stop, bowed their heads, and began walking gravely and demurely over toward the archbishop's tent outside the walls.

✠

The heated argument in the council chamber of the east tower had subsided and turned into a long discussion as a result of Arn's harsh words about the impossibility of mounting a crusade from the Gothic lands and Svealand. Both the king and the jarl were offended by the curt way he had dismissed the capability of Nordic men.

Arn had been forced to elucidate, and what he told the others made them both reflect and listen with dread.

Retaking the Holy Land now from the Saracens, since the fall of Jerusalem, would require an army of no less than sixty thousand men, Arn began. And an army that big would be difficult to keep supplied with food and water; it would have to be constantly in motion, plundering its way forward. So they wouldn't be able to survive without a strong cavalry, and that alone made the use of Nordic warriors impossible. And sixty thousand men was such an enormous number that it would take every man capable of bearing arms in the two Gothic lands as well as Svealand.

But what if they did only what the Church demanded, their duty before God, and contributed as best they could, scraping together as many men as possible? What would that mean?

Ten thousand foot soldiers, said Arn. If King Knut, after much effort and persuasion and threats, managed to convince everyone that God truly wanted all Nordic men who could handle a sword or at least a pitchfork to head off for Jerusalem for the sake of their salvation—*if* the whole country could be convinced—then exactly how would they get there?

They would sail, of course. On the way up from England just off the coast of Jutland, Arn and his ship had met a Danish crusader army of about fifty ships with three or four thousand men aboard, although without horses. Arn and Harald had agreed that all these men were on their way to their own slaughter. They would cause more trouble rather than be of any help, if indeed they even managed to arrive safely.

Let's say that King Knut, Arn went on, could indeed sail with a force of about that size. What would happen when they arrived in the Holy Land? Well, the only place where new crusaders could land was the city of Saint Jean d'Acre, the last Christian foothold in the Kingdom of Jerusalem, and it was now extremely crowded. Would thousands of Norsemen without cavalry be received with gratitude? No, they would just be more mouths to feed. And what use would they be to the Christian army? Perhaps they could run next to the cavalry, protecting the knights' horses. But the Norsemen could not be a fighting force of any importance, because there were too few of them to form their own army. And besides, they didn't understand Frankish.

It would not merely be certain death; it would be a death that was unnecessary and dishonorable. And those who died would not die with the firm conviction that death in the Holy Land would grant them forgiveness for all their sins and lead them to Paradise.

Birger Brosa attempted to object, but his earlier wrath had now vanished as if blown away on the wind. He spoke softly and often with a smile, balancing his ale tankard on the knee of his crossed leg.

"Knut and I are not accustomed to thinking of ourselves as lambs being led to the slaughter," he said. "At the start of the fight for the king's crown, in the years after you left, we beat the Sverkers in all our encounters except one. The final battle was outside Bjälbo, and our victory was great, although the enemy had a force almost twice as large as ours. Since then there has been peace in the kingdom. There were more than three thousand Folkungs and Eriks with our kinsmen standing side by side, one phalanx next to another. It was a formidable force. Yet you still think that we would be like lambs? That's hard to imagine. What if this force that stood outside Bjälbo in the battle of the fields of blood stood on the soil of the Holy Land?"

"There we would indeed have to stand," said Arn. "The enemy would be on horseback, so we couldn't attack, nor could we choose the time and place. The sun would reap its victims like willows in the summertime; the rain and the cloying red mud would drag us down into hopelessness and disease in the winter. The enemy would suddenly come from behind on fast horses, and a hundred men would die and another hundred be wounded and then the enemy would be gone. And there we would stand. The next day the same thing. None of us would have a chance to land a single sword blow before we were all dead."

"But if they come on horses," Birger Brosa mused, "then we could take them with arrows and lances. A man on horseback has twice as many things to keep track of; if he falls, he'll be dead, and if he rides into the lances he'll end up impaled."

Arn took a deep breath, stood up, and went over to the heavy oak table in the middle of the room. He cleared off the writing implements, seals, and parchment, and drew with his finger in the dust.

If the army were standing still out on the flat field with good visibility in all directions, the enemy would just make small sorties, since the sun and thirst would do the heavy work.

If the army didn't move it would die. If the army moved it would have to extend from the front to the rear, and then the attacks would come quickly from either direction. Saracen horsemen would ride up, shoot two or three arrows which almost all would strike home, and then disappear. After each such attack there would be dead and wounded to care for.

The Saracens also had some heavy cavalry with long lances, just like the Christians did. An inexperienced Nordic army would surely tempt the Saracens to use that weapon as well.

Arn described how the sky could suddenly darken with a tremendous wall of dust, how they would soon hear the ground shaking, and how they wouldn't be able to see clearly in all that dust before the cavalry struck with full force, riding straight in among the foot soldiers, storming forward without resistance straight through the army and cutting it in half, then turning and coming back again. Three thousand warriors on foot in the Holy Land would have died in less time than they'd been arguing and discussing in this chamber, said Arn in conclusion. Then he went back to his seat.

"I'm thinking of several things when I hear you tell all this, kinsman," said Birger Brosa. "Your honesty is great, I know that. What you tell us I believe to be true, which means that it could save us from the greatest folly."

"That is my hope," said Arn. "I have sworn our king *auxilium*, and that's not something I take lightly."

"No," said Birger Brosa with a smile reflecting his true nature, "that you do not. Tomorrow at the council we will therefore delight our archbishop and his followers with the decision to build a new cloister in . . . well, where do you think, Knut?"

"Julita," said the king. "It should be in Svealand, where the voice of God is heard least strongly, and that would probably satisfy our bishops the most."

"Then Julita it shall be, and perhaps we will finally have a moment of peace from the talk of a crusade," said Birger Brosa. "But this is our decision for the present. For the future there is another and bigger question. If a Saracen army could defeat us so easily, could a Frankish army do the same? Or an English or Saxon one?"

"Or a Danish one," said Arn. "If we encountered any of these armies on their home turf. But our land lies at the extreme end of the earth, and it would be no simple task to bring a large army all the way here. The Saracens will never come this far, nor will the Franks or the English or the Normans. But it's less certain with the Saxons and Danes."

"We should reconsider," said Birger Brosa, with a look at King Knut, who nodded in agreement. "Times are changing out in the world; we have learned as much when it comes to trade, which has served us well. But if we are to survive and flourish as a kingdom in this new age—"

"Then we have plenty of new things to learn!" the king completed his thought.

"Arn," the king went on earnestly, "my childhood friend, you who once helped me to gain the crown. Will you take a seat on our council? Will you be our marshal?"

Arn stood up and bowed to the king and then to the jarl, as a sign that he acquiesced at once, as he had sworn to do. Then Birger Brosa went over and embraced him, pounding him hard on the back.

"It's a blessing that you have come back to us, Arn, my dear nephew. I'm a man who seldom explains himself or makes excuses. So this is not easy for me."

"Yes," said Arn, "you surprised me. That wasn't the way I remembered the wisest man of all in our clan, the one from whom we all tried to learn."

"All the better that there were few witnesses today," Birger Brosa said with a smile, "and that they were my closest kinsmen next to my own sons and my friend the king. Otherwise my reputation would have suffered. As far as Cecilia Algotsdotter is concerned . . ."

He paused, trying to tempt Arn to object, but Arn waited him out in silence.

"As far as Cecilia is concerned, I have an idea that is better than the one I presented earlier. Meet with her, speak with her, sin with her if you are so inclined. But take some time, test your love and let her do the same. Then we'll speak about the matter again, but not for a long while. Will you accept this suggestion of mine?"

Arn bowed anew to his uncle and the king, and his face revealed neither pain nor impatience.

"Good!" said the king. "At the council meeting tomorrow we shall not speak of the abbess at Riseberga, as if we had entirely forgotten that matter. Instead we'll stuff the new cloister at Julita in the bishops' mouths and keep them quiet with that. We are glad that the storm is over, Arn. And we are happy to see you on the council as our new marshal. So, let me have a word in private with my jarl, who needs to hear some admonishments from his king. Without witnesses."

Arn and Eskil rose and bowed to the king and the jarl and then went out into the dark staircase of the tower.

Down in the courtyard tables and tents had been set up, and ale and wine were being poured. Eskil took Arn by the arm and steered him with firm steps to one of the tents, while Arn sighed and muttered about this constant drinking, although his displeasure was obviously feigned and only made Eskil smile.

"It's good that you're still able to joke after a storm like that," Eskil said. "And as for the ale, you might change your tune now, because here at Näs we serve the excellent ale from Lübeck."

As they approached one of the ale tents, everyone whispered and made way as before the bow wave of a boat. Eskil didn't seem to notice.

When Arn tasted the Saxon ale he agreed at once that it was far better than any he had managed to force down before. It was darker, foamy, and tasted more strongly of hops than of juniper berries. Eskil warned him that it would also go to his head faster, so he ought to be wary of growing unruly. That might cause him to bluster and draw his sword. They laughed and hugged each other in relief that the storm actually seemed to have passed.

They discussed what could have been the reason for Birger Brosa's unexpected loss of control. Eskil thought there were simply too many conflicting emotions all at once. Certainly the jarl was truly happy to see Arn return home alive. At the same time he had spent so many years considering how Cecilia Rosa—and

Eskil explained how Cecilia had gotten that name—might serve to counterbalance the insidious Mother Rikissa's lies about the queen's cloister vows. The combination of joy and disappointment was not a good drink; it was like mixing ale and wine in the same goblet.

Arn said that a battle half won was better than utter defeat. They were interrupted when one of the archbishop's chaplains made his way over to them.

The chaplain had a smug expression on his face, sticking his nose in the air in such a way that Eskil and Arn couldn't help from smirking at each other. Then the chaplain announced his business in Latin: His Eminence the Archbishop would like to speak with Sir Arnus Magnusonius at once.

Arn smiled at the amusing distortion of his name. He replied in the same language that if His Eminence summoned him, he would promptly appear, but for urgent reasons he first had to make a detour via his saddlebags. He took the chaplain politely by the arm and walked toward the royal stables.

After he had fetched his letter of release from the Grand Master of the Knights Templar, which he thought might be the subject of the archbishop's cunning move, he muttered something about wondering why he had been summoned. But the chaplain didn't understand what he meant, since he actually wasn't as familiar with Church language in daily speech as he had pretended to be with his nose in the air back at the ale tent.

Arn had to wait a moment outside the archbishop's tent while some business was finished inside. When a man with a dark expression and a Sverker mantle emerged, Arn was called in by another chaplain.

Inside, Archbishop Petrus loomed, seated on a throne with high arms and a carved cross. Stuck into the ground before him stood the archbishop's cross in gold with its silver rays. Another bishop was sitting next to him.

Arn stepped forward at once, knelt down on one knee, and kissed the archbishop's ring. Then he waited for his blessing before he stood up. He bowed to the other bishop.

With a smile the archbishop leaned toward his fellow cleric and said out loud in Latin, certain as usual that the men of the Church were alone in their understanding of it, that this could be a conversation as amusing as spiritually uplifting.

"Love is wonderful," said the other bishop in jest. "Especially when it can carry out the business of the Church, holding the Holy Virgin by the hand!"

The two worthies both had a good laugh at this jest. They paid no attention to Arn, as if they hadn't even noticed him yet.

Arn had seen this sort of behavior all too often in men of power to be bothered by it. But he was puzzled that these two, who spoke a Latin full of errors and with a strange Nordic sound to it, would take it for granted that he didn't understand what they said. He had to decide quickly how to handle this, with cunning or with honesty. If he heard too much it might be too late. He crossed himself and pondered what to do. But when the archbishop leaned toward his colleague again with a smile, as if he had thought of yet another jest, Arn cleared his throat and said a few words that were mostly intended as a warning.

"Both Your Eminences must excuse me if I interrupt your surely most interesting discourse," he said, at once gaining their astonished attention. "But it is truly balsam to the mind to hear once again a language which I master and in which each word possesses clear import."

"Why, you speak the Church language like a man of the cloth!" said the archbishop with eyes wide in amazement. His contempt for yet another lowly visitor had utterly vanished.

"Yes, because I am a man of the Church, Your Eminence," replied Arn with a bow, handing him his letter of release, which he assumed was the reason for this summons. The archbishop surely wanted to determine whether he was a deserter or not, a man obedient to the law of the Church or of the temporal world.

The two clerics put their heads together and searched in the various texts until they found the Latin translation from Frankish and Arabic. Then slowly and a bit solemnly they spelled their way through. They touched with something approaching reverence the seal of the Grand Master which showed the two brothers riding the same horse. When the archbishop looked up at Arn, he suddenly realized that the knight was still standing before them, so he called for a stool, which an astonished chaplain brought at once.

"It is a great joy for me to see you once again in our land, Fortress Master Arn de Gothia," said the archbishop kindly, almost as if speaking to an equal.

"It is a blessing for me to be home," said Arn. "Just as it is liberating to be able to speak the language of the Church and regain the free flight of the intellect, associations which move like birds in the air rather than crawl on the ground like turtles. When I attempt to speak my own childhood language it feels as though I have a piece of wood in my mouth instead of a tongue. Naturally this makes my joy even greater at being summoned to this audience, although no matter the occasion I would value the privilege of being presented to you."

The archbishop at once introduced Bishop Stenar from Växjö, whereupon Arn stepped forward and kissed Stenar's ring as well before he sat down.

"What does it signify that you are a Templar knight of the Lord and yet are dressed in a Folkung's mantle?" asked the archbishop with interest. It seemed that the conversation had now taken an entirely different turn than the two bishops had intended at first.

"That is a complicated matter, at least at first glance, Your Eminence," said Arn. "As will be seen from the document I presented, I am forever a brother in our order, even though my service in a fighting unit was restricted in time to those twenty years during which I was serving my penance. But I do retain the right to take up my Templar mantle again at any time, which may also be seen in the written words of the Grand Master."

"As a Templar knight . . . does one not also take cloister vows?" wondered the archbishop with a sudden concerned frown.

"Naturally, all Templar knights swear poverty, obedience, and celibacy," Arn replied. "But as may be seen in lines 4 and 5 of the document, I was released from these vows at the moment my temporary service expired."

The two bishops again leaned over the sheet of parchment, searching for the lines that Arn had indicated. They spelled their way through the passage and nodded in agreement. They also looked a bit relieved; Arn did not know why.

"So now you are free both to own property and to wed," the archbishop stated with a sigh of relief, carefully rolling up the parchment document and handing it to Arn, who bowed and slipped it back into its leather holder.

"But tell me," the archbishop asked, "if you do take up your white mantle, a right which you undeniably possess, to whom are you then subordinate? I have heard that you Templar knights are subordinate to no one. Can that really be true?"

"No, but there is a grain of truth to your supposition, Your Eminence. As a Templar knight, and being of the rank of fortress master, I am subordinate to the Master of Jerusalem and the Grand Master of our Order, and we are all responsible to the Holy Father in Rome. But in the absence of the highest brothers and of the Holy Father, I am subordinate to no man, as Your Eminence supposed. Wearing the Folkung mantle, I serve the king of the Swedes and Goths as well as my clan, as custom demands of us here in the North."

"So the moment you took up your white mantle again, you

would not be subject to any of our commands here in the North," the archbishop summed up. "That is indeed an exceptional situation."

"A fascinating thought, Your Eminence. But it would be entirely foreign to me as a true Christian back in my homeland to flee your jurisdiction by throwing a white cloak of invisibility over myself, as it is told in the Greek myths."

"So your loyalty is first to the Kingdom of God and then to your clan?" the archbishop asked quickly but with a cunning expression.

"Such dualism is a purely false conception of the difference between the spiritual and the temporal; nothing can ever take precedence over the laws of Our Heavenly Father," Arn replied evasively, a bit surprised by the foolishness of the question.

"You express yourself with admirable eloquence, Arn de Gothia," the archbishop commended him. At the same time he listened to something that Stenar of Växjö was whispering to him and nodded in confirmation.

"This conversation has been prolonged by a pleasant tone as well as unexpected content," the archbishop went on. "But time is hastening past, and we have souls waiting outside. We need to come to the point. Your time of penance was imposed on you because you sinned in the flesh with your betrothed, Cecilia Algotsdotter. Is that true?"

"That is true," said Arn. "And I served this time of penance with sincerity and honor until my last day in the army of the Lord in the Holy Land. I do not wish to imply, of course, that I was a man free of sin, but merely that the sin which brought about my penance has undergone purification."

"That is our opinion as well," said the archbishop, sounding a bit strained. "But your love for this Cecilia kept you alive and strong during all these years, just as her love for you burned with the same clear flame?"

"She has always been in my daily prayers to the Holy Virgin, Your Eminence," Arn replied cautiously, surprised that his innermost secrets were known to this somewhat rustic and unpolished archbishop.

"And every day you prayed to the Holy Virgin that She might protect you, your beloved Cecilia, and your child who was born as a result of your sinful relations?" the archbishop went on.

"That is true," said Arn. "As I with my simple powers of comprehension understand it, the Holy Virgin has listened to my prayers. She has delivered me unharmed from the field of battle back to my beloved just as I had sworn to attempt if it were not granted me as a Templar knight to die for my salvation."

"Every day for twenty years you could have died and entered into Paradise; that is the special prerogative of the Knights Templar. And yet you were led unscathed back to your homeland. Would not that be proof of the divine grace that has been granted to you and Cecilia Algotsdotter?" the archbishop asked.

"Earthly love between man and woman certainly has its place among human beings in their life on earth, as the Holy Scriptures tell us time and again. In no way does it conflict with the love of God," Arn replied evasively, now discerning the intention behind the turn the discussion had taken.

"Indeed, that is also my view," said the archbishop, sounding pleased. "In this somewhat barbaric part of God's realm on earth, in this *Ultima Thule*, humans do tend to ignore this miracle of the Lord. Here the holy sacrament of marriage, ordained by God, is entered into for entirely different reasons than love, is it not?"

"We undoubtedly do have such a tradition," Arn admitted. "However, it is my conviction and belief that Cecilia Algotsdotter and I were granted this grace by a miracle of love. I am also certain that the Holy Virgin allowed Her countenance to shine down upon us in order to show us something."

"Faith, hope, and charity," muttered the archbishop thoughtfully. "He who never wavers in his faith, he who never gives up hope in the benevolence of the Holy Virgin, shall be rewarded. In my opinion this is what She wants to show us all. Is that not your view as well, Arn de Gothia?"

"Far be it from me to interpret otherwise than Your Eminence this wondrous thing that has befallen us," admitted Arn, now even more amazed by the archbishop's knowledge and the good will he radiated.

"Then in our opinion," drawled the archbishop with a look at Bishop Stenar, who nodded in agreement, "it would be a grave sin to oppose the high will that God's Mother and thereby God have shown us in this matter. Come, my son, let me bless you!"

Arn once again stepped forward and knelt down before the archbishop, who motioned to one of his chaplains to bring a silver bowl of holy water.

"In the name of the Father, the Son, and the Holy Virgin I bless you, Arn de Gothia, who have been granted grace, who witnessed a miracle of love for the edification of all in this earthly life. And may the Lord's countenance shine down upon you, may the Holy Virgin ever after walk by your side, and may you and your beloved Cecilia soon harvest the reward of grace, for which you both, burning with faith, have thirsted so long. Amen!"

During the blessing the archbishop touched Arn's forehead, shoulders, and heart with the holy water.

Dazed and confused, Arn left the archbishop's tent and stepped out into the light that now struck him sharply in the eyes, since the sun had sunk low in the west.

On the way back to the castle courtyard, where he felt sure he would find his brother still at the ale tents, he pondered what had just happened.

He did not see the benevolent hand of Our Lady behind it,

although it was no doubt in accordance with Her will. He saw instead the will and intentions of human beings, but he didn't understand how it all had fitted together. Nor did he understand how a simple Nordic bishop could have so much information about the intimate secrets of himself, Cecilia, and Our Lady.

He did not see Cecilia again until the grand council feast in the great hall, where a hundred guests were assembled just after sundown.

On Queen Blanca's orders, branches of stock were raised at the head of the royal table, which made the women entering the hall whisper and titter happily.

The guests came into the hall in a specific order. The lowlier guests entered first and filled all the seats at the tables located farthest from the king's table. There could be much grumbling over the seating arrangement, but the king's ushers assiduously kept track so that nobody could seize a chance to claim a seat that was superior to his station.

Then came the guests who had seats at the king's table; they always wore the most colorful clothing. All who were seated craned their necks to witness the splendor, or to complain about some neighbor or acquaintance who was unjustly honored as a guest at the royal table.

Arn was among these guests, as was Harald, who made a point of complaining to his friend that he had not yet been introduced to either the jarl or the king, as if Norwegian kinsmen were not good enough. Arn whispered that there were reasons that had nothing to do with Harald's honor; discord and rancorous discussion had delayed the introductions.

Next to last came the royal family with golden crowns, and the jarl, also wearing a crown. The king and queen were dressed in the most magnificent, but unfamiliar, clothing that shimmered in all the colors of the rainbow. The whole family wore blue mantles bordered with ermine, even the three princes who walked along chattering to each other as if this were a perfectly ordinary meal.

When the royal family members were seated the archbishop and his retinue entered, and the splendor of their clothing was no less splendid. The archbishop first blessed the royal family, and then he and all the other bishops took their seats.

Arn could see Cecilia seated far away. He tried to catch her eye, but she seemed to be hiding among the castle maidens near her and didn't dare look in his direction.

When all the seats were filled but the two at the head of the table, the queen stood up, holding two leafy branches high over her head, one of birch and the other of rowan. An expectant murmur of approval at once rose in the hall, and the queen began to walk with the two branches, which she pretended to offer in jest or in earnest to first one, then another, then snatching them back as soon as a hand reached out. Everyone enjoyed this little drama, and speculated wildly about how it would end.

When the queen stopped next to Cecilia Rosa, who blushed and looked down at the table, they understood at least half the truth. Happy shouts and good wishes streamed toward Cecilia as she accepted the birch branch and with head bowed followed the queen to the vacant seat adorned with foliage.

Once again an expectant murmur arose when the queen held the rowan branch high above her head and slowly began walking toward the king's table. She stopped at Arn's seat; everyone knew him by reputation even if they had not had a chance to shake his hand, and loud shouts echoed from the stone walls, which were decorated only with banners of the Erik clan, showing golden crowns on a blue field.

Arn hesitated, not knowing what to do. But Queen Blanca whispered to him to hurry up and take the branch and follow her before it was too late. He stood up and followed along.

Queen Blanca led Arn to his beloved Cecilia, and there was such a great roar in the hall that no shout from king or jarl could have been heard.

When Arn, smiling uncertainly with his heart pounding as if before a battle, sat down next to Cecilia, the guests thumped their fists on the tables, raising a great commotion. The moment for the king or the jarl to do something had come and gone with the speed of a bird. The noise died down as the guests went back to their murmured conversations, thinking more about the anticipated meal than about the surprise they had just witnessed.

The jarl sat with his fists clenched, looking as if he were about to stand up, but he was forestalled by the archbishop, who raised both hands for silence. Taking out his white *pallium*, the holy sign of his high eminence, he slipped it over his back and chest and walked along the table until he reached Cecilia and Arn.

There he stopped and placed his right hand on Cecilia's shoulder and his left on Arn's.

"Behold now the miracle of the Lord and of love!" he announced in a loud voice, whereupon the whole hall fell silent, because what was happening was something entirely new. "This loving couple has in truth received the grace of Our Lady. They are meant to be together, for Our Lady has shown this more clearly than water. Their betrothal ale took place many years ago, so what occurs this evening is merely an affirmation. But when the wedding takes place, I promise that none of lower rank than archbishop shall be the one to read the benediction over you both at the church door. Amen!"

The archbishop walked with slow dignity and a look of satisfaction back to his place. On the way he exchanged a secret smile with the queen but avoided looking the king or the jarl in the eyes. He took off his *pallium*, sat down, and at once began speaking with the bishop sitting next to him. He acted as though the whole matter had already been decided.

And that was true. A woman could never become an abbess if her promise of betrothal had already been blessed by the archbishop. The sacrament of union between a man and woman was ordained by God, and what God hath joined together, let no man put asunder.

The jarl sat there, white with fury under his emblem with the Folkung lion, the only insignia that was allowed in the castle hall besides the three crowns.

Suddenly he stood up, angrily knocking over the ale that had been placed before him, and strode out of the hall.

Chapter 4

A stern and demanding new master came to Forsvik, the very day after he had sailed off to the king's Näs. No one had expected him back so soon.

Arn scarcely spoke to Eskil and Ellen when he arrived. He said nothing about what had happened at Näs and why he was returning after only one day. This behavior made it even more apparent that he was the new master of Forsvik.

The lovely summer repose that prevailed in Western Götaland, when there were only weeks left until the hay had to be harvested, was transformed at once into hard winter work. If timber was to be cut in the forest, it was preferable to do it in the wintertime when sleds could be used and the wood had a ringing dryness when it was felled. But as soon as he'd had something to eat after his unexpected arrival, Arn changed his clothes from lord to thrall by hanging up his chain mail and all the blue finery and putting on the leather clothing of a thrall, even though he still wore his sword. All the servants who could be spared from transferring cargo from the ships on Lake Vättern to the river-boats were ordered to work with him, as well as the five guards and the boys Sune and Sigfrid.

Much about his behavior was surprising. They were surprised to see Sir Arn working with the ax and draft oxen more than anyone else. It was also unusual that he commanded the five guards at Forsvik to work like thralls, just as he did Sune and Sigfrid, who not only were somewhat young for such hard work, but also Folkung boys who should be learning swordsmanship and good manners rather than thralls' work.

On the second day, when the amazement at these foreign customs had subsided, to be replaced by sweat and blistered hands, a few people began to grumble. Torben the guard, who was the eldest among his peers at Forsvik, dared to say aloud what everyone else was thinking, that it was shameful for guards to work like thralls.

When Arn heard this he stopped wielding the ax, wiped the sweat from his brow, and stood silent for a long moment.

"Good," he said at last. "When the sun has moved less than half an hour, I want to see all you guards fully armed and on horseback out in the barnyard. And make sure you're not late!"

They put down their tools in surprise and walked muttering toward the farm buildings as Arn finished up felling timber, loaded an ox-cart with two heavy pine logs, and drove them home. He told the servants and Sune and Sigfrid which two trees should be felled next and then stripped of their branches.

So Sune and Sigfrid were among those who were supposed to continue the logging work, but their curiosity was stronger than their will to obey Sir Arn. They waited until almost a half hour had passed, then sneaked down to the farm and up into one of the barns; from there they could peer out a vent hole down onto the barnyard. They would never forget what they saw and heard.

The five retainers were sitting on horseback in a square formation, with Torben foremost as the leader. They were sullenly quiet but also looked as though they were more nervous than they wanted to let on. No one said a word.

Then Sir Arn emerged from the stable on one of his small foreign horses. He rode two times around the barnyard at high speed, keeping a strict eye on the guards before he turned toward Torben and pulled up. He had put on his chain mail but wore no helmet. In one hand he held a white shield with a red cross, which made the two young spies shiver all over, because they knew quite well that this was the sign of the Knights Templar.

Instead of a sword Sir Arn held a heavy pine branch, which he tested by striking it against his naked calf as he watched the guards.

"All of you found working on construction unworthy of you," Arn said at last. "You want to do the work of guards, which you find more worthy. And so you shall. Whoever can knock me off my horse will be excused. But anyone I knock off his horse will have to go back to cutting down pine trees!"

He said no more, but his steed began to move to the side, almost as fast as a horse could move forward; when it neared one of the barns it turned, moved obliquely backward and suddenly forward again. To Sune and Sigfrid it looked like magic. They couldn't see what Arn was doing to make the horse dance like that. No one could ride a horse that way, and yet it was happening before their eyes.

Suddenly Arn attacked with two leaps forward, so fast that the guard who was closest didn't have time to put up his shield before he was struck so hard in the side with the pine branch that he slumped forward with a groan. Then Arn was suddenly upon him, toppling him to the ground with a single shove. In the next instant he had quickly backed away from Torben, who had come up behind him with his sword drawn and took a wild swing, striking nothing but air.

Before Torben could look around, Arn caught up with him from the rear and pulled him easily out of his saddle. Then he urged his mount forward in two quick leaps between two of the younger guards, who raised their shields in defense.

But instead of continuing forward, Sir Arn's horse turned suddenly and kicked to the rear so that the guards' horses shied and reared up, not regaining their composure before Sir Arn had doubled back and struck one of the guards on the helmet with his branch, and the other across his sword arm so that the guard bent forward in the saddle, moaning in pain.

Instead of bothering any more with the two he had struck, Sir Arn sprang toward the fifth guard and raised his branch as if to deal a mighty blow. His opponent in turn raised his shield to parry the blow, only to find the attack coming from the other direction, pushing him from the saddle with such force that he flew off and landed on his back.

Sune and Sigfrid no longer cared about hiding. With wide eyes they leaned so far out the vent hole up in the barn that they almost fell to the ground. Down in the barnyard things were happening so fast that they could hardly keep up, and they whispered to each other excitedly, trying to figure out how everything was done. Sir Arn was dealing with Forsvik's mighty guards as if they were kittens—anyone could see that.

"This is a guard's work at Forsvik," said Arn as he sat on his horse, the last man in the saddle, while the others were sitting or lying on the ground, or standing bent over with pain in body and limbs.

"If you'd like to continue working as guards, then gather up your weapons and get into the saddle again, and we'll start the game over."

Arn looked at them for a moment without saying a word. But none of them made a move to remount his horse. Arn nodded as though what he saw confirmed what he had believed.

"Then you can all go back to working in the woods. For two or three days, until Herr Eskil and my friend Harald arrive, we will work on the logging. Those of you who do good work will then be able to choose to join the guard at Arnäs or stay here at Forsvik. Anyone who chooses to stay here will be employed as a guard, but will not be as easy to beat as all of you were today."

Arn turned his horse without a word and rode it straight into the stable. Sune and Sigfrid sneaked down from their vantage point and dashed back to the logging area without being discovered. They talked breathlessly about what they had seen. They knew that Sir Arn had given them a glimpse into a knight's world. The sight was like a wondrous dream, for what young Folkung wouldn't give several years of his life to be able to do even half of what they had just witnessed a real Templar knight do.

Neither of them let on when Arn and the five bruised and silent guards came back to the work site in work clothes. The two boys now made an effort to do their very best, and they forced themselves not to ask any questions about what had happened in the barnyard.

When the two young Folkungs went to bed late that evening in their own wooden bunks up in one of the big ash trees outside the barnyard, they had a hard time sleeping despite their weary, aching bodies. Time after time they tried to describe what they had seen that afternoon. A horse that moved like a bird, just as fast and just as unpredictably, a horse that obeyed its rider as if it could be guided by thought alone and not by knees, reins, and spurs. And a rider who seemed to be one with his horse, so that the combination was like an animal from the sagas. If Sir Arn had been holding a sword in his hand instead of a tree branch, he could have killed the five guards as easily as killing a freshly caught trout. It was a terrible thought. Especially for someone who was merely a simple guard.

But it was a delightful, dreamlike thought for anyone who

hoped to be taught by Sir Arn and become a knight. Sune and Sigfrid did not lack for dreams as weariness finally vanquished their excitement.

✠

After three days of heavy toil a large quantity of pine logs was stacked up outside the barnyard at Forsvik. Nobody knew what was going to be built with all this lumber, nor had anyone dared asked the taciturn Sir Arn, who worked harder than any of them.

But on the third day Herr Eskil and Harald the Norwegian returned from the king's Näs, and the five retainers at Forsvik were then relieved of the manual labor. Arn told them that those who wanted to enter new service at Arnäs should prepare to depart that day. Those who would rather stay in his service at Forsvik to continue learning the art of war should speak up. Not one of them chose to stay at Forsvik.

There was a great commotion at the estate, because many would now have to move, traveling on riverboats to Arnäs and Kinnekulle. Erling and Ellen, who with their sons and closest servants would be leaving Forsvik for a much better estate, tried one last time to have a serious talk with their son Sigfrid and foster-son Sune about whether they really wanted to be separated from their parents at such a tender age. Erling scowled when he heard how they had both been put to work like thralls, and it shocked him that this affront seemed to have reinforced the boys' desire to serve Sir Arn. Yet there was still time for them to change their minds, since it was decided that both Sune and Sigfrid would accompany their brothers and parents on the river journey. There were apparently many horses that had to be ridden back to Forsvik from Arnäs. Sune and Sigfrid seemed to be looking forward to this task too; they said they had an idea what special sort of horses might be involved.

As soon as the welcome ale was drunk, Herr Eskil and his brother and the Norwegian went off to sit down by the lakeshore. They had made it clear that they were not to be disturbed, so nobody approached them except when Eskil called for more ale.

At first Eskil only half in jest complained about drinking ale with a brother who was both dressed as a thrall and smelled like one. Arn replied that it was one thing if sweat came from indolence and revelry, and quite another if it came from blessed hard work. As far as thrall clothing was concerned, there were few thralls who wore the sword of a Templar knight. But they had much more important things to discuss. Arn told them he'd been working so hard in order not to think about all the things he had not been able to understand on his own.

This was indeed true, for it wasn't easy to divine what sort of game had been played out at the king's Näs. But Queen Blanca had clearly had a hand in most of it.

Soon after the council feast she had summoned Arn. Her message was that everything was at stake, and so he was forced to comply.

He met her at sunrise up on the rampart wall that connected the west and the east towers at Näs. They had only a brief discussion because she explained that it would not be good if anyone saw the queen alone up on the ramparts with an unmarried man.

She said quickly what she had to say. Arn must leave Näs at once and take the boat to Forsvik, then wait there several days until the council meeting was over. At present there were many enemies and evil tongues arrayed against him, and it was especially important that there be no hint that Arn and Cecilia Rosa were able to meet in secret. Such gossip could ruin everything. But there would be a wedding, Queen Blanca assured him. And it would take place as soon as the three weeks had passed before Midsummer; during that time weddings were forbidden. Until then, Arn and Cecilia Rosa must not meet. Except possibly at the house of Cecilia Rosa's parents in Husaby, but only in the presence of many witnesses. Because this would be a wedding that many people thought would lead to war and destruction and should thus be prevented by any means necessary.

Arn told Eskil and Harald how these words from the queen had tormented him. There was no mistaking her gravity, or her wisdom. And yet it was not easy simply to take his leave.

Arn had even tried to object that he'd been promoted to marshal in the king's council and so could not leave Näs. Queen Blanca laughed heartily at this, telling him not to worry about that. Birger Brosa, in his wrath, had declared that he would not sit on the same council with the promise-breaker Arn Magnusson.

She would explain everything to Eskil, she told him as she hurried off, dismissing any further questions. And so Arn had taken her at her word.

Eskil too had objected that Arn's presence in the council was unavoidable, but she explained that Arn would never assume the rank of marshal of the realm. Any chance of that had been ruined as soon as the jarl declared that it would take place only over his dead body.

The council meeting had otherwise gone well, and the bishops were not in the least surprised that there was no further talk of a new abbess at Riseberga. They were pleased, however, to learn that the king had donated land and forests worth six gold marks for a new cloister at Julita in Svealand.

It was clear that the queen had been in cahoots with the archbishop. Eskil had no doubt that Arn had been as much in the dark as he was about what was happening behind their backs. What they couldn't understand was why the queen could do all these things that were so clearly contrary to her own benefit. If Cecilia Rosa really did go to the bridal bed with Arn, the whole idea of her bearing witness against the perjury of the evil Mother Rikissa would be dead. In that case it would be uncertain whether the queen's own son Erik could inherit the crown. Queen Blanca's husband and king might well view this as treason.

Yet there was no denying the shrewdness of the two Cecilias. In less than a day they had fooled all the men: the king, the jarl, Eskil, and Arn himself.

But there was a more important matter that was bothering Eskil. He now had the responsibility of arranging the wedding at Arnäs, for there and nowhere else should it be held.

If he arranged this wedding he would make an enemy of Birger Brosa; if not, his own brother would become his foe. It was not a good choice.

When Eskil explained his concern, Arn said, "I understand your anguish, but you could never be my enemy no matter what you decide. Naturally the bridal procession would be long and perilous from Cecilia's Husaby to Forsvik, instead of to Arnäs. But we could arrange it that way."

"No!" said Eskil bluntly. "You shall never choose Ingrid Ylva instead of Cecilia as our uncle wished. Nothing shall stop you and Cecilia Rosa. I no longer care why this is so, I just know it is. What must occur shall not take place in secret and shame. It shall take place at Arnäs with pipes and drums and wedding guests lined up three deep!"

When they got beyond this rough spot in the conversation, they soon began talking easily about what would be done in the immediate future. Harald had received a letter with both Birger Brosa's and King Knut's seals to take to King Sverre in Norway. The ship down south in Lödöse had to be outfitted and manned, for soon Harald must start his first journey to fetch dried fish, if he wanted to make two trips to Lofoten that summer before the autumn storms arrived with the north wind that made it difficult to sail so far north. But even two trips should produce a good profit, and Harald would not be left without a good share of it.

It was good that Harald needed a crew, said Arn. Because at

Arnäs there were five Norwegian retainers who would certainly want to sail with Harald, especially since he was traveling with a royal letter of safe conduct. And here at Forsvik there were five retainers who had lost all desire to continue in Arn's service. They could replace the five Norwegians at Arnäs as early as tomorrow.

Arn was also going to need some thralls skilled in construction from Arnäs, and he tried to remember the names of the two who had been among the best when he was a boy. Eskil thought hard and recalled that one of them was probably dead; the other, named Gur, was still alive but very old. Yet he still lived at Arnäs with full right to bed and board, even though he could no longer work. His son, named Gure, was just as skilled as his father had once been at masonry and wood construction. There were other thralls who were good builders, although Eskil couldn't remember their names at the moment.

Half of the foreigners at Arnäs would be moving to Forsvik, Arn went on. Only half of them were good stonemasons, but the others had skills that would be more useful at Forsvik.

After they had disposed of these matters, Eskil had a more difficult question for Arn. It was about Eskil's only son Torgils.

Naturally Eskil had wanted Torgils to turn out like himself, a man of trade and silver, wealth and cunning. He had pondered this matter long and hard, but he realized that he couldn't change Torgils. By the age of seventeen the youth was already riding in the king's retinue, and his reputation was more for his skill with the bow and sword than for any interest in trade, like his father. Instead Torgils was going to take after his uncle Arn. So it was, and nothing could be done about it.

"And what is it you'd like to tell me about this matter?" Arn asked.

"My son Torgils does not yet know that you've come back to our realm. He knows all the ballads about you, and there are times when I think he loves the saga about you more than he loves his own father."

"I'm sure that's not true. But young men would rather dream about swords than about counting chambers, and we can't take their dreams away from them. Nor should we, but rather turn their dreams to something good. Now to your question."

"Torgils is up at Bjälbo right now with the king's eldest son Erik and your son Magnus," said Eskil. "They're having a feast and competing in archery. That's why none of them was at Näs—"

"I already know that," Arn cut him off impatiently. "Cecilia told me about it. But now . . . your question?"

"May Torgils be apprenticed to you?" Eskil hastened to ask. "My thought is that if he has to live by the sword, then he ought to have the best of teachers, and—"

"Yes!" Arn interrupted him. "You don't seem to have noticed how close I was to asking you the same thing first, although I feared that such a question might displease you. Send Torgils to me and I'll make him the warrior he probably could never become among the king's retainers. Young Sigfrid Erlingsson and Sune Folkesson are already in my service!"

Eskil bowed his head in relief, gazing into his empty ale tankard. Suddenly an idea struck him.

"You're planning to build up a force of Folkung knights!" he said, his face brightening.

"Yes, that is precisely my idea," Arn admitted with a glance at Harald. "And now I must tell you something that no other ears may hear, except for Harald who is my closest friend. Here at Forsvik I shall build a cavalry that can stand against Franks or Saracens, if only I'm able to get the men while they're still young enough to learn. But they may only be Folkungs, for the force I'm planning must not end up outside our clan. And with your son Torgils that's especially important, since he will become the lord of Arnäs. It is he who one day shall stand on the walls and look down on the Sverker army. And by that time he will know everything that a victor must know. But only Folkungs, remember that, Eskil!"

"But what about Eriks?" Eskil wondered. "The Eriks are our brothers, aren't they?"

"At the moment they are, and I have personally sworn loyalty to King Knut," Arn said calmly. "But we know nothing about the future. Perhaps the Eriks and Sverkers will join forces against us some day, for reasons we can't predict. But one thing is certain. If we build Arnäs to be a strong fortress, and God blesses our efforts to form a Folkung cavalry, no one will be able to defeat us. In this way we can avoid war, or at least shorten it, and power will be ours. My friend Harald has now heard what we intended only for the ears of close kinsmen. But if you ask him, he'll agree that I'm right."

"What Arn says is true," said Harald. "Arn is the one who taught me to be a warrior, though I may have been too old when I went into his service. Arn taught many squadrons to wage war both forward in attack and backward in retreat, just as he and other knights like him do. He taught archers, sappers, foot soldiers, and both light and heavy cavalry, as well as the master armorers and sword smiths. If any clan in the North is taught these secrets of the Knights Templar, be they Birchlegs or Folkungs, Eriks or Sverkers, then all power will reside with that clan. Believe me, Eskil, for I've seen all this with my own eyes. Everything I say is true. I'm the son of a Norwegian king and I stand by my word!"

✠

Queen Cecilia Blanca did not give her husband the king a peaceful moment until she got her way. He sighed at the fact that the calm that usually settled over Näs after a three-day council meeting was scant this time. But no matter what objections he thought up, she had at least two counter-arguments for him. He found it much too great an honor for an unmarried woman such as Cecilia Rosa to ride with more than a dozen of the king's retainers as protection. That was befitting a jarl, not an unmarried woman.

But the queen replied that nothing prevented her from sending her own retainers, for Cecilia Rosa was her dearest friend in life and everyone knew it. Who could be opposed to that?

King Knut insisted that it was excessive to send so many armed men with one woman. It would be a sign that they were expecting foul play.

The queen countered that no worse fate could befall the kingdom right now than for something to happen to Cecilia Rosa on the perilous journey she was about to undertake. With a sigh the king said that Cecilia Rosa could probably do no more harm with her death than she was doing by going to the bridal bed instead of to Riseberga cloister.

Showing not the least wifely kindness, the queen told him what would happen to the kingdom if Cecilia Rosa were killed or wounded. It would divide the Folkungs at once, with Eskil and Arn Magnusson on one side, and Birger Brosa and his Bjälbo branch on the other. And where would Magnus Månesköld stand in the dispute? He was both Birger Brosa's foster kinsman and Arn Magnusson's son. And what if Folkung support for the crown began to waver? What would happen to the power in the kingdom then?

King Knut had to admit that the very thought of a schism among the Folkungs was a nightmare. It would throw him and his Erik clan into the midst of a conflict that could endanger his son Erik's claim to the crown. Even worse, the crown might soon sit loosely on his own head. In this much he admitted she was right. But a split had already occurred, since Birger Brosa had set off for Bjälbo with many harsh words for both Arn and Eskil.

Queen Blanca thought that time would soon heal this rift. Once God's will had made it clear that nothing could be changed, all the excitement would die down. But if anything happened to Cecilia Rosa before the bridal night, they would have a fearsome foe in Arn Magnusson.

King Knut had no problem with agreeing that things could not get any worse than that. In a world where so much was decided by the sword, it was crucial to have a man like Arn Magnusson on his side. So it was even worse that Birger Brosa in his unusual fit of wrath had sworn that he would rather resign the power of the jarl than welcome Arn into the council as the new marshal. Any way they twisted and turned these questions, the pain remained like a rotting tooth.

As if nothing more need be said, the queen replied that the only sure cure for a toothache was to pull the bad tooth, and the sooner the better.

⚜

For Cecilia Rosa the following weeks passed as though they had taken from her both her freedom and her free will—as if she were floating with the current without being able to make the slightest decision for herself. She couldn't even decide about something as simple as traveling between Näs and Riseberga cloister, as she had done so many times before.

Because she was accompanied by twelve retainers, the journey took two days longer. Normally she would have simply sailed north on Lake Vättern to Åmmeberg and continued from there in a smaller riverboat up to Åmmelangen and through the lakes to Östansjö. From there it would have been only a day's ride to Riseberga.

But with twelve guards and their horses and all their gear, it was impossible to take the water route. They had to ride all the way from Åmmeberg.

She usually would have ridden with one or two men over whom she had authority. Now the guards from the king's castle spoke of her like an item of cargo, although she was sitting on her horse right next to them. They called her "the wench," arguing about what was best for the wench's safety and how best the wench could seek lodging for the night. The journey kept being delayed when the leader of the guards ordered men to ride ahead to scout a stretch of woods or check a ford before they rode over it. With all this extra trouble it took more than four days to reach Riseberga.

At first she had tried to close her ears and turn inward to her own dreams, sending prayers of thanksgiving to Our Lady every hour. By the second day she could no longer stand being referred to and treated like a load of silver instead of a human being. She rode up alongside Adalvard, the leader of the expedition, a man from the Erik clan.

She told him that she had made this journey many times, and only once had encountered highwaymen. The highwaymen had let her pass undisturbed when she explained that she came from the cloister and that her cargo was merely manuscripts and church silver. The bandits, who were young and had few weapons, had not frightened her in the least. Then how was it that a royal guard riding with the sign of the three crowns in the lead, a sight which should have scared off most highwaymen, was making such a fuss and displaying such timidity at every bend in the road?

Looking surly, Adalvard replied that it was his job to judge what was safe or not safe on this route, according to his own experience and knowledge. Naturally a woman of the convent would know all sorts of things that he did not. But now they had to make it through the woods of Tiveden alive, and that was something he knew best how to accomplish.

Cecilia Rosa was not satisfied with this answer, but she let it drop when their retinue came upon a farm that seemed large enough to house a dozen guards, their horses, and a wench.

The next morning, when they had proceeded a short distance along the road, she rode up to Adalvard and complained that it was not flattering to be treated like a prisoner being led to the *ting* to be hanged. Those words made more of an impression on him than her queries about their safety. He excused himself by saying that they were all responsible for her with their own lives.

It was a while before she spoke with Adalvard again. She was on her way to her wedding with Arn because Our Lady had listened to their prayers and allowed Herself to be persuaded. She had spared Arn for some other purpose besides the direct path to Paradise achieved through a martyr's death. What sort of safety did Cecilia need on her simple journey to Riseberga, other than the gentle, protective hands of Our Lady?

Cecilia Rosa was well aware that such religious reasoning would hardly impress a man like Adalvard. He was acting under the king's orders, and his first priority was man's will, and then possibly God's will. Or perhaps he considered it a man's obligation to do his utmost and in that way fulfill God's will.

But something wasn't right. There must be some danger that she didn't understand, while the men accompanying her feared for their lives because they were aware of the peril.

Once again she left her place in the column and rode up next to Adalvard.

"I've been thinking a lot about what you told me, Adalvard; that you are all responsible for me with your lives," she began. "I certainly should have displayed less impatience and more gratitude. I hope you will forgive me."

"Milady has nothing to apologize for. We have sworn to obey

the king's orders to the death, and until then we do not lead a hard life."

"You can see that I ride with a stirrup on each side, like a man," Cecilia went on. "Haven't you wondered about this?"

"Yes, I have, because it is most unusual for a wench, milady."

"I ride a great deal on my errands from Riseberga. I might even spend as much time on horseback as a royal guard," Cecilia continued innocently. "So I've sewn a woman's outfit with two skirts, one around each leg. And over them I wear an apron. I look like a woman, but I can ride like a man. And you should know one thing. If the danger comes that you mentioned, I can flee faster than most of the guards here with their heavy horses. If you want to protect me from attack, we mustn't stand and fight but ride off as fast as we can."

Finally Cecilia had said something that made Adalvard regard her as a person with her own thoughts and not as a pile of silver. Excusing himself politely, he rode off and spoke animatedly to some of his men, waving his arms. Those he talked to fell back and spread the word.

When he rode back to Cecilia he seemed pleased and more amenable to conversation than during the previous part of the journey. Then Cecilia saw that the ground had been prepared for what she really wanted to ask.

"Tell me, Adalvard, my faithful defender, and as a man at the king's Näs who knows so much more than a simple woman from the cloister, why should I, a poor woman from the weak Pål clan, be the target of foul play?"

"Poor?" Adalvard laughed and gave her a searching glance, as if to see whether she was jesting. "That may be the case now," he grumbled, "but soon there will be a wedding and as the wife of a Folkung a third of his property will become yours. You'll soon be rich, milady. Anyone who kidnapped such a bride would also get rich from the ransom."

"Well, it gives me a safe feeling to have such powerful giants by my side," Cecilia replied, only half satisfied with what she had learned. "But that can't be the whole story, can it? To protect me from poor highwaymen and kidnappers with poor weapons it shouldn't take this many men. Wouldn't it be enough that they saw our banner with the three crowns?"

"Yes, that's true, milady," said Adalvard. And enlivened by their conversation he continued to explain, as Cecilia had hoped he would.

"I am of the clan of King Knut and his father Saint Erik. But my older brothers inherited all my father's farms, so becoming a retainer was my fate. I'm not complaining. Any man from the Erik clan knows how things stand in the kingdom when it comes to the struggle for power. Your life, milady, is in the center of this struggle for power—as is your death."

"I don't understand very much of the world of men," Cecilia said humbly. "So much the greater will be my pleasure at riding beside a member of the Erik clan if he can explain to me things that are beyond the comprehension of a cloister woman. What does my death or my life have to do with the struggle for power?"

"Well, I can't tell you anything that you won't find out later anyway," said Adalvard, pleased to be the one who possessed the truth about life. "You should have become the abbess; then I could never have spoken to you as irreverently as I do now. But as abbess you would have sworn against the testament of the previous abbess, and then King Knut's eldest son would have inherited the crown. But this is all something you already know, isn't it?"

"Yes, it is. But if that's not going to happen, then why would any of the Sverkers wish me any harm?"

"If they kill us all—you, milady, myself, and all my men—then every man in the kingdom would believe that it was the Sverkers who were responsible for the foul deed, even if it wasn't true,"

Adalvard replied with sudden distaste. He regretted the turn the discussion had taken.

"In that case wouldn't the wisest thing be to kill Arn Magnusson?" asked Cecilia without the slightest quaver in her voice.

"Yes, it would. Everyone knows that we Eriks would gain from such a murder, because there would be no wedding between the two of you. You, milady, could become abbess even more quickly since both grief and loneliness would drive you to the cloister. But I swear that we're thinking no such thing, because that would mean breaking our alliance with the Folkungs, which has been sealed with many oaths. If the Eriks and the Folkungs start to feud, both clans will have ceded all power to the Sverkers."

"So now the Sverkers would most like to kill Arn Magnusson and make it look as though you Eriks were guilty of the deed," Cecilia filled in his thoughts. Her voice was firm, but she felt a lightning bolt strike her heart when she spoke the words.

"That is true," Adalvard said with a smile. "If the Sverkers could kill Arn Magnusson and put the blame on us Eriks, they would gain a great deal. But who would they send to Arnäs or Forsvik to commit such a treacherous crime? Odin, who could make himself invisible? Or Thor, whose hammer could make the whole world rumble? No, there is no killer who can sneak up on Arn Magnusson in secret, you may rest assured of that, milady."

Adalvard had a long laugh at his suggestion of Odin and Thor. Although these jests seemed ill-placed to Cecilia, she still found great comfort in them.

When they finally arrived at Riseberga, Cecilia went straight to her chambers and stood a long while with her hand on an abacus, taking in the scent of parchment and ink. A room full of documents had a special smell that was unmistakable, and she knew that later in life she would always be able to recall it.

But she still had a hard time grasping that this was really a moment of farewell. She had lived so long among these account books that in her heart she had imagined doing so for the rest of her life. No, she had imagined it as the only life available to her in this world, while Arn Magnusson belonged in the world of dreams.

Her farewell was difficult and a bit tearful. The two Sverker maidens who had been granted asylum at Riseberga, despite the fact that Birger Brosa later disapproved of this action, wept more than the others. For they had stood closest to Cecilia and were the ones she had taught most lovingly about needlework, gardening, and bookkeeping. Now the two would be alone without the yconoma's protection, and their hope that Cecilia would return as the new abbess had been crushed.

Cecilia consoled them both as best she could, assuring them that they could always send her messages and that she would stay informed about what was happening at Riseberga. But her words did not offer as much solace as she intended. Yet she promised to keep them in her thoughts.

Now Cecilia had to take her leave. She considered the abacus that she had made herself to be her own property, and so she took it with her. She owned a horse, saddle, and tack. She had paid out of her own salary for her winter mantle and boots lined with dog furs. Beyond this she owned only the clothing she was wearing at present and a few garments for feasts held at Näs.

When she and Cecilia Blanca were young they had worn the same size clothes. But now, with seven childbirths separating them, it was only Cecilia Rosa who could wear the same clothes as in her youth. It may not have been only the childbirths. At Näs there was a constant diet of pork, or even worse, salt pork, which required a great deal of ale. In the cloisters where Cecilia Rosa had mostly lived in recent years, anything resembling gluttony was forbidden.

She also owned one and a half marks in silver, the wages she had earned honestly during the time she had been yconoma at

Riseberga as a free woman and not as a penitent. She took out the silver, weighed it, and made a note in the account book that she had now taken what belonged to her.

At that moment she realized how little she knew about her own poverty or wealth. It was as though she had long been heading toward taking the cloister vows. Because of this she knew much more about each and every *örtug* owed to the cloister than she knew about any wealth she herself might possess.

When her father Algot died, he had left only two daughters as his heirs, Cecilia and Katarina. So each of them should have inherited half of the estates belonging to the clan around Husaby and Kinnekulle. But Katarina had been sent to Gudhem convent for her sins and there she had renounced all earthly possessions. Had she also renounced her inheritance? If so, to whom had it gone, to Cecilia or to Gudhem? And how much, in either case, did Cecilia own of the estates around Husaby?

She had never asked herself these questions. It was as though she had never thought of herself as the owner of worldly goods, merely as the administrator of the Church's property.

The one and a half marks in silver that she held in her hand would be enough to buy a lovely mantle. But there was a Folkung mantle she had worked on for three years, the most beautiful of all, lined with marten fur. The lion on the back was sewn with gold and silver thread from Lübeck, and red Frankish thread had been used for the lion's mouth and tongue. No mantle in the entire kingdom had such a brilliant sheen; it was the most magnificent work she had ever sewn in all her years at the convent. And she had never been able to conceal her dream from those around her, or from herself: to see this mantle worn by Arn Magnusson.

Such a mantle, she knew very well, was worth as much as a farm with both thralls and livestock. The mantle belonged to Riseberga cloister, even though she had sewn it with her own hands.

But it had been her dream; it could never be worn by any but a Folkung, and by no Folkung other than Arn. For a long time she sat with the quill in her hand before she conquered her doubt. Then she wrote a promissory note for fifteen marks in silver, fanned the ink dry, and stuffed the note into the correct pigeon-hole.

Then she went to the storeroom and found the mantle. She held it against her cheek and breathed in the strong scent that was meant to keep moths away rather than to promote sweet dreams of love. She folded it up and put it under her arm.

At the farewell mass she took Communion.

✠

For young Sune Folkesson and his foster brother Sigfrid, the ride between Arnäs and Forsvik was like having their most fervent wish fulfilled.

Each was now riding one of the foreign horses; Sune on a roan with a black mane and tail, Sigfrid on a sorrel with mane and tail that were almost white. Sir Arn had carefully selected the two young stallions and tried them both out first, ridden them, and played with them before deciding which boy should have which horse. He had curtly but gravely explained that both horses were young, like their new owners, and that it was important for them to grow older along with their horses, that this was the beginning of a friendship that would last until death, for only death could separate them from a horse from Outremer.

Arn hadn't spent much time explaining the difference between these horses and Nordic horses, perhaps because he could see in the eyes of his two kinsmen that they already understood. Unlike grown men in Western Götaland, the two boys realized at once that these horses were almost like fairy-tale horses compared with the Gothic horses that the retainers rode.

Sune and Sigfrid, like nearly all their contemporaries from clans with a coat of arms, had been riding horses almost since they could walk; riding for them was like breathing or drinking water, something they no longer had to learn.

Until now, that is. Now they had to start over from scratch. The first difference they noted was the pacing. If they urged on these horses like a Nordic horse, the speed after only two or three leaps would be so dizzying that the wind filled their eyes with tears and swept their long hair straight back. The other difference they could see at once was the liveliness of their new steeds. Whereas a Nordic horse might take three steps to move sideways, these horses would take ten. This gave the rider the feeling of floating as if on water; he didn't feel the movement but simply noted the change in position. Where a Nordic horse would move straight forward, following his head, these horses would move to the side or diagonally as if they were frolicking their way forward. It was a bit like taking a boat down rapids without really being able to steer; the slightest careless movement could lead to totally different results than those one intended.

To this extent it was like starting over, learning to ride all over again, since there were a thousand new possibilities to learn to control. The boys recalled how Sir Arn had done just that in the barnyard at Forsvik when he rode his horse with movements that looked impossible, toying with the guards as if they were kittens.

They were thirteen men riding through the forest, if Sune and Sigfrid could be counted as men. At Arnäs, Herr Eskil had given them each a small, faded blue mantle for which he had no more use; he and his brother had worn them when they were young. So now there were three men riding in blue Folkung mantles, with Sir Arn in the lead.

The foreigners had wrapped themselves in several layers of cloth and wore either headdresses made of thick bundles of cloth or strange pointed helmets with cloth around the bottom. The ones who wore such helmets were the best horsemen, and they also carried peculiar curved swords, bows on their backs, and quivers at their hips.

The group rode in a loose circle formation, and in the center was the flock of horses with no riders. It wasn't easy to understand how this was done, but after only an hour it became clear that all the loose horses were following the slightest variation in course made by Sir Arn.

This cavalcade of horses toward Forsvik rode straight through the forest where there were no roads. It was hard to see how Sir Arn could be so sure of the direction in a trackless wood; now and then he glanced up at the sun, that was all. And yet toward the end of the day it turned out that he had ridden straight for the Utter ford on the River Tidan, just above where the Askeberga *ting* met. When the beech forest thinned out and the landscape opened, they could see the river below them like a long, glittering snake. And they approached it at precisely the spot where the horses could make their way across without difficulty.

As they neared Askeberga they rode past one riverboat after another bringing cargo from Arnäs, along with some of the foreigners who did not want to ride. It seemed as though some of their cargo was so precious that they did not want to be parted from it; they sat suspiciously atop the wooden crates that were securely bound with leather thongs. Sune thought it must be gold or silver that they were guarding so carefully, but Sigfrid disagreed, since such treasures would have been stored in the tower chamber at Arnäs. They told themselves they would find out soon enough, when the whole party arrived in Forsvik.

At Askeberga all the horses were unsaddled, curried, and watered. Sir Arn then came over to Sune and Sigfrid and demonstrated the care and love they would have to show their horses from now on. Every little burr had to be removed from their tails and manes, and every inch of the horses' bodies had to be in-spected and groomed, just as each hoof had to be scraped clean and examined to make sure there was no stone or root stuck in it. And while these tasks were being done, they had to keep talking to their friend, for such a horse was a friend for life, and the greater the friendship between a horse and rider, the bet-ter they would be able to work together. The friendship was more important than any movements they made with their legs and hands to command the horses. Soon they would have to learn far more than they could imagine, because not only would they have to be faster at a full gallop than any other rider in the North, they also had to learn to ride backward and to the side, as none of their kinsmen or friends could do. It would take time.

But during all that time they had to maintain the friendship with their horse and let that friendship grow from one day to the next; that was the foundation of all horsemanship.

Sune and Sigfrid felt at once a strong assurance that every-thing Sir Arn was saying was part of the great secret, even though to others' ears it might have sounded more crazy than wise. For the sight of Sir Arn on his horse out in the barnyard in Fors-vik had been incised into their memory.

An hour before prayers Arn took out his bow, strung it, and grabbed a quiver of arrows to go out and practice. He no longer lived according to the strict Rule which had been his guide for so many years that he could hardly remember his life without it. He was no longer a Templar knight; on the contrary, he would soon enter into the carnal union of man and woman blessed by God. But the Rule condemned idleness as much as pride—the indolence of not practicing the arts of war so as to be able to serve God in the hour of danger, and the pride of imagining oneself to be sufficiently skilled without practice.

He found the bale of hay that he and Harald had used as a tar-get the last time they were in Askeberga, and headed toward the river to find a place where he would not be disturbed. Young Sune and Sigfrid came sneaking after him in the belief that he, a Templar knight, would not discover that he was being followed. At first he was tempted to pretend not to notice them, just as he had done the time they saw him chastising the lazy guards at Forsvik. But he changed his mind and picked up his pace so that he managed to hide behind a thick oak. Then he grabbed the two boys by the scruff of their necks when they came padding after him.

He warned them sternly never to follow a knight in secret. For as they surely had heard at Arnäs, his brother Eskil would have preferred to see a retinue of at least a dozen guards on the way back to Forsvik, since it was rumored that more than one powerful man in the kingdom would gladly send secret assassins to avert the wedding at Arnäs. So Sune and Sigfrid could not have chosen a worse time to come sneaking up from behind. The boys were ashamed and hung their heads and begged forgiveness, but this lasted only a moment. Then they were eagerly offering to help their lord by retrieving the arrows after he shot each round.

Arn gave them a solemn nod but could hardly keep from laughing. He pointed to a rotten stump where they could set up the target. They were surprised at the long distance, but quickly obeyed.

When they returned and sat down expectantly on a large, mossy rock, Arn nocked the first arrow on the bowstring, pointed at the target, and said that this was the distance at which he had first noticed them following him. Then he shot five arrows in quick succession and motioned for them to run down and fetch them.

The arrows were grouped so closely together that Sigfrid, who reached the target first, could grab them all with one hand when he yanked them out of the straw. Then he fell to his knees and stared incredulously at the five arrows in his hand. Sune met his gaze and shook his head. No words were necessary.

Five times Arn shot, and five times Sune and Sigfrid ran down to fetch the arrows, which every time but one could be grasped in one hand. The boys' initial excitement was slowly replaced by a dejected silence. If they had to be able to shoot like Arn to become a knight, neither of them thought they would ever pass the test.

Arn saw their gloomy expression and guessed the cause of it.

"The two of you won't have to shoot with my bow," he explained in a light tone when they returned with the arrows the fifth time. "My bow is suited to me but certainly not to you. When we get to Forsvik we'll build bows that fit you, as well as swords and shields. You already have horses that suit you, and keep in mind that you're just at the start of a long path."

"A very long path," said Sune quietly with his head bowed. "No one will ever be able to shoot better than you, Sir Arn."

"Nobody in our land can shoot like that," Sigfrid added.

"There both of you are wrong. My friend Harald from Norway shoots like I do, and you will soon meet a monk who might shoot even better; at least he did once. There is no limit to what a man can learn except for the limits he creates inside his own head. When you saw me shooting, you simply moved that limit forward farther than you thought possible. And it would be ill advised to do anything less, since I shall be your teacher."

Arn laughed when he added this last remark, and he received hesitant smiles in return.

"He who practices most will be the one who shoots best, it's that simple," Arn continued. "I have practiced with weapons every day since I was much younger than the two of you, and if there were days when I didn't practice, then there was war and practice of another kind. No man is born a knight; he must work to become one, and I find that acceptable. Will you two work as hard as necessary?"

The boys nodded and looked down at the ground.

"Good. And you will certainly have to work. At first when we get to Forsvik there will be more building work than weapons games. But as soon as we get settled, your long days with sword, lance, shield, horse, and forge will begin. By evening prayers your bodies will be aching with fatigue. But you will sleep well."

Arn gave them an encouraging smile in order to make up a little for the true words he had spoken about the path to knighthood, which was a path with no short cuts. He felt an odd tenderness for them both, as if he could picture himself as a young boy in Brother Guilbert's strict school.

"What does a knight pray in the evening, and to whom shall we direct our prayers?" asked Sigfrid, looking Arn straight in the eye.

"You ask a wonderfully wise question, Sigfrid. Who of God's saints has the most time and the best ear for the prayers from the two of you? Our Lady is the one to whom I direct my prayers, but I have been in Her service and ridden under her banner for more than twenty years. You mentioned Saint Örjan before, he who protects worldly knights, and he would probably suit both of you best. But it's easier to say what you should pray for. It is *fortitudo* and *sapientia*, a knight's two most important virtues. *Fortitudo* means strength and courage, *sapientia* means wisdom and humility. But none of this will be given to you; you will have to work to achieve it. When you pray for this at the end of the day after working hard, it's like a reminder of what you are working and striving for. Now go to your beds and pray for the first time this prayer to Saint Örjan."

They bowed and obeyed at once. Arn watched them disappear into the twilight. At journey's end there would be a new kingdom, he thought. A mighty new kingdom where peace reigned with such great strength that it would no longer be worthwhile to wage war. And these two boys, Sune Folkesson and Sigfrid Erlingsson, might be the beginning of this new kingdom.

He gathered up his arrows in the quiver, slinging it over his shoulder. He did not unstring his bow but walked silently with it in his hand down toward the river, to the lovely spot for prayer under the alders and willows that he had found the last time he was in Askeberga.

He did not really take seriously the gossip he'd heard at Arnäs, that enemies who strove for power might now entertain the notion of sending secret assassins to kill Arn Magnusson. There was some logic to this argument, he thought, noticing at once that he had shifted to Frankish in his mind to be able to think more clearly. The assassin who could make it look as if Birger Brosa, for instance, were the instigator, would have much to gain. Internecine strife among the Folkungs would benefit the Sverkers in their ambition to seize the royal crown; it would also weaken the Eriks' positions. But all such thoughts were mere theories sodden by ale and wine. It was one thing to think up such plans, and another to carry them out. If someone was now approaching Askeberga in the twilight to murder him, where would the murderer look first? And if the killer were really in the vicinity now that light for shooting was about to vanish, how could he silently advance to use a dagger or sword?

And if the killer approached in the dark, he couldn't very well expect to find a sleeping and unarmed Templar knight, could he?

God's Mother had not held her protective hands over Arn for all these years of war, and She had not denied him a martyr's death and Paradise only in the end to see him murdered in Western Götaland. She had given him the greatest gifts of earthly life, but not without conditions, since at the same time She had presented him with the greatest of all tasks She could give one of Her knights. First he was to build a church that would be consecrated to God's Grave, to show humanity that God was present wherever people resided and did not have to be sought in war in foreign lands. The even bigger task She had given him was to create peace by building up a force that was so superior that war would be impossible.

Once again Arn found the place by the river where he could rest and pray. The brief hours of darkness had fallen; there were only a few weeks left until Midsummer when it would be dark for merely half an hour. There was no wind, and the sounds and smells of the night were strong. From the farms by the docks he could hear loud laughter when someone opened a door to go outside and piss. The oarsmen on the river were probably helping themselves to all the ale that the foreigners refused to drink. There seemed to be a nightingale in a thicket quite close by, and for a moment the bird's powerful song filled his soul.

He had never felt such peace before; it was as if God's Mother wanted to show him what heavenly bliss was still possible in earthly life. In everything that happened, big and small, he could now see Her will and endless grace. His father was well on his way to regaining all his faculties, and he would soon be ready to start walking again.

Ibrahim and Yussuf had moved Herr Magnus up to the large tower chamber as soon as it was cleaned like a mosque. With the help of some thralls they had built a bridge with two rails on which the sick man could shuffle along with the support of his arms. At first he moved slowly and laboriously, but well enough that they could see from day to day that soon he would be able to walk without support. And he had regained much of his good humor, saying that he would be sure to be walking in time for the wedding—perhaps like an old man, but on his own two feet. Until then, since there were only a few weeks left of the season forbidden for weddings, he would keep his blessing secret so that the power of the healing arts could be seen that much better by everyone who saw him at the wedding.

He also was able to speak much better now that he was practicing every day and had left any form of hopelessness far behind.

At first he had so stubbornly resisted when they began with a stone that he had to move from one hand to the other. But he now devoted himself with such zeal to the task that Ibrahim and Yussuf sometimes had to stop him so that he didn't overdo it.

To Arn he had said that it was like seeing and feeling at the same time how life returned to both his body and soul. But what he said that gladdened Arn even more was that he understood that this was no miracle, no matter what other people would believe when they saw him healthy once more. This was his own work, his own will, and yes, his own prayers, but most of all it was due to the skills of the two foreign gentlemen. And they were ordinary men, neither saints nor sorcerers, even though they wore odd clothes and spoke an incomprehensible language.

Then Arn had finally told his father the truth, that these men, Ibrahim and Yussuf, as their names were more properly pronounced, were Saracens.

Herr Magnus had sat in silence so long when he heard this that Arn regretted his earnest veracity. But at last his father had nodded and said that good skills from near or far were what made life better. He had seen it with his own eyes and felt it in his own limbs. And if the people of the Church had bad things to say about these Saracens, their words were worth nothing compared to what his own son had to say. For who knew better the whole truth: someone who was priest in Forshem or bishop in Östra Aros, or someone who had waged war against the Saracens for twenty years?

Arn took the opportunity to tell him that all the fortresses of the Knights Templar had employed Saracen medical men because they were the best. What was good for God's Holy Army of Knights Templar would surely be good in Western Götaland up in the North.

The good humor brought on by this insight made his father

ask Arn to accompany him out on the walls to take a look at the new construction.

Arn had feared that it was too soon for his father to go outside, even though he had his son to support him. He had also feared that his father would find the construction unnecessary and forbid it, now that he had regained his reason.

But his concerns were groundless. When Herr Magnus saw how a perfectly smooth and high wall was being formed around the outer portions of the castle closest to Lake Vänern, and when he realized that these walls were intended to surround all of Arnäs, he was struck dumb with joy and pride. He himself had improved the fortifications considerably in his younger years, but he had often regretted that he hadn't done better. Arn told him at length how everything would look when it was finished, and how no enemy could then threaten the Folkung clan. In all he recounted he received his father's eager support.

The only matter that caused concern during Arn's brief visit to Arnäs was Erika's state of mind. Since he had heard about the death of his unknown little brother Knut, Erika's son, he had spoken about this sorrow with her as he must. But she had made him angry by talking more about the revenge to which she had a right than about her grief. Even worse, she told him that she had offered thanks to Our Lady because a warrior of God like Arn had returned so that the days of that wretch Ebbe Sunesson were now numbered. For the law was clear. If Arn demanded a duel for the sake of the clan's honor, the villain could not say no. Erika grew so heated that she seemed both to cry and laugh at the same time when she described how Ebbe Sunesson would feel when he was forced to draw his sword against the older brother of the youth he'd slain and then watch his own death coming straight at him.

Arn hadn't been able to allay Erika Joarsdotter's desire for vengeance; he found that out as soon as he tried. Instead he prayed with her for the soul of his brother Knut. Even though she couldn't refuse such a prayer, she seemed to long more for revenge than for the peace of Knut's soul.

It was sad to find Erika filled with such a sinful obsession. During the long night by the river he prayed first of all for Erika's recovery and the forgiveness of her sin.

✠

It felt as though they were on their way to the heart of darkness. The farther the river journey took them, the more certain the Wachtian brothers felt that they were leaving the habitations of men behind them and approaching the inhuman and unnameable. The individual hovels they passed looked more and more shabby, and on the banks of the river the livestock and wild children romped about together so that it was hard to tell the animals from the people.

The inn where they were to spend the night was abominable and crowded with savage, filthy men who bellowed in their incomprehensible singing language and drank like beasts until they ended up in brawls or simply passed out. All the men from Outremer, Christians as well as Muslims, kept to themselves and made camp some distance away from the inn buildings rather than set foot inside. The food that the thralls brought them they had refused with disgust and horror, and when darkness fell they all prayed, the Prophet's people and the Christians separately, for forbearance.

In the morning it took an eternity to get going, since the sleeping oarsmen had to be rousted from the most unexpected places, wherever they happened to fall asleep. Red-eyed and grumpy, stinking of vomit and piss, these men had finally been herded together like beasts of burden to their oars. By then the sun was high, and it was said that Sir Arn and his band of riders had a lead of many hours.

Late that afternoon their boat glided up to the wharves at Forsvik. The unloading began at once, and Marcus and Jacob Wachtian were kept busy ensuring that nothing in their baggage was damaged by these ignorant and worthless souls.

Yet they agreed it could have been much worse, when Sir Arn called a meeting in the courtyard in the midst of the low gray wooden houses with the grass growing on the roofs. At least all the Nordic people around them were sober and relatively clean. At least they didn't stink like the oarsmen.

"In the name of God, most beneficent, ever-merciful, He Who is the God of us all even though we worship Him in different ways, I bid you welcome to my home," Sir Arn began as usual in Arabic. "This is the destination of our journey. Let us therefore, before we do or say anything else, offer prayers of thanksgiving that we have arrived safe and sound."

Sir Arn then bowed his head in prayer, and all the men around him did the same. He waited until all had raised their heads when they finished their prayer.

"What you see here at Forsvik will impress few of you, I know," Sir Arn went on. "But we have four years of work ahead of us until the time we have agreed on is over. None of us will recognize this place after those four years, you can be assured of that. We shall not build a fortress, but a caravanserai, a place of trade. We shall not build walls here as we did at Arnäs, but smithies, furnaces for making brick and glass, and workshops for the manufacture of saddles and tack, felt, leather goods, and clothing. But we can't do everything at once. Of primary importance are roofs over our heads and cleanliness, which will be the same here as in Outremer. Then we will put in order everything else in the sequence we find best. But roofs over our heads must be the first priority, for winters here in the North are of a quite different nature than anything you have ever experienced. When the first snow and cold arrives, I'm sure that none of you, even in silence, will curse me that in your first days you had to slave like simple builders, although your skills could be employed doing more difficult things than dragging lumber. The Prophet's people, peace be upon him, will not see any unclean food before them. Now we have hard work to do, but we will also reap the reward for it, because within less than half a year the first snow will fall!"

Sir Arn repeated his words in Frankish, as usual, and then he went over to the two field masters, Aibar and Bulent, and took them along to a smaller building which lay right next to running water.

"Some people are lucky enough to be spared the slaving on construction from the start," Jacob Wachtian muttered. "What skills do we have that will spare us?"

"Surely one thing and another, don't worry," said Marcus, unconcerned, taking his brother by the arm to study more closely the estate which would apparently be their workplace for several years to come.

They took a tour around Forsvik, and since they were both men who took great pleasure in learning new things about what could be built by the hands of men, they soon had much to discuss. They could see from the quantity of new timber that was still being dragged in by ox-teams from the nearby woods that several new buildings were planned. But the piles of stones and barrels of chalk and sand made them realize that the new structures would be built differently from those that were already here. Apparently it was going to be like the big wooden longhouse at Arnäs, where one gable was entirely of stone and had a huge fireplace at the end. If they heated up that much stone with the fire, maybe they could fight off the terrible cold of winter, Marcus reasoned. Unlike in Outremer, at least here they had unlimited quantities of wood for fuel.

Sir Arn strode over to the brothers, put his arms around their shoulders, and told them that now they would soon have a chance to work on what they were best suited for. But first he had to show them his idea. He seemed happy and sure of his plan, as if this Godforsaken spot at the end of the world were already a large and flourishing caravanserai.

First he took them down to the two waterfalls and described how they could get as much power from this water as they wished. He told them that water was much better than wind, because water flowed all the time.

At the smaller waterfall there were two mill-wheels. Arn took them inside the mill and showed them how the rotating power could be transmitted to the millstones.

"But this is just the beginning," he said. "We can build ten wheels like this if we like, and we can build them much bigger. The power produced will be slower but much stronger, if we should want to grind limestone to lime for use in mortar. Or we could obtain weaker but much faster power with smaller wheels. I want you to put your minds to work on this!"

He led them out of the millhouse, still cheerful and enthusiastic, and showed them where he wanted to build food storehouses out of brick, next to the larger waterfall so that he could run a cooling stream of water in along the floor and back out into the river.

Along the big rapids they would build a stone channel to harness all the power that would otherwise be wasted. That's where the row of workshops would be located, since the water power could drive both the bellows and hammers. To avoid having to haul all the charcoal and fuel back and forth, he thought they might as well build the brothers' workshops next to the smithies and glassworks. When Marcus muttered something about trying to think sharply about springs and gears, with all the pounding that would be going on next door, Sir Arn said with a laugh that he truly had not thought about that drawback. But in the wintertime it might be very beneficial to work right next to the smithies and glassworks for the sake of the warmth.

But first both of them, like Ibrahim the physician, had to start on a completely different project. During the fall with all the mud, and during the long winter, it would be hard to keep themselves and their dwellings clean if they didn't soon begin making soap. Sir Arn apologized with a laugh when he saw the insulted looks on the faces of the two Armenian brothers. Naturally such work would seem to be something for less knowledgeable men, he admitted. But here in the North they would have to choose. Anyone who wanted to stay clean in the wintertime would have to start burning ashes and gathering bone grease to make his own soap. Oil could be boiled out of the Nordic pines the same way it was done from cedar and pines in Lebanon. Sir Arn had already had the bark slashed on many trees in the vicinity, which were bleeding pitch.

Seeing the brothers' reluctant expressions, he assured them that he could set his own workers to the dirty task of collecting tree resin, but once it was in the iron cauldron even Armenian gentlemen would have to help out and continue the necessary work.

They looked so dismayed that Arn launched into a long, apologetic explanation. He began with something as simple as felt. Aibar and Bulent, the two Turkish feltmakers, had already begun their work. Even though most of the felt would eventually be put to military use, the surplus would be welcome in the winter.

What they had to understand was that everything that was taken for granted in Outremer was not readily available here. The same was true of soap, esteemed by both the followers of the Prophet, peace be upon him, and the Christians from Outremer.

So there were many simple tasks that had to be done before they could start on the real work: constructing crossbows, making arrows for the longbows, forging swords and helmets, extruding iron wire, and firing clay and glass.

Otherwise, Arn added with a smile, anyone who couldn't find work doing these small, simple tasks would have to assist with the construction and masonry work. This convinced the Wachtian brothers that they should begin working on making soap, as well as gathering the right sort of water plants for the ash that was needed for glassmaking.

But he asked them, whenever they had time, to think about the water power and what it might be used for.

This last was most encouraging to them. When Sir Arn left and hurried off to talk to other groups, the Wachtian brothers went back down to the water-wheels. Inside one of the millhouses they observed the turning stones and axles as they thought out loud to each other.

Saws, they thought at once. Up here in the North they split timber and smoothed it as best they could with adzes. But what if they could saw it evenly right from the start?

There was more than enough power, just as Sir Arn had said. How could they transfer that power to saws?

It wouldn't be easy to figure out, but this was the type of problem that put the two brothers in a better mood. They went to fetch ink and parchment at once. Both of them thought best when they could sketch their ideas.

Chapter 5

Upon her homecoming to Husaby, Cecilia soon found that she was an unwelcome guest; if anyone had wished her banished to the cloister more than Birger Brosa, it was her relatives.

She had not relinquished her inheritance from her father Algot. At least half of the ten farms around Husaby were hers. And her kinsmen circled around the matter like a cat around hot porridge when it came to her sister Katarina's inheritance. The question was whether Katarina had relinquished her birthright when she entered the cloister, and if so, whether the property would fall to the cloister, to Cecilia, or to her male kinsmen.

Husaby had been a royal estate ever since the days of Olof Skötkonung. But the Pål clan had been caretakers there for more than a century, so they reckoned Husaby as their own estate when it came to holding feasts for the clan, even though they always had to make sure that they had plenty of provisions in case the king himself came to visit. They also had to pay tax to the king.

Cecilia's homecoming was such a disappointment to her

uncle's son Pål Jönsson and his two brothers Algot and Sture that they could scarcely conceal their dismay. It wasn't hard for Cecilia to understand the reason for their sullen expressions or why they spoke to her only when forced to, preferring instead to sit by themselves. They stopped talking as soon as she came near.

Cecilia's wedding was going to cost them dearly, she was well aware of that. The law and custom were both simple and clear. The richer the bridegroom, the bigger the dowry. And a richer man than the son of Arnäs was difficult to find in Western Göta-land. At least that was what Cecilia surmised, without having any idea how much Arn might inherit from his father Magnus.

Cecilia had good reason not to discuss the dowry with her hostile kinsmen. It would be better to save that argument for the dowry ale when Arn's bridal representative, who would un-doubtedly be Eskil, came to arrange everything that had to be finished and decided by the wedding day. Very few would dare butt heads with Eskil.

Eskil had already sent over the old thrall woman Suom from Arnäs, since she was the most skilled in the sewing arts and could make a bridal gown better than anyone. Cecilia instantly became friends with Suom. They found great pleasure in each other's skill with needle and thread, distaff and loom.

Some of the things they could do in the convent Suom had never seen. But she knew other things that they didn't know at the cloister, so the two got on well together. And in this way Ceci-lia was spared keeping company with the unfriendly Pål brothers.

Eskil arrived at the appointed time on the day as promised, bringing a dozen guards. He quickly drank his welcome ale and explained that he didn't intend to stay overnight, so they had bet-ter take care of the business matters at once, without any more drinking.

The Pål brothers could offer no argument, but they blushed

with humiliation that this Folkung did not even care to share their bread and meat.

Things did not improve when Eskil said that he would prefer to have Cecilia included in the conversation so that she could speak her piece. This diminished the role of Pål Jönsson, which could hardly have escaped Eskil's notice.

In silence the three Pål brothers entered the feast hall of Husaby first and took their places together at the high seat. Eskil was careful to walk slowly, taking Cecilia's arm and whispering that she must remain calm and not worry about any of the things that now might be said. He had no chance to explain further before they moved further into the dim hall, which was still decorated with ancient runes and images of gods that were not Christian.

In silence the Pål brothers sat down in the high seat with Cecilia near them and Eskil facing them across the longtable. New ale was brought in by house thralls who said not a word, seeming to sense that this was a meeting that their masters did not particularly desire.

"Well, shall we set the date first?" said Eskil, wiping the ale from his mouth, as if he weren't talking about anything difficult or important.

"It's customary to decide on the date after everyone agrees on all the rest," Pål Jönsson muttered with annoyance. He was red in the face, and the veins bulged from his forehead as if he were as taut as a bowstring, anticipating what was to follow.

"As you like. We can talk about the dowry first," said Eskil.

"Half of the inheritance from my uncle Algot rightfully belongs to Cecilia. That's what she can take with her into the estate," Pål Jönsson said.

"Absolutely not!" Eskil snapped back. "Cecilia's sister Katarina was my wife, as you may recall, and she entered Gudhem cloister while their father was still alive. It was autumn, and during the subsequent Christmas feast Algot drank until he suffered a stroke and died. We all know this sad story, may he rest in peace. So Cecilia's inheritance is Algot's entire estate, all ten farms. She will take those with her into the estate."

"Doesn't Katarina's inheritance fall to Gudhem cloister?" said Pål, trying to be evasive.

"No, because when she entered the cloister she had no inheritance, since Algot was still alive," Eskil replied implacably. "And as far as Gudhem is concerned, I have paid out of my own pocket more for Katarina's admittance into the holy sisterhood than was ever required."

"So you're demanding that I and all my brothers leave our farms and property?" asked Pål Jönsson, wringing his hands. "That's an unfair demand when at the same time you expect to keep us as your kinsmen. Remember that this is my decision to make, since I speak on Cecilia's behalf regarding the dowry. And with conditions like those you have presented, I may decide to cancel the wedding altogether!"

Now it was finally said. It was evident when the three brothers took a deep breath that this was what they'd been planning for the past week.

Eskil's expression didn't change, but he waited an excruciatingly long time before he said anything. And then he spoke in a mild and friendly voice.

"If you break the agreement, no matter that it's an old one, you are the same as a bride-robber and will not live till sundown, my dear kinsman. That would not be a good start for this marriage. But I am not a disobliging man; I would like us to settle this for the best without bloodshed so that we can remain the friends that the union between my brother and Cecilia Algotsdotter demands. Let's say that Cecilia's dowry will be just the five farms and bordering lands to the north and west toward Arnäs and Lake Vänern. Then you can keep the other five farms and stay on as the king's hosts at Husaby. Would such a proposal suit you and your two brothers better?"

None of them could object to that, and all three nodded in silent consent.

"In return for relinquishing five farms, I may have to demand a bit more gold, let's say twelve marks in bullion in addition to the five farms," Eskil went on as if speaking of trifles, and giving more attention to the ale.

But this was no small matter he was proposing as compensation. Twelve marks in gold was a sum so large that not even all the farms of the Pål clan would have sufficed. And even if they had been a mightier clan, it wouldn't have been possible to produce such a sum in pure gold. The three brothers stared incredulously at Eskil as if unsure whether he or they had lost their minds.

"I need more ale," said Eskil with a friendly smile, holding up his empty tankard just as Pål Jönsson collected himself to speak, and his words did not look to be friendly.

But he had to wait until Eskil had his new tankard, and Cecilia thought that this delay may have saved Pål's tongue from behaving as the bane of his head.

"Well! Perhaps I should explain one more item before you say anything, kinsman," Eskil went on just as Pål opened his mouth. "You brothers would not be responsible for those twelve marks in gold; Cecilia will pay the sum out of her own pocket."

Once again Pål Jönsson was curtailed just as he was about to speak. All the anger that could have made him raise his hand to Eskil or say things that just as surely would have meant his death, now changed to gaping astonishment.

"If Cecilia, though I don't know how, can pay such an enormous amount as twelve marks in gold, I don't understand this discussion at all," he said, straining to keep his words polite.

"What is it you don't understand, dear kinsman?" asked Eskil, resting his tankard on his knee.

"Compared with you Folkungs, we in the Pål clan are poor," said Pål Jönsson. "And if Cecilia can pay twelve marks in gold, which is the largest dowry any of us have ever heard of, I don't see why you need to have five of our farms."

"It's a good bargain for us, because we want to have the land along Lake Vänern as part of our property," Eskil replied calmly. "It's a good bargain for you Pål brothers as well, if you think about it. You won't be left without any benefits. After this wedding you can bear a sword wherever you want in Western Götaland, because as Cecilia's representative you will become part of the Folkung clan by marriage. You can exchange your green mantle for our blue one. Anyone who harms you or your brothers will have harmed the Folkungs. Anyone who raises a sword against you will not live more than three sundowns thereafter. You will be united with us both in blood and in honor. Think on that!"

What Eskil said was true. But Pål and his brothers had been so stubbornly engaged in talking about their monetary losses, about five or ten farms in inheritance and how much better it would have been if Cecilia had gone into the cloister, that they hadn't thought about the significance of coming under the Folkungs' protection. Their lives would be changed completely after one wedding night.

A bit ashamed at their own simplicity, Pål and his two brothers now immediately submitted to all of Eskil's desires.

Cecilia would be given Forsvik as the morning gift, as her own estate in perpetuity, to be inherited by her progeny. At Forsvik she would also live with her Arn. As long as she saw fit to keep him there, Eskil added with a jocular glance at Cecilia, who looked surprised by these unnecessary additions concerning the legal right to all morning gifts.

It was decided to hold three days of celebration: the bachelors' and maidens' evening on the first Friday after Midsummer; the fetching of the bride and the traditional escorting to the bridal bed on the following Saturday; and the blessing of the bride at the mass on Sunday in Forshem Church.

✠

Four young men rode to the bachelors' evening. Even from far off everyone could see that these young men were not ordinary youths. Their horses were decked out for a feast in blue fabric, and three of the men wore surcoats with the Folkung lion over their chain mail, while the fourth bore the mark of the three crowns. It was a summer day in the midst of the hay harvest, so their mantles were rolled up behind their saddles. Otherwise it would have been obvious that the fourth among them, the sole Erik, had a mantle lined with ermine. And since it wasn't the king himself, it had to be his son Erik jarl.

Their shields hanging on the left side of the saddle were all newly painted in shining blue and gold around the lion and crowns. Behind them followed four royal guards and some pack-horses.

It was a beautiful sight with all the bright colors and the stout horses, but also a sight that would make every peasant in the lands of the Goths more than wary. If such a party happened to arrive toward evening and decided to spend the night, they would not leave much ale behind but a great void in the larder, for all power in the kingdom lay with the Eriks and Folkungs, and no one could refuse them anything.

The youngest of the four was Torgils, seventeen years old, the son of Eskil Magnusson of Arnäs. The eldest was Magnus Månesköld, who once had been reckoned Birger Brosa's son, but was now considered his foster brother. He was actually the son of Arn Magnusson. The fourth, who rode beside Erik jarl, was Folke Jonsson, son of Jon the judge in Eastern Götaland.

The four were best friends and almost always rode together in the hunt and during weapons games. Before this wedding they had spent ten days together while their riding clothes were cleaned and mended and their shields painted anew at the king's Näs. Each day they had practiced with their weapons for several hours, for it was not some ordinary test that awaited them.

For Magnus Månesköld it hadn't been easy to stay away from Forsvik for so long. When Birger Brosa came to Bjälbo, in a rage after the latest council meeting, he mentioned as if in passing that Arn Magnusson had returned to the kingdom. The first thing Magnus wanted to do was jump into the saddle and ride off to see his father.

But he restrained himself when he realized that Arn Magnusson was probably not a man he should seek out before first outfitting himself well and polishing all his weapons until they gleamed. And he wanted to practice even more with the bow, for Magnus had lived his entire young life hearing the sagas about how his father Arn was the best archer of all.

To himself he quietly admitted that he was a bit apprehensive at approaching Forsvik for such an unusual task. He was to be one of the young men to escort his own father to the bachelor evening. His friends had made much mirth about this. It was not granted to many men to drink their father under the table at the bachelors' celebration. He had not been amused by these jests and said so. Arn Magnusson of Arnäs was not some ordinary bridegroom. And the bride was no little weepy and terrified goose, but his own mother, a woman beyond reproach who was shown respect by all. With this wedding, it was more a matter of restoring honor than arranging favorable family alliances, and it was nothing to jest about.

Erik jarl had argued that among one's closest friends one could jest about anything and everyone. But he honored Magnus's wishes and avoided the topic. He himself was a jarl of the realm and thus highest in rank among the friends, but Magnus Månesköld was the eldest of the four, the best at weapons games, and often as wise as if he were truly Birger Brosa's son.

As they approached Forsvik the tension grew as the meeting with Arn Magnusson approached. They all knew him by reputation but had never seen him in person.

The first workers from Forsvik they met were the ones busy with the hay harvest, cutting grass and raising hay-racks. They all stopped what they were doing when they saw the gleaming trappings of the approaching riders. Then they lined up to kneel in greeting until Erik jarl ordered them back to work.

In one of the fields lying fallow close to Forsvik itself, a more surprising sight greeted them. Two young boys were practicing on horseback with two older foreigners. All four were riding in close formation, and at a cry from one of the dark-skinned strangers all four turned like lightning to the left or right or stopped short, rearing and turning on the spot in the other direction. Then they sped up and suddenly cast themselves all together in a new direction. It was a peculiar sight, a style of riding that none of the four friends had ever seen. The horses also looked foreign, smaller than regular horses but much quicker in their movements.

Soon they were discovered by the four riders practicing. One of the foreigners then drew an unusually narrow sword and yelled some warning to the other. He too drew his sword, signaling to the two boys to ride back into the farmyard at once. Then followed a moment of confusion when it looked as though the foreigners were preparing to attack, while the two boys protested and scolded without really being able to make themselves understood.

Erik jarl and his friends sat still, like their retainers, with their hands resting on the hilts of their swords. It was an astonishing sight, if what they were seeing was correct, that two men were preparing to attack a group of eight.

Before they managed to decide how to behave at this unexpected welcome, one of the two boys in the field spurred his horse and rode toward them at such high speed that it was hard for them to believe their eyes. In a few seconds he was upon them. Then he stopped abruptly and bowed.

"Forgive me, Erik jarl, that our foreign teachers took you for our foes," he gasped. "I am Sune Folkesson and am apprenticed here at Forsvik to Sir Arn, and that's my brother over there, Sigfrid Erlingsson."

"I know who you are. I knew your father when I was your age," replied Erik jarl. "Since you are the one who came to meet us, you may now take us to your lord."

Young Sune nodded eagerly. He wheeled his horse around with a single odd leap and rode ahead at a canter as he waved to Sigfrid and the two foreign teachers that there was no danger. The teachers bowed and turned their horses toward Forsvik.

The sound of hammers and axes thundered along with the ringing of metal from smithies as the four noble youths neared the bridge over the rapids with their retainers, the two boys, and the foreign riders behind them. They saw thralls and workers transporting timber although it was the middle of summer. Others were loading bricks and stones and carrying heavy yokes laden with masonry supplies in every direction. It seemed that no one had time to look up at the visitors.

They rode across the courtyard between the buildings, and nobody came to greet them; they continued out the other side where two new longhouses and two smaller buildings were being raised. Most of the residents of Forsvik who were not out at the hay harvest seemed to be there working together.

As the four visitors came around the gable of the new longhouse, they finally aroused the attention they had no doubt expected much earlier.

A man who was way up on the wall and dressed in dirty

leather clothes swung down from the wooden scaffolding in two long, nimble leaps. Everyone made way for him as he wiped the sweat from his brow and flung away the trowel, looking gravely from one visitor to the next. When his gaze fell upon Magnus Månesköld he nodded as if in affirmation and went straight over to him and held out his hand. Everyone was quiet. Nobody moved.

Magnus's head spun when he saw the warrior's filthy hand covered with mortar extended toward him, and almost with horror his gaze sought out the man's scarred face. His friends sat mute, just as amazed as he was.

"If your father offers you his hand, I think you ought to take it," said Arn with a broad smile, wiping the sweat once more from his brow.

Magnus Månesköld immediately dismounted, took his father's hand, and quickly dropped one knee to the ground. Then he hesitated before he fell into his father's embrace.

His friends instantly got off their horses and handed the reins to the servants, who now seemed wakened from their paralysis and hurried over from all directions. One by one the four youths politely greeted this Arn Magnusson who did not resemble any of the images they had envisioned and discussed with each other.

The guests' horses were taken away. Ale and wine, bread and salt were brought out, and then Arn and his four guests entered the hall of the old longhouse and sat down for a meal.

"I wasn't expecting you until tomorrow," Arn explained, motioning to his dirty work clothes. "A message came from Näs that you are the four who shall escort me to my bachelor evening, and for that honor I thank you warmly."

"It's an honor for us to do so," replied Erik jarl with a curt bow, but his expression did not match his words.

"You have come to a building site that is hardly suited for guests," said Arn after a moment. He had no difficulty seeing through their embarrassed reticence. "So I suggest that we leave at once, stop to rest in Askeberga, and arrive at Arnäs early tomorrow morning." He was expecting their astonished expressions.

"You probably shouldn't leave right away, Father," said Magnus glumly. "Thrall clothing and mortar in your hair are not the proper attire for a bachelors' evening."

"My thoughts exactly," said Arn as if not noticing that he'd been reprimanded by his own son. "So perhaps you might enjoy the meager entertainments that Forsvik has to offer today, while I change my attire for a new fate!"

He got up, bowed to his guests, and left, aware of the silence that remained in his wake. Their unmistakable disappointment was written in stone on their faces.

Arn was in a hurry when he came out of the longhouse. He was sure that they should all saddle up and get away from Forsvik as soon as they could. He called together all the workers and told them what he expected to see finished by the time he and his bride returned in less than a week. Then he ordered Sune and Sigfrid to ready his horse Ibn Anaza, decking him out like the horses of the four guests. Sune objected that there was no such Folkung caparison at Forsvik, so Arn went into one of the new buildings and fetched a white cloth that he tossed to the boys. Then he commanded that the guests' retainers be given ale, and he summoned the Saracen who was handiest with a razor and ordered hot water to be brought to the bathhouse.

Inside the longhouse Erik jarl and his friends were served smoked meat, bread, and ale, but all declined to partake of the wine that was offered.

Their good mood from the trip to Forsvik was gone. They had a hard time talking, since none of them wanted to add to Magnus Månesköld's embarrassment. Finding his father with a trowel in his hand was not something they envied him.

"Your father is as strong and agile as any of us. Did you see the way he came down from the top of the roof in only two leaps?" said Torgils Eskilsson in an attempt to say something positive.

"He must have fought many battles to have so many scars on his hands and face," Folke Jonsson added.

Magnus Månesköld at first said nothing, just looked down into his ale and sighed. Then he muttered something to the effect that perhaps it wasn't so odd that those who had lost the Holy Land had taken some lumps before it was over. His disappointment spread like the cold to the others.

"But it was he who once met Emund Ulvbane in single combat at the *ting* of all Goths, sparing the berserker but hacking off his hand," Torgils attempted to console him once more.

"Back then he was a young man like we are, and it wasn't a trowel he was holding in his hand," Magnus muttered.

Their conversation faltered even more.

Less than an hour had passed when a completely different Arn Magnusson stepped through the door. His face was rosy from a hot bath, his blond hair that had been a matted gray mass of mortar and dirt was slicked back shiny and clean, and his face was now free of whiskers so that the white scars gleamed even more clearly than when they first saw him. But this was not what had changed him most.

His chain mail was of a foreign type, shining like silver and clinging to his body like cloth. On his feet he wore a type of steel shoes that none of the four had ever seen before, and spurs of gold glittered at his heels. He wore the Folkungs' surcoat over his chain mail, and at his side hung a long, narrow sword in a black scabbard with a cross stamped on it in gold. On a chain from his left shoulder dangled a gleaming helmet.

"The horses have been brought out to the courtyard," he said curtly, motioning to them to get up and follow him.

Outside, the thralls stood holding the reins of five horses. Their retainers were already mounted and waiting a short distance away.

Arn strode straight over to a black horse with a silver mane and mounted it in a single leap as the horse turned and set off at a trot. It all seemed to happen in one fluid movement.

Just outside the barnyard Arn wheeled his horse around, and it reared on its hind legs as he drew his long flashing sword and shouted something in a foreign language. The many foreigners responded with shouts and cheers.

"He who judges too soon judges himself," said Torgils knowingly to Magnus as they hurried to mount their horses and catch up with Arn.

Magnus was just as confused by what he now saw as he was at his first meeting with his father. The man riding ahead of him was not the same one who had met him with the trowel in his hand.

The four urged their horses on until they came up alongside Arn, the way equal brothers ride through the land. Now they saw that it was not merely a white cloth covering his horse like those who lacked their own clan's coat of arms. On both hind-quarters shone a great red cross, the same as that on Arn's white shield. They knew what that meant even though none of them had ever actually seen a Templar knight in person.

They rode for a long while in silence, each man subdued by his own embarrassment. Arn made not the slightest move to start a conversation to help them out of this difficulty. He thought he had a good idea what their expressions had meant when they saw him *working like a thrall*, as they probably would have said in their language. But he had been so young when he was sent to Varnhem cloister that he hadn't had time to develop such pride. And yet he had a hard time imagining that he would have turned out like these young men even if he had grown up outside the cloister walls along with Eskil.

Then Magnus came riding up beside him and asked timidly about the long, light sword they all had seen when he saluted farewell to the farm folk.

"Hand me your sword and take mine and I'll explain," said Arn, drawing his sword in a lightning-quick motion and holding it out with his iron glove around the blade by the hilt. "But be careful of the blade, it's very sharp!"

When Arn took the Nordic sword in his hand he swung it a few times and nodded to himself with a smile.

"You're still forging in iron that you bend back and forth," he said before he explained.

Magnus's sword was very beautiful, he admitted at once. It also lay well in the hand. But it was too short to use from horseback, demonstrating with a swift downward slash. Yet the iron was too soft to cut through the modern chain mail and would easily get stuck in the enemy's shield. The edge was far too dull, and after a few blows against another man's sword or shield it wouldn't be of much use. So the important thing was to win quickly, and then go home and whet the blade anew, he said in an attempt to jest.

Magnus took some tentative swings with his father's sword and then cautiously felt the edge. He flinched when he cut himself. As he was about to hand back the sword, his eyes fell on a long inscription in gold that was impossible to read. He asked what it meant, whether it was only for decoration or something that made the sword better.

"Both," said Arn. "It's a greeting from a friend and a blessing, and one day, but not today, I'll tell you what it says."

The sun was on its way up to its zenith, and Arn surprised his young companions by leaning back in the saddle and untying his mantle, which he slung over his shoulders. Arn told the wondering youths that if it was heat they wanted to protect themselves from, they should do as he did. They all hesitantly did the same, except for Erik jarl, who had ermine lining his mantle and thought the heat was bad enough without wrapping himself in fur. By the time they reached Askeberga resting place late that afternoon, he was the one who had sweated most.

✠

On the day of the maidens' celebration at Husaby the entire royal estate was transformed into an armed camp. At least that was Cecilia's impression, and it made her even more agitated to hear the sound of horses' hoofs, clanging weapons, and rough male voices everywhere. A dozen retainers had been sent from Arnäs, and more than twice as many warriors had been brought from the villages that were subject to Arnäs. A ring of tents sprouted up around Husaby, groups of riders searched through the oak woods far and wide, and scouts were sent out in every direction. Nothing must happen to the bride before she was safely under feather-bed and covers.

During the weeks at Midsummer when Cecilia felt like a guest on her own land she had spent most of her time in the weaving chamber with old Suom. Their friendship, which had developed after such a brief time, was not usual between a thrall and an unmarried noblewoman. Suom could perform miracles with her loom, making the sun and moon, images of the Victorious Bridegroom, and various churches appear as if in their actual settings, with some close and some far away. From Riseberga Cecilia had brought some of the dyes she had worked with for many years, and a sort of blended linen and woolen yarn. Suom said she had never seen such lovely colors, and everything she had done in her life would have been so much better if she'd had this knowledge from the start. Cecilia explained the origin of the dyes and how to boil and blend them; Suom showed with her hands how to weave figures right into the cloth.

So the two got a late start on the most important task, to weave Cecilia's bridal mantle. When the bride was escorted along the road to the church for the blessing and on to the bridal ale, she was supposed to be clad in her own clan's colors. Cecilia had such strong memories of the blue color from her time in Gudhem convent. There she and Cecilia Blanca had been alone among all the Sverker daughters who wore red yarn around one arm as a sign of their common loyalty and hatred toward the two foes, Cecilia Rosa and Cecilia Blanca. She and her best friend had defied them by tying a small piece of blue yarn around their arms. And when the king and jarl came at last to take away Cecilia Blanca and make her queen, jarl Birger Brosa had done something that still warmed Cecilia's memory.

She had been summoned to the hospitium and there the evil Mother Rikissa had torn off the scrap of blue yarn. Cecilia had been close to tears at this affront and her own feeling of powerlessness. Then the jarl had come over and hung his own Folkung mantle around her shoulders, which was a sign of protection that no one could mistake. Since that day she had always thought of herself as wearing blue and not green, which was the color of the Pål clan.

With renewed vigor they went back to work on the bridal mantle. Suom wove in the sign of the Pål clan in the middle of the back, a black shield with a silver chevron, so that it was very prominent although it was not sewn on but a part of the weave. After many attempts Cecilia had developed a deep, shimmering green color which pleased them both. At last the mantle was done.

When Suom took her leave to return to Arnäs, Cecilia stood up, sweeping the loveliest of green Pål mantles around her, and headed over to the longhouse, where her kinsmen were now gathered for the brief evening ale that would start off the maidens' evening celebration. When she came in the faces of the three Pål brothers lit up with genuine joy when they saw the mantle she wore. They all admired it and wanted to feel the fabric, turning it this way and that in the light to see its shimmer. They also seemed relieved to have escaped the affront to the clan if she had decided to sew a blue mantle for herself for this grand wedding celebration.

Pål Jönsson himself handed her a small goblet of ale and was the first to drink with her. Afterward she drank with his younger brother Algot. Sture, who was the youngest and still a bachelor, had ridden to Arnäs to take part in the bachelors' evening as the only youth from the Pål clan. They all raised their tankards to the young Sture because, as Pål said, it would not be easy to spend the evening drinking with men who were all Folkungs and Eriks.

Then they began the arrangements for what was to take place during the maidens' evening. Six young women from the Pål clan came into the hall, taking Cecilia's hand and greeting her. She didn't know any of them, since they were so young. The priest from Husaby Church blessed all seven of the maidens and then the house thralls brought each of them a white shift and a wreath made of lingonberry twigs.

Cecilia had only a vague idea of what a maidens' evening was, and she had no idea how she was supposed to behave when these young women, whom she didn't know, lined up holding the white shifts in their arms, with the lingonberry wreaths on top. She decided that the only thing she could do was to pretend that nothing was unfamiliar and just follow the others. They were now slowly leaving through the open doors, stepping into the summer night.

Outside stood a row of retainers. Every third man held a burning torch in his hand to keep the evil spirits or the unblessed away from the maidens as they appeared at this most dangerous of moments in terms of the powers of darkness.

Cecilia came last in the procession, which slowly headed toward the oak woods and the stream a short distance away. There the bathhouse could be glimpsed in the glow of torches.

As they left the courtyard and took their first steps into the oak forest, the other maidens began singing a song that Cecilia had never heard before, even though she'd undoubtedly heard thousands of songs. She didn't grasp all the words, since many were old-fashioned, but she understood that it was a song to a female god from heathen times. Inside the forest menacing shadows reigned. But Cecilia didn't believe in sirens of the woods or gnomes as much as she did in apprehensive armed retainers.

As custom demanded, the seven maidens arrived at the washhouse at the darkest hour of the summer night. But since it was the week after Midsummer, it wasn't very dark. Even so, they were dazzled by the burning torches that were posted around the entire washhouse. Outside stood two long benches, and there Cecilia's escort, amid much giggling and laughter, placed their clothes so that one after the other they stood there naked. They also removed their headbands and then combed their fingers through their long tresses that fell over their shoulders and breasts.

Cecilia hesitated, blushing, although no one noticed in the dark. She had never stood naked before anyone, and at first she didn't know how she was going to manage.

The other maidens teased her by hugging their arms to their chests and shivering, telling her to make haste so that they might quickly step inside where it was warm. Cecilia then realized that there was actually one person before whom she had been naked, although a very long time ago; only one, and that was Arn Magnusson. And if she could show herself naked to a man, never mind the one she loved, then it ought to be much easier to do so before women. That was how she persuaded herself as she diffidently fumbled with her clothes, taking them off and placing them on the wooden bench.

Now all of them lined up, crossed their hands over their breasts and walked seven times around the bathhouse, singing yet another heathen song that Cecilia had never heard. Neither the melody nor the words were familiar. After that the first maiden to approach the bathhouse opened the door, and then everyone ran inside, shrieking and giggling in the steam.

There were big wooden vessels filled with hot or cold water, as well as buckets for pouring the water. After the first cautious attempts with a bare foot, it turned out that they had to pour some of the cold water into the hot vessel, which was so huge that it could hold at least two butchered oxen. Several of the maidens splashed cold water on some of the others, prompting more shrieks and laughter.

When one of them boldly stepped into the tub and hastily sat down, she gasped several times and then gestured to the others, who followed suit. Sitting in a circle, they grabbed each others' hands and sang more pagan songs. Some of the words made Cecilia's already flushed cheeks turn even redder. The songs were bawdy and dealt with things that were forbidden up until the wedding night but afterward all actually encouraged, although many verses implied that it was the forbidden fruit that always tasted best.

Cecilia felt as if she had landed in a big tub of chicken soup, but there was in truth not much that she could do about it, nor could she get out of it by sulking. That was a consoling thought, and soon she began to feel strangely cheerful and then almost feverish, as if the sorcery of the songs had truly affected her.

They sat there until the water began to cool and the light of dawn glimmered outside as the torches gradually went out. Then they hurried to perform the last tasks before they were allowed to start drinking. They all rushed out to the stream and jumped in, screaming shrilly at the ice-cold water, then dashed back inside the bathhouse, which now seemed wonderfully warm. There they lit new torches and helped each other to wash all over, even the most unclean parts of their bodies.

Afterward they quickly dried themselves with big pieces of linen and then went over to where they'd left their special clothing piled up. They put on the white shifts that they'd brought from the longhouse, pressed the wreaths down over their foreheads, and arranged their wet hair. A row of small ale tankards and a newly tapped cask were brought from the back of the bathhouse. They were soon drinking together like men, imitating the men as they walked around with their legs astraddle, swaggering barefoot across the wooden floor. Cecilia wished that she'd been able to mimic her friend Cecilia Blanca, who could belch and fart like an old man.

They had to empty the ale cask before they were allowed to leave. Otherwise, as one of Cecilia's young kinswomen named Ulrika explained, it would mean bad luck for the bride. But there was no cause for alarm on this occasion, since this was a night when the young maidens were allowed to drink as much as they liked.

The ale was warm and sweetened with honey, which better suited the women, and they soon began talking louder and louder as they drank almost like men.

And now the shyness that had existed between Cecilia and her young kinswomen disappeared. One of the maidens said that Cecilia shouldn't think that any of them thought ill of her because she had reached such an old age before drinking the bridal ale. Another said that whoever waited for something good never waited too long.

Even though these words were no doubt meant to encourage Cecilia, they suddenly made her feel embarrassed again. All of these young maidens were so much lovelier than she was; their breasts were firm and their hips softly rounded. On this evening when Cecilia had touched her own body with less modesty than ever before, she realized that her breasts drooped and her body was gaunt and angular.

The others saw at once this hint of nervousness in Cecilia's eyes, and before any of the others could speak, the maiden named Katarina said what she thought they were undoubtedly all thinking. For them this was a great day, for Cecilia had shown that a woman could decide much for herself. She was even able to defy her kinsmen and refuse to enter the cloister, despite the fact that a struggle for power was at stake. And she could go to the bridal bed with the one she loved instead of accepting someone chosen by her father.

Yet one of the maidens objected that it didn't matter with whom a woman went to the bridal bed, as long as she honored her clan. That started a heated quarrel that went on for a while, ending only when the maiden named Katarina and another named Brigida began splashing ale at each other. Finally Katarina picked up her tankard and dumped the whole thing over Brigida's head.

That sparked new laughter and the quarrel was ended and everyone poured themselves more ale. Katarina suggested that they demand another whole cask before they went to the longhouse to attend the night ale.

But when the first cask was empty, they put on their mantles over the white shifts and gathered up their other clothing. Carrying their shoes in their hands, they walked back to the longhouse. By then it was bright daylight, and a chorus of birds was singing, with promises of a beautiful wedding day.

To Cecilia's great amusement, the maidens now sang Kyrie Eleison; for the first time she could add her own voice to the song, sounding clearer and louder than all the others. These young maidens might well have breasts and hips more beautiful than the bride's, but she could sing better than any of them.

✠

Ten pounds of honey, 13 salted and 26 live pigs, 24 smoked wild boar hams and an equal number of shoulders, 10 salted and 24 live sheep, 16 live oxen and 4 salted, 14 casks of butter, 360 large cheeses and 210 small, 420 chickens, 180 geese, 4 pounds pepper and cumin, 5 pounds salt, 8 barrels of herring, 200 salmon and 150 dried Norwegian fish, as well as oats, wheat, rye, and flour, plus malt, bog-myrtle, and juniper berries in sufficient quantities.

Eskil was laboring to keep count of the provisions that came streaming into Arnäs, when Arn and his companions rode into the castle half a day earlier than planned. The next day over two hundred guests would fill Arnäs, but for the bachelors' evening more than a hundred were already expected, since there were many who were looking forward to the customary games, which this time promised to be particularly impressive. These were not just ordinary young men who were going to compete.

So far none of the guests had arrived, and Arnäs was deserted except for all the house thralls running back and forth as they tended to their tasks. The village of Arnäs had emptied out and every nook and cranny had been swept so as to provide lodging for guests who were too highborn to sleep in tents. Bowers of stock and rowan had been erected by the field on the other side of the moat below the western gate, and tables and benches had been hauled out there. Ale casks had been rolled across the castle courtyard, cartloads of birch and rowan branches had been brought in and unloaded to adorn the walls of the great hall. Tables were brought from near and far, while poles and canvas for tents set up and made taut.

Arn and his companions took no part in all this work, and after they handed their horses over to the stable thralls, Erik jarl decided that he needed to rest in order to gather strength for the evening's strenuous trials. Folke Jonsson agreed. Besides, those who arrived first could claim the best sleeping areas.

Arn thought he could make better use of his time by not sleeping, but he didn't say this out loud. Instead, he put his arms around the shoulders of his son Magnus and the young Torgils. Offering a few jests, but with great firmness, he led the two men toward the big tower. They both recoiled when he explained that they were now going to meet old Herr Magnus, because they had heard that the old man was no longer in his right mind.

Hence their great surprise when they climbed the tower stairs with Arn and found Herr Magnus out on the battlement. He was walking back and forth, muttering but resolute, with only a rough stick to lean on for support. A foreigner was attentively walking at his side. When Herr Magnus noticed the three visitors, a broad smile immediately lit up his face. He threw out his arms, even the one holding the stick, and offered up loud and incomprehensible words praising God for the grace that had now been granted him.

Magnus Månesköld stepped forward at once, took the old man's hand, and sank down with one knee touching the stone floor. Torgils then did the same, followed by Arn.

"You've regained your strength much faster and better than I dared hope, Father," said Arn.

"Yes, and that's why I'm both happy and vexed to see the three of you, even though it's been a long time since I saw you, Magnus, and you as well, Torgils. My two grandsons!"

"It was truly not our intention to vex you, dear grandfather," said Magnus Månesköld gently.

"Oh, you misunderstand me! I merely meant that I wanted to see all of you struck dumb with surprise at the bridal ale.

Everybody will be expecting to find me crippled and lying in my own piss somewhere, shoved aside where no one would see me. Instead I intend to give the bridal toast myself, because it has been a long time since I had that pleasure. So I ask all of you to promise not to say anything of this; then I will still enjoy my surprise."

His speech flowed freely and without slurring, perhaps a bit slower than in the past, but otherwise almost the same. Both Magnus Månesköld and young Torgils, who hadn't seen him in over a year, and then more to bid him farewell than to encounter any joy, now thought that they were beholding a true miracle. And it was not difficult for Herr Magnus to see what they were thinking.

"It's not at all what you two imagine," he went on as he took a little turn around the battlement to demonstrate again that he was able to walk almost as he had done previously. "It's this Frankish man who is knowledgeable in healing who has shown me the way, along with Our Lord, of course!"

Arn had been carrying on a brief and quiet conversation in an incomprehensible language with the foreigner, and what he learned was apparently favorable.

"You mustn't exert yourself too much today, Father," he said. "You don't want to get overtired, because it's going to be a long night tomorrow. And we all promise not to say a word to anyone about your surprise."

"Agreed?" he added, looking at the two young men, who immediately nodded solemnly.

"Father should rest for two hours now, then practice for an hour and rest again for two," Arn went on after another brief discussion with the foreigner. "We won't disturb you any longer right now."

The three men bowed and took three steps back before turning around and continuing along the battlement, with Arn in the lead. He wanted to show them the construction work that was going on.

But Magnus and Torgils seemed a bit too timid in his presence, and they soon said they wished to follow Erik jarl's example and rest before the evening's contests.

Disappointed by their lack of interest and concerned that there was something about the young men that he didn't understand, Arn went over to the side facing Lake Vänern where the tackle groaned and the stone hammers rang. He was genuinely surprised to see how fast the work had progressed and how evenly the stones were being fit together. He gave all the Saracen builders much praise before he explained that they would now have a three-day holiday for the wedding. They were all invited as guests, but they would need to dress accordingly. He said nothing about washing, since it would have been insulting to mention such a thing to the Prophet's people.

Yet he did offer a few jests about the matter to the sweaty Brother Guilbert, who had been a Templar knight for twelve years in the Holy Land, after all. Was he perhaps still obeying the Rule's ban on unnecessary washing? Brother Guilbert had a good laugh at this assumption, explaining that of all the regulations, he found the one prescribing that a man should stink like a pig was the least comprehensible. Unless Saint Bernard, in his inscrutable wisdom when he wrote the Rule, had thought that the Saracens would be more afraid of those warriors who stank like swine.

Brother Guilbert went off to get washed and change into his white monk's robes, because when he was toiling so hard he dressed as a lay brother. In the meantime Arn went looking for Eskil. He found his brother engaged in a palaver involving many different languages, although no one seemed to understand a single word uttered by the group of minstrels, pipers, and drummers who had arrived from Skara with four ox-carts. What needed to be negotiated was the payment and the location; in such matters people were apt to pretend that they understood less than they actually did. But when the leader of the minstrel group turned out to be from Aix-en-Provence, Arn was soon able to help his brother by clarifying the agreement regarding every silver coin, as well as the group's right to free ale and meat. In return, they would have to set up camp with their carts a good distance away from the fortress. In the end both parties seemed satisfied with the agreement, and the minstrels immediately returned to their ox carts to head for the specified camp area.

Eskil then took his brother to the bridal chamber, which was separated from the rest of the living quarters in the western end of the loft of the longhouse, with a stairway leading up to it from each side, one for the bridegroom and one for the bride. In the chamber hung the clothing that Arn would wear at various times during the days of the bridal ale. He would wear the garb of a warrior only when going to fetch his bride; afterward he would change into other attire. For the evening of the bridal ale, he would wear foreign clothing in blue and silver and made from cloth that was otherwise worn only by women. But now, for the bachelors' evening, he was to dress in a loose white surcoat with sleeves that reached only to the elbow; underneath he would wear a long blue tunic made of supple dyed deerskin, leggings of undyed leather, and soft leather boots with cross-gartering. He would wear his sword no matter what his attire.

After explaining these changes of clothing to a somewhat astonished Arn, Eskil sighed as for the thousandth time that day he remembered something that demanded his prompt attention. They were six men, but seven were needed for the evening. The group included Erik jarl, Sture Jönsson from the Pål clan, and four Folkungs: Arn, Magnus Månesköld, Folke Jonsson, and Eskil's own son, Torgils. They needed a seventh, and he had to be unmarried and not a Folkung.

Arn said he could offer no suggestions in this matter, since he had only a vague idea what a bachelors' evening was all about, although he assumed that an ungodly amount of ale would be consumed, as usual. Eskil explained with growing impatience that it signified youth's farewell to the free life, one last night together before one of them would leave his youth behind forever. Such was the custom.

Although this time the bachelors were unusually mature, he admitted, parrying Arn's mocking smile, and the bridegroom was a man who had already reached his best years, with both a son and a nephew among his kinsmen. A similar situation had doubtless never occurred before, since some of these unmarried men, in particular Erik jarl and Magnus Månesköld, were already well known in the land to be fierce and deft at wielding weapons, many people were bound to arrive to watch the start of this bachelors' evening.

With a sigh Arn then suggested that since Brother Guilbert was his oldest friend after Eskil himself, and he could not be said to be a Folkung, he would prefer to see the monk and no one else as the seventh man. For age apparently made no difference, and as far as being a bachelor was concerned, Brother Guilbert could certainly defend his position with greater conviction than some among these young roosters.

Eskil fretted about this decision. He thought that an old monk would be more an object of ridicule than honor to their friendship in the games that awaited them.

Even though Arn had some idea what was ahead and did not like it, he found it impossible not to comply with his kinsmen's customs. Still, he asked with an innocent expression what young roosters might be able to accomplish that Brother Guilbert could not.

Eskil replied evasively that there were seven games, seven different tests of skill with weapons, and that eternal honor would be won by the man who bested the others on a bachelors' evening. Hence, it would be all the worse for anyone, especially a close friend like this Brother Guilbert, who performed poorly.

When he heard this, Arn sat in silence for a moment on the feather bed, but not for the reasons that Eskil assumed. He truly had no desire to compete in weapons' games with tenderfeet and young boys; even less desire to do them harm. It reminded him of that unpleasant day when King Richard Lionheart had urged one of his young whelps, Sir Wilfred Ivanhoe was apparently his name, to joust with lances in the lists against a Templar knight. Such sport might end badly.

Boys should be taught and fostered; it was undignified to compete against them. He realized gloomily that not even this objection would seem reasonable to his brother.

"What sort of weapons games are we going to play and put our honor at risk?" he asked at last.

"As I said, there are seven different games," replied Eskil impatiently. "Three you will perform on horseback, and four on foot, involving ax, spear, bow, and quarterstaff."

"Three games on horseback and the quarterstaff?" asked Arn with sudden merriment. "This may be more fun than you think, and don't worry about the monk. He'll acquit himself well and offer much entertainment for those who are watching. But I have to go and talk to him first. Then I'll fetch bows from the tower that will suit the two of us and see to it that my mare is properly saddled, befitting a monk."

Eskil threw out his arms, saying that he relinquished all responsibility for this decision. Then he remembered another hundred things that he had to take care of and rushed down the bridegroom's stairs, all of a sudden in a great hurry.

Arn dropped to his knees and rested his face against the soft coverlet of the bridal bed, breathing in the scent of herbs. For a long time he prayed to God's Mother that she might hold Her protective hands over his beloved Cecilia for as long as there was still danger, and that he might not be struck by pride or injure any of the youths, especially not his own son, in the childish games that it seemed impossible for him to avoid.

⁜

By early evening more than a hundred guests had arrived at Arnäs to drink a toast to the bachelors' evening, but mostly to watch the youthful games. The castle courtyard was crowded with ale tents and the stages that had been set up on trestles so that the conjuror's tricks could be witnessed by all. Pipes and drums played, and the minstrels' children performed preposterous antics, contorting themselves to stick their heads between their legs and creeping like big lice over the boards, prompting both laughter and alarm. But the air was filled with anticipation and few could keep from talking about what was to come: youthful games unlike any in memory, in which a jarl of the realm and one of the Lord's knights from the Holy Land would both compete.

The drama began when the seven white-garbed men rode in from the stables on their horses, one after the other, and then circled round the courtyard with Erik jarl in the lead. A white-clad monk who aroused laughter and surprise came last. All rode magnificent stallions, except for Arn Magnusson and the monk, who rode small and lean steeds that already seemed skittish amidst all the crowds and tumult.

Erik jarl led the horsemen through the gate and down toward the pasture with the stock bower, where stable thralls held the reins of their horses as they dismounted. The guests at Arnäs gathered expectantly along the low western wall where the view of the playing field was so good that none of the spectators would miss any of the action.

Down on the field the seven youths—because according to custom that is what they were called even though at least four of them were full-grown men—chose Erik jarl to decide any dispute that might arise. Yet nobody believed that these men would squabble like real youths; each and every one of them was sure to behave with honor.

The first game involved tossing an ax, and the results would determine what came next. The man who won the ax game would be in charge of the following game and thus decide how to proceed.

A disk had been sawn from a thick oak log, and a red circle had been painted in the center of it as the target. Each of the men would be allowed three tries wielding old double-bladed axes from a distance of ten paces.

Arn and Brother Guilbert, who were standing together, joked that if a man held such a battle-ax in his hand, it was actually best to hold on to it. Once he let it go, he wouldn't be much use. Neither of them had ever seen or practiced this skill.

Erik jarl was first. His ax hurtled through the air and stuck in the red circle with a dull thud. Applause and an appreciative murmur rose from the spectators, since it would be no small matter for a member of the Erik clan to beat four Folkungs.

The second ax also struck the target well, but the third landed outside the circle.

Then came Magnus Månesköld's turn. He too landed two axes inside the circle, with the third just outside. Erik jarl and Magnus agreed that Erik's aim had been the better, and neither of them showed any sign of disappointment or joy in victory.

Young Torgils was next, and he managed to land only one ax inside the circle, although the other two he threw struck the oak plank hard and well. Folke Jonsson did not do quite as well as Torgils, and when it was Sture Jönsson's turn, a good deal of murmuring and laughter could be heard from the spectators up on the wall. It was hard not to jest about what would happen if a member of the Pål clan should beat both the Folkungs and Eriks.

That was exactly what he did, beating everyone who had tried so far. All three of his axes landed close together and inside the red circle. For that he received subdued applause.

When the stout monk stepped forward, there was again laughter accompanied by some scornful remarks; people yelled that there was no doubt of his bachelor status, but there wasn't much else in his favor. And as expected, only one ax landed fairly, and outside of the red circle, at that.

Everyone then fell silent with excitement as Arn Magnusson, the last contestant, stepped forward, holding the three axes in his hand. But the disappointment was great and many commented on his poor attempts, for two of the axes hit the target but the blades didn't lodge firmly, and the third ax landed outside the red circle, staying there only a few moments before it fell to the ground. This was not what anyone had expected from a man of the sagas.

Seven woven baskets were brought to the youths, who now filled them with last year's half-rotten turnips, the number depending on their placement in the first contest. Hence Arn had seven turnips in his basket, while Sture Jönsson had only one. At the end of the games, the man who had the least number of turnips would be the winner.

Now it was time for spears. And Sture Jönsson would decide who he would battle first, and with that the real game would begin. Because now it was not just a matter of being able to wield a weapon well; the man who would win also had to be able to plan cleverly. With an aim toward winning, Sture should compete with the best men first, so that they would receive many turnips for being defeated first. If on the other hand he merely wanted to make it through with modest honor, he should start at the other end and challenge the monk or Arn Magnusson, since they had both proved to have little skill at throwing axes.

As if he truly saw himself as becoming the evening's victor, Sture Jönsson arrogantly pointed his spear at Erik jarl.

He should not have done that. Because when they both cast their three spears at a bull's-eye on a bale of hay, Erik jarl was the winner and Sture Jönsson the one who could expect to receive seven turnips in his basket.

Erik jarl was out to win; no one had any doubt of that. Therefore it was only right and proper for him to point his spear at Magnus Månesköld, who was surely his best competitor; it would be best for him to receive as many turnips as possible.

It turned into a fierce battle between the two, both of whom were very skilled at throwing spears. Time after time appreciative murmurs would pass through the crowd of spectators up on the wall. Both men threw all three of their spears with such precision and so close to the target that it was impossible to decide the winner. And so they agreed to try again.

The second time Erik jarl determined that Magnus Månesköld had won. Magnus then pointed his spear at the monk and defeated him as easily as everyone had expected. After that he boldly pointed at his own father.

Arn Magnusson was defeated too, just as easily as the monk. Magnus Månesköld soon won the game, and many of the spectators were already convinced that he was the one who would finally have the least number of turnips of all and thereby win a crown of gold.

The next game was quarterstaffs on a plank. The two combatants had to balance on a plank placed over the moat and try to knock the other off using a long quarterstaff with its ends wrapped in leather. Before starting this game, it was customary to remove most of their clothing, since by the time the contest ended, all but one would have taken a bath in the moat.

Magnus Månesköld didn't even bother to take off his open white shift when he first pointed his quarterstaff at the monk, so confident was he of victory.

The monk couldn't very well remove his white woolen habit, and that prompted spiteful merriment among the spectators when he went to get his staff and took a few powerful practice swings through the air. But some also noticed that Arn Magnusson, standing there among the youths, was looking especially amused. He pounded the monk on the back and uttered a few coarse remarks that seemed to have something to do with taking an involuntary bath.

It was now that the games were turned upside down and became as unforgettable as the spectators had been hoping.

With a smile and shaking his head, the monk went out onto the plank where Magnus Månesköld was waiting with his quarterstaff lowered, as if expecting no threat from an old monk who could handle neither a spear nor an ax.

So quickly that no one even saw what happened, Magnus Månesköld landed in the moat, still wearing all of his clothes. The monk must have struck a lucky blow; that was what most people thought.

Brother Guilbert set down his staff and hitched up his habit around his white legs. Then he pointed at Erik jarl, who took off his white shift and stepped forward, a bit more cautiously than his friend. That didn't help him in the slightest. Almost with the same speed, he too landed in the moat. This time the people on the walls had paid more attention to what was happening. The monk had first directed a blow at Erik jarl's head, but halfway there he had lowered the staff with one hand and knocked his opponent's feet out from under him.

The monk just as easily dispatched the other three youths, each of whom took off more and more clothing, anticipating the bath awaiting them. Finally only Arn Magnusson remained.

Arn removed his woolen shift and the long blue tunic before approaching Brother Guilbert. They began a conversation that few of the spectators could understand, no matter how much they strained to hear, since it was conducted in Frankish.

"It's no wonder that you've grown a bit slow over the years, my dear old teacher," said Arn.

"Just remember that you've never even come close to defeating me, you young stripling," laughed Brother Guilbert as he raised his quarterstaff menacingly, feinting a blow. Arn didn't even flinch.

"Your problem is doubtless that I'm no longer a stripling," said Arn, and in the next moment the battle began.

The two fought for a long time and with dizzying speed, aiming four, five, or six blows with each attack, each of which was equally quickly fended off by his opponent. From the very beginning it was clear that these two were the superior combatants when it came to quarterstaffs on a plank.

At last it looked as if fatigue overcame the monk first, and Arn then increased his speed until he finally struck the monk's foot and won. At the same time, he stuck out his staff so that the monk, as he fell, could grab hold of it and swing his body over toward the edge of the moat where there was solid ground. In this way most of his woolen habit stayed dry.

From that point on, none of the youths would come even close to another victory, and this was already evident when the first game on horseback commenced.

The first contest involved riding toward each other holding a long leather sack filled with sand, attempting to knock the other man out of the saddle. Arn, who had won the quarterstaff on a plank game, and hence was to determine the sequence of this battle, dispatched all of the youths as easily as the monk had done with the staff. When only the monk remained, a protracted contest began with an exhibition of horsemanship conducted at dizzying speed and with skills that were almost impossible to comprehend. Arn won this time as well, and again it looked as if the monk had tired first, and that was the reason for his defeat.

The next game entailed galloping toward rows of turnips that had been impaled on posts, and slicing through the turnips with a sword. None of the youths was able to cleave even half of the turnips in their row before Arn was already done. He didn't bother to chop at them; he merely rode past with his long, slender sword stretched out like a wing, and all the turnips split in half. The first turnip hadn't even hit the ground before Arn had sliced off the next. The monk, who came last, tried to ride in the same manner, but his borrowed sword got stuck in the third turnip, and with that the game was over.

Whoever won the turnip-chopping would have an almost impossible time trying to win the next game, since it was a race on horseback. If he won the first, second, and third race, it would be difficult to urge his horse to top speed against the other, rested horses.

Apparently Arn Magnusson had thought about this. It looked as if he rode the first races by holding back, although he was always just slightly ahead of his competitor. Perhaps it would have been wiser to start with the monk, who was riding one of his own foreign steeds. Instead, Arn saved the monk for last.

Then both men rode at full gallop, as they had when they competed against each other in the games with the leather sacks and the turnip-chopping. But the rested mare easily defeated Arn Magnusson's stallion.

After that only the noblest of the games remained: archery. And no one had ever heard of monks who could shoot arrows. Yet no one had ever imagined that monks could ride like this Cistercian, let alone handle the quarterstaff and sword as he had done.

Perhaps the monk and Arn had decided between them how they would finish the games, because now things got very exciting. As soon as the monk tested the string on the bow that his friend Arn handed to him, it was easy to see that this was not the first time he'd held such a weapon in his hands.

The archery contest proceeded with two archers alternating shooting arrows at bales of hay adorned with the head of a griffin and set at a distance of fifty paces. When the targets were brought out, the spectators began snickering and murmuring at the audacity of choosing the coat of arms of the Sverkers as the target. It was not particularly honorable to jest in this way with the vanquished enemy.

Evidently without even exerting himself, the monk defeated first Sture Jönsson, then Torgils and Folke Jonsson. He had to make more of an effort to beat Erik jarl, and when it was Magnus Månesköld's turn, it looked as if the monk had to do his utmost with every shot, since they both seemed almost equally skilled.

Both archers were evenly matched, striking the black griffin head each time, until the ninth arrow. Then Magnus Månesköld's arrow landed outside, at the edge of the griffin, while the monk landed his arrow in the center of the target. With the tenth arrow, Magnus once again struck the center. Then it all came down to the monk's last arrow.

Brother Guilbert turned and said something to Arn Magnusson, who replied curtly, shaking his head, whereupon Brother Guilbert shot his arrow so that it struck the center of the target. And with that, the single arrow from Brother Guilbert defeated the best archer in all of Eastern Götaland.

With the archery contest, the situation was the reverse of the horseback race. It was a disadvantage to sit idle until the very end and an advantage to shoot against the lesser opponents before the decisive competition. And Brother Guilbert needed only to cast a glance at the youths to know in some strange way who was strong and who was weak, so he was able to take them in the proper sequence.

"Now, my young apprentice, you won't be able to rely on the power of your lungs or the strength of your legs to defeat your teacher," Brother Guilbert said, beaming and pulling the string of his bow taut several times as Arn stepped forward.

"No, that's true," said Arn. "I would much prefer that we conducted this contest just between the two of us if we truly wanted to know whether the teacher is still stronger than his apprentice. For which of us will now win?"

"Your son Magnus was very disappointed when he lost; I could see that, even though he chivalrously hid his feelings," said Brother Guilbert. "But what would be best? If he sees his father defeated by the same monk? Or if he sees his father become the victor, even though he has practiced his whole life to defeat you, or rather the shadow of you? He is truly very skilled."

"Yes, I could see that," said Arn reluctantly. "Truly very skilled. Imagine what he could have become with you as his teacher. In the meantime, I can't say who ought to win, you or me, or which victor Magnus would find it most difficult to stomach."

"Nor can I," said Brother Guilbert. Then he crossed himself as a sign that he was leaving this difficult decision to higher powers.

Arn nodded in agreement, crossed himself as well, and nocked the first arrow to the string of his bow. It struck the lower part of the griffin's head, which wasn't so odd, since this was his first shot, and it would either strike high or low before he had tested his bow.

For this reason Brother Guilbert took the lead until the seventh arrow, since they both hit the center of the target each time, until it was bristling with arrows. Brother Guilbert shot the seventh arrow too high, but not as high as Arn's first arrow had been too low.

There was utter silence up on the walls, and the other competing youths had unconsciously moved closer and closer to get a better view. They now stood in a semicircle right behind the two archers.

With the eighth arrow, both struck the center of the target. The ninth arrow, for each of them, again landed in the middle.

Arn shot his tenth arrow, which sliced off the fletchings of two other arrows, but still plunged into the center. Now everything depended on Brother Guilbert's last arrow.

He spent a long time taking aim; the only sound at Arnäs was the rush of wings from a flock of swifts flying past.

But then he changed his mind and lowered his bow, taking several deep breaths before he raised the bow once more and drew the string along his cheek. Again he spent a long time taking aim.

His arrow struck too high because he had taken too much time. And with that Arn was the victor of this youths' game that no one who was present would ever forget. Nor would it be forgotten by those who were not present, because they would hear so many accounts of it over the years that they came to believe they'd actually seen it with their own eyes.

Eskil immediately came over to the youths with the mistress of Arnäs, Erika Joarsdotter, at his side. She carried two glittering crowns, one of gold and the other of silver. They stopped and all the youths lined up in front of the couple, very close to the moat so that the guests would be able to see and hear everything that was about to take place.

"This bachelors' evening has begun well," said Eskil in a loud voice. "You have brought great honor to my house, because such a game of youths as we have seen today has never occurred before and never shall again. The victor's crown is gold, for a finer victory than this could not be won. To be miserly is not one of my qualities, and yet I am careful with my money. I am pleased, of course, that my brother has won since any other outcome no doubt would have taken a toll on his honor and reputation. I am also pleased that the gold will remain in this house, after a fashion. Step forward, Sir Arn!"

Arn was reluctantly shoved forward by Magnus Månesköld and young Torgils. He bowed before Eskil, and Erika Joarsdotter placed the gold crown on his head. After that Arn didn't know what he was supposed to do, so Magnus leaned forward and tugged at his shift, which aroused great merriment among the spectators up on the wall.

Erika Joarsdotter now raised the silver crown toward Brother Guilbert, because they didn't have to count turnips to know who had finished in second place.

Brother Guilbert protested and refused to come forward, which at first seemed like the feigned modesty of a religious man, but then he explained that in accordance with his monk's vows, he was not allowed to own personal possessions. To give him silver would be the same as giving it to Varnhem cloister.

Eskil frowned, agreeing that it might be unnecessary to present a youth's prize to a cloister to which he had already given more than enough in donations. A moment of indecision followed as Erika lowered the silver crown and looked at Eskil, who shrugged his shoulders.

But it was Brother Guilbert who came up with an unexpected solution. Cautiously he took the silver crown from Erika's hands and went over to the baskets belonging to Erik jarl and Magnus Månesköld to count the turnips. He soon returned and went over to Magnus.

"You, Magnus, are the best archer that I've ever seen in this land, after your father, of course," he said solemnly. "After myself, and I don't count since divine rules prevent me from being considered, you were the best. All right, young man, bow your head!"

Blushing but at the same time looking proud, and with the encouragement of his friends, Magnus complied. And so it was that father and son went to the bachelors' ale celebration that evening wearing crowns of gold and silver.

The youths held their own feast. They were to celebrate the bachelors' evening on their own, at the leafy bower, as custom dictated. Eskil and Erika Joarsdotter walked back up to the castle and their waiting guests while the youths went off to the banquet hall under the open sky. Stable thralls led away their horses and house thralls hastened to bring them mantles and dry clothing, meat and ale.

When they were finally alone, all seven began talking at once, since there was much to try and understand. Most puzzling of all was the fact that an old monk had been able to beat young Nordic warriors at their own weapons games.

Arn explained that this was no ordinary monk. Brother Guilbert, like himself, had been a Templar knight, and it would have brought both of them much shame if two Templar knights could not have put the young Nordic roosters in their place.

There was much shouting and everyone was in the best of spirits even before they partook of the ale. They all had reason to be pleased.

Magnus Månesköld was satisfied, even though he had come to the games fully intending to win. But the only men who had defeated him were two of the Lord's Templar knights, and everyone had seen on this day with their own eyes that everything recounted about these holy warriors of God was true. But Magnus had defeated all of his friends.

Erik jarl was also pleased, since he knew that he would need a great deal of luck to be able to beat Magnus Månesköld. But at least none of his other friends had managed to defeat him.

Torgils was satisfied because as the youngest contestant he had still succeeded in avoiding the last position. And Sture Jönsson was pleased even though he had come in last overall since he was one of two, not including the Templar knights, who had won one of the games, the one with axes.

Arn was pleased that he had won, even though it felt almost shameful to admit this. But since he clearly was going to have to fight to win his son's respect, this was a good step along the way.

Brother Guilbert was perhaps the most satisfied of all, since he had shown that as an old man he could keep up with a fellow knight. He was also happy that God had determined the archery contest for the best so that he and Arn wouldn't have to argue about the outcome.

Because so many lively youths had come for the bachelors' evening, it would cost Eskil a lot of ale, and many of the young men would pay with an aching head the next day. The whole night was theirs.

Food and ale was as plentiful as Brother Guilbert and Arn had feared. But at Arn's command a small cask of Lebanese wine was also brought out. He had made the wine himself, and two glasses were found for the two men who preferred wine instead of the bridal ale from Lübeck.

During the first hour, before drunkenness began to settle over them, the men talked mostly of various events that had occurred during the games. Soon someone dared to jest about Templar knights who couldn't throw axes or spears.

Brother Guilbert explained with good humor that the business of casting away a spear was not a knight's foremost concern; in fact, it was the last thing he would do. And as for the ax, he'd be happy to carry an ax on horseback and confront any youth. But not for the purpose of throwing it. After that he gave everyone present a stern and ferocious look, making the young men involuntarily recoil until he suddenly burst out laughing.

But as for the quarterstaff on a plank, he went on, that was an excellent exercise. That was the basis for everything—speed, agility, balance—and the many resultant bruises were a reminder that defensive actions were just as important as knowing how to attack. Consequently, this was the first lesson he had taught Arn when he was a little boy.

Arn raised his wineglass and confirmed at once that he spoke the truth. That was how things had been when he had arrived at Varnhem at such a young age. And he'd received a thrashing from Brother Guilbert every day for twelve years, he added, sighing heavily and bowing his head, which prompted everyone to laugh.

After they'd drunk a considerable amount of ale, the young men kept jumping up to go off and piss, while Arn and Brother Guilbert remained calmly in their seats. In this way a different young man would sit down next to the two older men as soon as a place was vacated. And for as long as the youths remained coherent, Arn and Brother Guilbert had the chance to converse with all of them.

By the time Magnus Månesköld came over to sit down next to Arn, the evening had progressed farther than Arn had expected. A shyness seemed to exist between the two of them, and a good deal of wine and ale was required to get past it.

Magnus began by apologizing for twice having misjudged his father, but he added that he had learned a great deal from these mistakes.

Arn pretended not to understand what he was referring to and asked for an explanation. Magnus spoke of his disappointment when he first saw his father, not as the knight of his dreams but as a thrall wielding a trowel, and how he should have known better as soon as they took to their horses and rode away from Forsvik. But he had been so foolish as to revive his disappointment when he saw Arn throw an ax without striking the target. And so the rebuke that he'd received was fully justified, and he'd never seen greater archers than the monk and his own father. So in that respect the sagas had spoken the truth.

Arn tried to dismiss the subject by jesting that he promised henceforth to practice strenuously at the art of throwing weapons. Yet such jesting did not suit Magnus Månesköld, who kept his solemn demeanor and only afterward dared to ask about something that he said had been puzzling him.

"When we arrived at Forsvik on horseback," he said, "and we came around the corner of the house, where you, my father, stood up on the ridgepole holding a trowel . . . when you leaped down and looked at us . . . how could you recognize me as your son so quickly?"

Arn burst into uncontrollable laughter, even though he would have preferred to keep a straight face.

"Just look at this!" he exclaimed, ruffling his son's thick red hair. "Who would have hair like your mother except you, my son! And besides, even if you'd been wearing a helmet, all I had to do was look at your shields. You were the only one who bore a half-moon painted next to our Folkung lion. And if none of that were sufficient, I would have looked into your eyes. You have your mother's beautiful brown eyes."

"Tomorrow I will become your legitimate son," said Magnus, suddenly sounding on the verge of tears.

"You have always been my legitimate son," replied Arn. "Your mother Cecilia and I may have committed a sin when we conceived you too early. It has taken a long time for us to be able to celebrate our wedding, because it was not as easy for my kinsman Knut to become king as he first thought, and he had promised to come to our wedding as king. The love between your mother and myself was great, our yearning just as great, and so we committed a sin, though we are not the only ones who have done so. But whether it was a great sin or not, we have both atoned for it with a harsh punishment, and we are now cleansed. And tomorrow we'll drink the bridal ale that was intended more than twenty years ago. But that's not when you will become my son, nor when I will be Cecilia's husband. I have always been hers, and you have always been my son, every single day in my prayers during a long war."

Magnus sat and pondered in silence for a moment as if he were unsure in which direction he should steer the conversation. All of a sudden there were so many things crowding into his head.

"Do you think the king will come to the wedding, as he promised?" he then asked, as if thereby saving himself from more difficult topics for discussion.

"No, he won't," said Arn. "Birger Brosa will not attend, that much we know, and I don't think the king has any desire to offend his jarl. And as far as the promises of kings are concerned, I've learned that it makes a difference whether they're given before or after the crown is in place. Yet it was wisely arranged for Erik jarl to be present to honor us, representing both the Eriks and the king."

"But Erik jarl is here because he's my friend," Magnus Månesköld objected without thinking.

"I'm glad that he's here, and I'm glad that he's your friend," said Arn. "But above all else, he is a jarl of the realm and our future king. In this way my friend Knut has solved his predicament. He is here as he promised me. And he's also not here, as he no doubt promised Birger Brosa. That is how a wise friend acts if he is king."

"Will there be war soon?" asked Magnus, as if on impulse or as if the ale and not his sense of chivalry were already guiding his speech.

"No," said Arn. "Not for a long time, but let's talk of that subject another time, when there's not so much ale-drinking going on."

As if Arn's words about the ale had reminded Magnus of nature's call, he excused himself and on slightly unsteady legs went off into the dusk to relieve himself. House thralls brought in tarred torches and more roasts.

A short time later Brother Guilbert and Arn sat alone, each holding a wineglass, while songs and bellows surrounded them on all sides.

Arn teased Brother Guilbert about the last arrow he had shot, saying that if a man spends that much time thinking before shooting, it's almost always sure to go wrong. It means that he wants something too much. And if you want something too much, then you take too much, and this was something that Brother Guilbert surely should know better than anyone else.

Yes, you would think that would be true, admitted Brother Guilbert. But he had been shooting to win. Or at least to do his best so that no one would think he had simply handed the victory to Arn. Yet Higher Powers had steered his arrow.

"*Deus vult!*" said Arn in jest, raising his clenched fist in the greeting of the Templar knights.

Brother Guilbert immediately joined in and struck his fist against Arn's.

"Perhaps we can compete again, on horseback and with more difficult targets that are moving," said Arn.

"Oh no!" replied Brother Guilbert crossly. "You just want to put your old teacher in his place. I'd rather go another round with you using the quarterstaff!"

At that they had a good laugh, but none of the youths were paying much attention to them any more, perhaps because they couldn't understand the conversation. Brother Guilbert and Arn, as if from old habit, had switched to speaking Frankish.

"Tell me one thing, brother," said Arn pensively. "How many Templar knights would it take to conquer the two lands of the Goths and Svealand?"

"Three hundred," replied Brother Guilbert after pausing to

consider the question. "Three hundred were enough to hold the Holy Land for a long time. This kingdom is bigger, but on the other hand there is no cavalry here. Three hundred knights and three strongholds and we could pacify the entire region. Aha! So that's what you're thinking! At this very moment I'm helping to build the first stronghold with our dear friends the Saracens. What a superb irony! And you're not afraid that our Saracen friends will cause problems? I mean, sooner or later these Nordic barbarians are going to figure out what sort of foreigners pray five times a day and in a less than discreet manner at that, if I'm going to speak of the matter with some delicacy."

"That was a lot to bring up at once," said Arn with a sigh. "Yes, this is more or less what I've been thinking: that if I build a cavalry force using the same exercises that we use as Templar knights, then we will have peace. More strongholds than are necessary, that's true. And as for the Saracens, my plan is for them first to display their skills; afterward people can choose between their demonstrated abilities and their own misconceptions about what Saracens are."

"That last part might be a dangerous game," mused Brother Guilbert. "You and I know the truth about Saracens. There's an explanation for that. But won't any one of this land's ignorant and primitive bishops drop dead, choked by bacon, as soon as he realizes the truth about your fortress builders? And to create peace with overwhelming strength, as you are planning, is both right and wrong."

"I know how it's right, but how is it wrong?" Arn asked sharply.

"It's wrong because the Nordic people don't understand the new cavalry force, how invincible it is. Once you have created such power, you will first have to demonstrate it before you can gain peace. That will mean war, in any case."

"I have pondered this very matter for a long time," Arn admitted. "I have only one answer and that is to make it a gentle lesson. Do you remember the foremost of the golden rules of the Templar order?"

"*When you draw your sword—do not think about who you must kill. Think about who you should spare*," replied Brother Guilbert in Latin.

"Precisely," said Arn. "Precisely. May it be God's will!"

Chapter 6

With thundering hooves the stout Nordic horses once again pounded the bridal path. Long lances glinted in the sunlight, and the clanging and ringing of weapons could be heard everywhere, as well as the harsh, heated words of warriors. A number of the horsemen bore the king's emblem, but most of them were Folkungs who had been summoned from farms and hamlets far and wide. A thousand armed men were to protect the bride and her procession. So many warriors had not been seen since peace had come, and it was almost like old times when the king called for a campaign.

From villages as far away as the region of Skara, every single person had come out, and since early morning crowds had lined the entire road between Husaby and Forshem Church. Some sat down to rest with ale and pork, others conversed with neighbors they hadn't seen in a long time, while the children leaped and played all around them. Everyone was there to see the bride riding to Forshem. But they'd seen bridal processions before, so this time most of them hoped to see something more. The portent had shown four suns, and many rumors circulated about evil machinations directed at the bride. Some had to do with perils threatening the bride from dark forces; others foretold that she would be stolen by Näcken the water spirit or be turned to stone by the siren of the woods or be poisoned by the troll. Other rumors were less imaginative and had to do with war and misfortune descending over the land—and it made no difference whether the bride ended up alive under the feather bed on this night, or whether she was killed or spirited away. Among the older and wiser men there was gloomy talk of how this wedding had much to do with the struggle for power in the realm.

No matter what happened during this bridal procession, it would in any case be a drama worth waiting many hours to see. And wait they did, because those who were supposed to fetch the bride were late.

When the sun was at its zenith, Cecilia was led out into the courtyard by her three kinsmen Pål, Algot, and Sture, who had arrived that morning from Arnäs still feeling the effects of the ale. Yet they were in good humor and had much to tell about the youths' games with the foremost archer in the land.

The three brothers were all clad in their most beautiful green mantles of the Pål clan, and yet their garb looked pale and simple in comparison with that worn by Cecilia. In the courtyard stood the bridal table and on top were five leather pouches of earth from the five farms along with a heavy chest; this was the dowry that those who came to fetch the bride would take with them. Also on the table was Cecilia's gift for the bridegroom, the blue Folkung mantle carefully folded; she hadn't yet shown it to anyone. The stable thralls held the reins of the groomed and festively adorned horses, and the six bridesmaids dressed in white held the long bridal veil in their hands. Cecilia would not be dressed in the veil until just before the men arrived to fetch her.

There they all now stood, but nothing happened.

"Perhaps Herr Eskil drank too much of his own excellent ale," said young Sture shamelessly. Like the others, he took it for granted that Eskil Magnusson would be the one to fetch the bride, since old Herr Magnus was now crippled.

For an hour they stood in the noonday sun without budging, because that would spell bad luck. At first Cecilia feared that something bad had happened; then her concern was replaced by a cool anger that Eskil had let her stand here so long. She thought that even though Eskil might be shrewd in business affairs, he could indeed be irresponsible when it came to the well-being of others.

Yet she would soon see that none of this was Eskil's fault.

From far off, at the bend in the road down by the stream and bridge, could be heard shouts from the waiting people. It was not the sound of surprise or alarm that they heard, but rather jubilation.

The tension grew among the three Pål brothers and Cecilia as they stood with their eyes fixed on the bend in the road where the one who had come to fetch the bride would appear.

The first thing they saw was a rider bearing the king's banner. Then came a glittering retinue with countless lance tips flashing in the sunlight.

"If *this* is the bride-fetcher we were kept waiting for, then everything is forgiven," Pål Jönsson gasped in surprise. He gestured for the bridesmaids to bring the white veil and drape it over Cecilia so that her hair and face and most of her body would be hidden.

Then she stood motionless and erect as the royal horsemen came thundering into the courtyard, taking up position in a wide circle with their swords drawn and their horses facing outward. Riding into the huge space formed inside this circle came the king and queen, both wearing ermine and crowns. They reined in their horses ten paces from the waiting Pål brothers and Cecilia.

Because Cecilia's face was now hidden under the veil, no one could see her eyes. And so she was unable to meet the gaze of her dear friend the queen, but she gave a little nod in return when Cecilia Blanca smiled at her with an expression that showed she realized this was not what Cecilia Rosa had expected.

The king raised his hand for silence as he delivered his greeting.

"Many years ago we, Knut Eriksson, king of the Swedes and Goths, promised that we would escort you, Cecilia, and our friend Arn Magnusson to the bridal ale. Promises should be kept, especially promises made by a king. We are here now and ask for forgiveness that it has taken so long to see this promise ful-fillled!"

With these words, the king dismounted from his horse and stepped forward to greet the three Pål brothers, one after the other. They all returned his greeting by swiftly falling to one knee. A bride's kinsmen rarely behaved in this manner upon handing over the bride. But it was even rarer to have the bride fetched by the king himself.

To Cecilia, King Knut merely gave a curt nod, and he did not touch her, for this would bring bad luck to both of them.

Men from the king's retinue were summoned to load the dowry and the bride's gift on a cart festooned with leafy boughs and drawn not by oxen but by two lively sorrel horses. The stable thralls then led forward the horses for the bridal party to mount. A stool was put in place to assist Cecilia. Since she would now be riding in her bridal attire and with the bridal veil, she could not avoid the women's saddle, which she normally found so loathsome.

Then they rode off from the royal estate of Husaby with the king and queen in the lead, followed by the bride and then the three Pål brothers. The royal retainers fell in on either side, and horsemen galloped ahead to clear the road of curious spectators who might be standing too near. Commands resounded through the air as the leaders of the retainers shouted back and forth. The Husaby thralls started in on the warbling, rolling song that was their way of sending along their best wishes.

A more magnificent bridal procession than the one now riding through the summer sunshine down the slopes from Husaby toward Forshem had not been seen in the realm since King Knut, many years ago, went to Gudhem cloister to fetch his bride. But that time not as many peasants had turned out to watch the festivities. And this time even many town-dwellers from Skara had come out. It was easy to recognize the town-dwellers, since they dressed like womenfolk, with feathers in their caps even though they were men, and they all talked through their nose.

As the procession approached Forshem, the riders slowed their pace, with the faster horsemen galloping on ahead, kicking up clouds of dust, in order to make inquiries and ensure that both processions would arrive at the church at the same time.

From a great distance Cecilia could see that the church hill was crowded with people, but that there were also red colors among the blue. The king and queen, who were riding in front of her, must have seen the Sverker colors too, and yet they didn't seem the least bit alarmed. So Cecilia quickly crossed herself, thinking that she was wrong in assuming there was any danger.

As she got closer, she understood the reason for all the red color. Waiting at the church door was the archbishop, and his retainers were almost all Sverker men.

The bridegroom's procession was now seen approaching from Arnäs. In front was the eldest leader of the Folkung retainers, who had come all the way from Älgarås for the honor of riding in the forefront of the Folkungs. Behind him rode Herr Eskil and Arn side by side, both in the garb of warriors, which seemed to suit Arn better than his elder brother. Arn had rowan boughs adorning both himself and his horse, since he had been greeted along his procession route by almost as many well-wishers as Cecilia had encountered. Behind Arn rode his groomsmen, which included a Cistercian monk dressed in white robes with the hood looking like a tall cornet on his head.

Everything could now take place in the order that custom prescribed. On the church hill the bride dismounted from her horse with the help of her kinsmen. The retainers of the king, the Folkungs, and the archbishop all formed a circle of shields and swords around the open area in front of the church door where the archbishop stood, wearing his finest vestments with two black-clad chaplains at his side and the white *pallium* draped over his chest and back.

The bride was led forward to bow her head briefly before the archbishop without touching him. Her three kinsmen dropped to one knee and kissed the bishop's ring.

From a distance Arn and his companions had been watching; now they too came forward to greet the archbishop. Arn also kissed the bishop's ring.

Then came the moment when Arn and Cecilia stood face-to-face in front of the archbishop, and Cecilia slowly removed her bridal veil to reveal her face. She had seen him through the cloth, but he had not seen her until now, as was the custom.

Then the wedding gifts were exchanged. Erik jarl stepped over to Arn and with a deep bow, which was an unexpected gesture that prompted much whispering, he handed the groom a heavy and costly belt made from heavy gold links, each of which was set with a green stone. Arn fastened the belt around Cecilia, fumbling a bit, which aroused great merriment. Then Cecilia turned around with her arms outstretched so that everyone who stood near could see the glittering gold that now encircled her waist, with one end hanging down the front of her skirt.

Pål Jönsson then brought Cecilia's wedding gift; even folded as it was, everyone could see that it was a blue mantle. Eskil reacted quickly and removed the mantle his brother was wearing; he then unfastened from the cloth the heavy silver clasp that had held it closed under Arn's chin. Cecilia slowly and solemnly unfolded her gift. Soon loud shouts of admiration and excitement issued from the crowds standing behind all the retainers as the people craned their necks to see. A more beautiful blue mantle had never been seen before, and the lion on the back gleamed as if made of gold, the three bars were as bright as silver, while the lion's mouth shone bright red. Together Eskil and Cecilia placed the mantle over Arn's shoulders.

Then he did just as Cecilia had done, spinning once around with the mantle stretched out over his arms so that everyone could see, and many more admiring shouts were heard.

The archbishop raised his staff, a bit galled that it wasn't met with immediate silence, though this had less to do with any sort of godlessness and more to do with the fact that so many people were talking all at once and with enthusiasm about the costly wedding gifts.

"In the name of God, the Son, and the Holy Virgin!" intoned the archbishop, and finally everyone fell silent. "I now bless you, Arn Magnusson, and you, Cecilia Algotsdotter, as you enter into a marriage sanctified by God. May happiness, peace, and prosperity follow you until death do you part, and may this union, ordained by the Lord God, contribute to the peace and concord of our kingdom. Amen."

He then took some holy water from a silver bowl, which one of the chaplains handed to him, and touched first Cecilia's forehead, shoulders, and heart; then he did the same with Arn.

If the archbishop had had his way, Arn and Cecilia would have then embraced each other as a sign that they had now entered into marriage. Arn and Cecilia both understood the hidden meaning of this blessing, which was that they had now become husband and wife, but neither had any desire to participate in this churchly show. For their kinsmen and before the law, they would not become husband and wife until after being escorted to bed. And if they were now required to choose between the archbishop's efforts to allow the church to rule, and the conviction of their kinsmen that old customs could not simply be dismissed, neither of them thought this was the proper moment to confront such a dilemma. It took only an exchange of glances for them to agree how they would act.

Rather vexed that the couple hadn't seemed to understand what he was so clearly indicating with his blessing, the archbishop abruptly turned and walked into the church to conduct the mass.

The king and queen followed him, then Arn and Cecilia, their groomsmen, bridesmaids, and kinsmen, as many as would fit into the small church.

The intention was to keep the mass brief, because the archbishop knew full well that everyone's eagerness to start the wedding celebration was greater than their thirst to commune with their God. Yet he received unexpected assistance from the bridal couple when it was time to sing the hymns, as well as from the Cistercian who was part of Arn Magnusson's retinue. When the final hymns began, those three simply took over. With increasing zeal, and finally with tears in the eyes of both the bride and groom, the three voices joined, with Cecilia's soprano singing the lead, and the monk's deep voice taking the third part.

The archbishop looked out over the enraptured congregation, who seemed to have forgotten all their haste to leave God's house and start in on the ale and entertainments. Then his glance fell upon Arn Magnusson. Unlike all the other men, he still wore his sword at his side. At first the archbishop was angry, as if this were a sign of ill intent. Yet he could see no trace of evil in this man's eyes as he sang as well as the best of church singers and with sincere rapture. Then the archbishop quickly crossed himself, murmuring a prayer to ask forgiveness for his sinful thoughts and his foolishness as he remembered that the groom was in fact a Templar knight, no matter the blue of his mantle. And a Templar was a man of God, and the sword in that black leather scabbard with the cross of gold had been blessed by the Lord's Mother; it was the only weapon that was allowed inside the church.

The archbishop decided to stay on good terms with Arn Magnusson. A man of God would more easily understand what needed to be changed for the better in this realm where raw fellows like King Knut and Birger Brosa reigned. It would no doubt be wise to have Arn Magnusson on his side in the struggles ahead between the ecclesiastical and the temporal powers. Surely the Knights Templar must have greater insight into such matters than any of his power-hungry kinsmen.

The thoughts that had begun for the archbishop as a mixture of malice and suspicion were now transformed into visions of a bright future as the three masterful singers voiced God's Own hymns.

Because the crowds of spectators had thinned out after the church blessing and the mass, the bridal procession now took only an hour to reach Arnäs. There was no longer as much need to fear for the bride's safety, since the worst was now over and no one sensed any serious threat to her life. All the warriors had now shifted position and kept the short stretch of road to Arnäs in an iron grip.

Leading the procession, after the horsemen carrying the banners of the king and the Folkungs, were Arn and Cecilia, riding side by side toward Arnäs. This was not actually the custom, but on this particular day there were many things that were not as usual. No one had ever heard of a king going to fetch the bride. Just as extraordinary was the fact that the bridal couple had sung the church hymns in such a way that outshone even the arch-bishop's retinue. And certainly no guest should ride in front of the host, but if that guest happened to be the king, with the queen at his side? This wedding had in truth turned many things upside down.

Inside the walls at Arnäs there were so many bright colors that the splendor seemed almost too much for the eye to take in. At the ale tents the bloodred mantles of Sverkers mixed with the blue of the Eriks and Folkungs. But there were also many for-eign garments in all manner of colors, worn by guests who had donned their finest in order to show their superior status, as hap-pens so often in the presence of a king. Some were also Frank-ish men that Arn Magnusson had brought home with him; they were apparently too highborn to drink ale, and the language they spoke was utterly incomprehensible. The pounding of drums and the sound of pipers could be heard from every direction; jugglers tossed burning torches high in the air, where they spun around and were then always safely caught. Singers accompanied by stringed instruments, stood upon elevated platforms and sang Frankish ballads. The archbishop was borne on his chair into the castle courtyard, but every now and then he would stretch out his hand, good-naturedly delivering blessings right and left.

Arn and Cecilia now had to part once again, since Cecilia was to ascend to a raised bridal seat that had been adorned with leafy boughs and positioned in the courtyard. Arn also had to take his place on a similar wooden structure along with his groomsmen. Eskil had decided on this arrangement so that everybody would be able to see the bride and groom, since later on only half the guests would be able to find seats in the great hall. For all those who had to partake of the feast outside in the courtyard, it would have been disappointing to be allocated such poor seats without even having seen the bride and groom. A similar raised platform had been constructed for the archbishop, the king, and the master of Arnäs.

Brother Guilbert quickly and nimbly clambered up the wooden structure to sit down next to Arn. At the same time he called to the Frankish lute players and singers to step forward and repeat the song they had just finished. Encouraged to hear that there were some among the spectators who actually understood the words of their songs, they obeyed at once. Both Arn and Brother Guilbert nodded to each other as they listened to the first verses. It almost looked as if Brother Guilbert could have sung along, even though such songs were forbidden to him.

The song was about Sir Roland, a knight who tried in vain before he died to break his sword Dyrendal so that it wouldn't end up in enemy hands. Inside the hilt were holy relics, a tooth from Saint Peter, blood from Saint Basil, and a thread from the kirtle that the Mother of God had worn. But the sword refused to break, no matter how hard the dying Sir Roland tried. Then the angels of God took pity on the hero and lifted the sword up to heaven, and Roland could sink down in the shade of a pine tree with his oliphant battle-horn at his side. He turned his head toward the land of the unbelievers so that Charlemagne would not find his dead hero with his face turned away in cowardice. And he confessed his sins, lifting his right gauntlet up toward God. Then Saint Gabriel came down to receive it and guide Roland's soul to heaven.

Arn and Brother Guilbert were both very moved by this song, since they could easily imagine everything that the words described, almost as if they had actually been present. Many were the accounts they had both heard about Christian knights in the Holy Land breaking their swords in half and lying down to await death as they surrendered their souls to God.

When the two Provençal lute players discovered that some of

their listeners were actually moved by the words of the song, they moved as close to Brother Guilbert and Arn as they dared and sang verse after verse, as if they never wanted to stop. The song about Sir Roland was quite long.

Not realizing that he should have offered a few silver coins in order to be quit of the singers, Arn finally grew tired of the endless singing and in Frankish called out his thanks, saying that now that would suffice. Disappointed, the singers fell silent and moved away to find a new audience.

"I suppose you should have paid them something," Brother Guilbert explained.

"No doubt you're right," said Arn. "But I have no silver on me, nor do you, so I'll have to put the matter aside until later. There is too much of the monk in me, and it's not easy to rid myself of those ways."

"Then you'd better make haste, since the wedding night is fast approaching," jested Brother Guilbert. But he regretted his words when he saw how Arn blanched at this simple statement of fact.

Finally the sound of a horn announced that the official festivities were to begin, and half of the guests headed toward the door of the great hall, while the other half remained in the courtyard without really knowing how to act so as not to seem offended that they hadn't been included among the foremost hundred guests. Only the Sverkers openly displayed their discontent, assembling together so that they formed one large red bloodstain in the middle of the courtyard. Among those entering the great hall, there were few red mantles, and those there were belonged to women.

The most beautiful of these red mantles was worn by Ulvhilde Emundsdotter, who had been the dearest friend of both Cecilias during those dark days at Gudhem cloister. The friendship of the three women was remarkably strong, even though there was spilled blood between them. Cecilia Rosa's future husband, Arn, was the one who had chopped off the hand of Ulvhilde's father, Emund. And Cecilia Blanca's husband, Knut, was the one who had killed him after a treacherous transaction.

The three women were the first to enter the great hall, staying close. Queen Blanca already knew where they were to sit during the banquet; all three would be seated together high up on the bridal dais with the six bridesmaids below.

Even though it was a bright midsummer evening, fires blazed on all sides as the guests entered. Above the high seat in the middle of the long wall of the room hung a large blue tapestry with a faded Folkung lion from the time of their ancestors. On either side of the high seat, to show respect, the house thralls had hung the two shooting targets used for the archery game on the bachelors' evening. Almost the first thing anyone noticed in the dancing shadows from the fires was the sight of two arrows embedded in the black Sverker griffins. Around the arrows in one of the targets hung a crown of gold, so that everyone could now see with their own eyes what the rumors had already reported. The bridegroom himself had shot ten arrows so close to each other that a crown could encircle them all, and he had done so from a distance of fifty paces.

Ulvhilde made no attempt avoid the sight. On the contrary. When she took her seat next to her friends high up on the bridal dais, she giggled, saying that it was most fortunate she hadn't been a guest on the previous day. She would have had to watch her back in order not to have arrows shot at her. For on the back of her red mantle, right in the middle, a black griffin head had been stitched with thousands of silk threads, the type of embroidery that the three friends had truly been the first in the realm to master during the time that they were confined to Gudhem under Mother Rikissa.

Cecilia Blanca was of the opinion that an insult was no bigger than one allowed it to be, and at the next shooting banquet

Ulvhilde ought to see to it that a lion was used for the archery target. Then those who had made this jest would be repaid in kind.

The bridegroom's dais was far away in the hall, on the other side of the first longtable, and in the middle of that table was the high seat. There Eskil and Erika Joarsdotter now took their places on either side of the archbishop. The king had decided to sit with the groom, just as the queen was seated with the bride. Such an honor had never been shown before to any bridal couple in the realm of the Eriks and Folkungs.

But when all had taken their seats, Erika Joarsdotter, looking worried, got up and went over to stand at the door while whispers and murmurs spread through the hall. The guests understood that something was not as it should be. And so their joy was even greater a few minutes later when old Herr Magnus came into the hall, walking next to his wife Erika. Slowly but with great dignity he made his way between all the tables all the way over to the high seat where he sat down next to the archbishop, with Erika on his other side. The house thralls brought the ancestral drinking horn with the silver fittings and handed it to Herr Magnus. He got up, standing steadily on both feet, and raised the horn. At once everyone fell silent with anticipation and amazement. They had all thought that Herr Magnus had been crippled for many years and was just awaiting the release of death.

"Few men are granted the joy that has been given to me today!" said Herr Magnus in a loud, clear voice. "I now drink with you my kinsmen and friends upon welcoming a son back from the Holy Land and upon gaining a daughter in my household, and because I have been granted the grace of renewed health and the joy of seeing kinsmen and friends join me in peace and concord. None of my ancestors have had any better reason to raise this horn!"

Herr Magnus drained the ale without spilling a drop, although those sitting closest to him noticed that at the end he was shaking from exertion.

There was a brief silence after Herr Magnus sat down and handed the ancestral drinking horn to his son Eskil. Then a great cheering began, swelling to a mighty roar as the hundred guests pounded their fists on the tables. The pipes and drums started playing at once, and the food was carried in by white-clad house thralls, preceded by minstrels who both played and frolicked merrily.

"With meat, pipes, and ale we'll manage to avoid a good deal of gawking, and that's much to be desired," said Queen Blanca as she raised her wineglass to Cecilia and Ulvhilde. "That's not to say that they don't have much to stare at, presenting as we do quite a marvelous sight up here in our green, red, and blue!"

They drank with abandon, and both Ulvhilde and Cecilia laughed heartily at their friend's daring way of dismissing the embarrassment of being the center of so much attention, which they had now endured for some time, amidst all the whispering and pointing.

"Well, if they're looking for red mantles in here, there aren't many of us," said Ulvhilde, pretending to be offended as she set down her glass.

"Don't worry about it, dear friend," replied Queen Blanca. "It's no small honor to be seated with the queen and the bride, and as luck would have it, you're sitting on that black rooster."

"Just as you're sitting on three crowns!" giggled Ulvhilde, continuing the game.

Next to Arn at the other end of the hall, in the place of honor on the groom's dais, sat the king on one side, with Magnus Månesköld and Erik jarl on the other. This was at the king's own request when he heard that Magnus had been the best in the warrior games, after the two Templar knights, who competed at an entirely different level, of course.

King Knut was sitting with one arm thrown around Arn's shoulders, recounting long stories about how much he had suffered by not having Arn at his side during the bloody years before the crown was securely placed on his head. He had never in his life had a better friend than Arn, for Birger Brosa was more like a wise father than a friend. That was something that he could admit now that nobody could hear what they said. He had not hesitated for a moment to decide to attend the bridal banquet of his best friend, bringing along all the banners and horsemen that he could muster. Nor had he doubted that this wedding between his two friends was taking place because it was God's will and the grace of Our Lady, as well as the reward for the years of faith and hope which Arn and Cecilia had never given up. And who was he, a poor and sinful man, to defy the will of the Almighty?

Since Cecilia Rosa and the queen were the dearest of friends in this world, the joy was even greater since now they would all live on neighboring estates. For those who lived at Forsvik, the closest church was the one located at Näs, and he and his queen would honor Forsvik with their visits. He also hoped that Arn and Cecilia Rosa would often be his guests at Näs, and on more occasions than to attend church.

Many were the gracious words that the king spoke to Arn early in the evening. At first Arn was both happy and relieved; he had lived so long in a world where lies and falsehoods were prohibited that he believed everything that was said to him. But somewhat later in the evening he happened to think about the Saracen saga regarding the ignorant Frankish physician who proposed smearing honey onto deep gashes made by a sword.

In people's minds, honey was the very opposite of wounds and pain, just as salt was the opposite of sweet. And since salt in a wound was what caused the most pain and harm, many believed in the honey remedy. It was also said that a thick layer of honey applied to a nasty gash did provide some relief in the beginning. But after a short time, the wound would get even worse and start to putrefy.

All of the Saracen builders were sitting together at the second long table closest to the bridegroom's seat. Arn had seen to it himself that they were placed there, since he wanted everybody to see that they were being honored for their work. He had also been careful to ask Erika Joarsdotter more than once to provide water in the clay tankards at that section of the long table; the house thralls were also told not to serve any pork to these foreigners. And he wanted to sit close to his builders in case any quarrels should arise.

And now it looked as if some sort of trouble was indeed brewing down there, although from this distance he couldn't hear what the row was about. Arn cast a glance at Knut, as if to indicate that it was about time for him to go out and relieve himself, and then he jumped down behind the groom's dais and headed toward the door, until he stopped near the Saracens, as if in response to the good wishes they wanted to offer him. And they did indeed express their congratulations as soon as he approached, and their quarreling quickly died out.

Arn felt unworthy, both in the eyes of the Saracens and in his own eyes, dressed as he was in the vain Frankish attire, which rustled under his mantle with every move. He also thought he could see a hint of derision tugging at the mouths of the builders, even though they did their best to hide it. He asked them candidly, following the Nordic manner rather than the Arab way, what the discord had concerned but received evasive answers that some of the gifts of the table might be unclean food.

He wanted to put a swift end to this dissension before rumors about these Franks who would not eat pork spread through the entire hall. There was only one way to win the immediate respect and loyalty of the Saracens. As if he were merely reciting passages from some ordinary foreign verse, he spoke to them with a smile, but using God's own words.

"In the name of God the Beneficent and the Merciful!" he began, and silence fell over the table at once. "Hear the first verse of sura Al Maidah! *Believers! Fulfill your obligations according to the agreements you have made! Permissible food for you is meat from all plant-eating animals. Or why not God's own words from sura Al Anam? Eat of all food over which God's name has been pronounced, if you believe in His message. Why should you not eat of food over which God's name has been pronounced, since you have clearly been told what He has forbidden except in a dire circumstance? Many people mislead others by what they in their ignorance believe to be right or wrong. Your Lord knows best who oversteps his commandments!*"

Arn needed say no more, nor did he have to explain how these words were meant to be understood. He gave a friendly nod, as if musing about something, as if he had simply recited some worldly verses to amuse his friends and fortress builders from the Holy Land. Then he calmly returned to his place, and more attention was paid to the most beautiful of all Folkung mantles in the land than to a bridegroom's unexpected decision to recite verses.

At the Saracens' table not a single spiteful grumble was heard for the rest of the evening.

As soon as King Knut began to get drunk, all honey was stripped from his speech and instead he started in on what was foremost on his mind. First he said that it was of greatest importance for Arn to be reconciled with his paternal uncle, Birger Brosa. Then he mentioned what he thought should be the next bridal banquet for the Folkungs, and that was when Arn's son Magnus Månesköld went to the bridal bed with the Sverker daughter Ingrid Ylva, and the sooner the better. Arn immediately filled his throat with wine.

"The bridal coverlet hasn't even been placed over me and Cecilia, but you're already hastening toward the next wedding. There is some purpose behind your words—what is it?" asked Arn after choking on the wine that had gone down the wrong way.

"That wily archbishop over there wants to make a Sverker, and more specifically Sverker Karlsson, the next king of the realm," replied Knut, lowering his voice even though no one nearby could hear them any longer over the great noise of the other guests.

"First of all, power is now in the hands of you Eriks and us Folkungs," replied Arn. "And second, I don't understand how we would appease the archbishop with my son's wedding to a Sverker daughter."

"Nor is that the intention," replied the king. "But our intent is to avoid war for as long as possible. None of us wants to relive what we saw in this kingdom during so many years of war. It's not the archbishop and his Danish friends that we need to appease, but rather the Sverkers. The more ties of marriage between us, the easier it will be to prevent another war."

"Those are the thoughts of Birger Brosa," said Arn with a nod.

"Yes, they are Birger Brosa's thoughts, and his wisdom has not failed us for more than twenty years. Sune Sverkersson Sik was the brother of King Karl. If the archbishop and his Danish friends want to go to war against us, they will have to win the support of Sune Sik. It will not be enough to have the backing of King Karl's son Sverker, whom they are fattening up to be king down there in Roskilde. Sune Sik would no doubt think twice about drawing his sword against his own son-in-law Magnus Månesköld. That is our royal wish!"

"We killed King Karl on Visingsö. His son Sverker escaped to Denmark, but now you wish us to tame him with a bridal ale. And thus it makes no difference whether I, as you and Birger Brosa first proposed, or my son Magnus should marry this Ingrid Ylva?"

"Yes, that is the arrangement we wish to make!"

"Have you asked Magnus what he thinks of this bridal ale that is planned for him?" asked Arn quietly.

But the king merely snorted at such a question and turned to the house thralls to order more salt beef and ale. The king was known for eating enormous quantities of salt beef, preferring it to fresh meat, since salted meat went better with ale.

Since Magnus Månesköld was sitting less than an arm's length from Arn, absorbed in a lively conversation with Erik jarl about some topic apparently dealing with spears and hunting, this question about another wedding could be quickly addressed. At least that was what Arn imagined when he leaned forward and placed his hand on his son's arm. Magnus interrupted his conversation with his friend and turned around at once.

"I have a question for you, my son," said Arn. "A simple question to ask, but perhaps more difficult to answer. Do you wish to enter into marriage with Ingrid Ylva, Sune Sik's daughter?"

At first Magnus Månesköld was speechless with surprise at this question. But he soon gathered his wits and gave a clear answer.

"If it is your wish, my father, and if it is also the king's wish, you may be assured that I will immediately comply," he said with a slight bow of his head.

"It was not my intention to command you but to ask you about your own wishes," replied Arn with a frown.

"My wish is to do as my father and my king will, in everything that is within my power. Going to the bridal bed is among the easier services that you might demand of me," replied Magnus Månesköld, almost as if he were reeling off a prayer.

"Would such a wedding make you happy or unhappy?" Arn insisted in order to get past his son's strange readiness to submit to their wishes.

"Not unhappy, my father," said Magnus Månesköld. "I have seen Ingrid Ylva only twice. She is a fair maiden with a slender waist and the black tresses that many of the Sverker women have, as did my own father's mother, from what I have heard. Her dowry would not be paltry, and she is of royal lineage. What more could I desire?"

"A great deal more if you had such affection for another that you prayed for her well-being every evening and awoke each morning with a longing to see her," murmured Arn with his eyes lowered.

"I am not like you, my father," replied Magnus Månesköld gently, and with an expression that was more sympathetic and loving than scornful upon hearing these strange questions, although he'd had to make an effort to answer them courteously. "The saga about the love between you and my mother is beautiful, and it is sung in the stables and fields. And this day has not diminished the beautiful song about faith, hope, and charity. I am truly happy about all of this. But I am not like you, my father. When I go to my wedding, I will do as honor demands, what my clan and my father and my king require of me. I had not thought to do anything else."

Arn fell silent, nodded, and then turned back to the king. But he stopped himself before saying what he had first intended, that a wedding with Ingrid Ylva could doubtless be arranged as soon as an agreement had been reached with Sune Sik. Several things made him hesitate. Foremost was his sudden insight that he himself would have to be the one to fetch the bride on such an occasion. He would be bringing home the daughter of the man whose brother he had helped to kill. Such matters required thought and prayer before acting hastily.

✠

The evening was hardly more than half over before the brief darkness arrived and it was time for dancing. With drums, tin plates, and pipes accompanying them, the six white-clad maidens got up from the bride's dais, took one another by the hand, and went in a line in between the tables, taking long sliding steps in time to the music. This was the farewell of youth to the maiden who would now leave her sisters behind. Seldom had anyone seen this dance with foreign minstrels and music, but most people thought the performance was even better.

When the maidens completed their first circuit around the tables, the music got faster and louder. For the third and last circuit the tempo increased even more, and some of the maidens had a hard time keeping their balance. According to custom, they were supposed to dance in a circle holding each other's hands and supporting one another during the fastest steps, but the hall at Arnäs was much too crowded for them to follow this tradition.

After completing three rounds, all the maidens stopped before the bridal seat, gasping and with flushed faces. They then invited Cecilia Rosa, the queen, and Ulvhilde Emundsdotter to come and join them. With Queen Blanca in the lead, followed by Ulvhilde and then the bride, the women slowly proceeded around the hall and out the door.

As soon as the doors were shut, shouts for more ale resounded from all directions, and there was a great tumult and murmuring; it was hard for anyone to hear even the person sitting right next to him without shouting.

No one had finished off more than a tankard before old Herr Magnus stood up. Supported by his son Eskil, he went over to the groom's dais. Holding out his hand, he invited his son Arn to come with him, then the king, Erik jarl, Magnus Månesköld, and also the monk.

Accompanied by shouts of joy and well wishes, including some brazen remarks of the type brought on by too much ale,

Arn slowly and with manly dignity walked through the hall, last in the group of men led by the king.

Out in the courtyard all of the guests were now standing atop the tables and benches in order to watch the escorting of the groom to the bridal bed. Torchbearers fell in on both sides of the short procession.

It was not a long walk, just to the far end of the longhouse where the stairs led up to the bridal chamber.

Old Herr Magnus had difficulty climbing the groom's stairs, but he was not about to admit defeat, and he brusquely refused all helping hands.

In the antechamber upstairs there was a great crush when everyone had come inside and began to undress Arn, a process that he at first tried to resist. His father jested that it was too late to turn back now.

They hung up his foreign garb and dressed him in a white, ankle-length linen shirt loosely fitted at the neck. Then the door to the bridal chamber itself could be opened.

There lay Cecilia in a long white shift with her hair unfastened and spread out around her and with her arms pressed to her sides. At the foot of the large bridal bed stood the queen, Ulvhilde, and the six bridesmaids. The king and Herr Magnus each took Arn by the arm and led him over to the bed, inviting him to lie down next to Cecilia. As he lay down, blushing with embarrassment as she was, he too pressed his arms to his sides. Then the men who had accompanied him went to stand at the foot of the bed with the women.

They all stood there for a long time without saying a word. Arn had no idea what was expected of him or of Cecilia, so he cast a nervous glance at her and asked a question that she was unable to answer. It seemed as if all their friends and kinsmen were waiting for something, although neither Arn nor Cecilia knew what that might be.

It seemed to both of them that they had spent an unbearable length of time in silence before they discovered the reason for the wait. It was the archbishop. They could hear his gasping breath on the stairs well before he appeared in the room, with a chaplain supporting him on either side.

Finally the time had come. The archbishop raised his hand and, still panting, gave them his blessing. The queen picked up one corner of the magnificent quilted coverlet, the king seized hold of the other, and together they gently drew it over Cecilia and Arn.

The escorting of the bridal couple had now been accomplished in the presence of twelve witnesses. Cecilia Rosa and Arn Magnusson were now husband and wife. According to church rules, until death did them part. According to the laws of Western Götaland and their ancestors, until such time as there was reason for them to part.

Their friends congratulated them and then, one by one, they bowed and left the bridal couple alone on their first night together.

The room was illuminated both by tarred torches set in the iron wall brackets and wax tapers. For a long time the two lay motionless in the bed, staring up at the ceiling and without speaking.

It had been a long journey to this bed, but now they were finally here, since it was God's will and the Holy Virgin had made them a promise. And both of them had prayed for this moment for more than twenty years. But it was also because the peace and concord of the realm demanded it, and because both of their clans had decided that it would be so. The king and queen had placed the wedding coverlet over them. No couple could be declared husband and wife in a more decisive manner.

Cecilia was thinking that the torment that had seemed so interminable, from the moment she first saw him riding to Näs and then all the hindrances that had piled up, had now vanished as quickly as the flight of a swallow. So much had happened to her because of others' wishes and the demands of custom that she had been helplessly swept away on a fast-moving current, like that leaf in the rushing spring stream that she had pictured during the ride between Näs and Riseberga. That moment when she happened to think of the leaf now seemed so long ago, and at the same time so recent. Time raced past at a dizzying speed; she tried to catch it and hold on to it by closing her eyes and conjuring up the memory of Arn riding toward her on his black horse with the silver mane. But when she shut her eyes the whole bed began to spin like a mill-wheel, and she had to open them at once.

Arn was thinking that the love he had felt so strongly for so many years, and that he had sworn never to betray, had lately been buried under all manner of things that had nothing to do with love. A short while ago, on this very evening, he and Knut had talked about a wedding as Birger Brosa's strongest means of preventing war, as if weddings had nothing to do with love. And Magnus, who was Cecilia's son and his own, had spoken of love in the same way when Arn asked him about marrying Ingrid Ylva. It was as if the constant struggle for power had dragged his love down in the dirt and sullied it.

As for the fleshly side of love, he had taught himself to push it aside through prayers, cold water, horseback rides in the night, and all sorts of other tricks. He had learned to regard it as sin and temptation, and yet it had now been blessed by God's Holy Mother herself. An entire banquet hall of guests was expecting him to unite his flesh with Cecilia's, for during the mass on the following day, the bride would go Forshem Church to be purified.

He tried to recall how it was between them when they were together and with such great desire devoted themselves to such pleasures, but it was as if the doors had been closed on that memory, bolted shut by too many prayers and nights spent in anguish in a little stone cell or a dormitory filled with brother knights.

He noticed that he was beginning to sweat, and he cautiously moved away the heavy bridal coverlet that the king and queen had pulled over them up to the tips of their noses.

"Thank you, my beloved," she said.

That was all she said, as if the shyness they both shared prevented her from saying more. But there was a sweet freshness to her words, especially as she uttered the endearment that they were now entitled to use.

"Imagine that we can now say those words: my beloved," he replied, his voice gruff. He decided at once not to let silence settle over them again. "Now that we have finally reached this day, shouldn't we first of all thank Our Lady for holding her hands over us during the long road we have traveled?"

Cecilia made a move as if to throw off the covers and sink to her knees beside the bed, but he reached out his hand to stop her.

"Take my hand, my beloved," he said, and for the first time he looked into her eyes as she turned toward him. "On this one occasion, I think that Our Lady would want to see us like this as we offer Her our thanks."

He held Cecilia's hand in his and recited a long prayer of thanksgiving in the language of the church, which she obediently and in a low voice repeated after him.

But after the prayer was done, it was as if their shyness returned. For a long time Arn studied Cecilia's hand he was holding, unable to say a word. This was the same hand as before, although the veins were more visible now, the fingers thicker, and the nails rough and cracked from all the work she had done to please God in His cloister.

She saw him staring at her hand and probably understood what he was thinking. She in turn studied his hand, thinking that it was the same as before, made strong by working with hammers in the smithy and by wielding swords in war, but with many disfigured knuckles and white scars, signs of all the privations and pain that his long penance had entailed.

"You are my Arn and I am your Cecilia," she said at last, since he didn't seem able to muster the courage to speak. "But are you the same Arn and am I the same Cecilia who parted with such great sorrow back then outside the gates of Gudhem?"

"Yes, we are the same," he replied. "Our souls are the same, though our bodies have aged; but the body is merely the shell of the soul. You are the Cecilia I remember, you are the Cecilia I tried to picture in so many dreams and prayers when I wanted to recall how you looked. Haven't you thought the same of me?"

"I have tried," she said. "I have always remembered you from that summer when you let your hair grow long, and in the wind it flew out behind you when you went riding; that is how I have always remembered your face. But I could never picture you differently, the way you would look when you returned home, the same Arn but older."

"For a long time I remembered your face as it was," he said. "Your hair and your eyes and every little sun freckle on your nose. But as the years passed I tried to imagine you older, the same Cecilia but older. It wasn't easy, and the image I had of you grew hazy. But when I saw you again for the first time outside Näs, I realized that you were much more beautiful than I had dared dream. Those tiny wrinkles at the corner of your eyes make you look both lovelier and wiser. Oh, if only I could say these things in Frankish! Forgive me if my words sound like rough wooden clogs when I speak our language that is now so unfamiliar."

"The words you speak are beautiful, and I understood them well, although I have never heard anyone describe words as wooden clogs before," she replied with a stifled laugh.

Her laugh came as a relief, and as if simultaneously, they both drew in a deep breath and slowly let it out. And with that they both ended up laughing, and Cecilia cautiously crept closer to Arn in the enormous bed.

"So what about my face?" said Arn with a smile. "Sometimes I feared that these wounds and scars would make me unrecognizable to my beloved when I finally returned home. But you didn't mistake me for someone else, did you?"

"I recognized you from the distance of an arrow shot, even before I could see your face close up," she replied eagerly. "Whoever has seen you on horseback will know that it is you and no one else approaching. It felt as if lightning had struck me though the sky was completely clear. I recognized you the moment I saw you, my beloved. I will never be able to explain properly how sweet it is to say those words."

"But when you saw my face at close hand, didn't I frighten you then?" Arn persisted. He was smiling broadly, but Cecilia glimpsed the concern in his eyes.

She drew her other hand from behind her back, wiped off the sweat on the coverlet, and reached out to touch his cheek, caressing the white scars without saying a word.

Finally she spoke. "You said that our souls are the same. But it is also said that the eyes are the mirrors of the soul, and your gentle blue eyes are the same as I remember. The Saracens have wounded you, sliced at you with their swords and lances for many years; that much I can see, as you well know. What are the wrinkles at my eyes compared to this! What serene strength your face shows, my beloved. Your wounds speak of the eternal battle against evil and the sacrifices that only those possessing great goodness and strong faith can endure. At your side I will always carry my head high, because a more handsome man cannot be found in all this kingdom of ours."

Arn was so overcome with embarrassment at these words that she saw he could find nothing to say. Afraid that silence would once again descend upon them, she leaned over and timidly kissed him, her dry lips touching first his forehead, then his cheek, and finally she closed her eyes and kissed his mouth.

He kissed her back, as if dreaming that they were once again seventeen and everything happened so easily. But it was not as easy as back then, and he felt a strange sense of despair growing inside him as he pressed his lips to hers and cautiously placed his calloused hand on her breast.

Cecilia tried not to tense and seem afraid, but she had kept her eyes closed so long that her head had started spinning unbearably from all the wine. Abruptly she had to pull away and dash outside to the stairs; there she vomited loudly without being able to stop herself.

At first Arn lay in bed, paralyzed with shame. But he soon realized that he couldn't just lie there idly while his beloved was feeling sick. He tumbled out of bed and went out to the stairway, putting his arm around Cecilia's shoulders to console her. Then he opened the door to the outer stairway and called for cold water. As he hoped, house thralls were posted outside, and they leaped up to obey at once.

A while later they were again lying in bed, both cooled by the cold water, each of them holding a big tankard.

Cecilia was deeply ashamed and didn't dare meet her husband's gaze. He comforted her with caresses at first, but soon with laughter. And it wasn't long before she too was laughing.

"We have the rest of our lives together to learn to make love as we once did," he said, stroking her damp forehead. "Such things are quickly forgotten in a cloister. The same is true for Templar knights, since we live as monks. But there is no haste to re-learn what we once did all too easily."

"Although not after drinking a cask of wine and eating an entire ox," said Cecilia.

"We'll try it with cold water instead," said Arn, but laughed at the same time as a fleeting thought passed through his wine-drenched mind.

Cecilia had no idea why Arn found the thought of cold water instead of wine so funny, but she laughed too, until they were both laughing hard and holding on to each other.

Late the next morning the twelve witnesses, bleary-eyed and unsteady on their feet, appeared as custom demanded. Arn had to get out of bed and accept a spear, which he was to hurl through the open window. Someone joked that the distance was so short from the bed to the window that not even Arn Magnusson could miss, even though he was known to be so poor at the sport.

Nor did he miss. The morning gift was thereby secured. Forsvik now belonged for all eternity to Cecilia Algotsdotter and her descendants.

Chapter 7

At Olsmas came the transition between the old and new harvests in Western Götaland. The barns normally stood empty, but the hay-making was going full speed and would be done by the feast of Saint Laurentius in twelve days' time. But during this unusually hot summer the crops had ripened much more quickly than normal, and by now all the hay had already been taken in. A month had passed since Arn and Cecilia's bridal ale, and it was time for the bride's third purification. The first took place the day after the wedding night, and the second one a week later.

This bride could not be more cleansed than she was already by having some priest say a prayer over her and sprinkle her with holy water, Cecilia thought. She felt a secret shame over her involuntary chastity which she had a hard time admitting to herself even in the brief moments of solitude and contemplation that she'd had during the first month at Forsvik. It felt like a reverse sin now that she and Arn were united in the flesh, and even though

Cecilia placed more of the blame on herself than on Arn, she had no idea how to improve the situation.

Arn seemed to be working like a maniac. He immersed himself in hard labor right after matins, and she saw him only briefly at breakfast and dinner; after vespers he would go down to the shore of Bottensjön and swim to remove the sweat and grime. By the time he came to her in their bedchamber it was already dark, and he didn't say much before he fell into a heavy slumber.

True, it was a special time, as he said, a time for harder work, since there was so much to do to get ready for winter. Many new souls had to have roofs over their heads as well as heat, especially heat, because the foreigners had never experienced a Nordic winter. Smithies and glassworks had to be ready by winter so that they could begin their real efforts then, able to work through the winter instead of merely eating, sleeping, and freezing the whole time.

Life at Forsvik was not easy, and the words between them were few, dealing mostly with necessities having to do with the day's or the next day's work. Cecilia sought solace in the knowledge that the need for such toil would soon pass, and the days would become calmer with the winter darkness. She was also happy about everything she saw being done, and each night when she entered their bedchamber she enjoyed breathing in the smell of fresh timber and tar.

Arn had decided that he and Cecilia would live by themselves in a smaller house that stood on stony ground a short distance away from the new longhouse, at the top of the slope leading to the shore of Bottensjön. The first day at Forsvik, before he felt compelled to spend months working every single hour between matins and vespers, he had taken her around to show her what was being built. And there was much to show, since a completely new Forsvik was rising up on either side of the old.

The greatest surprise was that he had built a separate house just for the two of them. Like her, he dreaded having to follow the old custom dictating that the master and mistress of the estate would sleep among thralls and servants in the warmest spot of the longhouse. Naturally he was used to sleeping in communal dormitories with his knight-brothers, he told her. But he had also had his own cell for many years. He didn't think either of them would be happy sleeping among all the others as if at a huge feast.

Their house was much smaller than a longhouse and divided into two big rooms; there was nothing like it in all of Western Götaland. It didn't take Cecilia long to be convinced of that.

When he took her in through the smaller door to the clothing chamber of the house, she was amazed at first to hear water running as if in a stream. He had conducted water through the house, flowing in a channel made of brick. It came in through a hole in one wall and ran out through the other wall by the door. In two places there were holes in the brick wall so that they could reach their hand down into the flowing stream. Above one of these holes there was an opening with wooden shutters. Next to it on the wall hung white linen for drying their hands and faces, and on a wooden tray under the linen was something waxlike that he called *savon*, which they could use for washing themselves. At the other opening the rough brick was covered with smooth-sanded wood so that one could sit down. At first Cecilia wasn't sure that she understood correctly, but when she pointed and hesitantly asked, he laughed and nodded that it was precisely what she thought it was, a *retrit*. Waste from the body was taken away at once by the stream of water and vanished through the brick wall to end a good way from the house in a stream that ran down to Bottensjön.

He said he wasn't sure that the water would flow all winter long, even though the channel had been well buried along most of its length. But at the point where the water entered the house it had to be conducted up onto a hollow wall which Arn had no

Nordic word for, so he called it by its Latin name of *aqueduct*. The difficulty was to ensure that the winter cold did not reach the stream of water when it came up from the ground. How well this system would work they would learn in midwinter, and if it didn't work on the first try they would have to redo it.

Cecilia was so excited by all these new things she saw in her new house that she forgot to go into their bedchamber and instead ran outside to see how the water stream was built. Arn followed her, shaking his head happily, and explained it to her.

It was like at Varnhem or Gudhem, the same idea of making use of running water and gravity. Here at Forsvik the water in Bottensjön was at a lower level than in Lake Viken, and every channel they dug from one to the other would create new streams of water.

Cecilia had many questions about this miraculous water system, but then she realized that she'd completely forgotten about the rest of the house. She ran back in with a laugh to look at the sleeping chamber.

This room had a gable built entirely of stone, and in the middle of the gable was a large open fireplace with two chimneys and a rounded vault of spiral wrought iron that held up the whole hood to catch the smoke. The floor was made of timber sealed with pitch and resin, flax and moss, just as the walls were. Although not much of the floor was visible because it was covered by large red and black rugs of tightly woven wool with foreign patterns.

Arn told her that he had brought a good many of these carpets home with him on the ship, not only for his own use but also so that his men from the Holy Land would be pleased on cold Nordic winter nights to have the floor covered as it was back home.

For the time being the space in front of the open fireplace was merely a depression cut into the timbers. Arn explained that the limestone to cover this portion of the room had not yet arrived. But they would be burning a lot of wood in the winter, and for several reasons it was best that all the flooring near the fireplace be covered with stone.

In the room stood a large bed like the bridal bed at Arnäs, as if Arn had ordered it built to match. The walls were bare except for the wall facing the east to Bottensjön. There she saw a large oblong window with shutters that could be closed from both inside and out. Arn explained that this would be improved as soon as they got their glassworks going. The advantage of having such a big window was that it let light into the room with the morning sun that would call him to his day's work; the disadvantage was easy to see, considering the cold and draftiness in winter. But with glass panes and secure seals around the window it would be much better.

The whole house smelled strongly of fresh timber, resin, and pitch. Outside the smell of pitch was even stronger, since all the new houses were covered with a thick layer. The intention wasn't merely to prevent rot, or to build for eternity the way the Norsemen built their churches, said Arn. It was important to stop up every little chink between the horizontal logs of the walls. They had to be especially careful when building with fresh timber, which wasn't the smartest thing to do because the wood would shrink as it dried. But they hadn't had much choice; it was either houses built of fresh wood or no houses at all. The thick layers of pitch would help to ensure that the walls were airtight.

They walked past the next house, which was for some of the foreigners, but the third house was surprisingly not for people, but for livestock. There more than thirty horses would spend the winter, and it seemed that each horse had its own chamber. The far end of the building was for the cows, and the entire upper floor above the low ceiling was to be used for storing winter fodder. For now the building had an earthen floor that eventually would be replaced with stone slabs since they were easier to keep clean.

All three of these new houses stood next to the gray houses arranged in a square with an inner courtyard. That was the old Forsvik. He took her into the barnyard and explained that the old longhouse would now be winter quarters for the thralls and farm hands, but that there was as yet no house to use for feasts or guests.

In one of the new houses, he had planned for Forsvik's yconoma to have her accounting chamber. Unless she would rather keep all such things in their own house, he quickly added to show that she was indeed the mistress of the estate and would decide for herself. Cecilia threw out both hands in dismay at the thought of doing work where they slept, so it was with relief that Arn took her around to see the growing row of smaller houses where the clang of work could already be heard in the various workshops.

And here they came to the greatest change at Forsvik, he announced proudly. Next to the new row of workshops was Forsvik's garden, which included apple trees and all sort of vegetables. Unfortunately all this would have to be dug up. The question was how someone knowledgeable about cultivation, which he understood she was, might save as many of the plants as possible and move them to another location in the spring.

Cecilia thought that now he'd gone too far in his eagerness. Whatever was to be built here would have to be built somewhere else, she insisted.

Arn sighed and said that what was to be built here could not be built anywhere else. Here they were to build a new stone-lined water canal.

Cecilia wanted to save her garden, but she was unsure whether to insist or not because she didn't understand the importance of this canal. She asked Arn to explain in more detail.

It was going to be a stone-lined canal in which the water would always flow with the same force in the spring, summer, autumn, and large parts of the winter. The power from the water would drive bellows and hammers in many of the workshops. His men from the Holy Land possessed all sorts of skills, he went on. They could work wonders if they had access to more power, and this was where it was, unfortunately, in the middle of the garden and orchard. But the canal would be the future of Forsvik; it would bring wealth and prosperity; it was the great endeavor that would lead to peace.

Cecilia tried to resist being swept along by Arn's eager enthusiasm. She asked him to sit down next to her on an old stone bench next to the garden to explain everything one more time, but more slowly and in detail. Because if she didn't understand what he was saying, she wouldn't be able to offer any help.

Her words stopped him, and he sat down obediently next to her, caressed her hand, and shook his head with a smile as if asking her forgiveness.

"So, let's begin again," she said. "Tell me what will be coming in to Forsvik on Eskil's ships. Let's start with that. What will we have to purchase?"

"Iron bars, wool, salt, livestock fodder, grain, skins, the type of sand we need to make glass, and various types of stone," he said.

"And all this we have to pay for?" she asked sternly.

"Yes, but it doesn't always mean we have to pay in silver."

"I know that!" she snapped. "One can pay in many ways, but that's a question for later. Now tell me instead what we will be producing at Forsvik."

"All the things that can be made from iron and steel," he replied. "All sorts of weapons that we can certainly make better than anyone in the kingdom, but also plowshares and steel-clad wheels. We can mill flour at any time, night or day all year round, and so much grain will be coming with Eskil's ships that we need never lack for it. We will make anything that has to do with leather and saddle-making. If we solve the problem with the clay, which now comes from too far away, the potters can work as steadily as the millers. But it's glass that will give us the best income."

"All those things together don't sound like income at all," Cecilia remarked with a frown. "It sounds like a loss. Because we also have big expenses maintaining the estate; there are many souls living here already, and there will be more this winter if I understand your plans correctly. And we have as many horses here as there are at the king's Näs, and we don't have enough winter fodder from our own fields. Are you quite sure, my love, that you haven't been overcome by pride?"

At first he was completely silenced by her words; he took her hand in both of his and raised it to his lips, kissing it many times. She grew warm inside, but was not in the least soothed when it came to their business affairs.

"In some respects you aren't the same woman I left outside Gudhem, my love," he said. "You are much wiser now than you were then. You see things instantly that none of your kinsmen would ever comprehend. There is certainly no better wife than you in our kingdom."

"And that is exactly what I would like to be, your good wife," she replied. "But then I must also try to keep track of all your ambitious plans, because you seem to be building more than you're thinking at the moment."

"That's probably true," he admitted without looking in the least worried. "I had probably thought to leave debt and loss, profit and expenses to be figured out later, even though I know it has to be done."

"That's a foolish way of thinking that could cost us a great deal, and many of us may pay for your recklessness with grumbling stomachs this winter," she said calmly. "Shouldn't you stop and think about everything a bit more?"

"Well, I can hear that I should leave the thinking about these matters to you," he said, kissing her hand again. "You know that in the beginning we can do business at a loss, don't you?"

"Yes, I do. I've done that myself, although back then it was not something I intended or even comprehended. But you'll need a thick layer of silver at the bottom of the coffer, and you must be sure that things will get better in the future."

"Here at Forsvik we meet both these conditions. But what sort of losses did you experience, my dear?"

"Cecilia Blanca, Ulvhilde, and I were the first to think of the idea of bringing in silver to Gudhem by sewing mantles, the kind that almost everyone in the kingdom wears nowadays. At first we sold them too cheaply, so we were spending more silver on buying pelts and expensive thread from Lübeck than we earned once we sold the finished mantles," she said.

"But then you raised the price and soon everybody wanted to have such fine mantles, so you raised the price even higher!" Arn suggested, throwing out his arms as though there was nothing to worry about either now or later.

"Yes, that's how we managed to correct our ways," said Cecilia, but her frown was back. "You said that we have silver, and you said that things will be better in the future. You'll have to explain that to me."

"Gladly," said Arn. "We have plenty of silver. What we can sell first is glass, but that income will be less than what we have to pay for all the other things. As soon as we can sell weapons, it will all even out. Then there is pottery, sawed timber, and several other things that will quickly turn our loss to profit, as soon as we get going."

"Weapons?" Cecilia asked suspiciously. "How are we going to sell something that people make for themselves on their own farms?"

"Because we'll make much better weapons."

"How are you going to make people aware of that? You can't just ride around displaying the weapons in your hand."

"No, but it will take some time to make all the weapons needed at Arnäs. They must have weapons and chain mail for a hundred men. And Eskil will have to pay for all of it. Then we have Bjälbo, and after that one Folkung estate after the other."

"Now that's a new way to do business," Cecilia admitted with a sigh. "But the most important thing is not the iron coming in from Svealand to Forsvik and finished weapons going out. More important is that all the wool we have from our own sheep has disappeared for your . . . what was the word?"

"Felt."

"Felt, yes. But we normally use the wool to make clothes for everyone, highborn and low. So now we have to pay for all that wool?"

"Yes, both for clothing and to make more felt."

"And we need more hides than we can get from our own slaughtered livestock," said Cecilia, "and more meat, especially lamb, than we have on hand now to get through the winter. And fodder for all the livestock, especially the horses."

"Yes, there you see, my love. You see everything so clearly."

"Well, one of us has to keep accounts so we can do the right thing at the right time, and that's not a simple calculation!" she declared at last when she had thought things over. She envisioned difficulties piling up like a mountain in the near future.

"Can I ask you, my own dear wife, to take charge of this?" asked Arn, a bit too eagerly, she thought.

"Yes, you can. I have my abacus, but this task will be more than anyone could hold in their head. I need writing implements and parchment in order to handle this work. And I'll have to talk to many people, so it will take some time. But if we don't start making calculations soon, we're going to starve this winter!"

He promised her at once that she would receive everything

she needed to begin keeping the account books. He added self-confidently that here at Forsvik they would never go hungry. After that he seemed to forget about the whole matter and went back to his own frenzied work.

✠

When King Knut told Arn that the castle church at his Näs would be the closest for residents of Forsvik, it was not entirely true. There were closer churches. But if the winds were favorable on Lake Vättern, it was still faster to get to Näs than to any other church, since King Knut still retained Norwegian oarsmen and sailors.

At Olsmas, early in the morning Arn and Cecilia went on board the ship called *The Snake*. Cecilia was glad when she saw the slender black ship, and she hoped that the helmsman was the same one she had met before. And it was, she soon found out, but his long hair had now turned white.

Arn was not happy to see this ship again. He had been aboard during its first journey, which had ended in the death of a king, but he said nothing of this to Cecilia or anyone else when he bowed his head, crossed himself, and climbed aboard. The Norwegian oarsmen smiled to one another, since they thought they had another West Goth passenger who had never sailed before. They still told the merry tale about the noble lady who asked Styrbjørn himself whether he wasn't afraid that he would get lost sailing on little Lake Vättern.

They had to row only for an hour before they caught a good wind and could set the sail. Then the crossing proceeded at a furious pace, with the white foam spraying up from the bow of the ship.

After the mass and the bride's third purification in the castle church, the two Cecilias went off by themselves, while Knut took Arn up to the battlement between the two towers. There he ordered benches and a table to be brought, along with food and drink, which he was unsuccessful in pressing on Arn on this holy day.

There was much to discuss and one day would not be enough, Knut explained sadly, stroking his almost bald head. But they might as well begin with the simplest problem, which was to arrange the wedding between Magnus Månesköld and the Sverker daughter Ingrid Ylva. Knut said that he understood that both Arn and the bride's father Sune Sik might be reluctant to have Arn act as the groom's spokesman and thus negotiate with the man whose brother he had helped to kill. But Birger Brosa had solved that problem as easily as cracking a nut in his hand.

Magnus Månesköld had grown up as Birger Brosa's foster son, and now was more of a younger brother. If Birger Brosa instead of Arn spoke on behalf of the groom, they would avoid all difficulties quite elegantly and insult no one. Besides, the king's brother Sune Sik would have the honor of meeting the jarl of the kingdom as his future son-in-law's negotiator.

Arn merely nodded his agreement and muttered that no more time need be wasted on this question if there was something that was more urgent.

The next matter to be discussed mixed pride with wisdom, so it could not be solved with wisdom alone. Still, Arn had to reconcile as soon as possible with his uncle, Birger Brosa.

Thinking that all the difficult topics of discussion had now been dealt with, Arn began asking eagerly how the kingdom was now being governed. He had understood that a great deal had changed since they were young, when everyone gathered at the *ting* of all Goths with the king, jarl, and judge and perhaps two thousand men. He hadn't heard a word about such a *ting* since he came home, so that must mean that the power had shifted away from the *ting*.

King Knut sighed that this was indeed true. Some things had improved with the new manner of governing the kingdom, others had grown worse.

At the *ting* free men decided now as before all matters amongst free men. At the *ting* they could present their disputes, determine fines for manslaughter, hang one another's thieves, and settle other petty matters.

At the king's council, on the other hand, matters were decided that dealt with the kingdom as a whole: who would be king, or jarl or bishop; taxes due to the king or jarl; building of cloisters; trade with foreign lands; and the defense of the realm. When Finns and Russians sailed into Lake Mälaren five years before, plundering and burning the town of Sigtuna, and killing Archbishop Jon, there was much for the kingdom's council to decide. It could never have been done at a *ting* with a thousand arguing men. A new city would have to be built to obstruct the inlet to Mälaren, at Agnefit where Mälaren met the Eastern Sea. Now a start had been made; defensive towers had been built, booms and chains had been stretched across the rivers so that no plunderers from the East could come back, at least not unnoticed as they did the last time. Such things were decided at the king's council. This was new.

Arn was well aware of where Agnefit was situated, since he had once ridden that way and past Stocksund when he was returning from Östra Aros on his way to Bjälbo. He once proposed that it was there the king ought to have his seat rather than down at Näs in the middle of Lake Vättern.

No matter how impatient King Knut was to find the discussion moving in a completely different direction from that he had intended, he couldn't help asking Arn to tell him more about this unexpected idea. What was wrong with Näs?

"The location," replied Arn with a laugh. Näs was built by Karl Sverkersson for one simple reason. The king wanted to have a castle that was so safe that no one with murder on his mind could reach him. Arn and Knut knew better than anyone how futile that thought was, since it was at Näs that they had killed King Karl, less than an arrow-shot from the place where they now sat many years later.

"The king should ideally have his seat where the gold and silver for the kingdom flow through," Arn went on. "Considering the present trade routes and how they might look in the future, this site should be in the east of the kingdom rather than in the west. For to the west lies Denmark."

From Linköping in Eastern Götaland they could certainly handle the affairs of the kingdom, especially trade with Lübeck, and better than from remote Näs. But Linköping had been the Sverkers' city from olden times, and for a king from the Erik clan that would be like seeking a home in a hornets' nest. Instead the king should build himself a new city, by the Eastern Sea, a city that belonged to no one else.

Knut argued that Näs was safer. Here they could either defend themselves or flee, and for a good part of the year it was inaccessible to any enemy. If they built a new city it could be taken by storm and burned. Arn countered that the site at Agnefit and Stocksund was suitable for building a city that could not be taken. Besides they had only one enemy, and that was Denmark; if the Danes wanted to go to war against Western Götaland they could simply take the land route north from Skåne. And sailing past the Danes from Lödöse down to Lübeck would no longer be possible if the Danes should deny them passage. Denmark was a great power. But the east coast of the realm was not as easy for them to reach. And from Agnefit it was closer to Lübeck than from Näs, if reckoned in the same way that Knut had reckoned when he said that the closest church to Forsvik was the one at Näs. It would be the same if they moved the power of the realm from Näs to the east coast.

They twisted and turned the idea of the new city by the Eastern Sea, but finally Knut wanted to get back to matters he had planned to discuss. Most difficult was the intractable Archbishop Petter, or Petrus as he called himself. Having a hostile archbishop on his neck was the worst thing that could befall a king. Archbishop Petter was a Sverker man, and he made not the slightest effort to hide his ties to the clan. And his ambition was clear. He wanted to tear the crown from his own king and hand it to Sverker Karlsson, who had lived his entire life in Denmark.

The king's council appointed every bishop in the realm, Knut explained. A bishop received his staff and ring from the king, and no one could become bishop without the king's will. Unfortunately it wasn't quite as simple with the archbishop, for the king could neither refuse nor appoint him. It was Rome that decided, but now Rome had assigned that power to Archbishop Absalon in Lund, which was the same as handing it to Denmark.

So the Danes decided who was going to be archbishop in the land of the Swedes and Goths. No matter how backward that might seem, nothing could be done about it. And even if Knut did what he could to cleanse the crowd of bishops of all Sverker men, those rogues changed their loyalty as soon as they received their ring and staff. Then they obeyed the archbishop regardless of what secret promises they had made to the king before receiving power. A cleric could never be trusted.

And that wily Petter never ceased arguing that Knut had not sufficiently atoned for the killing of King Karl. As long as the deed was not atoned for, it meant that he had unjustly seized the crown, even though he had been crowned and anointed. And a crown unjustly seized could not be inherited by the eldest son, Petter claimed.

There was also much grumbling about the claim that Queen Cecilia Blanca had actually taken cloister vows, so that her sons Erik, Jon, Joar, and Knut were all illegitimate. And illegitimate sons could not inherit the crown either, according to Petter. Arch-bishop Petter kept pulling on these two reins, sometimes in one direction and sometimes in the other.

Arn argued that the Church could not defy the king's choice of successor. If the council decided to name Erik jarl as king after Knut, the bishops could grumble about it, roll their eyes, and talk about sin. And of course they could refuse to crown Erik. But there had been uncrowned kings of the realm before.

Unless all the bishops then went off to Denmark and crowned that Sverker instead, Knut put in, sounding disconsolate.

"Then no man in the lands of the Swedes and Goths would take the matter seriously, and such a king in foreign service would never be able to set his foot in the realm," Arn said calmly.

"But what if such a king came leading a Danish army?" asked Knut, now looking anxious.

"Then whoever wins the war will triumph, that's nothing new," said Arn. "It's the same as if the Danes wanted to turn us into Danes today; who we select as king will not determine the outcome."

"Do you think the Danes could do that? Could they conquer us?" Knut asked, tears visible in his eyes.

"Yes, undoubtedly," said Arn. "If we were so foolish as to meet a Danish army on the battlefield today, they would enjoy a great victory. If I were your marshal I would advise you not to fight them."

"So we'd be lost, and also disgraced because we refused to fight for our honor and our freedom?"

"No," said Arn. "Not at all. It's a long way from Sjælland to Näs, and even further to the Swedes' Östra Aros. If a Danish army invaded our land, they would naturally want to have a quick and decisive victory, as long as the season was favorable and their supply lines were good. Now imagine if we didn't give them that opportunity. They would be expecting, just as you are, that we would immediately call for a campaign, that every man in the realm would put on his iron helmet and come with ax in hand to be crushed by the Danish cavalry. They would die bravely and with honor, but they would die. What if we didn't do that?"

"Then we'd lose our honor, and no one will follow a king without honor!" Knut replied with a sudden flash of wrath, pounding his fist on the table.

"No one follows a dead king," said Arn coldly. "If the Danes don't get the big battle they're hoping for, they won't win. They'll burn a city. They'll plunder villages, and it will cost us much misery. But then winter will come. Then their supplies will melt away, and we'll take them one by one and cut off their supply lines home to Denmark. When spring comes you'll be the great victor. More honor than that you cannot win."

"In truth you think like no one else when it comes to war," said King Knut.

"There you are wrong, absolutely," replied Arn with a smile that was almost impudent. "I think like a thousand men, many of whom I knew. In the Holy Land we were no more than a thousand men against a superior force infinitely greater than that which the Danes can mount. And the Knights Templar fought with great success for half a century."

"Until you lost!" King Knut objected.

"Quite true," said Arn. "We lost when a fool of a king decided to risk our entire army against a far superior enemy in a single battle. Then we lost. If we had been allowed to continue as we were accustomed to doing, we would have possessed the Holy Land even today."

"What was that king's name?"

"Guy de Lusignan. His advisor was named Gérard de Ridefort. May their names live in eternal infamy!"

⁜

For the brothers Jacob and Marcus Wachtian the journey to Skara was one of the strangest they had ever taken, and yet they were both well-traveled men.

Sir Arn had first intended that the brothers should travel with only a few of his thralls as guides, but they had refused this offer in fright and disgust, saying that they would have a hard time making purchases in a language they didn't understand. Actually it was the dark nights along the deserted riverbanks that they feared. This Nordic land was a land of demons, they were both convinced of that. And the people they encountered were often hard to distinguish from animals, and that was frightening too.

At first Sir Arn had been unwilling to leave his construction work, but he gave in to their objections and decided that both he and his wife would come along, since she had purchases to make as well. The brothers had pointed out that it seemed unwise to travel carrying the gold and silver necessary to buy such a long list of items when they had no armed horsemen with them. But Sir Arn had only laughed, giving them an exaggerated chivalrous bow, and assuring them that a Templar knight was at their disposal. He would be traveling in battle attire, taking with him his bow and quiver in addition to the sword and battle-ax he always carried.

As they loaded their cart with two oxen onto the ship, along with their horses and traveling accouterments, Sir Arn realized that they needed someone to drive the ox-cart when they proceeded further on land. He called over two boys who were full of eagerness; with bow and quiver in their hands they came running just as the ship was about to cast off.

They had engaged an empty riverboat with eight foul-smelling and sly-looking oarsmen for the journey. The Wachtian brothers thought they were risking their lives to venture out into the uninhabited and terrifying countryside with gold and silver right under the noses of such men. But they soon changed their attitude when they saw with what submissive and almost terror-stricken looks these river hooligans watched Sir Arn.

The route took them via Askeberga, the same way they had come, and on to the lake called Östansjö. From there they did not continue northwest toward Arnäs, but south for many hours on a different river, until they came to the place where everything had to be unloaded onto horses for the rest of the journey.

From the boat landing by the river the road to the nearest town passed through a dense forest. Because it was the only route and because those who wanted to go to the market in town had to travel this way, it wasn't hard to reckon what dangers might await them in the depths of the forest.

The brothers' premonitions were confirmed, for in the midst of the forest Sir Arn, riding at the head of the column, suddenly reined in his horse, raised his right hand as a sign to halt, and put on his helmet. He examined the ground in front of him closely, then looked up into the overhanging crowns of the trees before he called out something in a language that made the forest come alive. Robbers climbed down from the trees and appeared from behind bushes and tree trunks. But instead of rushing forward in an attack that would have gained them considerable riches if they had succeeded, the robbers lined up with heads bowed and weapons lowered and allowed the small column to pass without loosing a single arrow. They had never seen less effectual robbers.

Marcus jested happily about this when they emerged from the forest and saw a little town with a church in the distance. Robbers like these would not have been long-lived, and certainly not fat, if they had plied their trade in Outremer.

Jacob, doubting that this could be a typical way for Nordic robbers to behave, rode up alongside Sir Arn and asked him what had just happened. When Jacob fell back and slipped in beside his brother, he was able to explain with some amusement.

The robbers were not merely robbers, they were also tax collectors for the bishop in the town, and it seemed that the role they assumed depended on who came riding. From some people they collected taxes for their bishop; others they plundered on their own behalf, since they received no other payment for their work as tax collectors.

But this time it was to be neither taxes nor plunder. For when Sir Arn discovered the robbers waiting in ambush, he told them how it was. First, that he was Arn Magnusson and could single-handedly kill them all if he was provoked. Second, that he was of the Folkung clan. That meant that no robber, in service to a bishop or just out for his own benefit, would live longer than three sundowns after having loosed an arrow, even if he managed to escape from Sir Arn. The robbers had found this argument entirely convincing.

The clan that Sir Arn belonged to must therefore be almost like a Bedouin tribe, Jacob thought. This barbarian land did indeed have a royal power and church like all others. There were worldly armed forces and ecclesiastical ones. They had seen that at the wedding feast with their own eyes. So the law was upheld in much the same way as in other Christian lands.

But in what land could someone ride up to robbers or tax collectors and say that he belonged to a certain clan, and that statement alone would make them all lay down their arms? Only in Outremer. Anyone who attacked a member of certain Bedouin tribes could be assured that he would be hunted by avengers until the end of time if necessary. The same was apparently true here in the North. At any rate, these northern Bedouins could be considered safe company.

They rode right past the first stinking puddle of a town, which clearly housed a greedy bishop. They didn't even stop for food. Jacob and Marcus were both relieved and disappointed by this, since their buttocks ached from many hours' riding, but the smell coming from the town was extremely repellent to them.

But eventually they were rewarded for what they had endured, for a few hours later as the evening cold came sweeping in as a raw mist, they found themselves approaching a cloister. There they would stay for the night.

For the Wachtian brothers it was as if they had suddenly come home. They were quartered in their own room with whitewashed walls and a crucifix in the *hospitium* of the cloister. The monks who greeted them all spoke Frankish and behaved like real human beings, and the food that was served after vespers was first-class, as was the wine. It was like coming to an oasis with ripe dates and clear, cold water in the middle of a burning desert—just as astonishing, just as blessed.

Jacob and Marcus were not allowed inside the cloister walls, but they saw Sir Arn put on his white Templar mantle and go inside to pray. According to what his wife told them in her amusing and pure church Latin, he was visiting his mother's grave.

The next day they left a good deal of their clothing and traveling food at the *hospitium*, as they would be returning for another night after the day's bargaining in the town, which was called Skara.

They had been told that Skara was the biggest and oldest town in all of Western Götaland and thus their expectations were high. But it was hardly Damascus they rode into that morning. Here was the same stench of waste and foul air as outside the smaller town whose impossible name they had already forgotten; here were the same unclean people and streets without either cobblestones or gutters. And the primitive little church with the two towers that was called the cathedral was dark and oppressive rather than inspiring any sort of blessing. But as good Christians they couldn't refuse when Sir Arn and the rest of the party, his wife and the two boys, went inside to pray. Yet Jacob and Marcus felt that this was a church where God was not present, either because He had never arrived or because He had forgotten where it was. Inside it was damp and smelled of heathendom.

On the outskirts of the town there was a street that was clean and swept like a Frankish town or one in Outremer. Here there was a different aroma, of cleanliness and coffee and food and spices, which seemed familiar, and here Frankish was spoken, as well as some other languages which were not Norse.

They had come to the street of the glass masters, the coppersmiths, and the stonecutters. Samples of glass and stone and copper pots were displayed along the street, and interpreters came running from every direction to offer their services when they saw the fat money purses hanging from Sir Arn's belt. They soon learned that their skills were for once not needed.

They visited one booth after another, sat down and accepted cold water in beautiful glasses, politely but firmly declining the ale tankards that were also urged upon them. It was like a little Damascus; here they could converse with everyone in understandable languages, and learn about things that were impossible to discover outside this little street.

They learned how glass sand with copper inclusions or copper sulfate could be ordered from Denmark and Lübeck if they wanted to produce glass with a yellow or blue color. The substances for green or rose color, or colorless glass, were available locally if one knew the right place to find them. Sir Arn soon sent the two youths to fetch the ox-cart they had left with guards outside the cathedral, and then he went out buying. Eventually the cart was heavily loaded with substances for glass production; from some booths he bought everything they had on hand. There was also lead in great quantities, since the glassmasters worked mostly on church windows. Many merry bargains were concluded that day. Sir Arn spent a great deal of money without bothering to dicker about prices, which seemed to annoy his wife as much as it did the Wachtian brothers. It was an unusual day for these mostly Frankish glassmasters, as they were used to speaking through interpreters and selling finished glass, not speaking their own language with a Northerner who was as fluent as they were. Nor had they been involved in selling tools and materials for making glass instead of the glass they made themselves. But Sir Arn did buy a few glass pieces to take along, to be used as samples, as he said.

It was the same with the coppersmiths. Judging by the hammered and tin-plated vessels displayed outside the coppersmiths' booths, both the Wachtian brothers and Sir Arn could easily see that they could produce much better wares with their Damascene coppersmiths at Forsvik. Sir Arn did buy one vessel, but just to be polite. He bought mostly copper rods and tin ingots.

When their cart was already heavily loaded and they had visited every glassmaster and coppersmith along one side of the street, they returned slowly along the other side to meet the stonemasters or their servants and apprentices who were at home. Many of the masters themselves were out at church construction sites that required constant visits. Jacob and Marcus learned to their astonishment that the business of building churches was flourishing more in this small country than anywhere else in the world. Here more than a hundred churches were being built simultaneously. With so many orders for church construction, the stonemasters could charge twice as much as anywhere in France or England or Saxony.

One of the stonemasters was more expensive than all the others, and outside his booth drawings had been set up to show his commissions from the construction of the cathedral itself. They all went from one picture to the next guessing what they were seeing, which was often easy for those familiar with the Holy Scriptures. Sir Arn's wife in particular appeared to take a great interest in this master's artistry. Sir Arn then took his entire party inside to meet the master, who at first seemed peevish and dismis-

sive, complaining that he had neither the time nor the inclination
to converse. But when he grasped that he could speak his own
language with this buyer, his attitude quickly changed; he began eagerly explaining to them all the ideas behind his work and
what he would like to do. Sir Arn mentioned that he wished to
rebuild the church that belonged to his own clan, that it would be
new construction from the ground up, but it would also be consecrated anew. This church would be dedicated not to the Virgin
Mary, like almost all the other churches in Western Götaland,
but to the Holy Sepulcher.

The stonemaster grew even more attentive when he heard this.
For many years, as he said, he had carved the Virgin Mary in
every conceivable situation: gentle and good, strict and admon-
ishing, with Her dead Son, with Her Son as a babe, at the Annunciation by the Holy Spirit, on the road to Bethlehem, before
the star, in the manger, and in whatever other scenes could be
imagined.

But God's Grave? Then he would have to rethink the whole
design. It would take the right man, and it would also take time
to contemplate the design. But as to time, the stonemaster, whose
name was Marcellus, unfortunately had commitments all over
the land which would keep him occupied for a year and a half.
Before that it would be impossible to leave without breaking contracts.

Sir Arn didn't think that the delay would be any problem; it
was more important that the work would be beautiful for all
eternity, since what was carved in stone was meant to endure. So
he agreed to hire the stonemaster.

Both Marcus and Jacob felt alarmed when they heard how
hastily Sir Arn allowed himself to be persuaded to put down an
advance, and a shamelessly large sum at that. But they saw no
opportunity to interfere in the matter. The negotiation ended

with Sir Arn paying the outrageous sum of ten besants in gold as an advance on one year's work, and he promised another ten for each additional year the work would take. Stonemaster Marcellus was not slow in accepting this proposal.

On the return journey to Varnhem cloister in the early evening, it seemed at first that Sir Arn's wife reproached him, although mildly, for his irresponsible way of handling silver and gold. He was not in the least fazed by this, but answered her with a happy expression and eager gestures; even for someone who did not speak Norse it was obvious that he was describing his grandiose plans.

Finally he began to sing, and then she could not help singing along with him. It was a beautiful song, and both brothers understood that it was churchly and not worldly.

In this way they approached the cloister of Varnhem with heavenly singers leading the way before the sun set and the raw evening cold swept in. The brothers agreed that this journey had not only presented surprises, but also more good than either of them would have expected.

The next day their departure was delayed while Sir Arn's wife did business buying parchment and also roses that she bought in wet leather sacks with earth inside, pruned down so that only the stalks stuck up from the packing material. They didn't have to understand Norse to see that this woman was better than her husband at business. But they did have to wait while she and the cloister's garden-master bargained over every little coin. Sir Arn made no move to intervene. At last his wife had in the cart the plants she wanted, and judging by the roses climbing up the walls of Varnhem in red and white, she had purchased much beauty for the adornment of Forsvik.

✠

Between the bustling days of Bartelsmas, when the last of the harvest was brought in, and Morsmas, the summer returned briefly to Western Götaland with a week of stubborn south winds.

This time was just as busy for Cecilia as it was for Arn. Everything had to be harvested in the gardens, and then she had to try to save whatever she could. She toiled as hard as the thralls she had engaged to dig up the apple trees with their roots to replant them on the slope down toward Bottensjön. There the water would always be plentiful.

After supervising all the gardening work, she went to the Wachtian brothers at their workshop and asked about what they intended to start with and what would come later. She also persuaded them to accompany her to the smithies and pottery workshop to translate. Besides their own language and Latin the brothers had also mastered the completely foreign tongue that many of the men from the Holy Land spoke. They showed her arrow points of various types, some long and sharp as needles to penetrate chain mail, some with broad cutting edges that were meant for hunting or the enemy's horses, and others that served purposes she didn't understand. She visited the sword smithy and the workshop where they made wire for chain mail. And she went to the glassworks where she asked which of the glass samples that were set up along a bench they might make at Forsvik and which were still beyond their skill. She went to the stable thralls and asked how much fodder a horse consumed, to the livestock barn and learned how much milk a cow gave, and to the slaughterhouse to ask about salt and storage barrels.

After each such visit she returned to her abacus and writing implements. The best thing about their visit to Varnhem was not the purchase of the famous Varnhem roses, but the fact that she had laid in a good stock of parchment for making her account books. It was accounting, after all, that she knew best, even better than gardening and sewing, because for more than ten years she had kept books and taken care of all the business at two cloisters.

Finally she had everything in order and knew down to the penny the state of the economy at Forsvik. Then she went to find Arn, although it was only early evening and he was just finishing up his work with the cooling houses next to the big stream. He was happy to see her. He wiped the sweat from his brow with his index finger as was his habit, and immediately wanted her to praise the finished cooling houses. She couldn't say no but was surely not as effusive as he had thought she would be when she saw the big empty room clad in brick. Rows of empty iron hooks and rods hung there, waiting to hold food that they didn't yet have. She pointed this out so sternly that he almost ceased his lively chatter.

"Come with me to the accounting chamber and I'll explain everything to you, my beloved," she said with her eyes lowered. She was well aware that those words would soften him. But she also knew that they were true words and not merely the wiles of a woman. It was true that he was her beloved.

But that did not lessen the necessity of telling him the truth about all the foolishness she had discovered and could prove with numbers. She prayed to herself that he would have an under-standing of such things, even if thus far he had shown no interest in anything other than building for the winter.

"Look here, my love," she said, opening up the ledger to show how much was eaten and drunk each day by both humans and livestock at Forsvik. "This is what a horse needs in fodder every day. Here you see the total for a month, and here is what we have in our barns. So, sometime after Kyndelsmas in the midst of the bitterest cold of winter, we will have thirty-two starving horses. The meat we have slaughtered and can slaughter in the future will be gone by Annunciation Day. The consumption of lamb is such that we will have eaten it all before Christmas.

The dried fish has not yet arrived. You can see that this is true, can't you?"

"Yes, these seem to be very good calculations. What do we have to do?"

"With regard to feeding the people here, the dried fish must arrive as promised, preferably long before Lent. As far as meat is concerned, you have to hire some hunters, because there are plenty of deer and boars in the woods, and inside Tiveden Forest there is an animal as big as a cow that gives much meat. As for the horses, I assume you don't want to see them slaughtered by Kyndelsmas."

"No, of course not," said Arn with a smile. "Each of those horses is worth more than twenty Gothic horses or more."

"Then we'll have to buy fodder," Cecilia cut him off. "It's not normal practice to buy fodder for animals, since everyone usually takes care of his own. So you'll have to tend to this matter at once—before the ice begins to form and the time comes when neither boat nor sleigh can reach us. The earlier you begin in the fall, the easier it should be to buy fodder, I should think."

"I agree," said Arn. "I'll deal with that problem first thing tomorrow. What else have you discovered from your calculations?"

"That we have spent enough silver to equal almost the entire value of Forsvik without any income to balance our expenses. The gold alone that you advanced the stonecutter in Skara would have kept us alive and fat for several years."

"You cannot count that gold in your sums!" said Arn vehemently, but regretted it at once and smiled to appease her and excuse his temper. "I have enough gold to pay for everything having to do with the church in Forshem. It's in a coffer by itself; it has nothing to do with us. We can count that church as already paid for."

"Well, that changes thing a great deal for the better, of course," Cecilia admitted. "You could have told me this earlier, then I wouldn't have wasted so much ink. Because it's also about time you told your wife how much we own, or rather how much *you* own, since I own Forsvik, which increases in value with each drop of sweat you spill."

"I own approximately one thousand marks in gold," Arn said in embarrassment, looking down at the wooden floor. "That does not include what it will cost to build Arnäs into an impregnable fortress, which shall be a salvation for us all someday. Nor do I count what I have put aside to pay for the church in Forshem."

He squirmed when he said this last and still looked away, as if he were well aware that he had said something that no one with wit and sense would believe.

"A thousand marks," Cecilia whispered as if awestruck. "A thousand marks in gold; that's more than everything owned by Riseberga, Varnhem, and Gudhem combined."

"That may be true, my love," replied Arn softly, but it seemed as if he were more ashamed of his great wealth than happy about it.

"Why didn't you tell me this sooner?" Cecilia asked.

"I've thought about telling you many times, but it never seemed to be the right moment. It's a long story that isn't easy to understand, about how this gold came to be mine in the Holy Land. Once I got started I would have to finish the tale, and there is so much that needs to be finished before winter. Gold isn't everything; gold won't protect us from the cold, especially my friends from the warm countries. I hadn't intended to keep this from you. I imagined a long, cold winter night with the north wind howling outside, with you and me lying in the glow of our hearth without the slightest draft reaching us underneath our feather beds. That's when I would like to tell you the whole story."

"If you wait until winter you will wait in vain," said Cecilia with a little smile that lightened at once the gloom that had settled over them at this talk of riches.

"No, I look forward to the winter," said Arn, also with a smile.

"That won't prevent gold from offering poor protection against cold and hunger. As you said, tomorrow you must start buying fodder over in Linköping or wherever you can find it."

"I promise. What else have you found in the merciless logic of your numbers?"

"I have found that you should buy or build your own boat to transport clay."

"How so?" asked Arn, surprised for the first time in this conversation.

"For making bricks it takes so much fresh clay each time you fire them, that it isn't worth the effort to ship the clay here first instead of moving the work to Braxnbolet," Cecilia went on. "But with the clay for making pottery it's different. If you can get that sort of clay here, the potters can be kept busy all winter. It's merely a matter of keeping the clay damp, yet warm enough so it won't freeze."

He looked at her with an astonished admiration that he couldn't conceal, and she smiled back as if in triumph.

"Don't work anymore today," she said. "Stay with me. Let's ride off together just for a while to enjoy the fruit of our labor. The evening is so mild."

She went to change into her riding attire, but she frowned when she came out and saw him holding their woolen mantles over his arm as if to hide the long scabbard sticking out from under the cloth. But she didn't say a word.

They went first to the stable, which was empty this time of year, since all the horses were in the pasture. A long row of saddles with foreign signs above them hung on the wall, and Arn chose two. He handed her the mantles when he hoisted the saddles onto his shoulder and led her out to the horse pasture. The sun was low in the sky, but it was still as warm as a summer day, and the breeze was like a mild caress on their faces.

A black mare and her foal stood by themselves in a smaller pasture. They went there first, climbing in through the rails. Arn called the mare. She pricked up her ears and came toward him at once, tossing her head. Her foal trotted after her. Cecilia marveled at how affectionately her beloved and the mare greeted each other, how he rubbed his face against her muzzle, and how he stroked her glossy coat and spoke to her in a foreign language.

"Come!" he said, reaching out his hand to Cecilia. "I want you to make friends with Umm Anaza, for she shall henceforth be your horse. Come and say hello."

Cecilia went over and tried to do as Arn had done, rubbing her face against the mare, who at first seemed a bit shy. Then Arn talked to the mare in the foreign language, and she changed at once and yielded to Cecilia's touch.

"What language are you speaking?" she asked as she petted the mare and the little foal who timidly came forward.

"The language of horses," said Arn with a secret smile, shaking his head happily. "That was what Brother Guilbert told me once when I was a boy; back then I believed that there was a language that only horses understood. It's more correct to say that I'm speaking the language that these horses have heard from birth in Outremer. It's Saracen."

"And I who can only speak my own language or Latin with her!" Cecilia laughed. "At least I must know her name."

"Her name is Umm Anaza, which means Mother Anaza, and the little one is called Ibn Anaza, although that's what I used to call his father. Now the stallion whom we shall meet is called Abu Anaza, and you can probably guess what Abu and Ibn mean, can't you?"

"Father and son Anaza," Cecilia said. "But what does Anaza mean?"

"That's just a name," said Arn, swinging a saddle with a lambskin pad onto the mare. "Horses named Anaza are the noblest in all the Holy Land, and when the long winter nights come I will tell you the saga of Anaza."

Arn saddled and bridled the mare with amazing speed, and the mare didn't object in the least, but seemed eager to go out.

Cecilia was allowed to lead Umm Anaza down to the big pasture where the stallions were kept. Arn hopped over the fence and whistled so that they all looked up from their grazing. The next moment they were all galloping toward Arn so that the ground shook. Cecilia was startled but realized she didn't have to worry when the horses came to a halt the instant that Arn raised his arm in command. Then they all walked in a circle and crowded around Arn, who seemed to have a name for each horse and offered each a few friendly words. Finally he turned his attention to a stallion who looked much like Cecilia's mare, with a black coat hide and silver mane. It wasn't hard to understand that this must be Abu.

Cecilia couldn't help being moved as she watched her husband treat these animals with such tenderness. They seemed to be much more than horses to him, almost like dear friends.

No man in the North treats his horses this way, she thought, but realized at once that there was no man in the North who could ride like Arn. That was a good thought, that loving care made better riders than arrogance and harshness.

She felt something of this love herself as they rode out from Forsvik a while later, heading north along the shore of Botten-sjön. It was as though this mare enjoyed carrying her new owner, as if she spoke through her gentle movements which were not like those of other horses.

The sun had sunk below the treetops when they entered the endless conifer forest known as Tiveden. Arn led them up along a path and soon they were so high that they could see Botten-sjön, and off in the distance Lake Vättern glinted in the last light of evening. The smells of horses blended enchantingly with the sweet decay of late summer inside the conifer forest.

Arn came alongside her and said that now he was too old to stand up on his horse's back; he intended to stay in the saddle. At first Cecilia didn't understand what he meant, but then she remembered the time up on Kinnekulle when they were riding together for the first time and he stood up on his horse at full gallop. But he had his eyes on her and not on the road when his horse rode under a mighty oak branch. Arn had been swept to the ground and lay there lifeless.

"That time you almost made my heart stop beating," Cecilia whispered.

"That wasn't my intention," said Arn. "I wanted to win your heart, not stop it."

"By showing me what a rider you were? By standing up on a galloping horse you thought you could win my heart?"

"Yes, I did. And by doing whatever it took. If it had helped to stand on my head, I would have done that too. But it worked, didn't it?"

As he jested about courting her he raised himself on his arms in the saddle, slowly bent his body forward with his legs out to the side and finally placed them together as he stood on his hands in the saddle. All the while his stallion calmly continued on as if used to all manner of foolishness from his master.

"You don't have to show off like that," Cecilia giggled. "If I assure you that you have my heart as surely as if it were in a golden box, will you then sit down and ride properly?"

"Yes, in that case," said Arn, instantly spinning to sit in the saddle with both feet in the stirrups. "I feel I may be getting a bit too old for such tricks, so it's a good thing we're already man and wife."

"You must not belittle the goodness and divine will that have made us man and wife!" said Cecilia sternly, almost too sternly, she could hear. But she couldn't help thinking that such jesting went too far.

"I don't think that Our Lady will take it amiss that in our happiness we speak humorously about the time when our love first bloomed," Arn replied cautiously.

Cecilia scolded herself for unnecessarily bringing the fear of God into their conversation, when for once it had turned so carefree and playful. As she feared they now rode in silence, and neither of them could find a way out of it.

They came to a clearing by a stream where the moss shone magically green, welcoming the last light of day shining between the trees. Next to a thick and half-rotted oak the moss formed a big, inviting bed scattered with tiny pink woodland flowers.

It was as though Umm Anaza let herself be guided by Cecilia's thoughts, as if the mare had understood everything flowing through Cecilia's memory when she saw this spot, for she veered off without a word from Cecilia. In silence Cecilia dismounted and spread out her mantle over the green moss.

Arn followed, dismounted, and swung the reins around the forelegs of their horses before he came over to her and spread out his mantle next to hers.

They didn't need to say a word; everything was so clear between them, written on their faces.

When they kissed it was without fear, as if the difficult time after the wedding night had never happened. And when they both discovered their joy that the fear was gone, desire came back to them with the same power as when they were seventeen.

Chapter 8

A woman of the Folkung clan had been lamentably killed by her own husband and master. This heinous act occurred late one afternoon, and that evening the murderer saw the sun go down for the first time after committing his evil deed.

The name of this wicked man was Svante Sniving of the Ymse clan, and the name of his Folkung wife whom he had killed was Elin Germundsdotter from Älgarås. They had only one son, Bengt, who was thirteen years old.

After seeing his mother struck down by his father, young Bengt fled to the estate of his maternal grandfather, Germund Birgersson, at Älgarås. That same night, a summons was sent out from there in all directions to the Folkung estates within a day's ride.

It was daylight when the riders, who were young kinsmen clad in worn blue mantles, reached Forsvik. The unexpected guests were first offered bread, salt, and ale by Cecilia. They quickly quenched their thirst before explaining their errand, saying that they were carrying a Folkung summons for Sir Arn.

Cecilia said that she would quickly go in search of her husband, and she invited her guests to partake of ham and more ale while she was gone. Her heart pounding with alarm, she dashed toward the riding field where she could hear galloping horses. And there she found Arn along with the boys Sune and Sigfrid and the two Saracen horsemen. She waved urgently to Arn, who noticed her presence at once; he broke away from the other riders and raced across the field like the wind. He was riding Abu Anaza.

From a distance he'd already seen her agitation. When he reined in his horse and came to a stop, he dismounted at once and was at her side in one swift motion.

"A summons has arrived from the Folkungs," she replied to his wordless question.

"A summons from the Folkungs? What does that mean?" asked Arn, looking puzzled.

"Two young riders with solemn faces have arrived, saying only that they come bringing a summons," she replied. "I know no more than you do. Perhaps you should ask those boys over there."

Since Arn had no better suggestion, he did as Cecilia said and called over all four riders by whistling and uttering two loud shouts. They came at once, at full gallop, reining in their horses a few paces away.

"A summons has come from the Folkungs. Can either of you tell me what that might mean?" he asked Sune and Sigfrid.

"It means that all of us Folkung men at Forsvik must drop whatever we're doing at once, arm ourselves well, and go with whoever has brought the message," replied Sigfrid.

"No one in our clan can refuse a summons; that would mean eternal disgrace," added Sune.

"But you're only boys, and taking up arms doesn't sound like something that should be required of you," muttered Arn crossly.

"We are Folkungs all the same, young though we may be, and

the only two of our clan that you have with you here at Forsvik, Sir Arn," replied Sune jauntily.

Arn sighed and thought for a moment as he stared at the ground. Then he spoke, apparently delivering orders to the two Saracen horsemen, and pointed at the blue surcoats worn by the boys. The two warriors from the Holy Land immediately bowed their heads as a sign of obedience and galloped off toward the estate.

"Together let us seek out our kinsmen who have come with this message and find out what they want," said Arn. He walked over to Cecilia, pulled her up to sit in the saddle in front of him, and abruptly took off at a thundering speed for the old long-house. Cecilia alternated between shrieking and laughing during the short ride.

Inside the longhouse the two unknown kinsmen greeted Arn with a courteous bow as he came in. After a brief pause, one of them came over and fell to his knees; with arms outstretched, he held out the summons, which was in the form of a piece of wood with the Folkung lion burned into the surface.

"We hereby hand you, Sir Arn, your kinsmen's summons and ask you to follow us with all men that you are able to arm," said the young man.

Arn accepted the summons but didn't know what he was expected to do next. At that moment Sune and Sigfrid arrived, bowed solemnly to the two messengers, and then looked at Arn.

"I have been away in the Holy Land for many years, and hence I have no idea what you two are requesting of me," he said with some embarrassment to the messengers. "But if you tell me what this matter concerns, I will do what honor demands."

"It has to do with Svante Sniving. He's a man known for acting all too quickly, especially after drinking a great deal of ale. He beats the thralls and house servants, and even his own son," explained the other messenger, who thus far had not spoken.

"That does not speak well of Svante Sniving," replied Arn hesitantly. "But tell me what this matter has to do with me."

"Yesterday he killed his wife, Elin Germundsdotter, who was of our clan, and he has already seen the sun set once," explained the first messenger.

"A summons was sent out last night to all Folkungs who can reach Ymseborg before sundown tomorrow," clarified the other young kinsman.

"I think I understand now," said Arn, nodding. "What sort of resistance can we expect from Svante?"

"That's hard to know. He has twelve retainers, but we should be fifty men or more by tomorrow. But we must ride no later than tonight; preferably at once," replied the first man.

"We are only three Folkungs here at Forsvik, and two are mere boys. Can I take my retainers along with me?" asked Arn, and received eager nods in reply.

There was nothing more to ask or discuss. It took less than an hour to load up the packhorses and for Forsvik's five horsemen to dress for battle. The sun was still high in the sky when they rode off to the northwest.

It was shortly after the Feast of the Birth of the Virgin Mary, and the foliage in the woods gleamed red and gold. The nights had grown darker, which was good for the true believers, since their ninth month, the fasting month of Ramadan, had begun two days earlier. As they started off, Arn fretted about the exception to the Koran's laws, which stated that fasting need not apply during times of war. Yet this journey could hardly be considered war; as he understood it, they were merely headed to an execution.

He rode up alongside his Muslim companions and asked them candidly for their opinion. But they simply laughed, saying that there was nothing to worry about since it was the very beginning of the fasting month. Also, the weather was pleasantly cool and the sun had come to its senses so that it once again set in the evening. And, besides, they were forced to ride at a reduced speed because their two guides were so slow. Arn smiled and nodded in reply, thinking then that it was fortunate the fasting month had not occurred around Midsummer during the past few years. It would have been difficult for the Prophet's people to refrain from water and food from sunrise to sundown.

They continued riding for a hour after the sun disappeared and darkness descended, finally forcing them to make camp for the night. Ali and Mansour, who now rode with blue shirts on top of their leather-clad steel chain mail, gave no sign that they would have preferred to stop for food and drink as soon as the sun had set.

☩

The next day, when the sun was to go down for the third time since Svante Sniving's killing of a Folkung woman, five dozen riders had gathered outside Ymseborg. During the night the retainers up on the castle palisades had seen fires burning in all directions as a sign that escape was impossible. The estate's wooden gate was closed and up above perched four archers, anxiously gazing upon all the blue mantles that had gathered to confer less than a few arrow-shots away.

The leader of the Folkungs was Germund Birgersson, the father of the murdered Elin. At his side sat a grieving and bruised boy wearing a mantle that was half yellow and half black, which were the clan colors of Svante Sniving.

Arn had taken Ali and Mansour along for a short ride around the wooden fortress. They agreed that if required to take the castle, it could no doubt be easily accomplished with fire, but they wouldn't be able to simply ride through the wooden walls. And besides, Arn now realized that speed was essential, since everything had to be done by sundown.

When he returned to the group he went to talk to Germund Birgersson to find out more about what was planned. As far as he understood, the boy would inherit Ymseborg, so surely it would be unwise to burn it down.

Germund smiled grimly, saying that he didn't think it would be difficult to force open the gate. All he needed was for Arn, whose reputation had spread widely, also in this district, to help him persuade those who were standing guard. Arn replied that he had nothing against helping in any way he could.

"Good. You are a man of honor, and any other response would have greatly surprised me," grunted Germund Birgersson with satisfaction. With an effort he got to his feet, straightening the mantle around his shoulders. "Mount your horse and follow me; we'll soon take care of this minor hindrance!"

Somewhat puzzled, Arn went over to his horse, cinched the saddle tight, and rode up alongside Germund, who was now headed toward the gate of Ymseborg. None of the other Folkungs went with them.

They rode so close that they could easily have been struck by arrows, but no one chose to shoot at them.

The old Folkung chieftain cast a wily glance at Arn and rode even closer; Arn followed without hesitating, since hesitation is halfway to death.

"I am Germund Birgersson of the Folkung clan, and I come to Ymseborg for the sake of honor and not for war or plundering. I am mistress Elin's father, and I have come to demand my right, as have my kinsmen with me," said Germund in a loud and clear voice, almost as if he were singing his message.

No one up on the wooden wall replied, but neither did anyone reach out a hand to grab a weapon. Germund waited a moment before continuing.

"We would prefer not to harm Ymseborg, for the estate shall soon pass in inheritance to the young Bengt, who is our kinsman," he went on. "Hence this is what I now swear to you. We seek no man's death other than Svante's. We will not harm either buildings or thralls, nor house servants, nor any of the retainers; we do not intend to visit any sort of violence upon you once we have finished here. That is our vow if you open this gate in an hour's time and lay down your weapons. All of you will be in service to young Herr Bengt, or the one we choose to reside here as caretaker in his place. Your life here will continue as it was before. But if you should resist, I swear that not a single retainer among you will come through this alive. At my side is Arn Magnusson, and he makes the same vow to you!"

Then Germund slowly turned his horse around, and Arn followed, his expression grave, although he felt an unseemly mirth trying to force its way up inside him because someone had sworn death and destruction in his name with even asking his permission.

Not an arrow was shot at them; not a single jeer was heard.

"I have no doubt that we'll have this matter resolved by nightfall," said Germund Birgersson, groaning as he laboriously sank down at his former place in the encampment and reached toward the fire to pull out a piece of pork.

"What do we do with the bodies when we're done?" asked Arn.

"My daughter's body I will take with me to Älgarås for a Christian burial at the church nearby," said Germund. "Svante's body and his head we will stitch inside a cowhide and send to his kinsmen. Then we will choose a caretaker for Ymseborg, to reside here in young Bengt's place."

"What about the boy? It will be a sorrowful time ahead for him, after losing both his mother and father," said Arn.

"That's true. I shall do my utmost to see to it that young Bengt's life will be brighter from now on," said Germund pensively. "As young as he is, he still has the seed of a wastrel in his body. It is not his inclination to work the fields; instead he babbles on about knights and the king's retainers or service at Arnäs. All youths seem to be dreaming of such things these days."

"Yes," said Arn, his expression serious as he mused. "The young seem to set their sights more easily on swords and lances than on plows and flails. But you intend to shake that inclination out of him and turn him into a farmer?"

"I'm too old for such business," muttered Germund crossly at the thought that before the sun set he would have a thirteen-year-old boy foisted upon him, and he would have to try to turn the boy into a man.

Arn excused himself and went to seek out Sune and Sigfrid. He found both boys busy sharpening the tips of their arrows, their faces solemn. He took Sune's whetstone from him and showed him how the task could be done better as he told the boys about young Bengt's sorrowful fate. Not only was he without a mother, but he would soon be fatherless too, and then he would be forced to accompany old Germund home to become a farmer, as was the custom a hundred years ago. Perhaps, Arn mused aloud, it might not be such a foolish idea if Sune and Sigfrid stayed close to Bengt during the next few hours, since the three of them were the only retainers who were so young. And it would do no harm to tell Bengt a little about what they were learning at Forsvik.

Arn had a hard time concealing his smile as he abruptly stood up, leaving his two young squires behind.

An hour passed, and all the Folkungs mounted their horses and slowly rode toward the gate of Ymseborg, which opened before them as soon as they were within the distance of an arrowshot. They rode into the courtyard, lined up their horses, and waited. The place was deserted except for a few thrall children peering out from vents. A couple of maids dashed across the courtyard in alarm, looking for a stray child.

Silence descended over the estate; the only sound was the

snorting of the horses and the clattering of stirrups. No one spoke and nothing happened. They waited for a long time.

Finally Germund grew impatient and signaled to ten hale and hearty young men who dismounted, drew their swords, and went inside the longhouse. Soon shouts were heard, followed by a great commotion. A short time later they emerged along with Svante Sniving, whose hands and feet were bound. They forced him to his knees in front of the line of horsemen, where only one yellow and black mantle was visible among all the blue. That was young Bengt, his face expressionless, although the bruises from his father's fists could be seen from far away.

"I demand my right as a free yeoman in the land of the Goths and in accordance with the laws of the Goths!" shouted Svante Sniving, his voice slurred, indicating that he was no less drunk than usual, even though this would be the last time.

"Whoever kills a Folkung, man or woman, young or old, has no right but to live until the third sundown!" replied Germund Birgersson from where he sat on his horse.

"I offer double the man-price and will present my case before the *ting*!" Svante Sniving yelled in reply, as if he truly believed in his legal right.

"We Folkungs never accept a man-price, whether double or threefold, it means nothing to us," replied Germund with such contempt in his voice that laughter erupted from some of the stern-faced horsemen.

"Then I demand my right to God's judgment in single combat, the right to die as a free yeoman and not like a thrall!" shouted Svante, still with more fury than fear in his voice.

"To demand single combat will do you no good," snorted Germund Birgersson. "Among the kinsmen who have joined me in this matter is Arn Magnusson, here at my side. He would be the one to fight the duel for us. Then you would no doubt die faster than by the executioner's ax, though your honor would be no greater. Be glad that we don't hang you like a thrall; think now about the fact that your last honor in life is to die like a man without complaining or pissing!"

Germund Birgersson gave a signal, and several of the young men who had taken Svante Sniving from the longhouse brought forward a chopping block and ax. Germund silently pointed to the man who looked to be the strongest. Without hesitation he picked up the ax and the next moment Svante Sniving's head rolled out into the courtyard as two men held the twitching body pressed to the ground until the blood stopped gushing from the neck.

During this entire scene Arn kept a watchful eye on young Bengt's face. A slight flinching was noticeable as Arn heard the sound of the ax strike its blow, but nothing more. Not a tear, not even an attempt to make the sign of the cross.

Arn was not sure whether such a stony response was good or bad. But it was certain that this was a young man who above all hated his father.

The few things that still remained to do were quickly accomplished. Svante Sniving's body was dragged to the nearby slaughterhouse while another man followed, carrying his head; there both would be stitched inside a cowhide. In the meantime young Bengt dismounted from his horse and slowly walked over to the place where his father's blood was still trickling quietly in the oblique evening light.

He took off his mantle and dragged it along the ground through the blood.

The Folkungs sat on their horses, their faces expressionless as they watched the young man whose courage and honor were worthy of admiration. Germund Birgersson signaled to Arn to dismount and follow him as he went over to the boy.

Germund approached slowly until he stood behind young Bengt and placed his left hand on the boy's left shoulder. After a brief glance from Germund, Arn did the same with his right hand. They waited for a moment in silence while young Bengt seemed to gather courage for what he wanted to say. It was not easy, because he clearly wanted to speak in a firm and resolute voice.

"I, Bengt, son of Svante Sniving and Elin Germundsdotter, in the presence of my kinsmen, now take the name Bengt Elinsson!" he shouted at last, managing to say the words without any sign of quavering or uncertainty.

"I, Germund Birgersson, and my kinsman Arn Magnusson," replied Germund, "take you as one of our clan. You are now a Folkung and a Folkung you shall remain for all eternity. You are always one of us, and we will always be with you."

In the silence that followed, Germund nodded to Arn to continue. But Arn didn't know what to do or say until Germund leaned toward him and explained in an angry whisper. Arn then took off his blue mantle and wrapped it around young Bengt, and all of the horsemen drew their swords and pointed first toward the sky and then toward Bengt.

By swearing an oath of blood, Bengt Elinsson had been accepted into the Folkung clan. At Ymseborg, which now belonged to the boy, his maternal grandfather chose two caretakers to manage his inheritance. For Bengt had no desire to stay at Ymseborg for even one more day.

But what he did want was something that his grandfather soon learned as they rode away from the estate. All the Folkungs were then to take their leave at the encampment. With fervent zeal Bengt begged to go to Forsvik with Arn Magnusson, for he had heard from the two other young kinsmen who had come with Arn about all the wonders that were taking place there.

Germund thought that for once it might be best to make a quick decision. Young Bengt truly needed something else to think about, and the sooner the better. To ride to Älgarås for the funeral and week of mourning might be what honor demanded, at least of an older man. But a boy who in less than three days had lost both his mother and father could not be treated in the same way as others.

Germund went over to Arn Magnusson, who was speaking in a foreign tongue with his retainers, and he asked outright whether Arn might be able to comply with what the young and newly fledged Folkung so clearly wished. Arn didn't seem fazed in the least by this question, and he replied that it could be easily done.

And so it was that the three Folkungs who had left Forsvik in order to avenge the honor of their clan now returned with a fourth.

✠

During the first mild weeks of autumn a sense of order descended upon Forsvik so that not even Cecilia's stern vigilance noticed anything different. Every day boatloads arrived with winter fodder, which was stored in the barns and haystacks. From Arnäs dried fish from Lofoten began arriving in great quantities, which showed that Harald Øysteinsson had made a successful second trip with the great ship of the Templar knights.

With the third load of dried fish, new thralls arrived that Arn had requested from Eskil. They included Suom, who was so skilled at weaving, and her son Gure, who was said to be particularly proficient with anything that was to be made of wood. The hunter Kol and his son Svarte also came along.

For many reasons Arn and Cecilia had looked forward to the arrival of these thralls, and they welcomed them almost as if they were guests. Cecilia took Suom by the arm to show her the weaving room that was almost finished while Arn took the three men to the thralls' quarters to find space for them. But he soon realized that what he could offer them was much too paltry for the coming winter, and thus he ordered Gure to start his work at Forsvik by repairing the worst of the thrall lodgings. And when he was done with that, he should begin building new quarters.

Gure was given a work team of four thralls, whom he was to supervise according to his own wishes. If he needed new tools, he could simply go to the smithies and ask for them.

At first Arn wanted to give Kol and his son Svarte lodgings in the old longhouse. But they said they would rather live in the simplest of hovels, since they were used to keeping to themselves and hunters went out at different hours than workers.

Arn thought he remembered Kol from his youth, but he had to ask several times before this was confirmed. They had hunted together when Arn was seventeen and Kol was apprenticed to his father, who was named Svarte, like Kol's son. The old Svarte had died by now and was buried near the thralls' farm at Arnäs. That was why it had been easier to sell Kol and his son to Arn. At Arnäs it was not viewed favorably to leave old and feeble thralls without kin.

After these explanations, Arn refrained from asking any questions about the boy's mother. He was still not accustomed to the fact that he was the owner of human beings. From the age of five he had lived among monks and Templar knights, for whom the very idea of slavery was an abomination. He promised himself to speak with Cecilia about this matter as soon as possible.

He told Kol that the first thing of importance was to see to it that he and his son had horses and saddles so that they could make a survey of the region and find the best hunting areas. Kol and Svarte, whether morose by nature or dumbstruck with embarrassment, followed Arn over to the horse pastures. There Arn put halters on two horses that he chose for their calm nature rather than for speed and impetuous temperament.

Until the hunters became accustomed to their horses, the animals would be kept in the stable to rest instead of being released into the pastures with the others. Otherwise it would be difficult to catch them again, Arn warned as they led the horses up toward the estate.

Arn was pleased to see that Kol was overjoyed to see these horses, and he spoke eagerly with his son in the thralls' language as he gestured toward the necks and legs of the steeds. Arn couldn't resist asking Kol what he was telling his son. He learned that it was just such a horse that Sir Arn himself had once, long ago, brought to Arnäs, and all the servants had thought the animal a miserable beast. Even Kol and his father had foolishly believed the same until they saw Sir Arn ride the horse that was called Kamil or some such name.

"Shimal," Arn corrected him. "It means 'north' in the language of the land where these horses come from. But tell me, Kol, where do you come from?"

"I was born at Arnäs," replied Kol in a low voice.

"But what of your father, with whom I also hunted. Where was he from?"

"From Novgorod on the other side of the Eastern Sea," said Kol, sounding sullen.

"And the other thralls at Arnäs, where do they or their ancestors come from?" Arn persisted, even though he could see that Kol would have preferred to avoid any further questions on the subject.

"All of us come from across the sea," replied Kol reluctantly. "Some of us know this to be true; others merely believe it is so. Some say from the Byzantine Empire, other say Russia or Poland, Estonia or even the Abbasid Caliphate. There are many sagas but little knowledge about this. Some think that our fathers and mothers were once taken captive in war. Others believe that we have always been thralls, but I don't agree."

Arn remained silent. He stopped himself from saying at once

that Kol and his son would now be free men; he needed to think about the matter first and discuss it with Cecilia. He didn't ask any more uncomfortable questions, merely told Kol and his son to spend time getting to know the area and not to do any hunting unless the opportunity to shoot some animal happened by chance. But he assumed that right now the important thing was to find out where the hunting would be best.

Without speaking Kol nodded his agreement, and then they parted.

⁜

Arn had planned to say something to Cecilia about his concern regarding ownership of thralls during their journey to Bjälbo, where they were to attend the betrothal ale for their son Magnus and the Sverker daughter Ingrid Ylva.

But Cecilia had apparently also planned to use this journey, in particular the first idle hours on the ship crossing Lake Vättern, for a conversation that required both time and consideration. As soon as the ship left shore, she spoke at length and without stopping about the old weaver Suom and the almost miraculous skill that this woman possessed in her hands. As Cecilia had requested, Eskil had sent along a heavy bundle of tapestries that Suom had made; previously they had hung on the walls at Arnäs. A number of them Arn had already seen, since Cecilia had adorned the walls of their bedchamber with Suom's work.

Arn murmured that some of the images were much too strange for his taste, especially the ones that purportedly depicted Jerusalem with streets of gold and Saracens with horns on the foreheads. Such images were not true, and he could attest to this better than most people.

Cecilia seemed a bit offended by his comment and said that the beauty of the images was not simply a matter of truth; it had as much to do with how the colors were put together and the ideas and visions that the pictures conjured up if beautifully done. In this manner the conversation veered a bit from what she had intended to discuss, and they ended up quarreling.

Arn moved forward to the bow of the ship to see to their horses for a while and to speak to Sune and Sigfrid. The boys had been allowed to come along to tend to the horses even though they no doubt regarded themselves more as Sir Arn's retainers. When Arn rejoined Cecilia, she spoke at once about the matter she wanted to discuss.

"I want to free Suom and her son Gure," she said quickly, her eyes fixed on the planks at the bottom of the ship.

"Why? Why Suom and Gure?" Arn asked with curiosity.

"Because her work has great value that will produce silver many times the worth of a thrall," replied Cecilia at once, without looking at Arn.

"You can free anyone you like at Forsvik," said Arn. "Forsvik belongs to you, and therefore all the thralls are yours as well. But I would like to free Kol and his son Svarte."

"Why those particular hunters?" she asked, surprised that the discussion had already moved past the initial hurdle.

"Let's say that Kol and his son bring home eight stags during this first winter," replied Arn. "That will not only make our meals less monotonous, but it's more than the value of a thrall, and in only one winter. But the same can be said of every thrall. They all bring in more than their own worth."

"Is there something else you wish to say?" asked Cecilia, giving him a searching glance.

"Yes," he said. "It's a matter that I have been saving to discuss during this journey—"

"I thought as much!" she interrupted him, looking pleased. Then she clapped her hand over her mouth to show that she had no intention of saying more until Arn had finished.

"God did not create any man or woman to be a thrall; that is how I view it," Arn went on. "Where in the Holy Scriptures does it say that such should be the case? You and I have both lived in that part of the world, behind walls, where thralldom would be unthinkable. I imagine that we think alike regarding this matter."

"Yes, I think we do," said Cecilia solemnly. "But what I can't decide is whether I am wrong or whether all of our kinsmen are mistaken. Not even the thralls believe otherwise; they think that God created some of us to be masters and others to be thralls."

"Many of the thralls don't even believe in God," remarked Arn. "But I have had the same thought that you mention. Am I the one who is wrong? Or am I so much wiser and better than all of our kinsmen? Even Birger Brosa and Eskil?"

"Yes," she said. "You and I are in agreement about this matter."

"But if we do indeed agree, then what should we do?" Arn mused. "If we were to free all the thralls at Forsvik tomorrow, so that no one was allowed to own thralls anymore, what would happen then?"

At first Cecilia had no answer. She sat for a while, leaning her chin on her hand and pondering the matter. It occurred to her that the easy part was to forswear the sin, but the hard part was to clear up the confusion that might then arise.

"Wages," said Arn at last. "We free all of them, let's say sometime in midwinter so that cold will keep them sensible and they won't go running off in all directions with their freedom. Then we will institute wages. At the start of each year every thrall, I mean every man and woman, will receive a certain amount of silver coins. Another possibility, which my blessed mother Sigrid employed, was to allow freed men to work new fields and pay a tenant's fee each year. I suggest that we try to proceed along both these paths."

"But so much in wages would mean heavy expenses for us in pure silver," sighed Cecilia. "And here I was just beginning to see brighter prospects when it comes to our account books."

"He who gives alms to the poor performs a deed that pleases God, even when his silver pouch grows lighter," said Arn as he brooded. "It is the righteous thing to do, and you and I wish to live a righteous life. That alone is reason enough. Another reason is that those tenants that my mother freed from Arnäs worked harder. Without costing us any winter fodder, they increased our wealth. What if freed men always work harder than thralls, what if it would be good business to free them?"

"In that case, our thrall-owning kinsmen are not merely sinners, but also short-sighted," laughed Cecilia. "I can see that we both share a certain arrogance in thinking these thoughts, my dear Arn."

"We'll see about that," said Arn. "But you and I wish to cleanse ourselves of a sin, so let's do it! Whether the Lord will reward us or not, it is not our concern. And if we find it costly in terms of silver, then so be it. We can afford it. So let's try!"

"Yes, and we'll wait until midwinter so they don't go running off like chickens when they are freed," said Cecilia with a smile, as if picturing all the tumult that would then occur at Forsvik.

⚜

When they reached Bjälbo, Birger Brosa's estate, Arn and Cecilia were not as well received as they had hoped. When they rode in among the welcoming fires outside the church, they were received by house thralls who showed them into one of the guest houses, as if they were supposed to share lodgings with their retainers. They had not brought a large retinue with them, just the boys Sune and Sigfrid, who may have pictured themselves as offering protection to their master and mistress, but others saw them merely as boys.

This was one of the few things that Birger Brosa himself mentioned in a brief conversation with Arn. He said that it was not befitting for a Folkung to ride without retainers, especially since the Sverkers at this banquet might take it as an insult.

Ingrid Ylva's father was also cold in tone and handshake when he greeted Arn. Sune Sik said only a few words about the fact that the blood between them could not be washed away until after the bridal ale.

A grim mood reigned over the high seat since neither Birger Brosa nor his wife Brigida was willing to speak a single kind word to Arn or Cecilia, and the mood spread throughout the hall. As a betrothal feast, this gathering at Bjälbo was not going to be remembered as festive.

On all three evenings Arn and Cecilia withdrew as early as possible without offending the honor of their host. They barely had a chance to speak to their son Magnus or his future wife Ingrid Ylva, since the betrothal seats, decorated with leafy boughs, were far from the high seat.

They didn't stay even an hour longer than the three days that custom dictated.

Nor did Arn find the situation much better when they arrived at Ulfshem, the next estate they were to visit and the home of Cecilia's dear friend Ulvhilde Emundsdotter. It was in a beautiful location between Bjälbo and Linköping. There was wine for Arn and Cecilia, who both preferred not to partake of all the ale-drinking, and the meat that was served was tender. But there was a shadow between Arn and Ulvhilde that would not recede, and everyone saw it, although no one said a word.

And Ulvhilde's husband, Jon, who was more inclined to the law than the sword, had a hard time carrying on any sort of sensible conversation with Arn, since he assumed that Arn was a man who understood nothing but war. Arn constantly felt as if Jon were addressing a halfwit or a child.

For his part, Jon found it difficult to see his young sons Birger and Emund watching Arn with their eyes bright with admiration. In one sense the situation improved, though in another sense it did not, when Arn suggested that the young Sune and Sigfrid join Jon's sons outdoors rather than be forced to keep the older people company. The boys obediently retreated, but soon the clanging of weapons was heard from out in the courtyard, which didn't surprise Arn, though it clearly annoyed Jon.

On the second evening, which was to be their last at Ulfshem, Arn and Cecilia, Jon and Ulvhilde were sitting at the long hearth in the great hall. It was as if the two women discovered too late that while they had a thousand things to discuss, their husbands were less pleased with each other's company. On this evening the conversation also seemed sluggish, and the topics were inoffensive matters that would not lead to anyone's discomfort.

Arn was fairly certain what lay at the bottom of this dark lake, and at the beginning of the evening he was determined to leave it alone. But when the first few hours had crawled by with dreary talk, too many silences, and not a single laugh, he decided it was more difficult to carry on in this way than to lance the boil.

"Let's speak of the matter that lies between us, since it will not get any better if we pretend it's not there," said Arn in the middle of a discussion about the mild autumn they were now enjoying compared to the severe cold of the previous year.

At first there was utter silence so that only the crackling of the fire was heard.

"You mean my father Emund Ulvbane," said Ulvhilde at last. "Yes, it would be better to speak of him now rather than later. I was only a child when he was so treacherously killed, and perhaps what I know of the matter is not the whole truth. Cecilia

Rosa is my dearest friend, you are her husband, and between us there should be no lies. Tell me what happened!"

"Your father Emund was King Sverker's greatest and most loyal warrior," began Arn after taking a deep breath. "It was said that no man could defeat him. At the *ting* of all Goths at Axvalla, he offended my father Magnus so deeply that honor demanded a duel between the two, or with the son taking the father's place, as the law provides. My father has never been a swordsman and could expect a certain death at Emund's hands. He called for a priest, gave his confession, and said farewell to his kinsmen. But I fought against Emund in my father's place. I was only seventeen and had no desire to kill anyone. I did all in my power, and twice I offered your father the chance to withdraw from the duel when he was at a disadvantage. But it did no good. In the end I thought the only thing to do was to wound him so badly that he would have to yield, but with his honor still intact. Today I might have managed things better, but at the time I was too young."

"So you were not present when Knut Eriksson killed my father at Forsvik?" asked Ulvhilde after a long silence.

"No," said Arn. "My brother Eskil was there, but his only task was to handle the terms of the transaction when we purchased Forsvik from your father. Once the purchase was made and sealed, Eskil rode home to Arnäs. Knut stayed behind for revenge."

"For what purpose did he seek revenge upon my father?" asked Ulvhilde in surprise, as if she had never heard even a whisper about this matter before.

"It was said that Emund was the one who had chopped off the head of Knut's father, Saint Erik," replied Arn. "I do not know if that was true, but Knut was convinced of it. And so he killed Emund in the same manner as his own father had been killed."

"And yet Emund could no longer defend himself, since he had

only one hand, and you were to blame for that!" exclaimed Jon, as if to defend Ulvhilde.

"What you say is true," replied Arn in a low voice. "But when it comes to blood revenge in our land, I have learned that one hand or two, it makes little difference."

"Killings are to be taken up at the *ting* and should not lead to more killings!" replied Jon.

"That may be what the law says," admitted Arn, "but when it comes to the killing of a king, no laws apply; then it's the right of the strongest. And you are a Folkung, as I am, so surely you know that the killing of a Folkung is never a matter for the *ting*."

"That sort of justice is no justice at all!" declared Jon.

No one had anything to say against him in this matter. But after Ulvhilde had sat in silence for a while, she got up and solemnly went over to Arn. She took his sword-hand and pressed it to her lips, kissing it three times. That was the sign of reconciliation, according to ancient custom.

The evening did not get any merrier after that; there was no jesting or loud laughter. But it still felt as if the air had been cleared between them, as when the sun is about to reappear after a thunderstorm on a hot day in late summer.

And with that, Arn's first visit to Ulfshem did not end as badly as it had begun. And the enticement that he knew Sune and Sigfrid represented for all boys of their age also had its effect. After the visit Ulvhilde and Jon had no peace from their youngest son Emund, who tirelessly nagged them about going to his mother's ancestral estate of Forsvik. That he didn't intend to make a similar pilgrimage to his father's land was as clear as water. He had been infected with the dream of becoming a knight. And in the end his parents promised that he would be allowed to go as soon as he turned thirteen.

✠

Upon returning to Forsvik, Arn and Cecilia found that the estate had by no means suffered because the master and mistress had been gone for ten days. The newly purchased thrall named Gure had found many helping hands among the other thralls to repair their living quarters. And with the smiths, the fletchers, the potters, and the feltmakers the work was proceeding apace and without quarrel. Since it was nearly all foreigners engaged in these tasks, and all the crops had been harvested except for the turnips, there were many thralls available to work with Gure. He was a great asset to Forsvik, and the others were quick to obey his slightest command, as if he were their master and not their equal.

The Wachtian brothers had taken turns making lists of all the new goods that had come in, and they delivered these lists to Cecilia's accounting chamber so that she simply had to enter the items in her ledger books. The brothers were also eager to take Arn and Cecilia to the millhouse to show them a new tool they had built.

Jacob was the one who always came up with the first designs and ideas. Then Marcus went to the smithy and shaped these ideas into iron and steel.

The question that had long preoccupied them was how the water power might be used for a saw. Since the power consisted of a water wheel that turned axles, it had proved unfeasible to transform the circular motion into the type of back-and-forth motion used when sawing by hand. So then they had asked themselves whether they ought to concentrate on the rotating motion, and in the end they had created a saw that was round. They finally found a way to make the saw blade spin evenly without warping and with a cutting edge that could withstand the heat from the rotation. But then new problems arose. It turned out to be impossible to press a log by hand against the saw blade, since the force was too great. For this reason, they had built a sled that moved along the floor and carried the logs toward the blade. But the floor was uneven; when they solved that problem other difficulties appeared.

Now they thought it was ready, so they called for help from Gure and his work team. And in a very short time, before the childishly delighted Arn, they sawed a log into four boards, like the planking at the bottom of a ship.

When Cecilia asked them what the planks were for, they told her they were meant to be floorboards. Floors for the stone house at Arnäs was what they first planned. But perhaps also for here at Forsvik, since the rough-hewn logs that they were now using were not the best. But that could be decided later on. First it was a matter of putting in a good store of planks so they would dry over the winter and next summer; then they would see if the boards were actually an improvement over the old method. The amount of work hours would be only a tenth if they compared making a floor from these sawed timbers with using hewn limestone.

And this was only the first of many saws they wanted to make. When they dug a canal with new water wheels, they would be able to make more circular saws, both big and small. And the brothers claimed that it would save much time and make it possible to saw more timber than merely for their own needs.

Arn pounded them heartily on the back and said that such new ideas and tools were like gold for the estate, but also for those who had thought of them.

The following week Arn, along with Ali and Mansour, spent every morning teaching the three boys to ride. The afternoons were then devoted to archery and swordsmanship. At first Arn practiced several hours on his own and then with his three young warriors.

He had the smithies make several swords with dull blades that he let the boys wield almost as if they were real swords. Even though the weapons lacked real blades, they felt quite real in the hands of Sune, Sigfrid, and Bengt. Arn tested them until he judged that each boy had a practice sword of the proper heft since the strength of their arms varied. He also had chain mail made for them, which Cecilia found more childish than sensible, since surely no one would expect such young boys to go to war.

A bit offended, Arn had explained that such was not his intention, but he wanted them to become accustomed to moving in this heavy armor. When she insisted that they would soon grow too big for these costly trappings, he assured her that other boys would follow these three in learning the same skills. With time, Forsvik would have armor and practice weapons of every size, suitable for any age between thirteen and a full-grown man.

This gave Cecilia much to ponder. She had taken it for granted that it was out of kindness and Arn's inability to refuse that these boys had ended up at Forsvik; not because of his own wishes but rather because of their importunate entreaties. As if he were merely doing a favor for his young kinsmen.

But now she envisioned rows of chain mail and swords hanging like saddles in the stable with numbers written above. There was something menacing about the image, mostly because she didn't truly understand what she saw.

Arn was unaware of the puzzled distress that Cecilia felt, since he was busy brooding over how he should best train such young boys to handle weapons. His first mistake was to allow them to practice with each other after they had been given their chain mail. They set upon each other at once with great ferocity and wildness. Bengt Elinsson, in particular, fought with a fury that was almost frightening to behold, not only because Sune and Sigfrid both had bruises on their arms and legs, but more because of the hatred that Arn thought he could discern in the boy's heart.

Arn soon altered the sword exercises so that they struck at a post instead of each other. He set logs on end and with an ax made four marks in each post to represent the head, upper arm, knee, and foot of an opponent. Then he showed the boys the most common exercises and pointed to the various spots on his own body that might be injured by too much practice. In that instance, it would be best to stop. It didn't surprise him that Bengt Elinsson was the one who ignored the initial warnings that his body gave him and instead continued for so long that he made himself sick and reluctantly had to put down his sword and rest for a week.

Sooner or later, of course, they would have to practice fighting each other, but before that time, Arn planned to devise better protection for the head, hands, and cheeks. Pain during practice was fine, since it promoted a necessary respect for the opponent's sword. But if the young apprentices suffered too much pain and too many wounds, it might lead to fear. Perhaps things would be better when Brother Guilbert came to Forsvik during the winter, Arn thought, consoling himself. For Brother Guilbert had truly made a knight of Arn, and the ability to teach was now considered invaluable at Forsvik.

Thinking about Brother Guilbert also aroused feelings of guilt in Arn. For three months he had left Brother Guilbert to tend to the hard work of assisting the Saracen stonemasons at Arnäs. Yet Arn had not visited them even once, nor had he sent any words of encouragement.

He was ashamed by this sudden insight and set off for Arnäs at once with Abu Anaza, taking the direct route through the woods and across fields. By doing so he arrived by early evening on the same day he had left Forsvik.

When he saw his Saracen brothers toiling with the stone at Arnäs, his eyes filled with tears as he noticed that their clothes hung in rags and sweat glistened on foreheads and bare arms. Even the robe of a lay brother worn by Brother Guilbert had been ripped to shreds by many sharp stone edges and were so filthy with mortar that he too looked more like a thrall than a monk.

No matter how much Arn felt ashamed by his thoughtlessness,

he couldn't help riding around the walls to see what had been accomplished. And what he saw matched in every stone and line all his greatest hopes and dreams; in some cases even far exceeding what he had envisioned.

The shortest section of the wall facing Lake Vänern and the harbor was now done, with both corners protected by round towers projecting past the exterior. Above the gaping space of the portal facing the harbor loomed a rectangular tower, and they had finished building twenty paces of the longest part of the wall, the one extending west to east. Accomplishing so much in only a few months and with so few hands would have overwhelmed Saladin himself, thought Arn. This was in truth the beginning of an impregnable fortress.

He was torn from his dreams and brought back to his guilty conscience when the builders discovered his presence. He rode over to meet them, gesturing them forward with both hands. Then he dismounted from his horse and fell to his knees before them. They were all so surprised that none of them said a word.

"Brothers of the faith!" he said as he stood up and bowed. "Great is the work that you have done, and just as great is my debt to you. Great too has been my neglect, leaving you here as if you were slaves. But I must tell you that I have been working just as hard to see to it that you will be able to endure our hellish Nordic winter. I invite you now to finish this hard work before winter arrives, and two days from now, when you are ready, you will journey with me to the winter quarters where you will rest. The month of fasting will soon be over, and we shall celebrate together; it will be a memorable feast. One more thing I will tell you. I came to see you who are doing the building before I even sought out my kinsmen here at Arnäs!"

When he was done speaking, the Saracens still remained silent, glancing at each other with expressions that showed more surprise than joy upon hearing that their hard work was about to come to such an abrupt halt. Arn went over to Brother Guilbert and embraced him for a long time without saying a word.

"If you don't let go of me soon, little brother, you will bring shame upon us both, in the eyes of these believers, as you call them," grunted Brother Guilbert at last.

"Forgive me, brother," said Arn. "I can only say the same to you as I said to the Saracens, that I have labored hard and without interruption to ensure a good winter for all of us. I am sorry to see how much all of you have suffered here."

"Most of us have doubtless endured worse things than building with stone in cool weather," muttered Brother Guilbert. He was not used to seeing the full-grown Arn so easily moved.

"Perhaps we can leave here in a day's time instead of two!" said Arn, his face brightening. "What needs to be done in order to secure the building site for the winter?"

"Not very much," replied Brother Guilbert. "We've tried to arrange the construction with a thought to the coming winter. Or rather, that's what I have done. These friends of ours have no idea what cold, ice, and frost can do to a structure. We've been careful to seal it from the top, but much of the masonry is wet."

"What if we use hides to cover the top?" suggested Arn.

"Yes, that would probably be best," replied Brother Guilbert with a nod. "Do you think you could obtain lead in the spring?"

"Lead?" repeated Arn, looking puzzled. "Yes, but perhaps not in large amounts. What will you need lead for?"

"The joints at the very top," replied Brother Guilbert, taking in a deep breath. "Just picture us pouring molten lead from the top and down along every joint that's exposed to the open air. Does that help you understand what I have in mind?"

"Yes," said Arn, nodding. "If we could apply lead to the joints at the very top, then no water would run down . . . or ice. That's a good idea. I'll try to procure the lead that you need. But tell me instead that you are well and that your body doesn't ache more than it should after laboring so hard and that you forgive me for leaving you here."

"I'll wait with that until I've seen my winter quarters and had my first bite of ham, because during the month of fasting, there hasn't been much of that here," said Brother Guilbert with a laugh. And he gave Arn a shake, as had been his custom when he chastised his young apprentice at Varnhem.

"But surely Ramadan doesn't apply to you," said Arn, opening his eyes wide. "Because you haven't—?"

"By no means!" replied Brother Guilbert, cutting off the question before it might sound offensive. "But if I am to work with these unbelievers, I've found it best to fast along with them. That way there is no chance of any grumbling."

"No food between sunrise and sundown?" mused Arn. "And at the same time doing such hard work. How do you manage it?"

"A man just gets fat from all that eating," muttered Brother Guilbert, feigning ill humor. "And we spend the first hours of work pissing away all the water that we've drunk. Then we eat like genies as soon as the sun sets. We eat for hours, and it's fortunate that we don't wash down all that mutton with wine."

While Brother Guilbert took the Saracen builders with him to strike camp, Arn rode over to Arnäs and immediately found those he was looking for. Eskil and his son Torgils were sitting in the accounting room of the big tower. His father, Magnus, was up in the highest chamber with the physician Yussuf. They gave Arn a hearty welcome, and all three of his kinsmen began talking at the same time about the new construction work, which they wanted to show him at once. Arn didn't need any persuading.

They had to climb a bit over the scaffolding to reach the area where the work was being done, since the new walls were almost twice as high as the old ones. Up there they were able to proceed a short distance along the machicolations where all the arrow loops were built so that they were wide on the inside but only a narrow slit on the outside. Anyone could clearly understand the reason for this without any explanations from Arn. A man standing at the arrow slit could aim his bow or cross-bow with a good view in all directions, while anyone standing below on the other side of the moat would have a hard time shooting an arrow through the narrow opening that was visible from the outside.

But there were other things that did require explanations from Arn. The tower located above the great gate facing the lake jutted out from the wall. That was so that archers could shoot from there along the wall if the enemy attempted to raise scaling ladders.

But it would be difficult to raise such ladders around the gate tower here since the walls were twice as thick at the bottom as up near the machicolation. There were two reasons for constructing the walls with that sort of incline, Arn explained. If anyone tried to raise a scaling ladder, they would have to be long and sturdy or they would break in half as soon as the besiegers started to climb up. And the heavier the ladders, the harder it would be to position them quickly and with any degree of surprise.

The other reason for the sloping wall at this particular location near the harbor was that the enemy would encounter a more slippery foothold on the ice in the winter. If the enemy tried to use battering rams, he would have to hoist them up, and build a big sort of cradle where the ram could be swung back and forth. Because if he just struck against the slanting base of the wall, he wouldn't produce much result for all the trouble. But to build scaffolding for battering rams was no simple matter, since such work could not be done without meeting resistance from the defenders up on the walls and in the gate tower.

The entrance from the harbor was high up and in the middle of the tower, creating a small archway. There Arn showed his kinsmen how the gate itself would be constructed, first with a wrought-iron portcullis that could be lowered from inside the tower. That could be accomplished in a few minutes if an attack came quickly and suddenly. Afterward the drawbridge made of heavy oak would be raised so that it fit securely on the outside of the iron portcullis. The gates were always the weak points of a stronghold; that was why this gate was so high above the ground that it would be difficult to reach it with battering rams and other siege engines. Especially since anyone who attempted such an attack would be exposed to a constant barrage of arrows from the two corner towers. They would also have all sorts of things dumped upon them from the highest battlements of the gate tower.

For the time being it was still possible to walk a short distance from the two corner towers in the direction where the walls would eventually be constructed. Standing up there and looking at the site where the building was due to commence, it was easy to picture how it would look when everything was finished. At that time a mightier fortress would not be found in the entire kingdom.

Arn asked to have as many of the untanned hides as they could find to cover the tops of the walls and the machicolations for the winter. Both his father Magnus and Eskil said at once, and almost reckless in their swift response, that whatever he wanted they would readily agree to, provided it was something within their power to grant. For by now they had both doubtless realized what a new era was dawning with all this construction, a time when no power would be greater than that possessed by the Folkungs. In the midst of this lively and spirited discussion, Herr Magnus happened to mention that Birger Brosa would soon be coming to Arnäs to hold a *ting* for the clan.

The mood turned gloomy at once. Birger Brosa had specifically commanded that Arn Magnusson not be invited to this *ting*, since both his father and elder brother could speak on his behalf. There was nothing to be done about this. Birger Brosa was the leader of the Folkungs and the jarl of the realm. Whatever his command, it must be obeyed.

But at the banquet that evening, there was no sense of gloom, since there were a thousand things to talk about regarding the construction going on at Arnäs, as well as what Arn was accomplishing at Forsvik. By now both Eskil and Herr Magnus were aware that Forsvik was becoming the other support in the power structure of the Folkungs.

They had been discussing all these plans for the future only a short time when young Torgils reminded them of the promise that he would enter an apprenticeship at Forsvik. Arn replied tersely that as far as he was concerned, Torgils was welcome at any time. Torgils said that he wanted to leave at once. Eskil was clearly not happy with this decision, but he offered no objections.

Before Arn and his party boarded the ship that would take them up Lake Vänern to the reloading area for riverboats, he had a brief private conversation with the physician Yussuf. It was then decided that Yussuf would also accompany all of the Saracens to Forsvik; Ibrahim had already left with the first group of foreigners. For to be left here at Arnäs over the winter and to witness the dreadful gorging on pork, which was part of the Christmas celebrations, was not a welcome reward for a lone Muslim. Arn was fully aware of this, even though he didn't speak of it aloud. His father Magnus was now in such good condition that he no longer needed daily care. In spite of this, Arn still took his father aside to repeat in a courteous but firm manner everything that Yussuf had told him to do. Each day his father had to make sure to move about, not too much and not too little, but without neglecting a single day. In addition, he was to eat less pork and more salmon and veal, and he should drink wine instead of ale when the Christmas festivities began.

Herr Magnus muttered that he would have been able to think

of all this himself. It was a sad but well-known fact that Christmas ale presented a danger to all men of his age.

✠

During the time that Arn was away at Arnäs, Cecilia had grown even more bewildered by the foreigners at Forsvik. At night there was a great deal of commotion evident inside their longhouse, and from the smell of meat roasting and bread baking, it was clear to everyone that constant feasting was going on. They disdained the bread to be found at Forsvik after the great baking that took place every autumn. Instead, they had built from clay their own ovens, which looked like big upside-down wasps' nests. Every evening they baked their own bread shaped in big flat sheets. They got up late in the morning, and only slowly did they begin their work.

Cecilia could only guess at what this all meant, and she was inclined to think that it was Arn's absence that had encouraged this sort of idleness from the foreigners. Although this was not true of all of them. The brothers Marcus and Jacob worked just as diligently as always, as did the two English fletchers, John and Athelsten. She had long considered asking Arn about this and other matters that she hadn't really been able to understand. But the long winter nights seemed far away, in more than one sense. She had imagined that when the north wind whistled around the corners of the house, they would lie close together in front of the fire, and he would tell her about the many wondrous and horrible things in the Holy Land, and answer all her questions.

Ever since the time when they had gone out riding alone and Our Lady had gently shown them again the joyful rights of the flesh which they had once misused but were now fully entitled to, their nights had been so delightful that Cecilia blushed to even think of them. And so there had been very little time for talk of serious matters in their bedchamber.

When Arn returned on the river, it turned out that he had brought not only young Torgils along with him but also more foreigners, including all the stonemasons from Arnäs. They looked so wretched in their tattered clothes, but they seemed to have other and better clothing packed in big bundles. They had broken camp at Arnäs and were going to spend the winter at Forsvik. Cecilia was a bit miffed that she hadn't been told of this in advance, since she assumed that if this many free men came to Forsvik, they should be treated as guests. She grew almost angry when, with much laughter and shaking of heads, they all declined her attempts to welcome them with salt, ale, and bread. It was truly not the custom in Western Götaland to refuse such a greeting.

She was all the more puzzled on that first night after the new foreigners arrived to hear an ever greater commotion coming from the foreigners' house. Arn replied curtly to her questions, saying that it was a celebration called Laylat al-Qadr, which meant "the power of the night." She had then innocently asked what sort of power this meant, and she went cold inside upon hearing that it was a celebration of Muhammed's first vision.

Arn didn't even notice her stony reaction. Grumbling sleepily, he had shown a greater interest in the joys of fleshly love than in anything else. And since he had already displayed such an inclination, she couldn't very well jump out of bed to stamp her foot and say that right now she'd rather have a discussion about Muhammed. Instead, she soon found herself floating into his warm stream, and she forgot all else.

But two or three days later he asked her to put on her finest attire for the evening, since they had been invited to a banquet. She asked where they would be going, but he replied that it was not far and they could easily walk there in their banquet garb. When she cautiously tried to find out whether he was jesting, he showed her his own clothing, which he had laid out on the bed, with the blue wedding mantle underneath.

Just before sundown, the brothers Marcus and Jacob Wachtian appeared, dressed for the banquet, along with Brother Guilbert, wearing his white Cistercian robes. They had come to fetch Arn and his wife for the celebration. Out in the courtyard the smoke from roasting meat was already blending with the aroma of exotic spices.

Cecilia had not been inside the guests' longhouse since the time when Arn had shown it to her. But that was where they were all now headed, and when she stepped through the door, she could hardly recognize the place. Even more colorful rugs had been spread on the floor, and on the walls hung tapestries with the most fanciful star patterns. Benches had been arranged in a rectangle in the room, with heaps of cushions and pillows behind them. From the ceiling hung burning lamps made of copper and iron and colored glass, and before the long hearth stood gridirons in which trout from Lake Vättern were being grilled.

The physician Ibrahim, who was dressed in a long coat made of shimmering material and a headdress made of a length of fabric wrapped many times around his head, received the guests at the door. He then led them to the place of honor in the row of benches and cushions closest to the west.

Artfully made copper pitchers were brought forth, along with glasses made at their own glassworks; all of them were lined up along the benches. Cecilia was about to sit down on the bench, but Arn showed her with a laugh that she should kneel down among the cushions behind the long wooden bench. He also whispered to her not to touch either food or drink until someone else did so first.

They were waiting for the sun to set, and gradually the foreigners all took their places, except for a few who tended to the grilled fish, and old Ibrahim, who went out to the courtyard.

Much to her annoyance, Cecilia discovered that Brother Guilbert, the Wachtian brothers, and Arn all seemed able to cope with these unfamiliar customs and smells and showed no sign of discomfort. They talked and laughed quietly, speaking the language that Cecilia could now recognize as Frankish.

Arn soon noticed Cecilia's confusion, and with an apology to the other men, he turned to her and began to explain.

It was a clear and star-strewn night, one of the first nights with frost during this mild autumn, and outside in the courtyard, Ibrahim was now carefully scanning the sky to the northwest. When darkness fell, he would soon catch sight of the slender crescent moon that foretold a new month, and then the celebration called Eid al-Fitr would begin, heralding the end of the month of fasting.

Cecilia was about to object that the fasting month was in the spring, not in October, but she stopped herself when she realized this was not in truth the time for a conversation about church customs.

Ibrahim came in from the courtyard and made an announcement in his incomprehensible foreign tongue. Everyone in the room immediately said a short prayer. Arn then grabbed the tin-plated copper pitcher sitting on the table in front of him and poured a glass, which he handed to Cecilia. Then he poured some for Brother Guilbert and the Wachtian brothers. Everyone else at the table did the same, raising their glasses and drinking greedily before pouring another. Cecilia, who had been slower and more hesitant about raising the glass to her lips began coughing when she found that there was only water in the glass and not wine, as she had thought.

The meal consisted of roast mutton, goose, and trout, along with other small dishes that Cecilia didn't recognize; all of the food was served on large, round wooden platters. Strange-looking instruments were played, and someone began singing a song; others quickly joined in.

Arn broke off a piece of the soft flat bread and showed Cecilia how to dip it into the meat sauce surrounding the mutton. When she did so, her mouth filled with a spicy taste that at first made her hesitate. After a moment she found it palatable, and after a few more minutes, she found it to be utterly delicious. The mutton was the most tender she had ever eaten, and the trout tasted entirely different, spiced with something that reminded her of cumin.

Arn amused himself by taking tidbits from various platters and putting them in Cecilia's mouth, as if she were a child. When she tried to resist, he laughed and said it was merely a chivalrous way for a man to show affection for his wife or close friend.

At first all the foreigners ate quickly and voraciously. But after they seemed to have sated the worst of their hunger, most of the men leaned back on the cushions and ate more slowly. With their eyes half-closed, they seemed to be enjoying the melancholy music played by two men on stringed instruments that resembled those played by the Frankish minstrels at the wedding at Arnäs.

It didn't take long before Cecilia also leaned back against the comfortable cushions which several men, bowing politely, had brought to support her back. She no longer felt so nervous, and she slowly partook of all the delicacies, merely raising an eyebrow when she noticed how much of the estate's honey had been used for the sweet that was served after the meat and fish. The dessert was small pieces of bread with shredded carrots and filled with hazelnuts, drenched in honey. All the foreign aromas and smells were somehow soothing and made her feel sleepy; she even began to take pleasure in the music, although it had sounded off-key at first. She started imagining herself in foreign lands. What made this banquet so different from those she was used to was the fact that everyone became more and more quiet as the evening wore on, just as the songs played on the stringed instruments became more yearning and sorrowful. No one started brawling, and no one vomited. She brooded a bit over these foreign ways, until she recalled that it was water they were drinking and not ale or wine. She dozed and dreamed more and more about this foreign world until Arn took her arm and whispered that it would be good manners for the two guests of honor to leave the banquet first instead of last.

He led her over to the door leading to the house *lavatorium*. There he took her hand, bowed, and said something in the foreign tongue that made all the men in the room stand up and bow deeply in reply.

The night air was cold and frosty, and it revived her at once, as if breaking a spell. She thought that this was going to be the first of the winter nights when Arn explained all the foreign customs to her.

When he blew some life into the fire and they crawled into their big bed, she fluffed up their pillows so that they could sit side by side and look into the flames. Then she asked him to begin his account; the first thing she wanted to know was how it was possible that they had come to welcome the worst enemies of Christendom as guests in a Christian home.

At first sounding a bit reluctant, he told her that these Muslims, as the followers of Muhammed were called, had worked for the Christians in the Holy Land. They would have been killed by their own kind if they hadn't fled with him to the North. The same was true for the Wachtian brothers, who were Christians from the Holy Land. Their workshop and their trade had been on Al Hammediyah, which was the biggest business district in Damascus. So the question of who was a friend and who was an enemy in the Holy Land was not solely determined by a person's faith.

Cecilia found this incomprehensible, even though she offered only cautious objections.

Then he began his story, which would continue for many winter nights.

In the Holy Land there were great men whose eminence far exceeded that of all others. Arn was thinking in particular about two of them; the first was a Christian named Raymond of Tripoli, and some night he would tell Cecilia about him. But it was more important to speak of the other, for he was a Muslim and his name was Yussuf Ibn Ayyub Salah ad-Din. For the sake of simplicity, the Christians called him simply Saladin.

When Arn said the name of the worst enemy of Christendom, Cecilia involuntarily gasped. She had heard thousands of oaths, reeking of brimstone, pronounced over that name by nuns and priests.

Yet Saladin was his friend, Arn went on, undaunted by her expression of alarm. And their friendship had followed such a course over the years that not even the greatest of skeptics would see anything but God's hand behind it.

It all started when Arn unintentionally saved Saladin's life; upon closer examination, that could not have happened without God's hand. Because why else would a Templar knight, one of God's most devoted warriors and defenders of His Tomb, be the one to save the man who in the end would crush the Christians to the ground?

After that they had met as foes on the battlefield, and Arn had triumphed. But a short time later, Arn's life ended up in Saladin's hands when the Muslim arrived with an invincible army at the fortress in Gaza where Arn was fortress master among the Templars. And Saladin had, in turn, saved Arn's life.

Saladin had spared his life because of their friendship, and that was how he had become Saladin's prisoner and negotiator.

That was during his last days in the Holy Land, when Jerusalem was already lost, as were most of the Christian cities. And Arn was Saladin's prisoner but also occasionally his messenger and negotiator, as one of the worst villains that had ever set foot on the ground of the Holy Land arrived with an army to meet Saladin on the battlefield and recapture the Holy City of Jerusalem. This man, whose name was Richard Lionheart, a name that would live on in eternal infamy, had amused himself during the negotiations by beheading three thousand prisoners rather than accepting the last of the ransom that he had demanded for them, and rather than receiving back the True Cross for Christendom.

At that sorrowful moment Arn and Saladin had parted ways for all eternity, and Arn had received as a farewell gift fifty thousand besants in gold, which Richard had refused in favor of sating his thirst for blood.

And so it was that Arn could now afford to pay for the building going on at Arnäs as well as for the new church at Forsvik and everything else that was being constructed there.

And this was just a short version of the story, said Arn. Many winter nights would be required to give a fuller account. And it might take the rest of his life to understand the meaning behind everything that had happened.

There he stopped and got up to put more wood on the fire. It was then he discovered that Cecilia had fallen asleep.

Chapter 9

Filled with a sense of foreboding, Arn rode at the front of the groom's procession as it entered Linköping. From the bishop's stronghold to the cathedral three red Sverker banners waved, as if taunting the guests. And among the spectators watching with hostility, only red mantles were visible; there was not a blue one in sight. And not a single rowan bough was tossed toward the bridegroom to wish him well.

It was like riding into an ambush. If Sune Sik and his kinsmen wanted to turn this wedding into a blood feud, they would be able to kill all the foremost Folkungs except for the aged Herr Magnus of Arnäs, who had been forced to forgo this ride through the chill of autumn because of his health.

As they neared the cathedral they could hear the distant shouts greeting the bride's procession with much greater warmth. Birger Brosa was leading the way, as the one who had fetched the bride.

Even Erik jarl was riding in the groom's procession alongside his friend Magnus Månesköld, who had his mother Cecilia on the other side of him; his paternal uncle, councilor Eskil, rode behind him. All the powerful Folkungs and King Knut's eldest son as well were putting their lives at risk. If the Sverkers truly wanted to take back the crown by force, this was the time to do it.

But the Folkungs had not come to the enemy's city unprepared like lambs to the slaughter. From Bjälbo came a hundred retainers and kinsmen fully armed. They had drawn lots so that half of the men swore not to drink even one tankard of ale during the first day and night. Those who won the draw had sworn to remain sober on the second day and night. The Folkungs were not about to be slaughtered either by surprise or by fire.

Yet it was for Cecilia that Arn felt the greatest concern. He could easily ride through hordes of Nordic peasant soldiers or use his sword to slash his way through the ranks of retainers. But the question that he hardly dared even consider was whether his foremost duty was to stay by Cecilia's side or to save himself so that the Folkungs would not be robbed of all defenders and avengers when the subsequent war began.

When the first arrows were shot, it was Arn's duty to ride away to save himself. His loyalty to the Folkungs demanded this. There was no better man to lead their avenging army to victory, and he couldn't possibly deny this fact either to his own conscience or to anyone else.

Nevertheless he decided to break with the laws of honor if the worst should happen. He would not leave Linköping alive without Cecilia. She was riding a good horse, and her new gown allowed her to sit astride the saddle with solid support in both stirrups. She was also an excellent horsewoman. At the sight of a single glinting weapon anywhere, he would immediately ride up alongside and clear the way for her.

These were his thoughts as they approached the cathedral where the bridal procession was coming from the other direction, and his expression was more harsh and somber than would be expected of a bridegroom's father. People whispered and pointed at him, and he suspected that in their opinion, he was the one among the enemies wearing the blue mantles who ought to be felled first.

Outside the cathedral they dismounted. Stable thralls came running to hold the reins of their horses. Arn surveyed the area with suspicion, casting a glance up at the walls of the bishop's stronghold when he went to fetch Magnus, who was suffering terribly after the bachelors' evening at Bjälbo that had been almost as good as the one at Arnäs. Even better, according to Magnus, since this time he didn't have to compete against old men and monks. Hence in the last games of his youth he had salvaged the victor's crown that had been denied him at Arnäs.

The gift for the bride was a heavy necklace made of gold with red stones. Erik jarl brought it to Arn, who accepted it and then handed it to his son Magnus. With much fumbling the groom fastened the necklace around Ingrid Ylva's neck, over the red mantle that she wore.

Then Sune Sik himself brought forward the gift for the groom, a Frankish sword with a sheath adorned with gold and silver; the hilt was strewn with gemstones. A sword that was more suitable for a banquet than a battle, Arn thought to himself as Ingrid Ylva fastened the sword at Magnus's waist.

The bishop blessed the bridal couple, and both the bride and groom kissed his ring. After that everyone who could find room inside went into the cathedral for mass, which was kept brief since the wedding guests were thinking more of the feast than of heavenly joys. During the mass many men wearing red mantles cast angry glances at Arn because he kept his sword at his side even though everyone else had left their weapons outdoors.

There was no hint of danger or treachery on the road between the bishop's estate and the cathedral or onward across the bridge to the Stång royal estate where the wedding banquet was to be held.

The royal estate was old and drafty, but it was still the finest building in all of Linköping. No doubt Sune Sik lived in far better quarters, but it was just as certain that he wanted to show that when he was the host, it was as the king's brother at a royal estate. Here in Linköping all Sverkers regarded the royal estates as their private property.

Two rows of heavy wooden pillars supported the roof of the hall, and they had all been painted red, as if to conceal the ungodly images, still faintly visible, that had been carved into the wood. Crosses and images of Christ hung like incantations between iron brackets that held tarred torches out from the walls.

Arn and Cecilia were expecting a rather gloomy evening like the previous one they had spent at Bjälbo. Yet as soon as they took their seats, both Birger Brosa and the bride's father, Sune Sik, showed that it was their intention to make it a good evening among friends, even at the high seat. It was impossible to know what had made them change their behavior so dramatically. Cecilia tried to find out from Valevaks, who was Sune Sik's wife and the bride's mother, but she learned very little, since the woman spoke more Polish than Norse.

The bishop, who was seated far from Arn and Cecilia on the other side of Sune Sik, also seemed to want to show his goodwill and friendship. As soon as he had drunk a toast with Birger Brosa and Sune Sik, he turned to the groom's parents. There was no wine at this banquet, and although Arn and Cecilia had determined to leave the ale placed in front of them untouched, they were soon shamed into drinking it because of the unexpected friendliness streaming toward them from all directions.

Birger Brosa surprised Arn more than once by praising him as a close kinsman and friend to Sune Sik, and the jarl spoke so loudly that Arn couldn't avoid hearing.

Something had happened to change the game, but at the moment the only thing to do was to remain courteous and wait until the next day to find out what was going on.

Escorting the couple to bed began earlier than anticipated, since there were so many guests in the hall who wanted to have this custom out of the way; then they could breathe more easily. When Sverkers and Folkungs became united in blood through Magnus Månesköld and Ingrid Ylva, the risk of fire, treachery, and murder would be over.

The bridal chamber was in a separate house near the river Stångån, and it was guarded by as many retainers wearing blue mantles as wore red. The only difference was that those in blue were able to stand upright without difficulty because not a drop of ale had passed their lips.

After the ring dance in the hall, the bride was escorted out by her kinsmen. Those who remained inside suddenly fell silent, as if listening for the clang of weapons and shrill screams. But everything seemed calm outside.

Then it was time for the truly decisive moment when Magnus Månesköld and his Folkung kinsmen were to leave the hall.

With his right hand Arn pulled Cecilia close to his side as he cautiously loosened his sword. Then they walked out between the rows of dazzling torches. They didn't speak to each other, but both bowed their heads in prayer, asking for mercy.

Yet nothing untoward happened. Soon they were standing next to the bridal bed on which Magnus and Ingrid Ylva lay in their white linen shifts, looking merry and holding hands. The bishop said a brief prayer over them, and Birger Brosa and Sune Sik pulled the bridal coverlet over the beautiful, dark-haired Ingrid Ylva and the vigorous, red-haired Magnus Månesköld.

Everyone in the room secretly breathed a sigh of relief, and Sune Sik immediately went over to Arn and held out both hands, thanking God for this reconciliation that had now taken place and swearing that there was no longer any blood between them. For they were now both fathers-in-law to the other's offspring, and blood united them instead of separating them.

When the witnesses emerged from the bedchamber and stepped out into the courtyard, they were greeted with cheers of relief and joy, since this wedding had led to peace and reconciliation.

Now it would be easier to liven up the mood inside the hall. And such was the case as soon as the guests in the high seat returned to their places. Arn recalled that only once before in his life had he been sick from too much ale, and that time he had promised himself never to repeat such foolishness. To his embarrassment, Birger Brosa and Sune Sik quickly drank him under the table, as if they had both joined in some malicious drinking pact against him.

Cecilia displayed no pity for his miserable condition the next morning. On the contrary, she had a great deal to say about the recklessness of a swordsman who drank as much ale as some ordinary, rough retainer. Arn defended himself by saying that he'd felt such great relief the moment he saw the coverlet drawn over Magnus and Ingrid Ylva that the ale had more easily seeped in as his wits left him, because he no longer needed to think clearly.

But over the two following feast days, Arn was very cautious about the amount of ale he drank, and Sune Sik had also procured wine for him and Cecilia; no one ever drank wine in such manly quantities as ale.

✠

Ingrid Ylva had received the Ulvåsa estate as a morning gift from the Folkungs, and after the three feast days in Linköping jarl Birger Brosa rode at the head of the bridal procession to Ulvåsa, located on a promontory on the shores of Lake Boren.

Since Boren was connected to Lake Vättern, Arn and Cecilia would now be practically neighbors to Magnus and Ingrid Ylva. It was only a day's journey by boat between the two estates in the summertime and an even shorter journey by sleigh in the winter. Cecilia and Ingrid Ylva had already found it easy to talk to each other since Ingrid Ylva had spent many years at Vreta cloister, and they quickly reached agreement about many things having to do with visiting each other and the important holidays. Their husbands had very little to say about these matters.

The visit to Ulvåsa would be brief so that the young people, as soon as honor deemed it possible, would not have the burden of taking care of older kinsmen. After that the intention was for Arn and Cecilia to travel together with Eskil on one of his boats, first to Forsvik. From there Eskil would continue on to Arnäs.

But as they prepared to depart from Ulvåsa on the second feast day, Birger Brosa came to Arn, hemming and hawing, to say that he would like Arn to accompany him back to Bjälbo so that the two of them might have a talk.

If the jarl made a request, it could not be refused. Arn had no idea why Birger Brosa wanted to have this conversation, but he had no trouble explaining to Cecilia and Eskil that he would have to travel by a different route. They both assented without asking any questions. And Eskil chivalrously vowed that with his own life he would protect the life and safety of this Folkung woman. Arn laughed that this was so much easier to promise now that peace had been secured.

When Birger Brosa and his retinue made ready to ride back to Bjälbo, Arn apologized and said that he would have to follow somewhat later, as he wanted to take advantage of the moment to speak privately with his son Magnus. Birger Brosa couldn't very well object to this, but he frowned and muttered that it was a short journey to Bjälbo. He had no intention of waiting for his kinsman, since his time was precious. Arn promised not to keep his uncle waiting at Bjälbo; in fact, they would probably arrive at the same time.

"Then you'll certainly need a good horse!" snorted Birger Brosa and set off at a slow gallop with his retainers lagging behind in surprise.

"I'll be all right with *my* horse, dear uncle," whispered Arn after the retreating jarl.

It seemed most likely that Ingrid Ylva and Magnus thought they had spent enough time in the company of their kinsmen; they were already behaving with affection toward one another. Yet Magnus could not say no to his father's request for a short ride and conversation, just the two of them.

Ulvåsa stood in a beautiful location on the promontory, with water glittering all around and fertile fields tended by both the house thralls from the estate and people from the nearby village of Hamra, which now was also owned by Ingrid Ylva. The farm buildings were of the older type and would not be comfortable in the winter. Arn said nothing of this, although he was thinking that next spring he would send builders from Forsvik to repair the living quarters for both the house servants and thralls. But he would cross that bridge when he came to it; right now there were more important things to discuss.

Without making any digressions to talk about the wedding or the youth competitions at Bjälbo, which Magnus found it pleasant to brag about, Arn began describing his plans for Arnäs. Every Folkung within three days' journey was to go to Arnäs if misfortune were ever approaching, because there no enemy would be able to touch them.

Magnus objected sullenly that in such case one's own estate would be left to fire and plundering, and Arn nodded grimly that this was true. But if the enemy was strong, it was more important to save one's skin than a few timbered houses that could easily be built anew.

Magnus didn't seem to understand or show any interest in what his father wanted to tell him. There were no enemies for as far as the eye could see. Besides, now that peace between the Sverkers and Folkungs had been so strongly sealed, wasn't that the reason that they were able to ride together here at Ulvåsa with Ingrid Ylva waiting back at the longhouse? Wasn't the very idea behind this wedding to secure the peace? And hadn't he, without grumbling, agreed to the clan's demands, even though it was no hardship to go to the bridal bed with such a lovely, dark-haired woman as Ingrid Ylva?

Arn realized too late that he had been tactless in his timing as he tried to make his own son see the threat to the realm and how they needed to defend themselves. He answered evasively that no danger would befall them during the next few years, and it was true that this wedding offered a strong message of peace. He was merely trying to see further into the future. At that, Magnus just shrugged his shoulders. Arn then asked him about the youth games at Bjälbo.

With much greater enthusiasm Magnus seized upon this topic of conversation and described in detail everything that had taken place during each of the seven contests. In the end he had come out the victor, and Erik jarl was again defeated.

More than an hour passed, and Arn began to have trouble hiding his impatience even though he had arrogantly promised Birger Brosa he would arrive at Bjälbo when the jarl did. Only with difficulty did he finally turn down Magnus's suggestion that they have a tankard of ale before his departure. They said farewell out in the courtyard, and Arn set off for Bjälbo at once, at full gallop. Magnus watched his father ride away, thinking that no one could keep up that pace for long; no doubt his father merely wanted to show his strength as long as he was in sight, but he would have to slow down as soon as he was beyond the oak grove south of Ulvåsa.

Birger Brosa and his retinue did not have to make another rest stop before they reached Bjälbo, and they could already see the church tower in the distance when Arn suddenly came racing up behind them, riding one of his foreign stallions at great speed. When Birger Brosa was told that a rider was approaching, he turned around in his saddle and saw the Folkung mantle. At first he thought that Arn had doubtless sneaked up behind them in order to ride the last stretch of the way at this unreasonable pace. But he soon had misgivings when he saw that Arn's steed was lathered with sweat.

Arn was relieved to find that the young horse he had chosen to ride to the wedding turned out to be good enough, even though it was slow compared to Abu Anaza. But Abu Anaza was black, and it would not have been suitable to ride such a horse to a wedding. An animal of that color, according to what Cecilia had told him, was more appropriate for a funeral and would be considered bad luck at a wedding.

Birger Brosa led the way and came to a halt as soon as they entered the confines of Bjälbo behind the stockade. He first wished to don simpler attire, then he had to go to his writing chamber where people were waiting with all sorts of missives. Only then would he meet with Arn, and their meeting would take place in the tower chamber of the church where the clan *ting* would be held in former times. A brazier and ale, cushions and sheepskins were to be taken up there at once; in an hour's time no one but Arn was to be present. After issuing these brusque commands, Birger Brosa laboriously dismounted from his horse, handing the reins to a stable thrall without even glancing around. Then with determined strides he headed for the longhouse.

Feeling rather offended, Arn himself saw to the care of his horse, which needed attention after such a hard ride. He paid no attention to the fact that his presence in the stable caused much confusion and surprise among the thralls. The health of his horse was more important. After drying the horse's flanks and cleaning the hooves, Arn asked for several hides, which he slung over the back of the dapple-gray steed to make sure the animal wouldn't cool down too fast. And he spoke in a foreign tongue, whispering as he caressed and seemed to console the horse. The stable thralls shook their heads and exchanged glances behind Arn's back, keeping out of his way.

After Arn left the horse, he went at once to brush himself off. Then at the appointed time he went to the old tower room and waited. There was a rank smell of mold and mortar. Birger Brosa arrived a bit late.

"You are more trouble to me than any other kinsman, Arn Magnusson, and I will never make any sense of you!" Birger Brosa said in greeting in a loud voice as he climbed the stairs. And without further ado he sank down onto the largest seat, exactly where Arn had thought he would choose to sit.

"Then you must ask me questions, dear uncle, and with God's help I will try to help you understand," replied Arn humbly. He had no desire to quarrel anew with the jarl.

"It's much worse than that!" declared Birger Brosa. "And it will get even worse if I do understand, because then I will feel foolish that I hadn't understood at once. And that would not please me. Nor do I have any particular wish to apologize, and I've already been humiliated by you once before. Now I am doing that again, for the second time. This has never happened, and as God is my witness, I shall never again, for a second time, be forced to ask some rogue for forgiveness!"

"What is it that you wish me to forgive?" asked Arn in surprise at this fiery drama his uncle was now presenting.

"I've seen all the building that is going on at Arnäs," replied Birger Brosa in a different tone of voice, keeping his voice low. He threw out his arms in a gesture that almost looked like surrender. "I've seen what you're building, and I'm not foolish. You're building up the Folkung power to be greater than ever, you're building so that we will be lords of this realm. My brother Magnus and your brother Eskil have also told me about what you're doing at Forsvik. Need I say more?"

"No, not if you wish me to forgive you, uncle," replied Arn cautiously.

"Good! Will you have ale?"

"I would prefer not to. During these past days I've had enough ale to last me till Christmas."

Birger Brosa gave him a scornful smile and stood up. He took two ale tankards over to the ale cask, filled them both, and placed one of them in front of Arn before he went back to his seat. He settled himself more comfortably among the sheepskins with one knee drawn up; there he balanced his tankard, as was his custom. He gazed at Arn in silence for a while, but his expression was friendly.

"Tell me of the castle that you're building," he said. "How does it look today, how will it look when Arnäs is finished, and how will it look after several years?"

"It will take time to answer these questions," said Arn.

"Nothing is more important for the jarl of the realm at this moment. We have plenty of time, and we are alone, with no one else within earshot," replied Birger Brosa. He grabbed his tankard and took several good swallows before he placed it back on his knee. Then he threw out his hands without causing the tankard even to wobble.

"Today there is peace, and the union is between the Eriks and Folkungs," Arn began hesitantly. "The Sverkers are lying low, biding their time until King Knut is gone, and God willing, that will not happen for a long time yet. So I do not see a war taking place for many years."

"Then we think alike," said the jarl, nodding. "But what about after that? What will happen then?"

"No one knows," said Arn. "But one thing I do know: at that time there will be a greater danger of war. That doesn't mean that things will go badly for us. For if we now build fortresses that are sufficiently strong, during the peace that we now have, our strength may preserve the peace as well as a wise marriage does."

"True," said Birger Brosa with a nod. "But what is our weakness?"

"We cannot engage a Danish army on the battlefield," Arn swiftly replied.

"A Danish army? Why a Danish army?" asked Birger Brosa, raising his eyebrows.

"That is the only danger we face and hence the only problem worth fretting about," replied Arn. "Denmark is a great power, a power that resembles the Frankish kingdom more than us, and the Danes wage war in the same way that the Franks do. The Danes have laid waste to great sections of Saxony and won much territory, showing that they are able to defeat Saxon armies. When they've had enough of heading southward, or when they reach so far south that they can no longer keep their armies supplied, they may turn their attention to the north. And here we sit, a much easier quarry than Saxony. And in Roskilde sits Karl Sverkersson's son, raised as a Dane, but still with an inherited right to our crown. He could become the Danes' nominal king in our realm. That is how the situation looks if we try to imagine what might be the worst thing that might happen."

Birger Brosa nodded pensively, almost as if acknowledging to himself that these were his darkest thoughts and he would have preferred to ignore them. In silence he drank more ale, expecting Arn also to remain silent until he received another question.

"When can we defeat the Danes?" Birger Brosa asked abruptly, speaking in a loud voice.

"In five or six years, but it will cost us dearly. In ten years it would be easier," replied Arn with such confidence that Birger Brosa, who had expected a more lengthy explanation, was caught off guard.

"Give me a more detailed explanation," he said after another long pause.

"In five years King Knut may die," said Arn, swiftly raising his hand to prevent any interruption. "We don't know that, and it's a wicked thing to think, but wicked ideas also have to be tested. Then the Danish army will come here with a more or less eager Sverker Karlsson following behind. We have a hundred horsemen. Not the kind of horsemen that can counter a great Frankish or Danish army, but a hundred horsemen that can make their passage through our land a great misery. They never engage us in battle nor do they catch up with us, but we take their supplies, we kill their draft animals, we kill or wound a dozen Danes each day. We do our best to entice them to pursue us to Arnäs. There they are crushed in their encampment. That's what would happen in five years, and the price would be great devastation from Skara and all the way north."

"And in ten years?" asked Birger Brosa.

"In ten years we defeat them on the battlefield after first plaguing them with our light cavalry for a month," replied Arn. "But to make this possible, you will also have to exert yourself and pay for a great many things that will make big holes in your silver coffers."

"Why should I do this? Why not King Knut?" asked Birger Brosa, and for the first time clearly showed surprise during this harsh conversation.

"Because you are a Folkung," replied Arn. "The power that I am starting to build does not belong to the realm; it belongs to the Folkungs. It's true that I have sworn loyalty to Knut, and I will stand by my oath. Perhaps some day I will also swear loyalty to Erik jarl, but we don't know that. Today we're united with the

Eriks. But tomorrow? Of that we know nothing. The only thing that's certain is that we Folkungs will stick together, and we're the only power that can hold the realm together."

"I think you have understood this even better than you know," said Birger Brosa. "I must tell you something at once that is for your ears alone. But tell me first what you think I should do, as jarl or as a Folkung."

"You must build a fortress on the western shore of Lake Vättern, perhaps at Lena where you already own a large estate. The Danes will come from Skåne when they enter Western Götaland. At Skara they can continue on a northerly route toward Arnäs or take the unprotected road past Skövde and up to Lake Vättern and the king's Näs. They must be stopped at Lena, and I hope that you will take this upon yourself. Axvalla at Skara must also be fortified. We will have our warriors in three fortresses. And our horsemen can move back and forth between the three without allowing the enemy to attack us, preventing them from knowing where the next assault will occur. With three strong fortresses, one of which is impregnable, we will be secure."

"But Axvalla is a royal castle," objected Birger Brosa.

"All the better for the sake of your own expenses," said Arn with a smile. "If I build up Arnäs and you do the same with Lena, you, in your position as jarl, shouldn't have a hard time convincing Knut that the king ought to add his straw to the stack and fortify his own castle of Axvalla. He would do it as much for his own sake as for ours."

"I notice that you've begun to speak to me as if we were equals," said Birger Brosa, and for the first time he gave Arn a broad smile, which had always been a distinctive characteristic of his, ever since his youth.

"Now it's my turn to ask forgiveness, my uncle. I got carried away," replied Arn, bowing his head for a moment.

"I too got carried away," replied Birger Brosa, still smiling.

"But from now on I wish that you and I continue to speak with each other in this informal manner, except possibly when we attend the king's council. But now to what I wanted to tell you of a great and difficult matter. Perhaps I would like to see Sverker Karlsson as our next king."

Birger Brosa abruptly fell silent after speaking this treacherous thought. He may have been waiting for Arn to leap to his feet in anger, upsetting his ale and lashing out with words that were far from chivalrous, or at the very least gaping in surprise like a fish. But with equal parts disappointment and astonishment, he saw that Arn's expression did not change. He merely sat there, waiting for Birger Brosa to continue.

"I suppose you'd like to hear how I came to this conclusion?" he now said, sounding a bit cross and his smile fading.

"Yes," replied Arn tonelessly. "What you say may be either treachery or something very wise, and I'd like to know which it is."

"The king is ill," said Birger Brosa with a sigh. "Sometimes he shits blood, and anyone knows that is not a good sign. He may not even last the five years that we need in order to offer even the most token defense."

"I have men trained as physicians with me who have too little to do. I will send them to Knut after Christmas," said Arn.

"Men who are physicians, you say?" Birger Brosa replied, interrupting his train of thought. "I thought it was mostly women who tended to such matters. No matter. But shitting blood is a bad sign, and Knut's life rests in God's hands. If he dies too soon, we will be in a bad position. Isn't that true?"

"Yes," said Arn. "So let's consider the worst that might happen. What if Knut dies in three years? What do we do then? Is that why you're thinking of Sverker Karlsson?"

"Yes, that's where he enters the picture with his Danish men," confirmed Birger Brosa with a gloomy nod. "He has been married to his Danish wife, I think Benedikta Ebbesdotter is her name, for six or seven years. She gave birth to a daughter early on, but no more children since then; and more importantly, no son."

"Then I think I understand," said Arn. "Without waging war, we give the crown to Sverker. But we don't make such a gift without receiving something in return. He'll have to swear that Erik jarl will become king after him. Am I right?"

"More or less," said Birger Brosa with a nod.

"Much could go wrong with such a cunning stratagem," brooded Arn. "Even if Sverker Karlsson produces no son, some new kinsman might appear from Denmark with claims on our crown, and then we'd be in the same situation."

"But by then we will have won time, and many years without war."

"Yes, and that would be to the benefit of the Folkungs," admitted Arn. "We would gain the time we need to secure a victorious power. But the Eriks at Näs won't be pleased if you propose what you have now suggested to me."

"No, I don't think they will," said Birger Brosa. "But the Eriks find themselves in a difficult position right now. After Erik jarl is done ranting and calling us things that he will later regret, he'll discover that without the Folkungs no war will be waged for the sake of the king's crown. Without us there is no power. No doubt his father Knut will have an easier time understanding this. Of course much depends on Knut over the next few years, but if things get worse, I will find the right occasion to describe what we must do to preserve the peace, and thereby save Erik's head as well as his crown. Knut will yield if he is ravaged by disease and if the moment for such a conversation is chosen well."

"And after Erik jarl?" asked Arn with a scornful smile. "Where have you thought the crown should be placed then?"

"By then I will no longer be here on this earth," laughed Birger

Brosa, raising his ale tankard and draining it to the bottom. "But if my view from heaven is nearly as good—and considering how many prayers of intercession I've paid for my soul at three cloisters, I should have quite a nice view—it would be my greatest pleasure to see the first Folkung king crowned!"

"Then I suggest that you begin at once to marry off your kinsmen in Svealand rather than with Sverkers," said Arn, his face expressionless.

"That's precisely what I intend to do!" exclaimed Birger Brosa. "And it has occurred to me that your brother Eskil, who is a very tempting marriage prospect, needs to find a new wife very soon!"

Arn sighed, smiled, and pretending resignation raised his ale tankard toward Birger Brosa. He had great admiration for his uncle's ability to steer the struggle for power. Such men were rare, even in the Holy Land.

But he was also uneasy about the fact that no matter how many prayers of intercession had been purchased in three cloisters, even that might not be sufficient to procure a good vantage point in the next life, as Birger Brosa seemed so convinced that he had done. But Arn said not a word of what he was thinking.

⁜

The first snow came early and in great abundance that year. Among the foreigners at Forsvik, the snow and the increasing cold had a strange effect; some showed even greater diligence in their work, while others stayed indoors next to the hearth in the longhouse without doing any work at all. It wasn't difficult to explain the difference, since those who were hard-working were those who toiled in the smithies and glassworks where the heat was always so great that everyone worked in long, thin tunics and thick-soled wooden clogs with a rough leather cover across the instep, no matter how cold it might be outdoors.

The thralls at Forsvik took care of the other winter work, such as using the sled to collect more wood or keeping the courtyard clear of snow or shoveling snow passages between the buildings. They were better on their feet when tending to such tasks.

Jacob Wachtian surprised Arn during the second week of snow by asking that the section of water conduit stretching across the field to the house of the foreign guests be covered over with snow. Arn admonished him a bit indulgently that this might not be the wisest thing to do, since it would be difficult if the water froze. But Jacob insisted that it was precisely that occurrence that he wanted to avoid, and he claimed that snow was warmer than air, and that he'd heard this from kinsmen who lived high up in the Armenian mountains. Since Jacob refused to give up this idea, although he was insistent in a most chivalrous manner, Arn decided to try out his suggestion on one of the water lines. He allowed Jacob to choose which one it would be. Cloaking his words in many unnecessary courtesies, the Christian brother then explained that so many men lived in the longhouse, and since most of them had never even seen snow before, the damage would be all the greater if the water froze and they were all forced out into the winter night to relieve themselves; it would also be difficult to wash up in the mornings and evenings.

Arn then agreed to his request, although he didn't believe that this experiment would end well. Great heaps of snow were piled on top of the section of the water line running above ground to the longhouse.

A short time later the water stopped running into his own house, but when Arn went to see the Saracens in their longhouse, he found the water running as briskly as it did in the summertime.

Muttering and grunting, he had taken Gure outside to help break open his own water conduit using iron spits and pickaxes, and forcing boiling water into several places. Finally they managed to dislodge the ice plug, which went rattling through the house, and soon the water was flowing again. Arn then had his own water line covered in the same manner as had been done at the foreigners' house. After that everything was as it should be, even during the coldest time in midwinter.

Winter was a good time because the days weren't filled with such hard work that no one had any strength left to think. On the contrary, in winter people had time to reflect on matters.

For this reason Arn instituted *majlis* every Thursday after midday prayers in the Saracen longhouse. He also summoned the Christian foreigners to take part. At the first meeting he apologized for not establishing this excellent custom of having a council room and conversations much earlier. But as everyone no doubt realized, there was good reason to make haste with all the work that had to be done to shelter them from the winter. Yet now the cold had overtaken them, and what they hadn't been able to finish would not get done until spring. So, what should they talk about?

At first no one spoke. It was as if these Saracens, no matter how accustomed most of them were to the idea of *majlis*, had forgotten much of what they had been used to since everything in the North was so unfamiliar. In the worst case, thought Arn, this had happened because they saw themselves as slaves, subject to the mercy or disfavor of their foreign master.

Arn translated what he had said to Frankish when he realized that the two Englishmen didn't understand a word of Arabic; their Frankish wasn't particularly good either.

"Wages," said Athelsten Crossbow, who was the first to speak. "We work a year. Where is wages?" he went on.

Arn immediately translated his question to Arabic and saw that more than one man in the hall suddenly showed interest.

Work clothes could be another topic for discussion, said one of the stonemasons. Old Ibrahim, who was the most respected of the faithful and the only one who was allowed to speak for the others, added that they ought to solve the matter of God's day of rest, since there had been a good deal of confusion about this.

After a short time the reticence of the gathering had vanished; soon so many men were talking all at once that Ibrahim and Arn had to speak up to restore order.

The first decision had to do with wages. The general opinion was that it was better to receive wages after each year served than to get five years worth of wages all at once just before they traveled back home. There were some objections, including the fact that it might be difficult to store the silver and gold, since they had no use for it while at Forsvik. Another person who was more ingratiating said that there should never be any reason to doubt the word of Al Ghouti, and everyone's gold was doubtless better stored at Al Ghouti's home at an-Nes.

Nevertheless, Arn decided that after his next visit to Arnäs, which would take place during the most important Christian celebration, he would bring the wages for every man in gold coins.

The matter of work clothes was easier to solve. Most of the men in the hall knew full well what working with masonry and forges and glass entailed. Arn assured them that this would be the saddle-makers' most important task during the winter, since the masons in particular needed clothing that was reinforced with leather.

The question of a day of rest was more difficult to address; they had to discuss whether it should be Friday or Sunday. To slow the work in the smithies and at the glassworks would not be desirable. It was easiest to solve the problem with the smithies, since there were many Christians, especially if the thralls at Forsvik were considered Christian, who had no trouble working on Friday, just as the faithful could work on Sunday. It was not as simple at the glassworks, since all the skilled workers except for the Wachtian brothers were Muslim.

Then Arn asked Brother Guilbert how they had dealt with this matter when he was working with the stonemasons at Arnäs. Brother Guilbert muttered with great embarrassment that he had merely counted Sundays as Fridays, and no one had offered any protest. His words aroused much disapproval and many shocked glances among the builders who had worked on the fortress. Evidently they had been misled as to which days were Fridays and which were Sundays.

Arn quickly cut short the dispute that seemed likely to grow too big even for a *majlis*. He said that during the winter and at Forsvik, Friday would be a day of rest for every Muslim, while Sunday would be the Christians' day of rest, and so it would be. They would then think about what do at Arnäs when the masonry work resumed in the spring.

Not everyone who was present at this first *majlis* was satisfied with what had been discussed. But that was how it usually was and would continue to be.

Arn and Cecilia had more trouble in determining when they should free their thralls. For several evenings they sat with Brother Guilbert in his chamber so as to talk undisturbed about this matter, which they wished to keep secret until it could be realized. Just to be safe, they conducted the discussion in Latin.

Brother Guilbert had no reservations whatsoever about the idea of freeing the thralls; Arn expected no less of him. But the monk realized that such important news had to be delivered with care and wisdom. If they tried to imagine themselves as thralls, it was easy to understand how such news would be received. He was most concerned that the entrenched obedience of the thralls might lead to the opposite extreme. The poor, simple souls might lose their wits and fall upon each other with weapons in order to right old wrongs, in the belief that the person who was free was allowed to strike anyone at will. Or they might simply run off to the woods.

Cecilia remarked that in the middle of winter no one would run away from Forsvik to the woods. That was why the news should be delivered soon, during the coldest period.

Arn said gloomily that it would do little good to try and guess how a thrall thought, since it must be impossible to have a sensible opinion on the matter if someone had lived his whole life as a free man. Shouldn't they ask one of them?

Both Cecilia and Brother Guilbert objected at once, saying that if even the slightest hint of what they were planning got out, Forsvik would turn into a chicken coop of rumors and misconceptions before evensong. But Arn stubbornly insisted and asked them who they might suggest to ask for advice.

They both replied at once that they should ask Gure, Suom's son.

For Gure, who had not had a free moment since the snow began falling, busy as he was with hearths and drafty doors, this sudden summons to the master's house seemed an ill omen. He stopped his work at once and made his way from the thrall quarters to the courtyard, where he cut across the open space to Arn's house. He thought nervously that perhaps he had devoted too much time to the thralls and too little time to the stables and shelter for the livestock; harsh words were probably awaiting him. He did not fear the whip, because it had never been used even once at Arnäs; he knew from talking to everyone that not a single thrall had been whipped at Forsvik since the new master and mistress had arrived.

Outside Arn's house he paused in the snow for a moment, feeling at a loss. From inside he heard voices that sounded loud and ominous, as if Sir Arn and those he was talking to in a foreign tongue were not in agreement. What worried him most was not the fact that he was about to be rebuked, but that he didn't know the reason. He stood outside so long that he started to freeze, but no one came out to get him. He could not enter of his own volition; no thrall was allowed inside the mistress's chamber, and he could hear that she was inside. He stuffed his hands under his armpits and started stamping his feet in the snow to stop shivering from the cold.

He wondered to himself if this was his punishment, to freeze for his sins. But if that was the case, shouldn't he at least know why? What good was a punishment without knowing the reason behind it?

Brother Guilbert unexpectedly came to his aid; it might not have happened if he had remembered the *lavatorium* arrangement inside the master's house. But since he lived in the old longhouse, he was used to going outside to relieve himself. As he stepped outside and raised his robes, he discovered he was just about to spray his water on Gure waiting nearby.

Brother Guilbert quickly went about his business and then put his arm around Gure's shoulders and led him inside through the dark clothing chamber to the large room where the hearth kept it as warm as a bathhouse. The monk led him over to the great fireplace and pressed him down onto a stool a suitable distance away from the blaze while he said something to Arn in a foreign tongue.

Gure rubbed his hands to get warm as he kept his eyes on the floor, noticing how the master and mistress and the monk were all studying him, even though no one said a word. Suddenly Fru Cecilia stood up, took a tray with smoked ham on it from the bed, and carried it over to him with a knife.

Gure understood only that what had just happened could not have happened. A mistress did not serve food to a thrall, and he had no idea what he should do with the knife and ham. But she nodded and motioned for him to cut off a piece and eat it; reluctantly he did so.

"It was not our intention to keep you waiting outside in the cold, Gure," said Sir Arn at last. "We asked you to come here because we wish to ask you about a certain matter."

Sir Arn fell silent, and all three again stared at Gure. The smoked ham, which he had never before tasted, turned into a lump of wax in his mouth, and he was unable to swallow it.

"What we are about to ask you must stay with us here in this room," Fru Cecilia went on. "We want to know your opinion, but we don't want you to repeat our words to anyone else. Do you understand?"

Gure nodded, dumbstruck by what she said. He now guessed that something valuable must have been stolen and the master wanted to ask him about it, since he was the one who had the most oversight of all the thralls at Forsvik. He could tell that he was in a bad position since he knew nothing of this matter and they might not believe him. Thieves were hanged. But what happened to the person who protected a thief with lies?

"If we gave you your freedom, Gure, what would you do?" asked Sir Arn without the slightest warning.

Gure had to think carefully about this unexpected question. With great difficulty he finally managed to swallow the piece of meat in his mouth. He realized that he had to come up with a sensible answer, and at once, because the master and mistress and the monk were all looking at him, as if anticipating something remarkable.

"First I would thank the White Christ, then I would thank my master and mistress," he replied at last, as if the words simply spilled from his lips. Though he immediately regretted that he hadn't named his master and mistress before the White Christ.

"And what would you do after that?" asked Fru Cecilia.

"I would go to a church man to be baptized," he replied slyly in order to gain time. But he won only a few moments' delay because now the monk spoke up.

"I can baptize you tomorrow, but what would you do after that?" asked Brother Guilbert.

At first Gure had no answer. Freedom was a dream, but a dream that ended where it began. After that, there was nothing.

"What could a free man do?" asked Gure, thinking hard. "Wouldn't a free man have to eat? Wouldn't a free man have to work? If I, as a free man, could do the same building work that I now do, then I would. What else would I do?"

"Do the others think the same?" asked Fru Cecilia.

"Yes, we all probably think the same way," replied Gure, now more sure of his words. "People have been whispering for some time that we might be freed. Some have said they are sure of it; others have snorted at the rumor, which always spreads through farms. Freedmen can stay with their masters or work new fields; everyone knows that. If we could stay at Forsvik, then we would. If you drove us away, we would have to accept that decision; there is no other choice."

"We thank you for these words," said Sir Arn. "You are a man who thinks sensibly, and you have already understood what we are intending. So let me speak the truth to you. When your mistress and I come back from Christmas at Arnäs, where we will stay until dawn, we intend to free all the thralls at Forsvik. That is the truth. But we don't want you to speak of this matter to any of your peers, nor to anyone else, not even your own mother. This may be the last order I give you as a thrall, but you must obey."

"A thrall's word is of no worth, either before the law or in the view of others," replied Gure looking Arn straight in the eye. "Yet I give you my word, Sir Arn!"

Arn merely smiled without replying as he got up and motioned for Cecilia to do the same. That brought Brother Guilbert to his feet as well. Gure understood at once that this was a sign for him to go, but he didn't know how to take his leave; he attempted to bow and he slipped out.

As soon as Gure had shut the door behind him, Arn, Cecilia, and Brother Guilbert began talking all at once about the strange scene they had just witnessed. It was Arn's view that what they had just seen and heard with their own eyes and ears showed that the thralls were not nearly as half-witted as people said. Brother Guilbert talked about baptizing those who were freed, and that Gure should be made foreman of the freed thralls so that Arn and Cecilia wouldn't have to run around taking charge of every little matter. They both agreed about this, but Cecilia warned that perhaps not everyone was like Gure. For she had studied him closely as he spoke and thought she noticed something odd. Gure didn't speak like any other thrall she had ever heard; he spoke almost as well as they did. It had also occurred to her that he didn't look like a thrall, either. If Arn and Gure exchanged clothing, many might not be able to tell who was the thrall and who was the knight.

She didn't know what had made her say these words, but she regretted them at once when, for the first time, she saw anger flash in Arn's eyes. It didn't help matters that she tried to jest to banish her reckless words by saying that of course she meant that Gure looked more like Eskil, only thinner.

✠

The Saint Lucia celebrations were held around the darkest night of the year, when the forces of evil were stronger than at any other time, and so a great commotion was deliberately stirred up at Forsvik. A procession of house thralls plodded three times around the courtyard in the frigid midwinter night. Everyone carried blazing torches and wore horned masks made from woven straw. In spite of the bitter cold, many shivering Saracens peered outside in surprise or crowded onto their porch wrapped in mantles and rugs to watch the strange goings-on. It was so cold that the snow creaked loudly under the straw shoes that the thralls wore over their summer footwear.

Once again, the forces of evil were kept away from Forsvik on that night, and soon the frosty silence of midwinter settled over the estate anew; only the hunters were awake.

Arn and Cecilia, Torgils and the three boys, Sune, Sigfrid, and Bengt, and the Christian foreigners at Forsvik had all returned by sleigh from Arnäs after the dawn church service on Christmas Day. They had also attended the Christmas ale, which had been kept unusually moderate for the sake of old Herr Magnus. When they all returned, it was time for the big change.

On the following day, before the midday meal, all of Forsvik's thralls were summoned to the great hall in the old longhouse. They were more than thirty souls, counting a few nursing infants resting in their mothers' arms. Many of the thralls were workers in the fields or storehouses who had never set foot inside the great hall. The house thralls teased some of their kinsmen because of their wide-eyed amazement.

When everyone had gathered in the hall, Arn and Cecilia stood at the high seat. Arn was the one to speak, since Cecilia had requested that he do so, even though these thralls were rightfully her property and not his.

He briefly explained the reason for summoning them. He and Fru Cecilia had both decided that no one should be in bondage at Forsvik, since such a state was an abomination in the eyes of God. Hence they were now all free, and after their name they were allowed to add the name of Forsvik or call themselves Forsvikers, so that everyone in the villages and at other estates would know that they came from a place that had no thralls.

As free men and women, they would work for wages. Those who chose to remain at Forsvik would receive their first annual wages the following Christmas. For those who would rather work new fields near Forsvik as tenants, that too could be arranged.

After these words, Arn and Cecilia sat down. They were both surprised and disappointed that not a single thrall shrieked and no words of gratitude came streaming toward them. Nor did anyone say a prayer. They could see the startled looks on many faces, so they had no reason to believe that Gure had broken his promise to keep their secret. A few embraced the person standing nearest, and a few tears were also visible.

✠

Around New Year's the north wind began blowing, ushering in an entire week of snowstorms that wrapped Forsvik in a warm blanket of snow drifts, filling in all the crevices in the floors and windows of the old thrall houses, where the cold would have otherwise killed both those who were free and those who were not.

During the storms, not even the hunters went outside. At the smithies and glassworks, everyone continued their labors as usual, but it was impossible to conduct any riding practice. And since every vent and window of the stable was kept closed, they couldn't continue with the exercises that Brother Guilbert had started with the boys and Torgils Eskilsson. No one could shoot arrows or swing a sword in the dark.

But midwinter in the North was the time for sagas and tales. No dark night went to waste without stories or long conversations about topics that few had time for during the busier seasons of the year. In the thrall houses sagas were recounted that would have displeased the master and mistress. But most of the freed men and women thought that what they didn't hear wouldn't harm them.

✠

Arn and Brother Guilbert spent three days together in Arn and Cecilia's chambers while she stayed with Suom and some of the former thrall women in the weaving house. It stood next to the hot glassworks, which made it easier to keep out the cold.

The question that Brother Guilbert and Arn discussed at length had to do with the difficulty of imagining goodness through violence. Many faithful Christians during that time would have had trouble understanding such a conversation. But for two Templar knights, there was nothing difficult about seeing swords and fire as serving God's cause. Indeed, that was the role of the Knights Templar, given to them by God Himself and defended by His Mother.

Instead, the question had to be asked whether the strict Rule of the Templars could be applied to an ordinary Christian life.

Brother Guilbert was going to take a greater responsibility for training the boys in the use of weapons, because Arn was unsure that he himself was the best suited for the job. But this meant that they would have to take turns supervising the construction work at Arnäs, since the Muslim builders shouldn't be left alone in a land where the laws would not protect them. And quarrels might easily arise. Brother Guilbert had noticed a few thrall women at Arnäs hovering around the building site at night.

For Arn it would not be easy taking his turn away from Forsvik. On one of the long winter nights Arn and Cecilia lay under the covers just as they had imagined that they would, and he recounted his long stories from the Holy Land. Now and then they were disturbed by a gust of wind striking the hearth and sending ash through the bedchamber. It was on that night that she first felt something stirring inside of her, like a little fish flicking its tail.

She understood what it was at once; she had already sensed

but hadn't dared believe in such a miracle. She was over forty, after all, and she thought she was far too old for this blessing.

Arn was in the middle of a story from the Holy Land, recounting how he had just ordered that the banner be unfurled with the symbol of the Virgin Mary, the High Protectress of the Templar Knights. And he raised his hand to give the signal to attack, and in unison all the white-clad knights made the sign of the cross and took several deep breaths.

Then Cecilia quietly took Arn's hand and told him. He fell silent at once and turned to face her. And he saw that what she said was true and neither a dream nor a jest. Gently he embraced her and whispered that Our Lady had blessed them with yet another miracle.

⊹

Around the feast of Saint Tiburtius, during the time when the ice broke up in the lakes of Western Götaland, when the pike spawned and the riverboats started up with Eskil's trade between Linköping and Lödöse again, Arn and the stonemasons traveled to Arnäs to resume the construction work. According to what Cecilia had told him, he had a good month ahead of him before he needed to return to see his newborn son or daughter. Cecilia thought it would be a daughter. Arn thought he would have yet another son. They had promised each other that if it was a son, Cecilia would choose his name, but if it was a daughter, then Arn would decide.

The work on the wall proceeded briskly, and the builders seemed happy to get started after a winter that at first had seemed pleasantly indolent, but in the end much too long. They also claimed to be satisfied with the new tools from Forsvik's smithies and the work clothes that each of them had received in the proper size from the saddlemaker and the weaving house. They all wore leather garb from their shoulders down to their knees, and on their feet they had wooden clogs like those worn by the smiths, although with an iron cap around the toe and heel. Many had complained that dropping a stone could cause great misery if it landed on anyone's foot.

The winter had damaged some of the structures, but not as much as Arn had feared, and soon the summer would dry out the top joints of the walls. Then the workers would be able to seal them with melted lead, just as Brother Guilbert had suggested. What now needed to be built was the longest expanse of the wall from the harbor to the living quarters and village. It would be an easy task, because there was to be only one tower in the middle, and it was rewarding to see how the work progressed day by day.

The question of which day of rest should be honored had not yet been successfully resolved, or at least not everyone was satisfied. After long and tedious discussions at more than one *majlis* at Forsvik, Arn had grown weary of the issue and decided that at Arnäs Sunday should be counted as Friday. On Sundays the faithful couldn't work anyway, since that would offend those who lived at Arnäs and lead to quarrels about who had the true faith. And those kinds of quarrels were the worst of all.

Since God is the One who sees all and hears all, and is both merciful and beneficent, Arn thought that He would certainly forgive His faithful—who were forced into exile so far away in a foreign land but only for a short period of their lives—if they made Sunday into Friday. After a good deal of brooding and discussion with the physician Ibrahim, who had the most book-learning of any of the Saracen guests, Arn had found certain passages in the Koran to support this arrangement that had been made out of necessity.

The work was monotonous and the days empty of conversation, except when the exchange of words had to do with which of two stones should be hewn to fit best with the one next to it. Even though all the stones were nearly the same when they came from the quarry at Kinnekulle, most had to be trimmed and altered slightly in order to fit together as tightly as possible, the way both Arn and the Saracen builders required.

✠

Arn began counting the days and the hours till he would be able to return to Forsvik. He couldn't leave until Brother Guilbert arrived, and he came a day later than they had agreed, a very long day for Arn. But he heard that everything was well with Cecilia, and nothing untoward had happened at Forsvik while he was away. The day she would give birth was approaching, but according to the womenfolk who knew about such matters, he should have no trouble getting there in time.

He took a hasty farewell from both his kinsmen and the builders. Never had he thought that a boat could move so slowly as it did on that day, and as he stopped for the night at Askeberga, he considered borrowing a horse to continue on through the light spring night at once. But he changed his mind when he saw only dray animals and slow Gothic steeds in the stable.

After the feasts of Filippus and Jacob, when the livestock was turned out to pasture and the fences mended in Western Götaland, Cecilia Algotsdotter gave birth to a healthy little girl at Forsvik. Afterward a celebration was held for three days, and no one did any work, not even in the smithies. All free men and women at Forsvik took part with equal joy, since this blessing upon the house was now important to them all.

Arn decided that the child should be named Alde, a foreign name from one of his sagas, but also a beautiful name, Cecilia thought when she tried it out for herself as she lulled the little one to sleep at her breast. *Alde Arnsdotter*, she whispered.

Now the happiest time began for Arn and Cecilia since the day they were married. That was how they would always remember it. During that summer Arn, looking like a boyishly proud father, rode with his daughter in his arms nearly as often as he rode with those who were to become knights. And at that time there was no hint of the dark clouds gathering far in the distance, where the heavens and the earth met in the southwest.

Chapter 10

There was nothing about death that frightened Arn; he seemed to be out of the habit of even thinking about it. Or perhaps he had seen too much during his twenty years on the battlefield in the Holy Land, where he had certainly killed more than a thousand men with his own hands and had seen many thousands of others die close at hand. A bad or arrogant commander could raise his arm and in the next instant send off a squadron of sixteen brothers against a superior force pursuing them. They would ride off without hesitation with their white mantles fluttering behind them, never to be seen again. Yet there was consolation in the knowledge that they would meet these brothers in Paradise. A Templar knight never needed to fear death, because victory and Paradise were his only choices.

But it was a different matter when death came to a man as a slow, withering and stinking torment in slime and his own shit. For three long years Arn's friend Knut had dragged himself through life, growing steadily skinnier until finally he looked like a skeleton. When Yussuf and Ibrahim looked at him they could only shake their heads and say that the tumor eating at the king's body from inside his stomach would keep growing until it devoured his life.

Now Knut lay stretched out in his bed in his childhood home of Eriksberg, and his arms and legs were as thin as hazel twigs. Under the covers the tumor was visible as a bulge in the middle of his stomach, which in an odd way was reminiscent of a pregnant woman. He had lost all his hair, even his eyebrows and eyelashes, and in his mouth could be seen big black holes where his teeth had fallen out. The stench of him filled the entire room.

Arn had come alone to Eriksberg. Unlike all others who traveled to the king's deathbed, he could sit there for hours without minding the stench or even noticing it.

The king was still quite lucid. The tumor was eating his body but not his mind. It wasn't hard for Arn to understand that he was the person the king preferred to talk to during his last days, but it probably surprised many others waiting at Eriksberg. With Arn the king could talk about the Inscrutable One and the Vengeful One as well as he could with Archbishop Petrus; the difference was that Arn didn't look both expectant and impatient at the same time. For the archbishop it was a divine blessing that Knut was finally going to die; his death was a premonition of the new order about which the archbishop had said so many sincere prayers. According to King Knut, Sverker Karlsson in Denmark had already begun packing up for the journey, so it was really not much use to lie here and resist.

For large parts of his life Knut had lived out at Näs in the middle of Lake Vättern, constantly surrounded by stone walls and guards so that he wouldn't die the same way so many other kings had done, including the one he had killed himself. Now that death sat in the waiting room with his hourglass in which the sand would soon run out, there were almost no armed men offering protection. The estate at Eriksberg was like any other normal large estate, without any walls or even a stockade of sharpened stakes, and the church that Saint Erik once had begun to build provided little defense. Nor was it necessary, for who would come to kill a man who already had one foot in the grave?

"It's still not fair," said King Knut in a weak voice and for at least the seventh time as Arn sat by his bedside on the second day. "I could have lived another twenty years, and now I have to go to my ancestors having suffered an ignominious death. Why does God want to punish me so? Am I a greater wretch than all the others? Just think of Karl Sverkersson, whom that archbishop Petter claims is the reason for my suffering. But why him? He was the one who had my father Saint Erik murdered! Isn't the murder of a saint the worst possible sin?"

"Yes, indeed it is a grave sin," said Arn with an almost impudent smile. "But if you think about it a bit, then you'll probably understand that you're grumbling about the wrong thing. How long had Karl Sverkersson been king when we killed him? Six or seven years? I don't recall, but he was young, and you've been king five times as long as he was. Your life could have been more miserable and much shorter. You have to accept that. You have to be reconciled with your death and thank God for the grace He has shown you."

"I should thank God? Now? Here I lie in my own shit, suffering worse than a dog? How can you, who are my only true friend . . . just look around you, there's nobody else here. But where was I? Oh yes, how can you say that I should thank God?"

"At this hour it would at least be wiser than to blaspheme," replied Arn dryly. "But if you really want an answer, I'll give you one. You shall soon die, that is true. I am your friend, that is also true, and our friendship goes far back in time—"

"But you!" the king interrupted him, pointing with a finger so emaciated that it looked like a bird's claw. "How can you sit here healthy and feeling fine? Isn't your sin just as great as mine when it comes to the killing of my father's murderer?"

"That's possible," said Arn. "When I traveled to the Holy Land I had two sins with me in my saddlebag, heavy sins for my young age. Without the blessing of marriage I had joined together in the flesh with my beloved, and before that I had lain with her sister Katarina. And I had participated in killing a king. But these sins were atoned for over twenty years wearing the white mantle. You may think it's unfair, but that's how it is."

"How gladly I would have changed places with you in that case!" the king snarled.

"It's a little late to think of that now," said Arn, shaking his head with a smile. "But if you keep your mouth shut for a moment I'll try to tell you what I think. The sin that Karl Sverkersson committed when he caused the death of your father, Saint Erik, was something he had to atone for immediately. Now we come to you. You killed and partially atoned for the sin, but not wholly. Yet you have maintained a longer peace in the realm than any king I have heard of, and that will be reckoned in your favor in Heaven. You have five sons and a daughter, a charming wife in Cecilia Blanca, more than that, for in her you won a true queen who has been a great honor to you. You strengthened the power of the Church in the kingdom, something I don't think you are entirely happy with just now, but that too will be reckoned in your favor. If you look at all this together, you have not lived a bad life and have not been ill rewarded. However, a debt remains to be paid for your sins, and better now than in Purgatory. So don't complain, but die like a man, dear friend!"

"What is Purga . . . what you said?" asked King Knut hopelessly.

"Purgatory, the cleansing fire. There your sin will be burned away with white-hot irons, so it might be time to repent."

"Can a Templar knight give me absolution for my sins? You

are a type of monk, aren't you?" asked the king with a sudden spark of hope in his eyes.

"No," Arn said curtly. "When you confess for the last time and receive extreme unction from Archbishop Petrus, you will receive forgiveness for your sins. As glad as he will be about your death, it would surprise me if he didn't show you all conceivable kindness at that moment."

"That Petter is nothing but a traitor; if I weren't dying he would want to see me killed!" snapped King Knut, coughing and drooling. "And if he's in such a good mood at my deathbed he'll refuse to give me absolution, and then I'll lie here as powerless as a child and deceived as well. What won't that cost me in Purgatory?"

"Nothing," said Arn calmly. "Now think carefully about this: God is greater than everything else. He hears all and He sees all. He is with us now. Your state of mind is the important thing; if Archbishop Petrus fails you then he in turn will have to pay for it. But you must trust in God."

"I want to have a priest who will give me forgiveness for my sins. And I don't trust that Petter," the king muttered.

"Now you're being as stubborn as a child, and that doesn't become your dignity. If you believe that you can stay alive a few more days, then I'll call Father Guillaume here from Varnhem. He can take care of the extreme unction, confession, and forgiveness of your sins. After all, you will be going to your eternal rest at Varnhem, and that will not happen without some silver coins with your father's picture on them. If you wish, I will ride to fetch Father Guillaume, but then you must promise to stay alive for a few more days."

"I don't dare promise," said the king.

"Then we're back to the only thing that can truly save your soul. You have to trust in God," said Arn. "This is your moment to turn to God the Father; you are a king on his deathbed, and

He will listen to you. You don't need to take a detour through the saints or His Mother. Trust in God, only in Him!"

King Knut lay silent for a while, pondering what Arn had said. To his astonishment he actually did find solace in his words. He closed his eyes and clasped his hands and tried to say a silent prayer directly to God Himself. Naturally he realized that this was like a drowning man grasping at the last straw, but it didn't hurt to try. At first he felt nothing inside but his own thoughts, but after a while it was as though a warm flood of hope and solace filled him, as if God replied by briefly touching him with His Spirit.

"I'm complaining too much about my situation!" he said, suddenly opening his eyes and turning toward Arn. "I hereby consign my soul to God, and with that enough about me. Now to my sons! Do you swear that you are among those who will make Erik jarl the next king after the Dane?"

"Yes, I am among them," said Arn. "If Birger Brosa didn't tell you all this already, I will tell you what has been decided. We have an agreement with the one you call the Dane, Sverker Karlsson. He has no son. After him comes Erik, your eldest son. After Erik come his brothers, first Jon, then Joar, and then Knut. This must any Sverker swear before taking the crown. It's not God Who gives him the crown, but we free men in the lands of the Goths and Svealand. If he swears the oath then the rest of us will swear him loyalty as long as he stands by his oath. That is how it will be."

"And is this a good solution or a bad one?" asked the king through clenched teeth, overcome by intense pain. "I'm going to die, and you're the only one who will speak honestly to me. Tell me the truth, dear Arn."

"If everyone stands by his oath all will be well," Arn replied. "Then Erik jarl will become king at about the same time he would have been crowned if you had lived as long a life as my father or

Birger Brosa. The cost to us will be the humiliation of having to live under the red mantles for a time. What we gain is that we save the realm from a devastating war that we could win only with great difficulty, at a high price in dead warriors and burned buildings. And so this is a good solution."

"Will you be part of the royal council?"

"No, Birger Brosa has sworn that I will never be allowed to be part of the council."

"But I thought you two had been reconciled."

"That we have. But I'm not suited to be a member of the Danes' royal council."

"Why not? I myself missed your services in the council. No king in our land could have a better marshal than you."

"That's just it," said Arn with a secretive smile. "Birger Brosa and I are indeed completely in agreement, and we have spoken more than once about the matter. If I sat in King Sverker's council as his marshal, and also bound by my oath of fealty to him, I might do him more harm than good. Now Birger Brosa and I are pretending that our discord continues, and I am being kept at Forsvik. There I will continue to build the power which shall be that of the Eriks and Folkungs."

King Knut thought carefully about what he had just heard, and found that it was precisely as wily as could be expected from Birger Brosa. Once more he felt a warm stream inside him, as if God were reminding him with a slight touch.

"Will you swear to me and to Erik that you are his marshal and no one else's?" he asked after long contemplation.

"Yes, but we have to be cautious with our words," said Arn. "Remember that I must first swear the oath of allegiance to the Dane as all the others do. But that oath applies only as long as he keeps his word. If he breaks it, there will be war. In such a war I will be Erik Knutsson's marshal, that I swear, and I can swear that to both of you!"

As Arn said this he knew that he had promised nothing more than what was obvious. But since the dying Knut seemed to believe that there was great importance in such an oath, he had his son Erik summoned to the room. The king took both their hands, pressed them to his dying heart, and extracted from them a mutual vow of loyalty. Erik jarl had a hard time tolerating the stench from his father, and his eyes filled with tears from both sorrow and disgust as he swore the oath to Arn. For the first time Arn saw something he didn't like in Erik jarl—his inability to keep a dignified demeanor at his father's deathbed. But he swore obediently on his life, his sword, and his wisdom to do his utmost to save the kingdom's crown for Erik jarl the moment that Sverker Karlsson did not honor his word to the *ting* of all Swedes and Goths and the royal council.

King Knut Eriksson, son of Saint Erik who would be the patron saint of the new kingdom for all eternity, died quietly at his ancestral estate of Eriksberg in the year of Grace 1196. He was buried at Varnhem cloister as the first of all Eriks. No great retinue followed him to his last repose, since he was a king who had lost power several years before his death. But he was given a distinguished resting place, next to the founder of the cloister and donor, Fru Sigrid, the mother of Arn and Eskil.

Many prayers of intercession were said at Varnhem for the peace of King Knut's soul, since the royal gifts to the cloister had been considerable, and it was promised that in times to come this church would be the burial site of the Eriks as well as the Folkungs. Birger Brosa had declared that here the connection between the three crowns and the lion would last forever.

So in time the friends Knut Eriksson and Arn Magnusson would rest close to each other.

✠

There were two harbors in Forsvik, one for the larger ships on Lake Vättern to the east and one for riverboats on the other side on the shore of Lake Viken. At both places there were now so many people in constant motion that it took about a day to find and catch the stowaways. Young stowaways in particular, boys with a knapsack on their back who had run away from home with big dreams, often heading for Forsvik. Rumors about all the wonders for youths seeking to become men had spread from farm to farm throughout the land. Many felt called, but few were chosen.

As a rule the younger ragamuffins were caught and put on a boat back in the direction they had come. Gure the foreman even used to toss the helmsman a silver coin for his trouble.

Sigge and Orm were twelve and thirteen years old when they arrived in this way at Forsvik just in time for King Knut's burial at Varnhem. Like everyone, they had known that the king was going to die for about a year, but they had no idea that he had now passed away. As a result of the funeral at Varnhem, however, neither master nor mistress was at Forsvik.

Whatever Sigge and Orm had imagined about reaching the Forsvik of their dreams and seeking out Sir Arn himself, all their hopes were dashed at once by everything they saw. Perhaps they had expected a great house with carved dragon-heads sticking out from both ends of the ridgepole, with Arn the knight riding in the barnyard with his flashing sword surrounded by young men and boys trying to act as he did. What they found was a village with four streets, a throng of people all hurrying back and forth, and a buzz of foreign tongues.

To their relief they discovered that there were many youths of their own age wearing clothing like themselves of gray homespun. But everywhere they also saw young men, some almost as young as they were, wearing full weaponry with chain mail and blue surcoats as if it were the most natural thing in the world. On their way down the longest street they stopped first at a big open building without walls but with a roof overhead. There at least two dozen young boys were practicing with sword and shield while older boys corrected them, demonstrated the correct methods, and then forced them to repeat the exercises time after time.

Farther down, near the end of the street, there was an open field with a fence around it, and from there came the loud thundering of horses' hooves. Soon Sigge and Orm were perched on the fence rails, watching as if in a dream how young men moved at lightning speed back and forth across the field to commands shouted by older men. And all those on horseback wore armor as if they were going to a noble's feast or to war. So it was true that one could learn to be a knight at Forsvik.

They sat too long at their outpost, like all the young stowaways. After what could have been hours or no time at all as far as Sigge and Orm were concerned, the riders out on the field broke off their practice, lined up in a long row, and strode off to the largest street in the village. Then the two boys were discovered and grabbed by the scruff of the neck by a young man who dismounted from his horse. Showing no kindness, he began pulling them along toward the harbor.

Then Sigge grew angry and said without the slightest shame that he and his brother had no intention of leaving on any boat, because they had both received Sir Arn's own word that they could come to Forsvik.

At first their captor laughed at these preposterous words, but Sigge refused to back down. Planting his heels stubbornly in the dirt, he snarled that both he and his brother could swear before God and all the saints that they had been given a promise by Sir Arn himself that they could come here. Their guard then grew more wary, since he was used to captured stowaways acting submissive and whining rather than impudent. He got up on his

horse, told Sigge and Orm not to move from the spot, and galloped over to the head of the riders. There he stopped before a
man who bore the Folkung mantle and was one of those who had
barked the commands out on the field.

At once the Folkung came riding toward the boys at a gallop with the young man who had caught them close behind.
He leaped to the ground, handing his reins to the other rider,
and went over to grab Sigge and Orm by the scruff of the neck.
They were once again caught in a hard grip, this time in hands
that were wearing iron gloves.

"Forsvik is for Folkungs and not for runaway thrall boys!"
he said sternly. "What are your names and where do you come
from?"

"My name is Sigge, Gudmund's son from Askeberga inn, and
this is my brother Orm," said Sigge crossly but flinching under
the stony grip. "What's your name?"

In astonishment the Folkung loosened his grip. He too was
unprepared for such candid insolence.

"I am Bengt Elinsson and one of those in charge here at Forsvik next to Sir Arn himself," he replied not at all unkindly as he
observed the two urchins. "Gurmund at Askeberga I have met,
and so have all of us who have business between Forsvik and
Arnäs. Gurmund is a freed innkeeper, is he not?"

"Our father is a free man and we were both born free," replied
Sigge.

"Well, at least we'll be spared the trouble of sending you back
bound hand and foot. But you did run away from home, I pre-
sume?"

It was quite true that they had, since their father Gurmund had
not been willing to listen to their entreaties to be allowed to move
to Sir Arn's estate at Forsvik. When they persisted he had beaten
them, and finally so assiduously that they had run away, as much
for that reason as because of the dream of mantles and swords.

Sigge was ashamed to say anything of this, merely nodding to confirm what had been said.

"Your father has beaten you, that is all too obvious from looking at you, and that indicates his lack of honor," said Bengt Elinsson, his voice no longer as stern. "I know a lot about how it feels to be your age, and don't think that I aim to cause you more harm. But you are not Folkungs, so there are no jobs for you here at Forsvik, at least not the sort of jobs you have in mind. You'll both have to return home. But I shall send a message to Gurmund that he must never again lay hands on you, unless he wants to contend with Bengt Elinsson next time."

"But we have Sir Arn's word," Sigge insisted hesitantly. "And Sir Arn is a man who stands by his word."

"Yes, you are certainly right about that," said Bengt Elinsson, trying with difficulty to conceal a laugh behind his hand. "But when and where did Sir Arn give you two, sons of a freedman, such a promise?"

"Five years ago," said Sigge boldly. "He spoke to us in the barnyard and showed us a sword that was so sharp it made my finger bleed just to touch it. And then he said we should seek him out in five years, and now the five years have passed."

"What did the sword look like?" Bengt Elinsson asked, suddenly quite serious. "And how did Sir Arn look?"

"The sword was longer than other swords, in a black scabbard with a golden cross. It was shiny, with magical runes in gold," said Sigge as if the memory were altogether fresh. "And Sir Arn had kind eyes, but many marks from blows and cuts on his face."

"Sir Arn is at the king's funeral and won't be back at Forsvik for a few days or perhaps a week," said Bengt Elinsson in a completely new and friendly way. "Until he returns you shall be our guests at Forsvik. Follow me!"

Sigge and Orm had never in their lives been called guests, nor could they understand what had made the mighty Folkung change his mind so abruptly. They stood there without being able to take a step. They must have looked extremely foolish, for Bengt Elinsson then put his arms around their thin shoulders and swept them along with him toward the harbor.

They were taken to a powerful blond man named Gure who was at work building a house. He in turn accompanied them to a row of smaller houses where there was much noise from hammers and saws. Inside one of the houses sat four boys of their own age and two older men at a long table making arrows. A big pile of arrow tips of various types lay in the middle of the table among bowls of tar, goose feathers, linen thread, and various sorts of knives. Gure explained that such young guests at Forsvik were not only to eat sweet bread; they must also make themselves useful. Some of the arrow-making was simple work, and there they could begin. But two of the other boys would show them around Forsvik so that they could learn where things were and could see where they would sleep and eat. He pointed to two of the young boys at the table. They stood up at once and bowed to him as a sign that they had understood and would obey. Then Gure left without another word.

The two boys who were going to show Sigge and Orm around were named Luke and Toke, and both had hair cropped as closely as Sigge did, which was a normal way to cut thrall children's hair because of the lice. So Sigge took it for granted that the other two weren't free, and that he was superior; he tried to order them to stop staring and instead do as they were told. The one who looked older and stronger told him at once to shut up and remember that he was new at Forsvik and should refrain from putting on airs.

So at first there was little conversation among the four boys as the two Forsvikers began showing the others what there was to see. They started at the smithies; there were three of them located next to one another, but the boys were soon admonished not to get in the way. They continued through the glassworks, where small drinking glasses in shimmering blue and bright red stood in long rows; the older masters had four or five apprentices each. Inside a thundering furnace the glass lay like a big glowing loaf of dough; the masters and apprentices stuck in long pipes, caught up a piece of the dough and began rolling the pipe round and round as they ran over to wooden forms that they wetted with water before they began to blow and turn at the same time. It looked like very hard work, but the great quantity of finished glasses that stood on shelves around the walls showed that they must be very successful in their work. The heat soon drove the boys onward to the saddlery, where men were working with both saddle tack and many other items in leather; then to the weaving rooms where there were mostly women of all ages; to the cooperage; and to two other workshops where the work seemed similar to that of making arrows, but everyone was working with crossbows under the guidance of two foreign masters whose language was impossible to understand.

Sigge and Orm's eyes were so big that it made the other two boys more kindly disposed toward them, and when they headed over to look at the stables and practice halls for the warriors, Luke and Toke became more talkative. Luke said that he and his brother were freed as children, since they had been born as thralls at Forsvik. Now there were no thralls here any longer. Nor was the land at Forsvik used for anything other than pasture for winter fodder for horses and livestock. So a great deal in their lives had changed, more than just being given freedom. If everything had been as it was before, most would have grown up working the land. Instead all young people now were allowed to be apprentices in the workshops, which was like Heaven compared with toiling their whole lives out in the fields.

The two big stables were almost empty because most of the horses were kept outside as long as there was forage. But here and there a horse stood and stared at them suspiciously as they passed by, and saddles and weapons hung along the walls in long rows. Those were the weapons of the young noblemen, and nobody from the workshops was allowed to touch them.

The young nobles came from Folkung estates near and far and trained for five years. Each year new ones arrived, small and nervous, and in later years a number of them went home, self-confident and mortally dangerous with lance or sword. The young nobles also had their own longhouse, the largest at Forsvik. Ordinary folk were not allowed inside, but Toke said that there were more than sixty beds.

Next to the young nobles' longhouse stood the foreigners' house, and there it was not advisable to enter either. And beyond the foreigners' house stood Sir Arn's and Fru Cecilia's own house. Outside a whole little forest of white and red roses grew, and below the house on the slope toward Bottensjön stood rows of apple trees. The fruit would soon be harvested, and the gardens were full of all sorts of root vegetables and herbs.

The tour concluded where it began with the arrow-making workshop, and Sigge and Orm had to learn the first simple job, to bore holes in the arrow shafts where the points would be fastened, using tools they had never seen before. Luke told them that they had now made more than ten thousand arrows at Forsvik, and most of them had been sent to Arnäs in great casks with a hundred arrows in each. Every day at least thirty new arrows were produced at Forsvik.

With the two new apprentices in the arrow workshop the tasks were reassigned so that Sigge and Orm were occupied only with the simple work of boring holes for the points. Luke and Toke then fastened the points in place and wound them with linen thread which they dipped in tar. Then the arrows were sent on to the two foreigners who worked with the most difficult task, putting on the fletches.

This was not the way Sigge and Orm had dreamed of their new life with Sir Arn at Forsvik. But they could sense that it would not be a good idea to tell Luke and Toke that they intended to be apprenticed among the young nobles.

But when Orm, who till then had been too shy to say almost anything at all, let slip a few words about his dreams at the late supper of bread and soup, he was mocked by all the workers at the table. Only Folkungs went into apprenticeship to be warriors, not freedmen with names like Sigge, Toke, Luke, or Orm. With a name like that a boy never got beyond the workshops.

Sigge clenched his teeth and said nothing. He had received a promise from Sir Arn himself, and he intended to remind him of it as soon as he got the chance.

⊁

Arn rode for the first time with a squadron of retainers from the funeral ale at Varnhem to Arnäs. Sixteen men including Sune, Sigfrid, and Torgils Eskilsson had accompanied Cecilia on the alternate route down to Varnhem, along the shore of Lake Vättern.

The young retainers from Forsvik had drawn many curious looks at Varnhem; only the three eldest had reached the age of eighteen. Their horses were not saddled and equipped like those of others; their flanks and chests were covered with cloth in the Folkung colors. A few people had stepped forward to look at the stout black leather straps running beneath the cloth; they also pinched here and there and found that beneath a thin layer with the Folkung colors was a thick layer with chain mail sewn in as protection from arrows. The fact that only three of the retainers had reached the age of grown men also seemed odd, but even the very young in Arn Magnusson's retinue carried their weapons with great self-confidence, and they rode like few men in Western Götaland could ride.

Arn realized that with this unavoidable display he had opened up a new reservoir in the flood of rumors about what was going on at Forsvik. But he hadn't wanted to call Cecilia to the king's funeral without providing her with the protection on the road that honor demanded.

In a single day they had ridden from Varnhem up to Arnäs without straining themselves or the horses very much. As usual, Cecilia was using a regular saddle with a foot in each stirrup. Riding her own Umm Anaza she had no difficulty keeping up with the group of young squires.

They did not stop in Skara because they had brought no carts to carry any purchases. All their baggage was tied up in saddlebags on two extra packhorses. Outside Skara the road was swarming with peasants on their way in and out of town with their carts since it was market day, and the blue column drew much attention and astonished glances as it thundered past. There was an ominous, secret power about these riders, and everybody could sense it. They could see that these horsemen represented a growing Folkung power. But whether it was a good or bad power, whether it was protection for the peace or a portent of war, no one could tell.

They took the road over Kinnekulle to visit stonemaster Marcellus, who was now working at the quarry on the adornments for the new church in Forshem. He already had many sculptures ready, one that roused the admiration of all, and one that made Arn blush and stammer in a way that no one had seen before.

The image that they all admired was intended to sit above the doorway of the church; it showed the Lord Jesus giving to Saint Peter the keys to the Kingdom of Heaven and handing to Saint Paul the book with which he was to spread the Christian teaching all over the world. Above Lord Jesus's head there was a Templar cross and a text carved in good Latin which read: "This church is consecrated to Our Lord Jesus Christ and the Holy Sepulcher."

Both the picture and the text were meant to inspire devotion in the onlooker. It was as though they were looking at the very moment itself, though it never could have taken place in the realm of the senses. But for God, time and space did not exist; He was everywhere at the same time, so the image was just as true as it was beautiful. Arn felt a great emotion in his breast, almost a trembling sensation, at being granted the grace to be involved in building this church dedicated to His Grave. Even though the construction of the church itself had a long way to go, this image was a portent of what was to come.

But the image that stunned Arn and made him feel alternately ashamed and incensed, showed the Lord Jesus accepting the keys to the church from a knight and then blessing the church with his right hand; a stonecutter sat nearby, bent over with a hammer and chisel as he worked on the church. It was obviously supposed to represent Arn giving the church to God, while Marcellus built it. It was not outright blasphemy, but it was an unreasonable way to boast of his deed.

Marcellus took a lighter view of his sculpture. He thought it merely expressed a worldly truth and a good example for human beings. For a thousand years rapturous observers would see how Arn, a Templar knight, had donated this church. Wasn't that precisely the thought that should be expressed by dedicating the church to God's Grave? Instead of seeking out God's Grave in war and death in the Holy Land, true believers should seek it out in their own hearts. They had discussed this the first time they met and concluded their agreement in Skara.

Arn did not remember exactly, but he thought that exalting himself in an image standing next to the Lord Jesus was sheer pride, and that was a grave sin.

Marcellus said again that there was no pride in saying that Arn Magnusson built this church and dedicated it to God's Grave. That was simply the truth.

Arn was glad that there was plenty of time to change things before the church would be finished and consecrated.

The travelers stopped at Arnäs for only one day, mostly because Arn wanted to walk all the way around the fortifications and examine all the details. Everything to do with the outer defenses of the castle was finished. From now on they could spend as many years as they liked on the inner defenses and household comforts rather than war. The residence, which was three stories high and built of stone, was almost done; they would be able to move in this winter. All that was left to build were the big storehouses for grain, dried fish, and fodder for the horses and livestock; enough to withstand a long siege. The rest were simpler tasks for which the most skilled builders in the world were no longer needed. The outer walls, towers, gates, and drawbridges were ready. That was the important thing. At Forsvik the work on the thick chains for the drawbridges and portcullises had just been completed.

The old tower keep at Arnäs had now become an armory for the storage of weapons and valuables. In the high chamber there were several rows of wooden casks stuffed full of more than ten thousand arrows; the chamber below held crossbows, swords, and lances. Even now Arnäs was ready to resist a siege from a very strong foe. But as it looked at the moment, no war was on the horizon, so there was plenty of time to finish up everything they had planned. Soon Arnäs would be an impregnable fortress where many hundreds of Folkungs could seek shelter, regardless of who was threatening outside the walls.

Torgils, who had not been home to Arnäs since Christmas, decided to stay for a few days with his father Eskil, and Arn's party then set off toward Forsvik. They left at the crack of dawn in order to complete their journey in a single day instead of spending the night at Askeberga.

When they neared Forsvik that evening, the alarm was rung

on the big bell, and within moments all the young men and grooms stormed out toward the horses. When Arn and Cecilia and their party rode into Forsvik, three squadrons stood lining the main street. Bengt Elinsson, who was the only commander left at Forsvik, had positioned his horse three paces in front of the others. He first drew his sword, and then the others did the same, and that was how they greeted Sir Arn and Fru Cecilia's return.

Arn rode up to Bengt, thanked him briefly, took over command, and ordered all the young men to return to whatever they were doing before the alarm sounded.

✠

The following days at Forsvik were heavy with the bittersweet sorrow of parting. The five years for which Arn had hired his Saracen men were now over. Those who wanted to leave would do so soon, for the big ship with dried fish from Lofoten was expected in Lödöse. With that ship those returning home would sail to Björgvin, the largest city on the west coast of Norway. From there ships went constantly to Lisboa in Portugal, and then they would be almost in the lands of the faithful.

Only half of the foreigners wanted to return home. Among them were the two physicians Ibrahim and Yussuf, who were sure that their services would prove much more useful in the Almohad Empire in Andalusia. The two Englishmen John and Athelsten also wanted to leave, but for them it was easier, since ships occasionally sailed between Lödöse and England, where Eskil had in recent years begun to expand his trade routes.

Half of the builders who worked on Arnäs would travel the same way as Ibrahim and Yussuf; they found it difficult to live with the true faith in a land whose very existence God seemed to have forgotten. The other half of the builders perhaps had a more forgiving view of God's memory, although their decision to stay was probably due to the fact that many of them, like Ardous from Al Khalil, already had a wife and children.

The two feltmakers Aibar and Bulent were also unwilling to leave. They knew they could get from Björgvin to Lisboa, but from there it was an unfathomably long journey to Anatolia. Besides, their home villages had long since been burned and laid waste by both Christians and the faithful. They no longer had any other home.

The brothers Jacob and Marcus Wachtian had long since begun to adopt Nordic customs; both had been speaking the local language fluently for quite a while.

Surprisingly, Jacob had also come back from one of his trips to Lübeck with a wife to whom he claimed to be lawfully wedded before God. Her name was Gretel, and she was rumored to have been deserted by her betrothed in Lübeck on the very day of their wedding. But she found swift consolation in the arms of the foreign Armenian merchant Jacob. There was something not quite credible about that story, but no one at Forsvik found any reason to argue. For Jacob's part it would be unthinkable to leave. His Gretel refused to return to her own country for some reason; nor did she want to go to Armenia, and besides, she was expecting a child.

Marcus had no desire to travel alone. He had no woman to amuse himself with as his brother did, which he furtively pointed out to Arn from time to time, but life at Forsvik was good. And it was a delight to invent new ways to use water power, or build new weapons or tools for their work. Although with a woman it would certainly be easier.

Arn decided to accompany the faithful and the Englishmen to Lödöse so that no harm would come to them on their last journey through the land of the infidels. He reckoned that the faithful would be safe as soon as they boarded the ship for Björgvin, and he had no qualms about leaving the Englishmen to themselves in Lödöse.

It was a somber farewell, and many friends who had worked hard together for five years wept openly when the travelers went aboard the riverboats that would take them to Lake Vänern and then on bigger ships to the Göta River. It was a relief for all when the farewell was done and the riverboats disappeared around the first bend on the way out onto Lake Viken. Arn and Cecilia were both glad that so many of the foreigners had chosen to stay, for their work and skills were invaluable. It was still difficult to get the apprentices among the freedmen to do the tasks that took many years to learn well.

Arn had a heavy heart when he returned from Lödöse a week later. The most difficult had been parting with old Ibrahim and Yussuf, and the turcopoles Ali and Mansour; the art of those physicians could never be replaced at Forsvik. And even though the young men who had been in service longest had developed commendable skill on horseback, especially when compared to other men in the North, it would be a long time before they could ride like such Syrian warriors as Ali and Mansour. For them, weapons and horsemanship were their daily bread.

But contracts were contracts and had to be upheld. It was a consolation that half of the Saracens had chosen to stay, and Arn had to consider how much had been accomplished to secure the peace during those five years.

And yet he was not in the best of moods when he sat at the table eating and Gure came to him with two workshop lads that he didn't recognize. At first he doubted the explanation they managed to stammer forth. He didn't remember promising that they could be apprenticed at Forsvik. They were not Folkungs, and it was evident from far off that they were thrall boys or the son of a freedman. First he asked them sternly where they got these dreams from and whether they knew it was a grave sin to tell a lie. But then they recounted how he had come to Askeberga the first time, how they had called to him in the doorway, and how he had spoken with them in the barnyard. Then he finally remembered the incident. It made him thoughtful, and he pondered silently for a good while before he made his decision. Sigge and Orm waited with great anguish; Gure was clearly surprised.

"Gure, take these boys to Sigfrid Erlingsson," he said at last. "Say that they shall start in the youngest group of tenderfeet, and see to it that they receive clothing and weapons in due time."

"But master, these boys are in no way Folkungs," Gure objected.

"I know that," said Arn. "They are only sons of a freedman. But we had an agreement, and a Folkung must always honor his word."

Gure shrugged and took Sigge and Orm with him. They both looked as if they wanted to yell and jump for joy; only with great difficulty did they manage to restrain themselves.

Arn sat at the table for a long while, his plate of food half eaten. He was asking himself a very strange question that had never occurred to him before. Could a person only be born a Folkung, or could he become one? Certainly not everyone born a Folkung was superior, while all others were inferior.

The Rule of the Knights Templar said that only a man whose father bore a coat of arms could be admitted as a brother in the order. Others would have to be content to be sergeants. On more than one occasion he had seen knight-brothers who would have made better sergeants, and vice versa.

And what rule said that you couldn't make good men into Folkungs, just as you could inject new blood into a breed of horse? By breeding the heavy, powerful Gothic horses with the fast, agile Arabian horses they were about to develop a new breed that would be more suited to heavy cavalry. That was the next big venture they were going to start at Forsvik. It was a matter of combining the best of the Arabian and the Gothic breeds, just as they worked with different layers of iron and steel when making swords at Forsvik. Why not make Folkungs the same way?

Although he did have to see to it that those two lads were re-baptized, if they had ever been baptized at all. No Folkung horse-men could be called Sigge and Orm.

✠

Sverker Karlsson arrived at Näs, traveling with a stately retinue of a hundred horsemen from Denmark, intending to move in with his people. He had waited with his journey until the end of the year when the ice lay thick and solid on Lake Vättern.

After the New Year he summoned all the prominent men among the Folkungs, Eriks and Swedes to the king's Näs to elect him after he took his oath. Three days of feasting would follow.

Never had so many red mantles been seen at Näs, not even during the reign of King Karl Sverkersson. It was not merely the Sverker color, for also among the Danes red was most common. Erik jarl, who had been at Näs when the Sverkers arrived, whis-pered in disgust to Arn that it looked like a river of blood had come running across the ice.

Birger Brosa, his brother Folke, and Erik jarl were the only worldly men in the king's new council who were not Danes or Sverkers. Eskil had been forced to give up his seat on the council when Sverker declared that such serious matters as the trade of the kingdom must be left in the hands of more knowledgeable Danes. For marshal he appointed his friend Ebbe Sunesson, who was related to the Folkungs at Arnäs, since his kinsman Kon-rad was married to Arn and Eskil's half-sister Kristina. Sverker thought that this kinship was like a bridge between the Danes and the Folkungs.

Archbishop Petrus beamed like a sun and praised God over

and over because finally, in His infinite wisdom and justice, He had brought home the son of the murdered King Karl to the crown of the Goths and Swedes. With that, God's will was done, Petrus assured them.

But Sverker would not be allowed to wear the crown before he swore in front of the whole council and the royal *ting* of notables to uphold the law and justice with the help of God. He also had to swear that he renounced all claim to the crown for his kinsmen, since Erik jarl was the one next in line for the crown. And after Erik jarl followed his younger brothers Jon, Joar, and Knut, who would now live in the realm with all the rights pertaining to sons of the king.

Archbishop Petrus, who administered the oath, had in several places attempted to skip one thing and another but was immediately reprimanded by both the Swedes and Goths. Only when everything was truly legal did the *ting* of the whole kingdom swear its allegiance to King Sverker for as long as he lived—and as long as he kept his vow.

During the three days of feasting, the Danes showed how a royal feast was conducted out in the great world, with jousting between knights who rode at each other with lance and shield. Only the Danes took part in these games, since the new masters took it for granted that no man up in backward Western Göta-land or Svealand could fight on horseback. And judging by the many admiring and astonished expressions that King Sverker could observe among his new subjects, these knightly arts, which had already been long established in Denmark, were something no one had ever seen up here in the North.

Arn watched closely, keeping his face expressionless as he observed the actions of the Danish knights. Some were not half bad, others were as lax as he had expected. None of them would have passed muster even as sergeants in the Order of Knights Templar, but on Nordic battlefields they would be hard to combat. If they were going to overcome these Danes out on the open field, it would require another few years of training at Forsvik. But their lead was no bigger than that.

During the feast days King Sverker and his marshal Ebbe Sunesson spent their time mostly in the great hall surrounded by Danish courtiers, summoning the important men in the kingdom one by one for discussions. Birger Brosa made the introductions. King Sverker was always careful to be friendly and to treat Folkungs and Eriks like his own Sverker kinsmen.

When it was Eskil and Arn's turn to go before the king and his Danish courtiers, Birger Brosa announced that Eskil was a merchant and previously sat on King Knut's council and was the heir to the estate Arnäs. About Arn he said only that he had spent much of his life in the cloister, also in Denmark, and now was the master of the forest estate of Forsvik.

Arn exchanged a quick, puzzled glance with Birger Brosa about his somewhat incomplete description of what Arn had done in between his childhood years at the cloister and his present life at Forsvik. Birger Brosa merely winked back, unnoticed by anyone else.

King Sverker was happy to speak with someone who had no difficulty understanding the speech of the Danes; many of the slow Swedes seemed to find the language incomprehensible. And for Arn it was easy to fall back into the language he had spoken as a child. He still sounded more like a Dane than a Gothic man.

At first the conversation revolved around innocent topics such as how beautiful it was on the shore of Limfjord near the cloister of Vitskøl, and about the mussel cultivation they had tried at the cloister without much success, since people living on the fjord believed that it was contrary to God's word to eat mussels. That was no longer so, King Sverker assured him. Then he invited Arn and Eskil to visit Denmark with his letter of safe passage so that they might see their half-sister Kristina. When the brothers did not look as though this journey was of great interest to them, the king promised instead to invite both Kristina and her husband Konrad Pedersson to Näs sometime next summer. He was clearly trying to demonstrate that all old animosities had been forgotten.

So it seemed both tactless and unnecessary of marshal Ebbe Sunesson to remember suddenly how he had once gotten into a little fight at Arnäs with one of their kinsmen. But of course they bore no hard feelings about that, did they?

He had spoken calmly but with an irritating smirk on his face. Birger Brosa shook his head to warn Arn, who with great difficulty controlled himself before he replied that the one who had died was their brother Knut. He said that they both prayed for their brother's soul, but that neither of them had a mind for revenge.

There Ebbe Sunesson should have let it rest. He may have drunk too much during the festivities, or perhaps he was elated because he had been the victor in the jousting contest. Or it could be that he and his friends had already convinced themselves that they had become lords of folk that were not worthy of respect. For what he now said made both Birger Brosa and King Sverker blanch, although for different reasons.

With open scorn he explained to Arn and Eskil that they didn't need to feel in the least embarrassed. If it was so that they had not received their just honor after their brother's regrettable death, he would gladly meet one of them with the sword. Or why not both at once? Then it would only be a question of whether they had enough honor and enough courage.

Arn looked down at the stone floor and with great effort stifled his first impulse to propose a duel. It must have looked as if he were ashamed because he dared not take up the challenge that had been delivered with words as clear as a slap in the face.

When the silence had become unbearable, he raised his head and said calmly that upon reflection he found it unwise for the new king and his men to begin their time in the land of the Swedes and Goths with blood. In either case, whether Herr Ebbe killed yet another Folkung from Arnäs, or he himself killed the king's marshal, this would not benefit King Sverker or the peace they all desired.

The king then placed his hand on Ebbe Sunesson's arm and prevented him from answering, which he seemed all too eager to do. The king said that he felt honored that among those who had sworn allegiance to him there were good men like Eskil and Arn Magnusson who understood how to place the peace of the realm before their own honor.

They did not reply, but bowed and left without another word. Arn had to step outside in the cold air at once, since he was boiling with humiliation. Eskil hurried after to assure him that nothing good would have come of it if a Folkung, in the very first week of King Sverker's reign, had killed his marshal. And besides, these insulting words could have been avoided if Birger Brosa had been a bit more accurate in his description of what sort of cloister life Arn had lived. As things now stood, the arrogant marshal had no idea how close to death he had come.

"I still can't understand what God had in mind by placing our brother's murderer within a single sword-length of me," Arn muttered between clenched teeth.

"If God wants to bring the two of you together with weapons, then He will do so. That was apparently not His intention just now," said Eskil, at a loss.

Chapter 11

The only news from Näs during King Sverker's first two years which pleased the Folkungs and Eriks was that by the second Christmas ale, Archbishop Petrus had eaten himself to death. Otherwise they heard very little, either good or bad. It was as if whatever had to do with the highest power in the realm was no longer of any concern to the Folkungs and Eriks.

Not even when King Sverker sent a crusade to the east did he find any reason to ask for help from the Folkungs and Eriks; instead he allied himself with the Danes and Gotlanders. Of course it was not much of a crusade. The intention was for the Sverkers to be sent by ship to Courland to save the country once again for the true faith and bring home anything of value that they might find. But a southerly storm drove the two hundred vessels with the crusaders north so that they landed in Livonia instead. There they plundered for three days, loaded their spoils of war on board ship, and then went home.

Surely it was of little importance to have missed out on three days of plundering, but the Swedes up in the dark North Woods were especially insulted that they hadn't been trusted to send a single *fylking* of troops or a single ship, and that the king and his Danes thought so little of them.

For the Folkungs at Arnäs and Forsvik it was actually an advantage that the new king disdained their services, because it meant that they could spend their time on more useful endeavors. At Arnäs, villages were built inside the walls as wells were dug and the storehouses were completed. At Forsvik Cecilia's ledgers were finally showing a profit.

This was partially due to the glass from Forsvik that was now being sold in Linköping and Skara, Strängnäs, Örebro, Västra Aros and Östra Aros, and even in Norway. And a considerable number of young men had spent so many years as apprentices that it was now time for them to return home. When they did so, it was their responsibility to equip their own estates and teach their own retainers and archers. They then purchased all of their new weapons from Forsvik. In this way an ever-growing number of the weapons that had been produced for many years without payment in order to arm Arnäs and Bjälbo now began to provide Forsvik with an income. Unlike the story in the Holy Scriptures, they had endured seven lean years before the fat years had come. But when the tide indeed began to turn, Cecilia at first did her calculations several times, since she thought there must be some mistake. Instead of silver flowing out, it had begun to flow in, and at an increasingly rapid pace.

These last years before the turn of the thirteenth century, which according to some doomsayers and prelates would bring the end of the world, were tranquil times for the Folkungs, but they also involved a good deal of traveling and many wedding ales.

It no longer seemed of any use for them to marry members of the Sverker clan; that was the opinion of Birger Brosa as well as his brothers Magnus and Folke. And because Eskil had finally had his marriage to the treacherous Katarina annulled, and she had been banished to Gudhem convent for the rest of her life, he had to set a good example. With courtship in mind, he went to Västra Aros and the regions around the town of Sigtuna. There he soon found what he was seeking in the person of Bengta Sigmundsdotter from Sigtuna. Her husband had been killed several years earlier when the Estonians arrived on a plundering expedition. But she had been wise, almost as if she had been able to see into the future. Although she and her husband owned the largest trading house in Sigtuna, she had refused to keep all of the riches they had acquired in the city. Instead, she had ordered them transported north to her parents' home. In this way she became one of the few residents in Sigtuna to emerge from the fire as a rich woman.

It might well be that she was not so rich that she could provide a dowry worthy of a marriage with Eskil, but it was unlikely there was such a woman anywhere in the realm. And with widows, the clan was not as strict about such matters; nor was a betrothal ale required, since widows made their own decisions regarding marriage. The bridal ale could be celebrated immediately once Eskil and Bengta had come to an agreement.

The bridal couple were fond of each other, and it was everyone's opinion that they seemed particularly well-matched. For a woman, Bengta was unusually capable of handling business matters, and trade was after all Eskil's great joy in life. From the first day they met they had already started talking about leaving the business in Sigtuna and moving Bengta's trading house either to Visby on Gotland or Lübeck. In that way they would strengthen each other's dealings.

To find a woman from Svealand for young Torgils Eskilsson turned out to be more difficult. But the dowager queen Cecilia Blanca was from there, and after the death of King Knut she

could no longer bear to live at Näs even though the new lord,
King Sverker, had ingratiatingly told her that she could stay as
his guest as long as she liked. Yet that was not the impression
that the new king's contemptuous Danes displayed. Her sons
Erik jarl, Jon, Joar, and Knut were to be kept more like prisoners in a gilded cage at Näs, but she herself was allowed to leave.
She had pretended to set off for Riseberga cloister, which was a
befitting residence for a dowager queen with no power, but at
Forsvik she had disembarked from the boat, having decided to go
no further. The two Cecilias were soon making plans for young
Torgils' wedding, and they had decided that the daughter of a
chief judge would be best, for judges held a very strong position
among the Swedes; it would be important to establish ties to that
sort of power.

Once the two Cecilias had decided something, that was how
it would be. And so during the following summer a great deal
of traveling went on between Western Götaland and Svealand.
After celebrating his own wedding, Eskil set off with his son Torgils, Arn and his son Magnus Månesköld, and a large retinue
to Svealand. On their way north to the betrothal ale in darkest
Uppland, they stopped to visit many powerful men who were
either members of Eskil's new clan or were related to Cecilia
Blanca. The betrothal ale between Torgils and Ulrika, who was
the daughter of Leif, the judge at Norrgarns estate, a day's journey from Östra Aros, took place around the feast of Saint Laurentius before the harvesting began in Uppland. The bridal ale
was celebrated over five days at Arnäs later in the autumn.

But the women also did much traveling during this tranquil
time. They usually met at Ingrid Ylva's home at Ulvåsa, since it
was halfway between Forsvik and Ulfshem. This meant that the
two Cecilias and Ulvhilde would have only one day's journey in
order to meet. Ingrid Ylva and Ulvhilde were both Sverker daughters, Cecilia Blanca was of the Svea clan, and Cecilia Rosa was

of the Pål clan from Husaby. Hence the four of them could meet without constantly thinking about Eriks or Folkungs, though they had all married into one of these clans. Ingrid Ylva had already given birth to two sons, and she was expecting her third child that summer when the women spent more time alone than with their husbands. Since Ingrid Ylva's eldest son Birger would soon turn five, the same age as Cecilia Rosa's daughter Alde, there was much talk about how these two must soon be given booklearning and how it might be arranged for them to learn together. Earlier in the year Ulvhilde had sent her boys to a cleric in Linköping, but it would not be wise to send young Folkungs to the Sverker stronghold during the evil times that were now upon them.

Finally Cecilia Blanca decided that Birger and Cecilia Rosa's little Alde could be given schooling at Forsvik if they could persuade the old monk there to spend less time with the swords and horses, which would do him good. Cecilia Blanca also thought that she, as a queen with nothing to occupy her time, might be of use in a way that would arouse no objections if she too participated in teaching the children. They all found this to be such a good idea that they decided the very next day to take the first of Eskil's boats to Forsvik and speak with the monk themselves.

And so it was that before long Brother Guilbert found himself in an unexpected position in Forsvik's new great hall. He didn't require much convincing to agree, partly because it was an occupation pleasing to God to teach young children, and partly because such work would cause less wear on his old body than working with swords and horses. But he grumbled that this was not the task he had been given by Father Guillaume at Varnhem.

Cecilia Blanca dismissed this objection as easily as swatting a fly by saying that what Father Guillaume wanted or did not want when it came to Folkungs and Eriks depended more on the purse of silver than on the spirit.

No matter how much Brother Guilbert may have agreed with such an impudent statement, he went on to say that he also had an agreement with Arn. Then it was Cecilia Rosa's turn to address him, saying that she and not Arn was the owner of Forsvik.

As if grasping for the last straw, Brother Guilbert said finally that he couldn't very well promise anything until Arn came back home. He was instantly urged to admit that if Arn had no objections, he would comply.

And with that the stubborn women smiled contentedly and exchanged victorious glances before they began drinking a great deal of wine and talking so much that Brother Guilbert soon withdrew.

✠

When King Sverker's Danish wife Benedikta died of the fever, there was little cause for sorrow among the Eriks and Folkungs. King Sverker's only daughter Helena was no threat to the crown.

But their dismay was all the greater when a rumor began to spread that jarl Birger Brosa had fetched his last daughter Ingegerd from Riseberga cloister to marry her to the king. As far as anyone knew, Ingegerd was a healthy woman who looked as if she could give birth to any number of sons. Many said that this was the only foolish thing that Birger Brosa had ever done in his long life, and that black clouds were now gathering over the realm.

After King Sverker's first cautious years in power he began concocting bolder plans, and it was also obvious that he had decided to ingratiate himself to the Church and the crowd of bishops. This became almost ridiculously clear when he imitated King Knut of Denmark by promulgating a new law completely on his own, without consulting the council or the *ting*.

King Knut had declared that he was king by the grace of God,

so he could make any laws he desired. Naturally King Sverker
didn't dare make such a statement, but he did claim that he now
chose to make laws because he had received what he called "divine inspiration."

What exactly he meant by that was obscure, except that of
course it had something to do with God. But his action was also
futile because the new law had already been in force for many
years. It stated that the Church did not have to pay tax to the
king.

When it turned out that the ominous rumor was true about
how Birger Brosa himself had provided a fertile, child-bearing
woman to the Sverker king, the Folkungs decided to hold a clan
ting. The meeting would be held at Bjälbo, since Birger Brosa
pleaded old age and poor health. Most people guessed that he
would rather be rebuked at home on his own estate, acting as a
host rather than as a guest among kinsmen.

He did indeed have to endure many harsh words for this last
foolhardy marriage arrangement of his. Those who spoke with
him admitted that most previous marriages that the old jarl had
arranged had been wise and served the cause of peace, but this
time it was just the opposite.

Birger Brosa sat slumped in his high seat and at first did little
to defend himself. That had always been his approach in his most
powerful days, holding back until the end of a conversation and
then summing up what the others had said and sticking the sharp
sword of his tongue into the crack he would always discover between quarreling kinsmen.

This time no such crack was discernible, and he had to start
explaining his actions much earlier. As so often before he tried to
get the hall to quiet down by speaking in a low voice, but this time
he was merely admonished to speak louder. He cautiously raised
his voice and said that if a king became a widower at a young age
as Sverker had, then he was certainly bound to get himself a new

queen. And if that had to happen, wouldn't it be better if this queen were of the Folkung clan rather than a foreigner?

Such a course of events was by no means certain, said an angry Magnus Månesköld. For if a king became a widower, he might just as easily decide to marry some dowager queen, and an old crone from Denmark would have been more tolerable to everyone than a lively child-bearer, fetched healthy and ready from safekeeping in the convent.

Then Eskil took the floor and said that a blunder that was done could not be undone. Now that the bridal ale had already been celebrated, to attempt to break the betrothal would be an affront that might even lead to war. King Sverker could then say that the oath of allegiance everyone had sworn him was broken. So they would have to keep their promise and pray that Ingegerd gave birth to a long series of daughters before Sverker's member slackened.

At the mention of the word "war," several of the younger kinsmen in the hall livened up, and they began murmuring that it might be better to forestall than to be caught napping. They turned to Arn to hear his opinion. So many youths from so many Folkung estates had already been trained at Forsvik or were there even now; everyone was confident that Arn Magnusson would be the leader in the next war.

Arn replied that they were all bound by their oath to King Sverker until he broke his. If Sverker made a Folkung woman his queen, he would certainly not be breaking any oath. So there was no acceptable reason to go to war right now.

Besides, it would be unwise. What would happen if they set off at once for Näs and killed the king? That might mean not only war with Denmark, but Archbishop Absalon in Lund might excommunicate a number of Folkungs. Regicide was punishable by excommunication nowadays. Even an argument over who should be archbishop or who should crown the king could lead to excommunication. Only if King Sverker broke his oath could they go to war against him without encountering such risks.

Arn's objections were both so unexpected and thought-provoking that the clan *ting* soon calmed down. Then Birger Brosa tried to recapture some of his former power, saying authoritatively that even if the war might be getting closer there was still plenty of time to wait. They could best use the time to prepare themselves well. He mentioned specifically that more youths should be sent to train at Forsvik, and that more weapons should be ordered from there for every Folkung estate.

There was nothing wrong with the wisdom of these words, and everyone realized that. But it seemed that Birger Brosa's long hold over the clan *ting* was broken. And he too seemed aware of that fact as he left the hall first, as was the custom. His hands and his head trembled as though in terror or as if fast approaching his deathbed.

⳨

The year of Grace 1202 became the year of death. It was as though the Lord's angels had come down to burn the dry grass and prepare the ground for entirely new powers. King Sverre of Norway died that year, mourned by as many as rejoiced. That made the alliance of both the Folkungs and the Eriks with Norway weaker and more uncertain.

King Knut of Denmark also died, and his brother Valdemar was crowned, who had been nicknamed "the Victor." He had been given that name with good reason. He had recently conquered both Lübeck and Hamburg, which both paid tribute now to the Danish crown, and he had made several trips with warriors to both Livonia and Courland. Everywhere his armies had marched to victory. He would be a truly formidable foe.

As if God were jesting with the Folkungs, Eriks, and all other people in Western and Eastern Götaland, however, there was no danger that Valdemar the Victor would come north from Skåne, pillaging and burning. For King Sverker was the Danes' man, and his land did not have to be conquered as long as he was king. For him it did not seem vexing that all trade between his lands and Lübeck would be taxd by the Danes in the future. As Eskil Magnusson once muttered between clenched teeth as he sat at his account books, now they were paying a tax on peace.

But the greatest sorrow for the Folkungs came in January of that year when Birger Brosa died. He wasn't long on his death-bed, and few kinsmen managed to come and say farewell. But more than a thousand Folkungs accompanied the revered jarl on his last journey to Varnhem. They gathered at Bjälbo and pro-ceeded as a long blue-clad column of warriors across the ice of Lake Vättern to Skövde and on to Varnhem.

From most of the Folkung estates came only the men, since it was a bitterly cold journey. From Arnäs, Forsvik, Bjälbo, and Ulvåsa came all the family members. Wives and children and some of the elderly, like old Herr Magnus of Arnäs, were trans-ported in sleighs tucked under many pelts from wolves and sheep. And many riders probably wished they were riding in the sleighs, because their chain mail was like ice against their bodies, and every rest stop became more torment than respite.

From Forsvik rode Arn Magnusson first among forty-eight riders. They were the only ones in the funeral procession who didn't seem bothered by the icy wind, even though they were rid-ing in full armor. They had special combat clothing for winter use and absolutely no iron or steel next to their bodies. Not even their iron-clad feet seemed to suffer from the cold.

King Sverker did not come to Varnhem. There were various opinions about the reason for this. He hadn't been able to get together a greater retinue than two hundred men, and that would have looked paltry compared with the number of Folkungs who had gathered. And people were often unruly at wakes; in their grief, who could say what would happen if someone in a red mantle let his tongue run away with him so that the first sword was drawn. It was no doubt wise and cautious of King Sverker not to show himself at the burial of the old jarl.

And yet it was hard not to think that the king had shown disdain for Birger Brosa and thus all Folkungs by viewing the jarl's death only as an occasion for his own clan.

Birger Brosa was laid to rest near the altar, not far from King Knut whom he had served for the cause of peace and the kingdom's welfare for so many years. His funeral mass was long, especially for those of his kinsmen who could not get a seat inside the church but had to stand outside in the snow for the entire two hours.

But soon three hundred of those who had followed Birger Brosa to Varnhem had to return on a similar errand. Old Herr Magnus of Arnäs had not fared well during the cold journey when his brother was buried. He began coughing and shivering by the first day back at Arnäs, and he was put to bed next to a big log fire on the top floor of the new residence. He never did recover. His kinsmen barely had time to summon the priest from Forshem for extreme unction and the forgiveness of sins before he died, because he kept brushing off all premonitions of the worst. A Folkung should be able to stand a little cold, he assured them time after time. Someone said that those were his last words.

Sorrow lay heavy over Forsvik during the forty days of Lent before Easter. Work continued apace in the millhouse and workshops, of course, but the usual laughter and jokes were no longer heard. It was as though the master's sorrow had spread to everyone else.

Arn spent less time than normal with the practice sessions for the young noblemen. Fortunately many of them had now become full-grown men and already had several years' experience training their younger kinsmen. Sune, Sigfrid, and Bengt had all chosen to stay on as instructors at Forsvik rather than return to their own estates.

The fact that there were new instructors for the young men had also made the absence of Brother Guilbert among the riders and at swordplay exercises less noticeable now than at first. He spent most of his time in the little sacristy of the newly-built church, where he taught Alde and Birger Magnusson. Already all the *lectionis* were held in Latin.

Yet Brother Guilbert's instruction had not been accepted without question once Cecilia discovered that he had been in the workshops and fashioned two small bows for the children. She found him standing behind the church and urging them to try to hit a small leather ball that he'd hung by a thin cord. To Cecilia he had defended himself by saying that archery was an art that sharpened the mind, and that the children would have great use of that capacity when they eventually had to delve into Aristotle's logic or grammar. When Cecilia suspiciously went to Arn to ask him about the topic, he agreed much too eagerly with Brother Guilbert's words, which did nothing to lessen her suspicion.

Cecilia thought that there were great differences between Alde and Birger. Alde would eventually become the mistress of Forsvik or some other estate. No one could know for sure what awaited Birger Magnusson in the future, but as the eldest son in one of the most distinguished Folkung houses and with a mother of royal lineage, it was easy to imagine that archery, horses, and lances would assume great importance in his life. But it did not follow from this that their daughter Alde should be trained in war.

Arn tried to calm Cecilia by telling her that archery was not only for war but also for hunting, and that there were many women who were excellent hunters. No woman should be ashamed that she could singlehandedly bring home a duck or deer she had shot to the table. And as far as Birger was concerned, his schooling for life would change a great deal from the day he turned thirteen and joined the young men's beginners' group.

Cecilia contented herself with that explanation until she discovered that Brother Guilbert had also made small wooden swords, which Alde and Birger were using to attack each other with gusto in front of their eagerly gesticulating teacher.

Arn agreed that handling a sword might not be what he most wanted his daughter to learn. But the children's schooling was not easy, and Brother Guilbert was a very demanding teacher; he knew that from his own experience. And surely it wasn't wrong to shift now and then from grammar to a little play. A sound mind required a sound body, that was a basic human truth.

There had also been tears and a squabble when Birger got his first horse at the age of seven, and Cecilia forbade Alde to ride before she was at least twelve. Horses were not only for harmless play, and they knew that especially well at Forsvik, where over the years there had been many injuries and cries when young riders fell and hurt themselves, sometimes so badly that they had to spend time in bed. For young men learning to be warriors that was a danger they had to accept. But of course that didn't apply to Alde.

Arn found himself caught in the middle between a mother and daughter who were equally determined, and both of them were used to wrapping him around their little fingers. But in the matter of when Alde should be given her first horse, only one of them could win, and it was Cecilia.

He tried to console Alde by riding with her in front of him in the saddle, slowly and calmly while they were within sight of Forsvik, and at the dizzying speed that Arabian horses were capable of when they were out of sight. Then Alde would shriek with delight and was appeased for the moment. Although Arn began to suffer from a guilty conscience because he had tempted

Alde with such great speed. There was a clear danger that she might try the same thing as soon as she got her own horse, and speed was something one ought to try last, not first, when learning to ride.

At Easter the little wooden church at Forsvik was decorated with dark tapestries made by Suom, depicting Our Savior's suffering on Golgotha, His path up the Via Dolorosa, and the Last Supper with His disciples. Arn still had a hard time getting used to a Jerusalem that looked more like Skara, and Jesus' disciples that looked as though they had been brought from the nearest *ting* site in Western Götaland. He also had a hard time seeing pictures in God's house, because he thought that such things disturbed the purity of thought.

Spring arrived late that year which would be remembered as the Year of Death, and the ice around Forsvik and on the river was too thin to walk across but too thick for boats. So Christians had to stay where they were and celebrate the Easter masses themselves at Forsvik. But Brother Guilbert could handle all of the priestly duties, and besides, he had excellent singers to help him; not only Arn but the two Cecilias knew all the hymns by heart. Even though Forsvik's church didn't look like much to the outside world, resembling as it did a Norwegian stave church, it was likely that the Easter masses held there in the Year of Death 1202 were sung more beautifully than in all other churches in Western Götaland, except for those at the cloisters.

After they had sung praises to the Lord and the resurrection on the third day, an Easter dinner of lamb was held for all the Christians in the new banquet hall. The clouds of sorrow seemed to disperse, and not only because Lent was over and Our Savior resurrected. The Saracen method of preparing lamb won the admiration of all.

Now was the first time they could celebrate the fact that Marcus Wachtian had found himself a German wife. Her name was

Helga and she was also from Lübeck. When his brother Jacob had his own child and became more unwilling to make long journeys twice a year to the German cities, Marcus had volunteered to take over for him. Naturally he had brought back things that were both pleasurable and useful to Forsvik, everything from huge anvils that they could not cast themselves to sword blanks from somewhere called Passau which were marked with a running wolf. These sword blanks were made of extremely good steel, and they could quickly and easily be forged into finished swords. When Cecilia calculated what it cost to make swords from scratch versus buying them half-finished, she found that the latter method was more economical. She was counting not only the outlay of silver but also the time they could save and use for other smithy work that also brought an income in silver. It was a new way of reckoning, but both the Wachtian brothers and Arn agreed with Cecilia's view that it was probably better and more feasible.

Of everything that Marcus brought back from Germany, though, Helga was what he prized most highly. And not only because, as he said in jest, he hadn't been forced to pay Danish toll on her when he brought her home.

It was a good feast, with the first laughter that had been heard in a long time at Forsvik. Arn sat in the high seat between the two Cecilias, with Alde and little Birger below them. Next to the Wachtian brothers and their German wives sat the foreman Gure, who had decided to be baptized as soon as he was freed, and Brother Guilbert. Farther away in the hall at two longtables sat almost sixty young men in Folkung colors, growing louder and louder as the ale was consumed in great quantities.

Then Cecilia ordered wine and glasses to be brought to their house, inviting all the older folks to continue the Easter feast over there, since the noise coming from the young men would not diminish as the evening wore on.

They drank and talked until the small hours, but then Arn excused himself by saying that he needed to get some sleep because he had to get up early to do some heavy work. The others gave him surprised looks, so he explained that early in the morning, just after dawn, there was going to be a strenuous exercise on horseback with all the young men. They had apparently learned how to drink ale like men. Now they also had to learn what it cost in headaches if they had to show up and perform.

✠

It was Alde and Birger who found Brother Guilbert. He was sitting with his quill pen in his hand, calmly leaning back in his sacristy where he had the morning sun, and he looked like he was asleep. But when the children couldn't wake him they went to Cecilia and complained. Soon there was a great commotion at Forsvik.

When Arn understood what had happened he went without a word to his clothing chamber, taking down the widest of the Templar mantles he could find; he fetched a needle and coarse thread from the workshops and sewed the dead man inside the mantle. He had Brother Guilbert's most beloved horse saddled, a powerful sorrel stallion of the type they used in practice for the heavy cavalry. Then with no special ceremony he draped the body of his dead friend over the saddle in the great white sack that the mantle formed, with arms and legs hanging down on either side. As the stable workers saddled Abu Anaza, Arn dressed in full armor, not in Folkung colors but in those of the Knights Templar. Around the pommel he hung a water bag of the type only horsemen from Forsvik used, along with a purse of gold. Half an hour after the body had been found, Arn was ready to set off for Varnhem.

Cecilia tried to object that this could not possibly be an honorable and Christian way to take a lifelong friend to the grave. Arn replied curtly and sadly that indeed it was. This was how many a Templar knight returned with a brother's help. It could just as well have been Brother Guilbert riding this way with him. Nor was it the first time that Arn had brought home a brother in this manner. Brother Guilbert was not any ordinary monk, but a Templar knight who was traveling to the grave as many brothers had done before him and many would do after him.

Cecilia understood that it was clearly useless to object further. Instead she tried to arrange for Arn to have some food to take along on his journey, but he refused it almost with contempt and pointed at his water bag. More was not said before, with bowed head, he rode out from Forsvik, leading the horse carrying Brother Guilbert.

Losing both his father and uncle within such a short time had been as grievous for Arn as for anyone else. And Arn himself had believed that if Death immediately thereafter had sunk his claws into a lifelong friend, the pain would be greater than anyone could stand.

But Arn had not ridden very long in Brother Guilbert's company before he realized that this grief was both greater and easier to bear. No doubt it was because Brother Guilbert was a Templar knight, one in an endless series of dear brothers whom Arn had lost over a long span of years. In the worst case he had seen their heads stuck on lance-tips in the hands of Syrians or Egyptians howling with the intoxication of victory. The death of a Templar knight was not like that of an ordinary man, because the Knights Templar always lived in Death's anteroom, always aware that they could be the next ones called. For those of the brothers who were granted the grace to live a long time, without fleeing or compromising their conscience, such as Brother Guilbert but also Arn himself, there was no reason to complain in the slightest. God had now considered that Brother Guilbert's life's work was done, so He had called one of His most humble servants home. In the midst of his good work, with his quill pen in hand and having just finished the Latin grammar he had written for children, Brother Guilbert had quietly lowered his hand, blotted the ink one last time, and then died with a peaceful smile on his face. It was a blessing in itself to die like that.

On the other hand there were much more difficult things to try and understand when it came to the path that Brother Guilbert had taken in his earthly life. For more than ten years he had been a Templar knight in the Holy Land, and few fighting brothers lived longer than that. Whatever sins the young Guilbert had behind him when he rode out to his first battle in his white mantle, he had soon atoned for them more than a hundredfold. And yet he was not granted the direct path to Paradise, which was the greatest reward for a Templar knight.

God led him instead to a backwater of the world to become the teacher of a five-year-old Folkung, to raise the lad to be a Templar knight, and then against all sense and reason to work with him again toward utterly different goals twenty years later.

As Arn understood his own path, nothing was inconceivable, since God's Mother Herself had told him what he should do: build for peace and build a new church that would be consecrated to God's Grave. This he had also tried to obey as best he could.

He who sees all and hears all, as the Muslims said, must have known what was going on in the heart of the deceitful and bloodthirsty Richard Lionheart when he chose to execute several thousand captives rather than accept the last payment of fifty thousand besants in gold for his hostage. God must have known that this gold would come to Western Götaland, and what would happen to it there. In hindsight one could often follow and understand God's will.

But now as they were riding toward Varnhem and Brother Guilbert's grave, the future was still just as hard to discern as always. Brother Guilbert's service in his earthly life was concluded, and Arn had no doubt that such a good man, who had also served more than ten years in God's Own army, would have a place in the heavenly kingdom as reward.

What awaited Arn himself, he could not see. Did God really want him to vanquish the Danish king, Valdemar the Victor? Well, then he would try to do so. But he would rather see the armed force he had built prove strong enough to keep war at bay. The best thing that could happen to Arnäs would be that the castle's strength was so great that no one ever dared besiege it, and not a drop of blood was ever spilled on its walls. The best that could happen to the cavalry he was creating was if it never had to go on the attack.

If he tried to think clearly and coldly past his own wishes, things did not look particularly bright. Right after Birger Brosa's death, King Sverker had elevated his and Ingegerd's newborn son Johan to the jarl of the realm before the council at Näs. That honor rightfully belonged to Erik jarl and no one else. What King Sverker's intention was with his newborn son was not hard for anyone to see. And Erik jarl and his younger brothers were being held at Näs more as captives than as royal foster sons.

Prayer was the only path to clarity and guidance, Arn realized dejectedly. If God willed it, Sverker would fall dead at any moment, and everything would be over without war. If God willed otherwise, the greatest war that had ever ravaged Western Götaland was on its way.

He began to pray, and he rode most of the way to Varnhem in prayer. He stopped for the night in the middle of a forest, made a fire, and placed Brother Guilbert next to him, continuing to pray for clarity.

On the road between Skövde and Varnhem where it was no longer wilderness, many people were astonished to see the white-clad knight with God's emblem, with the lance behind him in the saddle and with his head bowed grimly. He rode past without either looking at anyone or greeting them. The fact that the body he was transporting behind him was dressed in the same foreign mantle as he was also caused astonishment. Thieves could be taken to the *ting* like this, but never an equal among nobles.

Arn stayed for three days inside Varnhem cloister before the funeral mass and the burial. Brother Guilbert was honored with a grave site under the transept, not far from the place where Father Henri rested.

When Arn returned to Forsvik almost a week after he had set out, he had a young monk with him who suffered severe riding cramps on Brother Guilbert's horse. This was Brother Joseph d'Anjou, who would be Alde and Birger's new tutor.

✠

Death did not soon loosen his grip over Forsvik in that sorrowful year of 1202. Just before All Saints' Day, foreman Gure's mother, the weaver Suom, lay dying. Gure and Cecilia kept watch by her bed, but she sternly turned away Brother Joseph until her strength failed and she let herself be persuaded by Cecilia and her son to be baptized and confess her sins before she died. She did not object to the baptism, but it seemed harder for her to confess sins, since it was her opinion that anyone who had lived the greater part of her life as a thrall had not had many opportunities to commit such acts that the gentry reckoned as sins. But finally Brother Joseph spoke with her in private and heard her confession so that he could administer the forgiveness of sins and prepare her for the life after this one.

His face was pale when he emerged, and he told Cecilia that although the confession had sealed his lips, he didn't know which would be better, if this woman was allowed to take her great secret to the grave or if Cecilia could try to coax it out of her.

Such a strange statement, which according to Arn when he heard about it was a violation of the secrecy of confession, naturally left Cecilia no peace. What sort of secret did a woman carry inside who had been a thrall since birth and free only in the last years of her life?

Cecilia made an effort to persuade herself that it was not simple curiosity but the desire for clarity that drove her to start questioning Suom, who was growing steadily weaker. If something was wrong, those who survived her could possibly put it right again; Cecilia certainly owed Suom that favor, she reasoned. Suom had brought much beauty to Forsvik with the ingenuity in her hands. It had brought in silver, and already two of the young weavers were following in Suom's footsteps. If it were possible to resolve any problems that Suom left behind, then it would be done, Cecilia decided.

But what she finally found out made her hesitant. Now she had inherited a secret that she could not simply carry silently inside her. It was not something that would be easy to tell Arn, particularly since she had been immediately convinced by what she had learned, and she did not want to start the first quarrel with her husband. Because it might come to that, she realized.

She went first to the church and prayed alone at the altar to Our Lady for support in doing what was right and good, and not what was wrong and merely showed selfish concern for the earthly life. She believed that Our Lady showed constant kindness not only to herself but also to Arn, and for that reason she prayed that Arn would control himself and wisely accept the news he would now receive.

Then she went straight to the sword house without walls, where she knew that Arn normally was at this time of day, along with the eldest of the young noblemen. He noticed her at once out of the corner of his eye, although he seemed so intent on his swordplay. He bowed to his young opponent, sheathed his sword, and went over to greet her. It wasn't hard to see by her expression that she had come with important news, and he took her aside into the barnyard where no one could hear them.

"Nothing has happened to Alde, has it?" he asked, and Cecilia shook her head. "Is Suom dead, do you want her buried here at Forsvik or somewhere else?" he went on.

"I have heard from Suom's own lips what she confessed to Brother Joseph," Cecilia whispered into Arn's shoulder, as if she didn't really dare look at him.

"And what might that be?" he asked, gently pushing her away so that he could look into her eyes.

"Gure is your brother and Eskil's; Herr Magnus was the father of all three of you," Cecilia hastened to reply, turning her face away as if ashamed to say the truth. For in the same moment she had heard Suom's account she knew that it was true.

"Do you think this is true?" Arn asked softly, without the slightest hint of anger in his voice.

"Yes, it is," she said, looking him straight in the eye. "Consider that Gure is six years younger than you. When your father sought solace after your mother Fru Sigrid died, Suom was young and certainly the most beautiful woman at Arnäs. And the resemblance between Gure and you and Eskil is so great that only our knowledge that he was born a thrall has prevented us from seeing it."

She took a deep breath now that she had said precisely what she knew Our Lady had advised her to say, the truth and nothing else, without evasion.

Arn did not reply. First he nodded pensively to himself, almost in confirmation, and then he turned on his heel and strode off to the church, closing the door behind him. Cecilia felt both relieved and warm inside when she saw how he took the news. She was sure that inside at the altar awaited a wise and gentle Mother of God for one of the sons on whom She had bestowed so much of Her love.

Arn was not gone long. Cecilia sat on the well lid in the center of the courtyard and waited for him to emerge. He smiled at her and held out his hand. They went together to Suom's bed, where Brother Joseph and Gure were kneeling and praying for her. Both of them stood up when the master and mistress came in. Without a word Arn went up to Gure and embraced him; Gure was quite embarrassed by this but not as startled as one might expect.

"Gure!" said Arn loudly so that Suom could hear him too. "From this day you are my brother and Eskil's, with all the rights and obligations that entails! I only wish that I'd known the truth sooner, because it is not much of an honor to have held my own brother as a thrall, even if it was for a short time."

"If a thrall could choose his master, which thralls are seldom granted, then I didn't choose so badly," said Gure shyly, looking at the floor.

They heard a groan from Suom, and Arn went at once to her bed, knelt down and said straight into her ear that she was leaving a great gift behind and that Gure would be elevated to a Folkung at the next *ting*. She did not reply but only smiled. That smile did not fade, nor did she ever regain consciousness.

Suom was wrapped in a Folkung mantle before she was laid in her grave near the new church. All the Christians at Forsvik drank to her at her funeral ale, and then Gure sat for the first time in the high seat between Arn and Cecilia.

His admission into the Folkung clan went quickly. Only a week after Suom's death a judge's *ting* was called at Askeberga for the northern part of Western Götaland, which meant that all free yeomen there could present their case. In recent years these *ting* meetings had come to be more esteemed and were attended by many. There was much to discuss, and even though the *ting* had lost a great deal of its import since the power had shifted to the king's council, it had become even more important for Eriks and Folkungs, who felt themselves pushed farther and farther away from the king and his councilors at Näs.

Arn rode to the judge's *ting* at Askeberga with Gure by his side and a squadron of the eldest young men, including Sigurd who was once called Sigge and Oddvar who was once called Orm.

To induct a man into the clan at the *ting*, an oath was required from the man who sponsored him and an oath from sixteen men in the clan. A squadron from Forsvik was precisely sixteen men, and even though they were young they were Folkungs. They all stepped forward as one man and gave their oath in a firm voice.

In the presence of the *ting* Arn then wrapped the Folkung mantle first around his brother Gure and then around Sigurd and Oddvar, who from that day forth did not need to dress differently than the other young warriors at Forsvik.

Eskil was also at the *ting*. He did not seem as pleased as Arn was about having acquired a new brother, although he consoled himself by the fact that there would be no inheritance from their father Magnus, since it had already been legally divided between himself and Arn.

In this situation it was unthinkable that anyone at the *ting* would utter a word about those whom Arn had admitted to the clan. If he wished, he could now make the stones in the field into Folkungs, so strongly had the clan's hopes been pinned on him. For everyone believed that war with the Sverker followers and their Danes was inevitable.

✖

Sune Folkesson's life had changed so dramatically that it now almost resembled a dream. He wouldn't have been able to imagine what had happened to him in recent years, even in his best or worst moments. No young Folkung could have felt the same torment in his breast and at the same time such devouring fire.

Two years had now passed since the day Sir Arn had called him over in his own house at Forsvik, carefully closed the door, and told him the astounding news that he was going to be sent off as a traitor. Sune was to forsake Forsvik, to which he had devoted nine years of his life and where he was now one of the three highest commanders under Sir Arn himself, and he was to flee to Näs and seek service with King Sverker.

At first he didn't believe his ears when he heard these words, which Sir Arn spoke quite calmly and kindly. Soon the situation was made more understandable, but no less surprising.

Since jarl Birger Brosa had died, Sir Arn went on to explain softly, the Folkungs had no information about what was happening with King Sverker. With their confederates, the Eriks, they were also unable to consult, because the leader of the clan, Erik jarl, was being held as a "guest" at Näs and was never expected to escape.

Information was half the victory, or defeat, in war. Perhaps there would indeed be war, because everything indicated that King Sverker sooner or later would break his oath to the council and royal *ting*. The king had made his son Johan the jarl of the realm when he was but a babe, and it was not difficult to understand that he saw Johan and not Erik jarl as the next king of the realm. He had also joined forces with Valdemar the Victor, who was the most fearful opponent there was in the North. However, King Valdemar was no Saladin, nor was he incapable of being beaten. Hence information was even more important.

Sune Folkesson had better chances than anyone else of taking on this heavy yoke and pretending to be a traitor. His mother was Danish, and he owned neither goods nor gold in the lands of the Goths. So it would be easy to believe that he, as half Danish, would be tempted to seek a more ambitious position than as a simple retainer at a Folkung forest estate.

Sir Arn emphasized that he would have to present himself just like that—as a simple retainer and not as the commander of three squadrons of light cavalry of the sort the Knights Templar employed. Also, when they tested him with sword and lance, he should avoid showing more than necessary of his true skills. That might arouse suspicion and curiosity. He didn't need to be the best to become a royal retainer at Näs, because it would be sufficiently tempting for the Danes to take in a Folkung with Danish blood.

Worst of all to endure was the fact that this stratagem they had now agreed on must remain a secret, known only to the two of them. Even Sune's own brothers among the young nobles at Forsvik must believe that he had simply deserted them; they would spit after saying his name if it were ever mentioned.

Why it had to be this way was not easy to accept. But if only Sir Arn and Sune himself knew the secret, that he hadn't deserted his clan or his brothers and was only a spy at Näs, he could never be betrayed. If the two of them met at Näs they would avoid looking at each other or show mutual contempt.

And they could never meet or exchange words even in deepest secrecy before the day came when Sune had to flee Näs to bring word to Forsvik. And then it would not be about some trifle, but information about where and when a foreign army would invade. He should flee back to his kinsmen when it was a matter of life or death, but not before. During his time at Näs he would naturally take note of everything he saw—how the Danes rode, what sort of lance tips they used, or anything else that might be of value. Such information was important but not reason enough to flee.

Arn would leave a sealed letter with his son Magnus Månesköld in which he told the true story. So if he should be killed while Sune was still on his dangerous mission, the truth would be passed down and remain in the hands of the Folkungs.

Sune must be careful to show restraint before he left Forsvik, and seek support in prayer. He could not take along anything to Näs except his practice weapons. And to none of his brothers could he disclose the secret before he set off. He could easily steal a little purse of silver coins to take along, Sir Arn concluded, handing him the purse.

Sune had been especially quiet after this meeting and spent more time than any of the young nobles in church. In the early hours of one November night he stowed away on a boat among sleepy sailors taking a load of flour and glass to Linköping. Then he jumped off at Mo and proceeded down the east coast of Lake Vättern until he found a trout fisherman to take him over to Visingsö, paying the man well.

Everything that Sir Arn had surmised about his reception at Näs met their expectations and more. When Sune reported to the leader of the royal guard the next morning the man laughed at him, because he seemed so young and destitute. But when he told them he was a Folkung on his father's side and Danish on his mother's, and that he had already served a long time as a guard, they changed their tune. He was told to wait until the marshal himself, a Danish gentleman named Ebbe Sunesson, had time to receive him. Then everything went more smoothly than he could have imagined. Ebbe Sunesson knew his mother well, because she had remarried to a man in the Hvide clan. And the marshal didn't want to criticize this Danish woman because when she returned to her fatherland she had left a son behind. Who could know how hard it might have been to wrest a son from the hands of the savage Folkungs? They should also keep in mind that if she had succeeded with this, young Sune would have grown up as a Dane. Perhaps they should view it as God's will that he had now returned to his kinsmen.

But blood was not everything. Sune also had to show that he was skilled enough to be a royal guard.

The tests he found easy, and he had to make an effort to remember Arn's words about not showing too much or to let his pride run away with his reason. The Danish guards who were ordered to swing their swords at him were easy opponents; a lad of seventeen at Forsvik would have had no trouble defeating them.

The very first day at Näs he'd been given the red Sverker uniform to wear, and it was the most humiliating moment of his life. In the evening he was invited to sit at the king's table, since it was joyous news that a bold Folkung had joined the king's guard.

It was on that first evening that his eyes fell upon the king's daughter Helena with the long, golden hair. And she looked often at him. But after that night he was not allowed to sit at the king's table; instead his task was to wait on those seated there. Many were the differences between the customs of the Danes and the Goths; the Danes preferred not to have house thralls or freedmen waiting on the king's table in the evening, but young men whom they called pages. So Sune began his life at Näs not as a guard, which he had expected, but as a person who did the work of house thralls. Naturally he could have asked someone whether this was an affront or not, but that question soon lost all importance because he got to see Helena every evening. Even though he never had a chance to speak to her, their eyes continued to meet in secret understanding.

At the royal table, King Sverker always sat in the high seat along with his new Folkung queen Ingegerd Birgersdotter and Helena. Next to the high seat sat the king's Danish marshal Ebbe Sunesson, and sometimes the queen brought her little son Johan jarl with her; she always dressed him with a little crown on his head.

She seemed to be well aware that this was a clear insult to the four Erik sons, who all sat in an inferior place at the table. She always spoke loudly of her son Johan as the jarl, while she addressed Erik jarl as Erik Knutsson. It was not hard to see what Queen Ingegerd thought about who should be the next king.

Erik jarl and his brothers Jon, Joar, and Knut never showed any joy at the table, since every meal was yet another affront to them. When the king happened to mention them as his dear guests, toasting them and feigning happiness at having them so close, many of the Danes in the hall laughed in a vulgar manner. The Erik sons were captives at Näs and nothing more.

To Sune they showed only hostility and contempt and were unwilling to be served by him; they said they had sensitive noses and the smell of a traitor did not go well with ale and roast meat. They often drank themselves senseless, and sometimes they had to be dragged from the table. King Sverker was more than willing to let this go on, and he was often the one who ordered more ale just as they looked to be finished drinking for the evening.

During the first autumn, winter, and spring it was almost impossible for Sune to get a single good night's sleep. He lay in a damp, cold stone room with ten other snoring and foul-smelling guards, and tossed and turned in his bunk. The shame of treachery burned inside him, as did the sorrow of seeing the Erik sons drinking their honor under the table and constantly showing him their contempt. But the flame that Helena Sverkersdotter had ignited in him was even more consuming, so that he felt trapped between fire and ice. If he dreamed anything when he finally fell asleep, it was of her face, her long hair, and her lovely eyes. Sleep came as a liberator when he finally was able to succumb to it.

Just before Midsummer Helena celebrated her eighteenth birthday, and there was to be a great banquet at Näs. In her honor there would be Danish and Frankish games, contests with quarterstaff and sword—things that simple Swedes and Goths could not even imagine.

Sune was well aware that he ought to stay away from these

festivities, just as Sir Arn had warned him. But then it was announced that the victor of the games would have the honor of being prince for two days and even wear a crown as he sat by young Helena's side for the rest of the feast. Then Sune could no longer keep his reason stronger than the longing of his heart.

The contest would be held as a Frankish game in which anyone who felt himself called could participate, although at his own risk. The inner courtyard at Näs was cleaned and high wooden bleachers were erected along one wall, where the king and his guests would have a good view of the games.

Sune suffered great anguish when he heard the other guards talking about the games, which most of them intended to enter with horse and battle-club. No guard could win such a contest; that honor would fall to one of the Danish noblemen. But it was a great honor for anyone who made it to the final stages of the competition.

The more the others talked about the contest and how it would proceed, the more impossible it became for Sune to resist the temptation. Finally he dressed himself like the others, grabbed a red shield, a battle-club, and the horse he was most accustomed to riding.

Horns blared and drums thundered as the forty horsemen with shields and clubs rode in a circle before the king and his guests. When an hour or so had passed, only one of them would still be on his horse. As if to egg them all on, the king got to his feet and held up the victor's crown; all fell silent and the contestants prayed a *Pater Noster* for themselves. Then a loud horn blast transformed the castle courtyard to a shouting and thundering melee of horses and warriors ferociously hacking at each other. A full dozen men fell to the ground at once.

Sune had cautiously moved toward the outermost circle of horsemen and at first was more concerned about keeping himself away from the swinging clubs than trying to knock someone else out of the saddle. With a horse from Forsvik, he thought, he wouldn't have had to raise a hand to any of them, but simply ride off until he was the last one left. But his Danish horse was too sluggish for such a simple fight and had to be continually urged forward with a jab from his spurs.

As the guards fell they were dragged off by stable thralls who also tried to catch the loose horses. When half of all the guards had fallen, the Danish nobles concentrated more on one another. They all reckoned that the victor could only be one of them and that any remaining guards would be easier to handle when they had more space and there was less risk of a surprise blow delivered from behind.

So Sune had a very easy time of it for the first half hour. He kept out of the fray and stayed alert, always in motion so he would never be a ready target.

When only ten riders were left, Sune knocked his first man out of the saddle with a blow to his helmet from behind. This brought laughter and a surprised gasp from the onlookers, because it was one of the Danish nobles who fell. But now the others also seemed to have discovered Sune and began to take him seriously, because he was one of the last three guards still in the saddle. Suddenly he was everybody's prey; they chased him around the courtyard, which was not without risk for his pursuers, since several of them were struck by men lying in wait and riding in the opposite direction.

When only four nobles and Sune remained, it would have been wisest to let himself be vanquished. Yet it seemed that the intention was for the king's marshal Ebbe Sunesson to win, because no one dared attack him even if the situation was favorable. But Sune's burning will to sit next to Helena was much stronger than his reason. He had reserved his energy and so far displayed only half the skill of which he was capable. Now the decisive moment was approaching and if he didn't want to lose he would have to assert himself.

When two of the nobles charged him side by side while Herr Ebbe and the fourth remaining Dane just sat still and watched, Sune knew that he could actually win the game. He rode around once with the two pursuing him. Then he cut across obliquely and stopped his horse abruptly in the middle of the courtyard. The steed reared up and turned in the air so that one of the nobles was knocked off by the horse's front hooves and the other was struck in the face by Sune's battle club.

Ebbe Sunesson then surprisingly knocked off the man sitting next to him. The man had both hands on the pommel and was obviously taken completely by surprise. It was as if Herr Ebbe wanted to show that he truly needed no help now that he was going into battle in earnest. Twice he rode back and forth before the king and his guests at a canter, waving his hand and receiving great applause before he turned toward Sune waiting in the middle of the courtyard.

Slowly and sure of victory, Herr Ebbe began to walk his horse toward Sune to decrease the distance before he attacked. Sune decided to try a simple and devastating trick that everyone at Forsvik knew. If his opponent was not prepared for it or underestimated the danger, Sune would win. If he knew the trick or managed to see through it, Sune would be lost.

As if he were afraid of the Danish marshal, Sune let himself be chased twice around the courtyard at high speed until Herr Ebbe, tasting victory, closed from behind and the onlookers roared with excitement. Then Sune stopped short, lowered his head to the horse's back so that his opponent's club whistled through the air. At the same time he turned and landed a blow right on the chest of his pursuer. Herr Ebbe flew back a lance length before he slammed into the ground on his back and buttocks.

Sune gathered up his reins and removed his helmet before he rode before King Sverker, his face solemn, and bowed with his right hand pressed to his heart as a sign of loyalty. For a few moments he gazed into Helena's eyes before he straightened up. If his wits were already clouded, the look he received from Helena did not improve matters.

In a rage Herr Ebbe came hobbling over, yelling that this rogue of a guard had won by luck that was not worthy of a victor. As the second-place contestant he now demanded his right to settle the matter by the sword.

The king at first looked around in confusion because he had never heard of this special rule. But some of the Danes around him nodded gravely, confirming that in cases when the victory was unclear, one could proceed to an unequivocal decision by the sword. King Sverker could do nothing but ask Sune whether he agreed to continue fighting or wished to cede the victory to Herr Ebbe, since it could be dangerous to meet such a swordsman.

As close as Sune was to spending two evenings at Helena's side, no reason in the world could make him decline the challenge. The king sighed and decreed that the combatants would meet man to man, with sword and shield and helmet within one hour.

Sune had to lead his horse to the stable himself, while guards took care of Ebbe's mount. When he reached the armory behind the stables, it was full of guards all talking at once, eager to give him good advice. Most of it seemed to be about watching out for his left foot, because sooner or later Herr Ebbe always swept his sword low toward that vulnerable spot. Others thought it was especially important to watch out for Herr Ebbe when he pretended to lose his balance and halfway turned his back, because then he would strike either at his opponent's left foot or head when he finished his twisting movement.

In the armory were several Folkung shields, though they had

not been repainted in a long time and the damaged sections had not been repaired. But the temptation was too great when Sune discovered that one of these shields fit him almost as well as his own back at Forsvik. Among the swords he didn't have to search very long before he found one that suited him, because the Danes did not use Nordic swords as in the lands of the Goths but Frankish or Saxon ones, which were like those at Forsvik.

Sune was the same height as Herr Ebbe, but the onlookers were deceived by the fact that the latter had attended at least a thousand more banquets, so he looked all the more powerful in his armor when they stepped forward and bowed to the king and queen. Sune looked into Helena's eyes when he raised his gaze.

In the first moments of the contest Sune felt himself turn cold and almost paralyzed with fear. There was a mighty weight and strength in Herr Ebbe's blows, and he attacked with hatred in his eyes as if they were enemies on a battlefield. And their swords were not for practice, but honed sharp. When he realized that it really was death he was facing, he cursed his own pride. For a good while he did not connect with a blow of his own, but had to concentrate on parrying and staying away from Herr Ebbe.

Everything that the guards had told him seemed to be true, for in quick succession he had twice seen his opponent strike at the left foot, and twice how Herr Ebbe seemed to wobble to the side only to spin around and in rage aim for Sune's head.

The king and his guests did not like what they were seeing, for a feast day should not conclude with blood and death. But honor forbade even the king from interfering in a duel man to man once it had begun.

After the fight had gone on a while, Sune noticed that he was beginning to think more clearly because the attacks were coming more slowly. With his heart in his throat he had done everything he'd practiced since he was a boy without even thinking, merely counting one, two, three to himself and then moving just as he said three to watch the edge of the sword swish above his head or past his left foot. He grew more self-confident, knowing that he was a Forsviker and that what he could do at home in Forsvik he could also do here.

He stopped merely defending himself and went on the attack. Soon he was driving Herr Ebbe back and giving him no quarter to strike either at his foot or his head. Now Sune also had to start thinking about the end. How one could lose a duel of this type was not hard to imagine. But how to win? Should he, who had been entrusted to gather information and who had been warned by Sir Arn not to draw too much attention, actually kill the marshal of the kingdom?

The longer they went at it, the wearier Herr Ebbe grew and the more he gasped. The opportunity to inflict on him a serious wound became ever more frequent. Sune decided not to kill his opponent but to let the fight continue until the other man could fight no more, because it was evident that Herr Ebbe was twice as old and twice as tired.

Some of the Danish nobles had already approached the king and whispered that the fight against all custom had to be stopped before it came to a disastrous end. Ebbe would certainly not grow less exhausted by continuing, and the young Folkung could have killed him already if he had so wished.

But the king didn't need to intervene. Suddenly Herr Ebbe held up his hand and went over to the king to say that he pardoned the young warrior. Because it would certainly be ill advised, he said, out of breath, if he were forced to kill such a hearty young man who should be serving his king rather than going to an early grave.

Without even the hint of a smile the king nodded pensively at these apparently noble and wise words and waved Sune over. He then asked him whether he could accept victory on these conditions. A bunch of foolish replies flew like swallows through

Sune's head, but he managed to bite his tongue and replied with a bow that it was a great honor to receive this mark of favor from the mightiest swordsman he had ever met or seen.

This was certainly the biggest lie that Sune had uttered since he arrived at Näs. But with only a sliver of wit remaining he tried to make up for his foolhardy behavior.

And yet it may have been Sune's foolishness that actually saved the future kingdom. For as events now unfolded one after the other, many lives were saved, although many more were wasted.

For two long evenings Sune was allowed to sit with his crown of victory next to Helena. That time was more than enough for the fire that had merely smoldered within them to flare up into a full blaze.

During these two evenings, when they sat together in full view of everyone and had to behave accordingly, they not only confessed their burning feelings for each other but also made more practical plans. They agreed to meet in private, or as close to private as they dared.

Helena was the daughter of a king, and it was still far from decided what the best marriage would be for her. King Sverker no doubt had his hopes that he could marry her off to the Danish king Valdemar the Victor. But there was not much hope of that, since such a mighty king would probably find a wife in the Frankish or German kingdoms. But as long as Valdemar the Victor remained unmarried, hope was not lost.

In the worst case Helena could marry in her own land for the sake of peace, to some Folkung or even an Erik. As long as no decision had been reached, she was allowed to remain unattended, becoming ever more beautiful. Actually King Sverker should have consigned her to one of his own clan's cloisters, to Vreta or Gudhem, to better prepare her for the bridal ale with the man he eventually selected. But she was too dear to him. She reminded him of a time when he was happier than now in his position as king. Her mother Benedikta had been a lovely and fair woman, while his new queen Ingegerd was hard and coarse of mouth and as hungry for power as a man. As soon as she bore him a son she had played all sorts of tricks so that she no longer had to take him to her bed. And she constantly nagged him both about petty matters and about intrigues that were dangerous enough to cost them all their lives. Helena was like a beautiful memory and a constant reminder of happier times. That was why he didn't want to send her to a convent.

But he would have done so in an instant if he knew who she was meeting at night. Now these rendezvous were certainly chaste, for Helena had sworn to God never to let any man enter her bedchamber at night. Her room had once served as the council chamber of the realm, but now it was much too small for the growing royal council. It was situated high up in the eastern tower at Näs, and a wild vine grew on the wall, enabling an eager young man to climb up to the window.

Helena lit two candles in her window as the signal. After his victory in the warrior games Sune had been given command of part of the guards. So it was no problem for him to visit the walls at night, as if he were going to check that all the guards were attending to their duties.

Many were their passionate meetings at her window; he may not have entered her bedchamber but he did enter her heart. He would stay until his arms grew numb from holding on to the wild vine, which took a long time because he was stronger than most and more eager than them all.

They refused to reconcile themselves to the fact that she was the daughter of a king, destined to be married to someone better than a guard. They found it utterly irrelevant that she was a Sverker and he a Folkung, and they promised each other eternal faithfulness after only two weeks when he ventured to lean forward and kiss her for the first time.

Because their love was as hopeless as it was great, Helena also told him things that would have been viewed as treason if anyone had heard. But she had only one person in whom to confide.

So one night in late summer Sune learned that the days of Erik jarl and his brothers were numbered. Queen Ingegerd had demanded their lives for the safety of her own son Johan and his legitimate inheritance of the crown of the realm. Often she had dripped her venom like the Serpent in the king's ear, and she claimed to have discovered that the Eriks were merely waiting for the right moment to kill him. She was constantly seeing secret signs that a conspiracy was growing at Näs.

Finally King Sverker gave in. The Eriks would be drowned and delivered to Varnhem for burial, and there would be no mark on their bodies from either sword or dagger wounds. The story would be that they were out fishing for trout and that an unexpected autumn storm on Lake Vättern had blown up and taken their lives.

Sune was doubly filled with sorrow when he heard this news. The lives of the Erik royal brothers may not have been his greatest concern, but the information he had now received was such that he would have to return to Forsvik. That meant being separated from Helena. Otherwise he would have to find a way to warn the Eriks.

At evening meals he often sat right next to Erik jarl and his brothers, although they all refused to talk to him. They treated him as if he were invisible, as a traitor deserved. Loudly so that everyone could hear, Erik jarl had complained more than once that Ebbe Sunesson hadn't been able to lop off Sune's head, but it might not be too late.

As if it were a special insult to have to sit near Sune, the Erik brothers took turns. One evening when it was Erik jarl sitting beside him, the moment came that Sune had been waiting for with growing trepidation. Now he could not falter; it had to happen now.

"The king intends to drown you all and say that the storm took you while fishing. You don't have much time to flee," he said in a low voice but with a smile as he handed a piece of meat to Erik jarl with a polite bow.

"And why should I believe a traitor like you?" Erik jarl snorted, but not loudly.

"Because I am Sir Arn's man and not the king's, and because I would be a head shorter if anyone heard these words pass between us," replied Sune as he courteously poured the jarl more ale.

"Where can we flee?" whispered Erik jarl, suddenly tense and serious.

"To Forsvik. There is shelter there and riders with Sir Arn," said Sune, raising his ale tankard. "But you must hurry, you don't have many nights left."

Erik jarl nodded gravely and to his brothers' astonishment raised his ale tankard to Sune.

Two days later the commotion was great when it was discovered that Erik jarl and his brothers had escaped. Nobody knew where and nobody knew how, and it did no good to whip the guards who had been on duty that night.

The suspicious Queen Ingegerd cast long, suspicious looks at Sune. She thought she had seen Sune and Erik jarl having a brief, whispered conversation, contrary to their habits not so long ago. King Sverker thought it impossible that Sune, the brave and faithful warrior, could have warned the Erik brothers. For how could he have known what was going on in the minds of the king, the queen, or the marshal? Which of the three would have betrayed such a plan? Could Ebbe have confided in Sune, when his feelings about the guard were no secret after the ignominious defeat? If not, could he himself or the queen have done such a thing? No, the Eriks had been lucky and that was all. Besides, it was clear as water that they had not had occasion to thrive at Näs.

The king then did the only thing he could do. He promised two marks in pure gold to anyone who could bring him information about where the Eriks were hiding, because they certainly hadn't been swallowed up by the earth.

It took a year before he learned that all four of them were hiding at an estate in the northern part of Western Götaland, a Folkung estate called Älgarås. Then he ordered Ebbe Sunesson to equip a hundred horsemen and bring the four back alive, although just their heads would suffice.

Sune found out that the Eriks had been discovered and were doomed to die. The same night that Sune heard this news, he was thrown into the tower dungeon by order of the queen, who had always suspected him. From the tower dungeons he heard the rattling of stirrups and weapons. It meant that the king's hundred riders were preparing to leave at dawn, and he cursed himself. He had pursued this game too long, and he lamented the fact that love had brought him not only his own death, but that of the four royal sons. It had also led to despair, which was a great sin. He who despaired dug his own grave. He began to pray to Saint Örjan, the protector of knights and the noble-minded.

When the night was at its darkest there was a rattle of keys at his cell door, and two men in dark clothes came in and took him gently but silently up the stairs. Helena was waiting for him. They said a hurried and whispered farewell. She was now going to be sent to Vreta cloister, and she wanted him to swear to fetch her from there. He had at first trembled and hesitated at the thought of stealing a maiden from a convent, which was one of the lowest deeds a man could commit. But she assured him that, first, she would not take the vows; she was a king's daughter and not intended to be a nun. And second, the day she saw blue mantles approaching Vreta she would run to meet them.

He then swore that he and his kinsmen, a squadron in number, in blue mantles and in the middle of the day so that they could be seen from far off, would rescue her from Vreta cloister.

They kissed, weeping, and then she tore herself away with a sigh and hurried off into the darkness.

Down below the castle a small boat awaited. The wind was from the south and should take him to Forsvik in one night.

✠

At dawn Sune was dropped off outside Forsvik clad in tattered, filthy Sverker clothing. His two companions quickly left the harbor and set a course for the north. They would never again set foot at Näs, nor did they need to. Helena with her gold jewelery had paid them more than enough to live a good life elsewhere.

At that early hour there were few people about at Forsvik, but when one of the young nobles on his way out to the privy caught sight of Sune, he at once ran to ring the alarm. A few moments later Sune was surrounded by armed and angry young men cursing him as a traitor. Soon he was dragged, bound hand and foot, over to the big bell that was the gathering place in case of an alarm. There he was forced to his knees while everyone waited for Sir Arn, who came running over half-dressed in chain mail.

When Arn caught sight of Sune he stopped, smiled, and drew his dagger from his belt. There was complete silence as he went over to Sune and cut off the ropes binding his hands and feet. He embraced him, kissing him on both cheeks.

Almost all the young warriors had now gathered, with only a few more running up as they tried to get dressed. Their ire had dissolved and they looked at one another in wonder.

"Think on the words of the Lord, all you Forsvikers!" said Arn as he raised his right arm in a command for attention. "What you see is not always what you see, and don't always judge someone by his clothes. This is your true brother Sune Folkesson, who in our service and at the risk of his life has been our informer with Sverker at Näs. It was Sune's words that saved the life of Erik jarl and his brothers. That was why they came to us and escaped death at the hands of the deceitful king. Everyone who thought evil of Sune should first beg forgiveness from God and then from Sune himself!"

The first to come forward to embrace Sune were Bengt Elinsson and Sigfrid Erlingsson. Then all the others followed in turn.

Arn ordered the bathhouse to be heated up and for new Folkung clothing to be brought there. The red rags that Sune was wearing would be burned. Sune tried to object that he had urgent news and had no time for a bath, but Arn just shook his head with a smile and said that nothing was ever so urgent that a man should not stop to think before rushing off. He understood that it was no small matter that had convinced Sune to leave his service at Näs, since Sune had dared to remain in his perilous mission even after he had rescued Erik jarl and his brothers.

Sune hastened into the bathhouse and was still pulling on his Folkung clothes as he rattled off greetings to everyone on his way to Arn and Cecilia's house. Inside awaited fresh Saracen morning bread and strong lamb soup. Sir Arn and Fru Cecilia embraced him with tears in their eyes and welcomed him home.

As they ate, Sune quickly told them all the most important news. King Sverker had finally found out that Erik jarl and his brothers were hiding at Älgarås, and he was sending a hundred fully armed men to kill them. If it was true that the Erik brothers were at Älgarås, there wasn't much time.

Arn nodded grimly. It was true that on Bengt Elinsson's advice they had moved the men to Älgarås because there were no Sverkers in the vicinity, and because the king would probably search toward Eriksberg in the south rather than in a Folkung village in the north. Erik jarl had also been wise enough when he arrived to tell Arn in private about the warning he had received from Sune. He hadn't said a word to anyone else about it, but Arn had confirmed that it really was true that Sune had always been a Forsviker, although he dressed in the red mantle at Näs. Erik jarl had also recounted the strange way that Sune had behaved so as not to draw attention to himself. But that was a matter for another conversation, because now in truth they did not have much time.

Three fully armed squadrons, two of light cavalry and one of heavy armored riders, left Forsvik that morning. At the mustering before their departure, Arn had given a brief speech and said that this was no longer practice. What was now about to happen was what they had been training for. That was why all their practice swords had been exchanged for sharp ones, the arrows were not blunt, and the lances were not fitted with round points but with triple steel points.

Perhaps they would have been more successful if they had ridden from Forsvik with only light cavalry and not with a squadron of heavy armor that delayed the others. In hindsight they could have drawn that conclusion, but hindsight is always the wisest jarl of all fools.

What Sune had to tell about the Danish knights' horses and weapons had convinced Arn that at least one heavy squadron was necessary, because they were meeting a force that was twice as large as their own.

Älgarås was ablaze when they arrived; they had seen the smoke and flames from far off. Yet Arn had sternly made them all follow his pace at a calm trot so as not to arrive exhausted to a confrontation with the Danes and Sverkers.

After a slow ride which tried all their patience, they finally came within striking distance, and they could see the red-garbed warriors on their way in through a big breach in the stockade wall of sharpened poles. Now there was no time to lose. Arn positioned the heavy cavalry foremost in order to attack with speed and power, ordering Bengt Elinsson to wait outside the walls with his squadron and clear the entire area of all the red troops.

King Sverker's men were so excited about entering the stronghold that they discovered too late the noise of the blue-clad riders coming at them in formation with lances lowered. The Folkungs crushed all before them on their way into Älgarås.

In a corner of the estate a small group was crowded together with Erik jarl in front. The heavy riders who had led the break-in moved off to the side, and behind them the squadron led by Sigfrid Erlingsson attacked. Most of the fleeing Sverkers and Danes were caught outside the walls by Bengt Elinsson and his squadron of light cavalry. No prisoners were taken. A few of the enemy escaped, among them Ebbe Sunesson.

Erik jarl was the only survivor among his brothers, and he was wounded in more than one place. Everywhere in the estate lay dead Folkungs, young and old alike. Even house thralls and livestock lay slaughtered.

Erik jarl showed his fortitude and honor in the hour of sorrow. He staggered with exhaustion and his face, hands, and one thigh were bleeding, but still gasping he had a brief whispered conversation with Arn. Then he wiped off his bloody sword, called over the three squadron leaders Sune, Sigfrid, and Bengt and their closest men—Sigurd, who was once called Sigge, Oddvar who was once called Orm, and Emund Jonsson, Ulvhilde's son. He ordered them to kneel and in his capacity as the new king of the Swedes and Goths, he dubbed them knights.

They were the first to be knighted in the new kingdom that was now on its way.

Chapter 12

It was a whole week before the riders who had left Forsvik returned. They had found much that needed cleaning up after the battle at Älgarås where more than ninety Danes and Sverkers were laid in a common grave, and all those from the estate who had been slain were taken to the church for a Christian burial.

Two Forsvikers had fallen in the conflict, while four were badly wounded, two of them so gravely that Arn didn't dare take the responsibility of transporting them to Forsvik to tend to their wounds. Ibrahim and Yussuf were no longer at the estate, at a time when their skills were sorely needed. With a fervent appeal, and in his capacity as a Templar knight, Arn wrote a brief letter on the only piece of parchment that he could find at Älgarås to the brothers of the Order of St. John in Eskilstuna. He sent the two wounded men by cart to Örebro, and from there it was an easy journey across Lake Hjälmaren to the brothers' hospital.

The bodies of two Forsvikers who had fallen were wrapped in Folkung mantles and sent to their kinsmen.

Since many Forsvikers left to accompany wounded and dead kinsmen, it looked as if the force had been cut in half when they returned to the estate. And the tidings were ominous, judging by the somber expressions of both Erik jarl and Arn as they entered the courtyard ahead of the other Forsvikers. The alarm had already been sounded when the horsemen were spotted far in the distance. Erik jarl and Arn brought the saddest news of all to the dowager queen Cecilia Blanca, who was the first to step forward when everyone anxiously appeared to greet the returning men. Three of her sons had been killed, all on the same day. They were wrapped in their mantles on a cart at the back of the procession.

Cecilia Blanca turned pale as she sank to the ground and silently rocked back and forth, tearing her nails bloody scratching at the earth. Finally she uttered a scream that stabbed like knives into everyone's heart. Erik jarl led her inside the church, where they both stayed for a long time.

Arn gave orders for the horses to be looked after, for the weapons to be put away, and for the three Erik sons to be taken to the cool room made of bricks that was used to store meat. It was not a dignified place for the fallen sons of a king, but the bodies had already begun to smell, and they needed to be buried soon.

He took his wife Cecilia to their own house and closed the door. Then he briefly and in Cecilia's eyes rather coldheartedly recounted what had happened. Three royal sons had been killed by Sverker's people. The Forsvikers had slain almost all of the one hundred men sent out by Sverker; only a few had escaped. And so it was that war had come to the Göta lands, even though it would be a relatively long time before the real battles began. The important thing right now was to bury Erik jarl's brothers. Arn suggested the church at Riseberga cloister, since it was the closest, and at the moment a journey to Varnhem would be dangerous as well as too long and hot for those who had already been dead a week.

Cecilia had a hard time replying to Arn's question about Riseberga, since she felt confused by the fact that she didn't really recognize him. His eyes had grown narrow and cold, and he spoke
in a terse and harsh manner. After a while she realized that this
was a different Arn than the one she knew; this was not her beloved and gentle husband or Alde's father, this was the warrior
from the Holy Land.

She saw the same change in Erik jarl when he appeared with
his arm around his trembling mother, leaving her in Cecilia's care
as if she were a child. Then he took Arn aside at once to exchange
only a few words about how and when they ought to ride to Riseberga.

That very day the funeral procession set off from Forsvik.
Most of the young noblemen who had been part of the force that
went to Älgarås now stayed behind at Forsvik. In Arn's opinion,
the talkativeness that had come over them after participating in
and winning their first armed conflict would not be fitting at a funeral. Instead, three cavalry squadrons were formed and armed
from those who had remained behind at Forsvik when their kinsmen rode off to Älgarås. But the six who had been knighted by
Erik jarl had to come along, since honor demanded their presence.

At Riseberga cloister the three sons of the king were buried,
and a large sum was donated for prayers of intercession on their
behalf. Erik jarl borrowed the money from Arn and Cecilia Rosa.
Cecilia Blanca, as the mother of the dead men, remained at the
cloister when the funeral procession returned to Forsvik. Neither
she nor anyone else knew how long she might stay there, whether
for a short time or forever.

During that autumn and early winter, many Folkung and
Erik riders headed off in all directions. Erik jarl went to Norway to attempt to win the support of warriors there. Eskil and
his son Torgils, along with Arn and Magnus Månesköld, made a
long journey through Svealand, where news of the ignominious

murder of the three Erik sons aroused great anger. The Swedes seemed to consider the Erik clan as their royal clan. Relics from Erik jarl's paternal grandfather, St. Erik, were carried around the fields in Uppland to bring a good harvest. At the judge's *ting* at the Mora Stones outside Östra Aros, the Swedes voted unanimously to take up their swords at once. The Folkungs from the south managed to dissuade them, since a Svea army would undoubtedly need better footing than the autumn mire to do full justice to their bravery, as Arn cautiously presented the matter. What he had seen of the Svea warriors at the *ting* did not persuade him that they'd be able to accomplish much against the Danish cavalry. After a lengthy and loud discussion, they finally agreed that the Swedes should go in force to Östra Götaland to join the warriors at Bjälbo in the spring, between the feast of Saint Gertrude and Annunciation Day.

On their way home the Folkungs stopped at Eskilstuna, where Arn donned the attire of a Templar knight to visit the hospital of the Order of St. John. If he had hoped to find Hospitaller knights of the order in Eskilstuna, he was soon disappointed. The brothers there devoted themselves almost exclusively to caring for the sick, and he had to give up any idea of acquiring reinforcements from the best warriors in the world besides the Templars. But he was courteously received by the brothers, and they had done their job well, almost as if they had been Saracens, with regard to Arn's two wounded young men. They would both be able to return to the saddle by spring.

After the New Year, a *ting* was called at Arnäs for the Folkung clan, and Erik jarl returned from his Norwegian travels in order to attend. It had been a disappointing journey because the Norwegians were once again at each other's throats; they had their hands full with their own war. But Erik jarl brought greetings from Harald Øysteinsson, who had now become jarl of the Birchlegs in Nidaros and had been granted several large estates.

Harald had promised that as soon as he was victorious in Norway, he and his kinsmen would come to the aid of the Folkungs and Eriks. That was a promise of questionable value.

Before the start of the *ting* of the Folkung clan, Erik jarl took a tour of the walls with Arn because he hadn't been there in many years. He offered much praise for the mighty strength of this castle, but he also had to admit that it made him uneasy. When Arn asked him outright what he meant by this, Erik jarl said that no one could help seeing how Arnäs had grown. It was evident that the power of the Folkungs was much greater than that of anyone else. The horsemen that Arn had trained at Forsvik so that they could easily defeat an enemy force of twice their numbers at Älgarås had merely reinforced their power. So who was he, Erik jarl, leader of the much weaker Erik clan, to think that he might set his father's crown upon his own head?

Arn didn't take this concern seriously but jested that if Erik found himself a good marshal he would have fewer worries. Erik jarl didn't understand the jest but replied almost angrily that he thought Arn was his marshal.

"Yes, such is the case," replied Arn with a laugh, placing his hand on Erik jarl's powerful shoulder. "Surely you haven't forgotten what we swore to each other at your father's deathbed. I am your marshal. For me, you are already king. Such was my oath."

"Why don't you Folkungs seize power now that it's within your reach?" asked Erik jarl, not entirely reassured.

"For two reasons," said Arn. "First, we have all sworn to fight for your crown, and the Folkungs do not take their oaths lightly. Second, you have the Swedes on your side, but we don't. Your axes and few horsemen may not frighten many Danes, but I have no doubt of their bravery, and besides they are many in number."

"And if I didn't have the Swedes on my side?" said Erik jarl, throwing out his hands.

"Then we would still stand by our word and you would become king. But who will succeed you is less certain; perhaps Birger Magnusson."

"Young Birger who is the son of your Magnus Månesköld?"

"Yes, he is the most lively of the brothers at Ulvåsa, and he has a good head. But why should we be thinking of those days that will come long after we're gone? The future is in God's hands, and right now we have a war to win. That should be our first thought."

"And will we win this war?"

"Yes, most certainly. With God's help. The only question is what will happen afterward. Sverker has no strong army supporting him; we'll vanquish him by spring. Even the Swedes could accomplish that. If he falls in battle, it will be over. If he manages to flee to Denmark, we will have Valdemar the Victor upon us. And then we'll have to pull back a bit."

"So it would be best if we kill Sverker in the spring?"

"Yes, that's my view. It's the only sure way of preventing him from bringing in the Danes."

⚜

Not much came of the first war against King Sverker. In the spring of 1206, a large and noisy horde of Swedes came south to Eastern Götaland, threatening to plunder Linköping if King Sverker refused to meet them on the battlefield. While they waited for his answer, they drank up all the ale but otherwise spared the town.

King Sverker, his most loyal supporters, and his retainers then fled from Näs and headed south to Denmark. The Swedes had to return home without delivering a single blow from their axes. He left behind his daughter Helena at Vreta cloister, where she was confined with the novices.

Erik jarl then moved with his mother and kinsmen to his childhood home at Näs and henceforth called himself King Erik, since both the Swedes and the Folkungs recognized him as such. Arn thought the king ought to have sought the protection of Arnäs instead, but he sent three squadrons of young Folkung riders to join the king's retainers at Näs.

Now the question was not if the Danish army would come, but when. For now King Erik's tenuous kingdom was secure, since during that year Valdemar the Victor was busy with a new crusade. He was plundering the Livonian islands of Dagö and Ösel, killing many heathens or those who were not sufficiently Christian, and taking much silver back to Denmark.

The workers in the weapons smithies at Forsvik were now toiling day and night; the fires were doused only on the day of rest devoted to God. That year young Birger Magnusson began training with the largest group of young Folkungs that had ever been taken on at Forsvik. New houses were also built, including a separate house for the six knights that King Erik had dubbed after the victory at Älgarås. And as a belated gift from the king, all six men had been given spurs of gold. In their hall hung both Sverker and Danish shields that they had seized in their first victory.

Not until late in the autumn of 1207, after the first snowfall, did word come that a large enemy force was on its way north from Skåne. King Valdemar the Victor was not leading the army himself, perhaps because he didn't want to offend his tributary King Sverker. But he had sent all his best commanders, including Ebbe Sunesson and his brothers Lars, Jakob, and Peder. And with them were twelve thousand men; it was the mightiest army that had ever been seen in the North.

Arn sent out a call to the Folkungs and Eriks, telling them to gather at two strongholds, the one at Arnäs and the one at Bjälbo, which was more of a fortified estate than a fortress. After that he made ready to take four light squadrons from Forsvik and ride at once to meet the enemy.

Cecilia felt equal parts dread and admiration when she saw the zeal displayed by Arn. She couldn't understand that there could be any joy in riding to face an impossibly superior enemy with only sixty-four young men. Arn then made time to speak with both her and Alde on the last evening before his departure. It was not his intention to engage in a real battle, he assured both of them. But for some inexplicable reason the Danes had chosen to come in the wintertime, and that made their heavy horses even slower. Danish riders would never be able to catch any Forsvikers; it would be a matter of flying past them at a safe distance. But it was necessary to obtain information about their intentions, their weapons, and their numbers.

What he told Cecilia and Alde was undoubtedly true, but it was far from the whole story.

Arn and his men got their first view of the enemy south of Skara. It was a few weeks before Christmas; the fields were snow-covered, but it was not yet really cold. The Forsvikers hadn't needed to put on the bulky garb that they wore in the winter, with thick layers of felt over all the steel and iron. They rode annoyingly close to the Danish forces, moving in the opposite direction, at first partly to count the number of men, partly to see where they could do their enemy the most damage. Now and then the Danes sent a group of heavy riders with lances toward them, but they easily rode out of range. They saw that King Sverker and Archbishop Valerius were situated in the middle of the army, surrounded by a strong force carrying many banners. Arn decided that an attack on the king himself would not be worthwhile. Their own losses would be too great, and they couldn't be certain of killing the king. In addition, most of Arn's young men had never been in battle; they needed to experience a few victories in several lesser assaults before he could order them to put their lives at risk.

But an hour's ride along the convoy he found easier targets.

There most of the Danes' provisions and fodder for the horses were being hauled on sluggish ox-carts through the mire created by all the riders up ahead. It would have been easy to ride up to the draft animals and kill enough of them, while also setting fire to the fodder, so that the enemy army would have been significantly delayed.

But there was no need to make haste with such action, and besides, now would be a good time to teach the young men more about war in general. Arn had no doubt that on the small scale, in terms of protecting their own lives and limbs, he could rely on the Forsvikers. Without releasing a single arrow or making any attempt to attack even if only to instill fear, Arn and his riders withdrew for the night to a village that was far enough away from the Danish army. They treated the villagers with consideration, taking only what they needed for an evening meal. Nor did they strike or harm anyone who complained.

Arn spent the evening and much of the night describing how they would destroy the Danes' provisions. Yet there was not much point to such action now because the enemy convoy had the city of Skara ahead. If the army arrived there starving, angry, and without fodder for their horses it would not bode well for those who lived in Skara. But as things now stood, it was uncertain what Sverker and his Danes intended to do after Skara. Arn speculated that the reason they had arrived in the winter was that they planned to reach Lake Vättern when it was frozen over so as to reclaim for Sverker the royal castle of Näs. That would not be much of an achievement, but kings often had a tendency to think like children. If Sverker once more occupied Näs, he would again feel like the king. But how was he going to provide for such a large Danish army at Visingsö in the middle of the lake? And if it wasn't possible to find supplies for them there, what was the next step?

Arn laughed and seemed in high spirits, and this wasn't just because he wanted to infuse courage into his young and inexperienced warriors. He understood full well what it felt like for a small force of sixty-four men to ride past an army that was three hundred times as large. But on the following day they would gain more self-confidence.

After a long and good night's sleep, since the days were short at this time of the year, Arn told his men that they would now be going into battle. Not against oxen and supply carts but against the best of the Danish horsemen, who were no doubt those riding in the lead. The reason for this was simple. They were going to teach the Danes that whoever pursued the faster enemy would not come back alive.

The first time they carried out this simple plan, everything went as expected.

Arn took only one squadron, riding toward the front of the enemy army where many banners could be seen and where there was a large contingent of heavy cavalry. At first the Danes couldn't believe their eyes when they saw a mere sixteen men come riding at a slant toward their vanguard, getting closer and closer. Finally they were so near that the horsemen could shout jeers at each other. Then Arn pulled his bow from his back, calmly strung it, and placed his quiver at his side, as if he was planning to stay for a long time. Then he nocked an arrow and took aim at the foremost of the banner carriers, who raised his shield at once. Arn abruptly changed his aim and felled a man much farther back who was sitting there gaping in surprise rather than bothering to protect himself. Only then did all of the Danes raise their shields, and furious commands resounded over the entire advance group with fifty heavy riders gathered to stage a broad attack. Arn laughed loudly and told his sixteen men to nock their arrows.

Naturally that was too much for the Danes, who immediately launched an attack with lowered lances and the snow spraying

out from the front hooves of their heavy horses. Almost indo-
lently the sixteen Folkungs and Arn turned their horses and
headed for the nearest grove of trees with their pursuers only a
few lance-lengths behind, a distance they were careful to maintain.

From the Danish army loud, triumphant laughter arose as the
soldiers saw what a sorry spectacle the enemy made, chased away
into the woods.

But not a single Danish rider returned, because among the
trees they had encountered three squadrons of light riders who
approached at close range and then shot their arrows, finishing
off any survivors with their swords.

This sort of cunning wouldn't work on a second attempt since
the Danes didn't dare pursue the chase after the taunting and
fleeing enemy. But by now the Danish army had already been delayed because of the loss of some of their heavy riders, since such
horsemen were often highborn men and they had to be tended
to after death, unlike the bodies of ordinary foot soldiers. The
Danes were now hungry for revenge, of course, but since they
were traveling with riders in the vanguard because of the deep
snow, they had no foot soldiers up front with bows. And their
horses could not keep up with the lighter and faster steeds of the
Forsvikers.

The next day Arn rode close to the head of the Danish army
with all sixty-four of his men. He had chosen a spot where the
landscape opened up just beyond two high hills, and there was an
expansive view in all directions, so the Danes wouldn't suspect
an ambush.

The Forsvikers quietly approached, moving in so close that
they were certain of being able to strike home with their arrows.
But this time they aimed not at the iron-clad horsemen or their
shields but at their horses. Every horse that was hit was as good

as dead, and that meant a horseman on foot, especially if the arrow struck the horse's belly. The heavy snowfall had prompted the Danes to ride without chain mail for their horses.

Once again the Forsvikers' attack enraged the Danes, who lined up a hundred horsemen with lances to stage a counterattack.

The Forsvikers now seemed to be frightened and hesitant, and they turned around to flee; with that, the Danish riders attacked at once. And so they rode out into the snow, getting farther and farther away from the rest of the Danish army until the heavy pursuers began to falter, having used up most of their strength and that of their horses. Then Arn suddenly turned his fleeing forces and divided them into two groups, which surrounded the Danish riders and went on the attack, using arrows that pierced right through the chain mail. They managed to kill most of the horsemen, or to cause terrible wounds with their swords before they once again had to flee from the reinforcements sent by the army. But this time they didn't succeed in enticing their pursuers to their deaths.

A thaw set in, and the soft, knee-high snow was like a blessing for the Forsvikers but a curse for the Danish cavalry.

Over the following days the enemy grew more discriminating when it came to making a sortie against the Forsviker forces. Not much was accomplished by either side, but according to Arn, that was the whole intention.

The Danes stopped for a short time in Skara but did not carry out extensive plundering before they moved on toward the southeast. They didn't even bother to besiege the fortress of Axvalla. That was an important piece of information; they truly were headed for Lake Vättern and Näs. Along the way stood the castle of Lena. Despite his grumbling over the expense, Birger Brosa had indeed followed Arn's advice to have it fortified. The Danes would either take the castle or besiege it in order to secure the route to Näs. So the real battle would take place in the vicinity of Lena. There they would gather to see if it was possible to set a trap for the entire Danish army. Arn sent off four riders with messages for Arnäs and Bjälbo, summoning all Swedes and Goths to Lena.

Then it was time for the Forsviker cavalry to cause serious delays for the Danish army so that their own forces would have plenty of time to assemble. It helped that they would soon be several days' ride from Skara.

The first time the Forsvikers switched to the new way of attacking, they killed more than a hundred of the oxen and other draft animals; they also burned most of the fodder at the very back of the Danish column. Then they cut off the supply line to the rear, so that everyone who was sent on foot to Skara to fetch new animals disappeared, never to be seen again.

When heavy riders were dispatched back to protect the columns that were supposed to procure new supplies and draft animals, Arn immediately moved his men up toward the head of the army and began harassing the standard-bearers by riding close and shooting either the men or their horses. Now the Danes no longer dared send any of their forces to pursue these tormenters.

Every third day Arn sent one squadron home to Forsvik to tend to their minor wounds and tack, to sharpen their weapons and rest, while the next squadron went into service. The most important thing that the Forsvikers achieved during these weeks as they constantly plagued the Danes with their pinpricks was to delay the army and make them frantic with longing to use their superior force for a decisive battle. The cold grew worse every day, and that too ought to make the Danes more inclined to go into battle with all their troops or to proceed across the ice of Lake Vättern to Näs.

The nights were becoming unbearable for them, and the snow meant that the enemy could approach in silence, even on horseback. Anyone who emerged from his tent at night to stand by the fire would certainly have the blessing of warmth, but he was also blinded by the blaze and couldn't see where the arrows were suddenly coming from. Every night the winter-clad Forsvikers crept up close with their bows.

When the Danes were within a day's ride from the castle at Lena, their blue-clad tormenters suddenly disappeared, but the tracks in the snow clearly led toward the castle, which King Sverker and his men knew well. It looked as if the Swedes and Goths were finally preparing to fight like honorable men.

And such was truly the case. At Lena the entire Swedish army had assembled, consisting of three thousand men on foot, along with all of the Folkung riders.

But of even greater importance was the fact that from every Folkung estate thralls and stable hands, peasants, caretakers and smiths had arrived in great numbers; even some house thralls had come. Most brought their own longbows with them and five arrows. But anyone who needed a new string or even a new bow or arrows was well supplied. More than three thousand of these lowborn archers had gathered at Lena.

The Forsviker cavalry was one hundred and fifty strong; a third of them were heavy riders, the rest were light. Two hundred crossbowmen from Arnäs and Bjälbo and other Folkung estates were also there, as were a hundred men with long horse lances and steel-clad horse shields.

As the Danish army approached Lena, the Folkungs, the Swedes, and the few Eriks who had managed to get past the Danes, took up position in the valley at the foot of Högstenaberget. In the vanguard stood the heavy riders, mostly to tempt the Danes into what appeared to be an easy assault. Behind them stood the light cavalry, and behind them a defensive wall of shields and long horse lances. Only a few paces in back of the line of shields stood the two hundred crossbowmen, and then the entire roaring and battle-ready army of Upplanders and other wild Swedes who were the foot soldiers.

At the very rear were the more than three thousand longbow archers. They were the key to either victory or defeat.

Arn had brought with him King Erik and two squadrons of his own horsemen to ride out to the Danes and induce them to turn in the right direction. With King Erik rode his standard-bearer, and the three golden crowns against a blue background could be seen from far away on that clear and cold winter day. It was a signal to the Danes that they were now confronting the real enemy for a decisive battle.

Arn and the king and their retinue didn't need to show themselves to the Danish army for very long before the Danes began doing what they had hoped. The troops came to halt high up in the valley in order to have a downward slope for their first overwhelming attack with the heavy cavalry. They must have been very pleased when they found that the enemy didn't seem to realize what a disadvantage it was to offer the possibility for such a descent. Now the site of the battle had been determined, but it would take several hours before the Danes established order among their forces.

Arn rode with King Erik back to their own army. Together they made the rounds so as to instill courage in their men, since they could all see what a mighty force had begun to rally up on the slope. Time after time Arn and the king tried to impress upon all their men that if everyone did as they were ordered, they'd be able to win victory faster than anyone could guess. But no one should have any doubts or lose their courage, since that was not only a great sin but also halfway to defeat.

To the line of big, rectangular horse shields and lances, they said that each man must stand firm. If a single man started running when the ground shook with horses thundering forward, a gap would appear that could be seen from far away by the attacking riders; that was exactly what they were waiting for in order to get through. But if everyone stood his ground, they would not get through; it was as simple as that.

To the crossbowmen they said time and again that they should take up position only when the enemies were so close that they could see the whites of their eyes. Then, and only then, should they take aim and shoot. Anyone who shot without taking aim would merely lose a bolt, but if everyone did as ordered, more than a hundred riders would fall before the lances, blocking the way for all the riders coming behind them, if any actually came.

But it was difficult to talk any sense into the Swedish army. These savage men looked more as if they were shaking with impatience, wanting to rush out onto the battlefield as fast as possible and get themselves killed.

On the other hand, there were important words to say to the longbow archers who stood at the very back and represented the largest force in the army. Arn explained that they and no one else would secure the victory. If every man did as he had practiced, then the victory was theirs. Otherwise, they would all die together here at Lena.

After King Erik and Arn had spoken with so many longbow archers that their mouths were dry, they noticed that a commotion had started up among the Danish troops, as if they were preparing to attack. Silence fell over the battlefield, and everyone prayed to God and the saints that they might see victory and survive. The Danes already sensed victory within their grasp, since from their viewpoint high on the slope, they could see that the enemy they were about to fight had an army only a third the size of their own, and less than a third as many riders.

The faces of the Goths, Eriks, and Folkungs turned pale, while the Swedes merely seemed even more impatient to get started.

Arn rode over to the longbow archers and ordered one of the

best archers, whom he knew from the village outside Arnäs, to shoot an arrow with red fletches to the height and in the direction that all had been ordered to shoot.

One lone arrow soon sailed high and far over the battlefield, landing close to the mid-point between the two armies. Coarse laughter was heard from the Danes up there; they seemed to think that some frightened archer had lost his wits. But they had never encountered longbow archers. Arn breathed a sigh of relief and said his last prayers.

When the heavy Danish riders set off, the mighty sound was heard of thousands upon thousands of horses' hooves pounding through the snow. Arn thought that it would have been much worse and more terrifying if the ground had been hard and free of snow; then the roar would have been deafening. But even without the rumble of attacking heavy riders, it was a mighty wall of death and steel that now came pouring down the slope.

Arn sat on his horse near a small hill across from the longbow archers. He ordered them to nock their first arrow and aim as they'd been taught, which was halfway between heaven and earth. There was a great rustling as three thousand bows were pulled taut.

The clang of weapons and the thunder of horses' hooves in the snow came closer, but the snow also sprayed up in an ever-growing white cloud, which was an advantage that Arn only now perceived. He cast a stern glance at the distant arrow with the red feathers, and the wall of horsemen in the snowstorm as they approached it. Then he raised his hand and shouted at the top of his lungs that everyone should wait . . . and wait . . . and wait still more!

"Nowwww!" he bellowed as loudly as he could, and dropped his right hand.

And then the battlefield grew dark with a great black cloud that at first rose up and then sank toward the attacking riders;

there was a whistling and roaring in the air, as if a thousand cranes had lifted off at once.

When the first salvo of arrows struck the storming Danish army, it was as if God's iron fist had dealt them a blow from above. Hundreds of horses fell, shrieking and kicking in the great cloud of snow that blinded those who came behind them, causing many who weren't even struck by arrows to fall to the ground. By then the next black cloud of arrows was already on its way.

A thin line of the vanguard Danish riders had passed through the deadly rain of arrows and continued forward with undiminished speed. They never realized that they were now only a small part of their own cavalry force.

Arn had ordered the third and last salvo of longbow arrows against the foot soldiers, who came running behind their own horsemen. Then he had ridden forward to the crossbowmen and commanded all the heavy and light riders in front of them to move to the sides to get out of the way.

He positioned his horse in the midst of the crossbowmen and shouted both to them and to the men with the horse lances that victory was now very close at hand if they would just wait until the right moment. Then he ordered the crossbowmen to stand up and aim as he raised his hand.

At a distance of twenty paces, almost all of the last Danish riders, numbering now barely a hundred, fell to the ground. A few came sliding through the snow all the way up to the lances and were quickly speared.

Now the untouched Folkung cavalry could go on the attack; the riders moved like a plow through the devastated Danish army and soon reached the foot soldiers, who turned to flee.

Arn didn't even need to give the Swedes a command before they were on their way forward amidst wild war cries, swinging their axes overhead. Arn had to swiftly move out of the way in order not to be mowed down by the Swedes. He rode over to join

King Erik, who had taken up position with a squadron of light Forsvikers on a hill with a view of the battlefield.

"May God grant us victory on this day!" shouted King Erik as Arn rode up alongside.

"He has already done so," replied Arn. "But Sverker and his Danes up there don't know it yet, because they probably can't see through the clouds of snow."

Arn called his light riders back from the battlefield since they were no longer needed among all the Swedes, who were assiduously hacking at the enemy with their axes. Arn moved the riders into position near the place where he and King Erik were watching the battle, which was now more slaughter than war. The Swedish warriors were advancing fiercely, having now been thrown into the type of battle that suited them, with the enemy on foot and most of them already dead or wounded, and in slushy snow.

It was time to seize the victory. Arn took King Erik and his standard and all the light Forsvikers up past the hill where the Danes had stood when they launched their attack. There he divided his forces into two groups and commanded the rider Oddvar and the rider Emund Jonsson to take their men and encircle the royal Danish standard-bearers that were visible some distance away, and cut off any retreat.

King Sverker and his men didn't seem to have fully grasped what had happened. For when Arn and King Erik and their standard-bearer with both the three crowns and the Folkung lion slowly approached, the Danes couldn't believe their eyes. And when they started getting uneasy and cast a glance behind them, they saw that they were surrounded.

The victors took their time, advancing slowly toward King Sverker and his men, among whom they recognized Archbishop Valerius and the marshal Ebbe Sunesson and several more from Näs.

When the circle of Folkung riders closed ranks around Sverker and his men, the Danes were still scanning the battlefield looking for reinforcements. From down there the shrieks of dying men and horses could still be heard. King Erik and Arn approached until they were within two lance-lengths before they stopped. King Erik was the first to speak. His voice was calm and filled with great dignity.

"Now, Sverker, this war is over," he began. "You are at the mercy of my favor or disfavor, and I hold your life in my hands like a baby bird. The same is true of the men who are with you. All the others are dead or will be soon; that is what you are hearing from down below. Tell me what you would have done if you were in my position now."

"He who kills a king will be excommunicated," replied King Sverker, his mouth dry.

"So you think that you have God on your side?" replied King Erik with an odd smile. "Then He has shown you His mercy in a very strange manner today. You came to us in cowardice with a foreign army, and God rewarded you as you deserved. But now I will tell you what I have decided, and God knows that I have thought a good deal over what I should do when this moment arrived. Your father killed my paternal grandfather. My father then killed your father. Let it end there. Give me the crown that you bear on your helmet of your own free will. Go back to Denmark and never return to our realm. Take your men and your archbishop with you, except for Ebbe Sunesson, for he has a debt to pay. The next time I will not spare your life. This I now swear before all men and before God."

It was not a difficult decision for King Sverker to make. With only a moment's hesitation, he took the crown from his helmet, rode forward to Erik, and handed it to him.

But the marshal Ebbe Sunesson, who realized that now his life had little value, demanded in a loud voice and displaying no fear that he should be allowed to defend himself in a duel, preferably against the cowardly Folkung who hadn't dared to fight him; the one whose brother he had already humbled.

King Erik and the Folkungs were all surprised when they understood that it was of Arn Magnusson the Danish marshal was speaking. They exchanged uncertain glances, as if they couldn't have heard correctly.

"It's true," said Arn, "that I have previously refused to kill you as revenge because you murdered my brother for the sake of your own amusement. I had sworn an oath of loyalty to Sverker, but I have now been released from that vow. I thank God for choosing me to give you the reward that you deserve."

With these words Arn rode off to the side and drew his sword. Then he bowed his head in prayer, which looked more like a prayer of thanksgiving than a plea for his own life.

Ebbe Sunesson was one of the few men present who had no idea of the reputation of the combatant he had chosen for the duel. With a triumphant expression he now drew his sword and galloped toward Arn. A moment later his head fell onto the snow.

Sverker Karlsson, his archbishop Valerius, and a few other men went back to Denmark. They were among the twenty-four who returned. The army that Valdemar the Victor had sent against the Swedes and Goths had been more than twelve thousand strong. The killing and plundering at Lena went on all night in the blaze of fires and continued into the next day.

King Erik, who now withdrew for the winter to his castle at Näs, had received the crown from Sverker's own hand. Erik had been wise to handle the matter in this way, because not even the Holy Roman Church could contest that he was truly the new king of the Swedes and Goths.

But he had also spared Sverker Karlsson's life, in spite of the fact that he easily could have killed him. That was a noble act, worthy of a king. But not a wise decision, as circumstances would show a few years later.

✠

The victory at Lena was the greatest in man's memory in the North, and it was given many heroes. For the Eriks, most of whom had found themselves cut off in the southern part of Western Götaland and unable get to Lena, the victory belonged without a doubt to King Erik alone. He had withstood a difficult trial and proved himself worthy of the king's crown.

In the view of most of the Folkungs, it was the new Folkung cavalry that had been decisive. And if anyone objected that it was mostly the longbow archers who had crushed the Danes, every Folkung would reply that in that case it was their own house servants, thralls, caretakers, and peasants who had done what their masters ordered them to do.

Yet the strangest explanation for the remarkable victory at Lena came from the Swedes. It was during this time in Svealand that the saga spread about how the god Odin, after long absence, had reappeared. Many Swedish warriors said they had seen Odin with their own eyes; he was wearing a blue mantle and riding his steed Sleipner to lead the Swedes out to the battlefield.

This blasphemous explanation about the pagan god Odin as sire of the victory galled all the bishops in the three lands. As if with one voice and from Östra Aros, Strängnäs, and Örebro, to Skara and Linköping the bishops preached that God the Father, in His inscrutable mercy, had granted this victory to the Swedes and Goths and King Erik. There was one good thing about this conviction so loudly proclaimed by the bishops; it meant that King Erik had triumphed with God's support and clearly demonstrated will. For this reason, the bishops all showed up to a man at the council meeting at Näs to assure everyone that Erik was now the incontestable king of the realm. But when he then asked them to set the crown on his head, they argued that such could be done only by the archbishop. And the one who would appoint a new archbishop to succeed Valerius would be the new Danish archbishop Andreas Sunesson in Lund. Yet no sign of good will could be expected from him; he was not only King Valdemar the Victor's man, but he was also the brother of the felled Danish commanders Ebbe, Lars, Jakob, and Peder. The only one of them to be given a Christian burial back in Denmark was Ebbe Sunesson, although he had to travel home missing his head.

The fact that Denmark was to appoint the archbishop for the Swedes and Goths was certainly unreasonable, and a better arrangement would no doubt be made after a letter was sent to the Holy Father in Rome. Yet it was not something that could be accomplished quickly.

Nevertheless, it was reassuring for the young king to have the bishops of the realm on his side from the very beginning. This newly established goodwill on the part of the bishops was also of benefit to the Folkungs because the clerics now stopped their surly resistance toward consecrating the church at Forshem to God's Grave. The church had been finished several years ago, but could not yet serve as the house of God. King Erik himself rode to Forshem to honor Arn Magnusson, his marshal and the one who commissioned this church, at the consecration.

The friendship between King Erik and Arn had grown even stronger. In Arn's eyes, Erik had quickly changed from a youth greedy for simple pleasures into a man of great solemnity and dignity. For Erik, who had now seen his marshal in a war against overwhelming enemy forces, there was no doubt who was the true architect of this victory. And he didn't hesitate to give full credit to Arn before the worldly members of his council, although in the presence of the bishops he found it wise to declare that the victory had been given to them by the hand of God.

Arn was not opposed to encouraging the bishops to talk of David versus Goliath, since every such more or less astute comparison from the prelates served to reinforce the idea that Erik had triumphed through God's will and was thereby entitled to wear the crown.

But in his own heart Arn had more doubts. Earlier in his life he had seen far too many apparently inexplicable victories or defeats to be genuinely convinced of God's intervention in every little human struggle on earth. In Arn's experience, it was foolish commands on one side of the conflict that usually spelled victory for the other side.

And the Danes had been foolish in more ways than one, as well as arrogant. They had seriously underestimated their enemy, and they had depended almost exclusively on heavy cavalry, even though they should have realized that they would encounter snow. Their greatest mistake was not anticipating the longbow archers, and thus they had forced their entire army to ride to its death all at once. So many serious misjudgments could end only in defeat.

Yet as the marshal of the realm, Arn's chief responsibility was to warn against pride. Such a great victory as occurred at Lena could never be repeated if the Danes decided to return. No doubt they wouldn't come back soon, since it would take time to replace such a large army; so many riders, horses, weapons, and armor had been lost.

After the Swedes had finished their plundering of the battlefield at Lena, which went on for two days, all the equipment, saddles, and arrows collected were transported on fifteen fully loaded ox-carts to Forsvik. The plundered goods were more than enough to outfit two hundred new heavy riders.

They also obtained important information from the conquered armor. The Danes had a new way of protecting themselves against arrows and swords. Their helmets were stronger and offered better protection for the eyes. And some of their chain mail was not made of linked rings but rather from whole steel plates, like the scales on a fish; not even the long needle-sharp arrow points could penetrate such armor.

This information created many new tasks for the Wachtian brothers, prompting them to replicate the best of the Danish armor and also to think up new weapons that might work better than those they already had. One new weapon was the long war hammer, with a hammerhead on one side and a short, sharp pike on the other, which could puncture a hole in any type of helmet. Another weapon that they spent much time discussing with Arn was a light crossbow for riders that required only one hand for shooting arrows. It took time to develop this weapon, since it had to combine seemingly incompatible traits. It had to be strong enough to pierce steel plates and yet light enough to shoot with one hand from horseback, since the rider's other hand had to hold the reins and his shield.

After much effort the Wachtian brothers finally produced a weapon that would allow a light rider to move in close to a heavy enemy and slay him with a single, infallible shot.

The marshal of a realm needed to prepare for the worst. That was Arn's firm conviction, and he was quick to say so whenever given the opportunity. Other councilors and kinsmen seemed convinced that they were now living in favorable times and with eternal peace, since the victory at Lena had been so monumental.

The worst that might happen would be for the Danes to return with just as many heavy riders in the summer; this time they would not underestimate the enemy or be enticed into the sun-dimming cloud of arrows shot by the longbow archers.

The Danes' greatest weapon was the number of heavily armored horsemen. An attack launched by a large group of such riders would strike like an iron fist through any army, provided they were sent into battle at the proper moment.

The lack of heavy riders was the greatest weakness of the Goths, but it was worse for the Swedes. This simple but grim conclusion brought about a thorough change in the exercises carried out at Forsvik during the next few years. All adult Folkung men were sent there to obtain new armor, both for themselves and their horses. Then they had to practice in the fields around Forsvik that had been turned into an arena, where no grass grew any longer. Arn's own son, Magnus Månesköld, was among the many men who arrived to learn the methods required for this new way of waging war.

It was of course easier to train heavy riders. They needed to do little more than ride close together with lowered lance, but without hesitation when the battle started. The trick was not to send them into the wrong situation. For this reason Arn thought the young riders at Forsvik should take responsibility for them. But the foremost of the Folkungs thought this was an unreasonable demand. Men like Magnus Månesköld and Folke jarl couldn't possibly take orders from youths young enough to be their own sons. Such an arrangement would never have worked in the lands of the Goths or the Swedes.

In the new knights' hall at Forsvik, Arn had requested that a big box of sand be brought in. There he gathered the young knights and squadron commanders a couple of times each week, shaping in the sand hills and valleys, using pinecones and spruce cones to represent cavalry or phalanxes of foot soldiers. By this simple device he tried to teach them what he knew of what had happened on the battlefield. But only the young men wanted to learn such things; all of the older Folkungs believed far more in their own courage and that of their kinsmen rather than in anything they could learn from pinecones.

Another way to prepare for the war that no one thought would come, not even Arn, was to establish new Forsvik schools. Sir Sigfrid Erlingsson had inherited his own estate on Kinnekulle, and there he began to train young men, as well as at least a hundred longbow archers from among the peasants and thralls. Sir Bengt Elinsson now had two estates, since he had inherited Ymseborg from his parents and Älgarås from his maternal grandfather. At Ymseborg he created his own school, and he sold Älgarås to Arn and Eskil. They in turn gave the estate to Sir Sune Folkesson, provided he took it upon himself to train at least three squadrons of light riders and two hundred longbow archers. Forsvik itself was becoming more and more a school and weapons smithy for heavy cavalry.

It was particularly hard for Sune Folkesson to part with Arn and Cecilia. In confidence he told them the whole story of the great love between himself and King Sverker's daughter Helena, how their love could have cost them both their heads, and how he had sworn that one day he would take a squadron of Folkungs to fetch Helena from Vreta cloister. There she still sat, withering away, even though her father had fled with his tail between his legs to Denmark.

Cecilia and Arn were probably the two people in all of Western Götaland who would be most moved by such a tale. They had never betrayed their love for each other, nor had they ever lost hope, and their virtue had been rewarded.

Yet Arn responded with great harshness toward Sune's hopes of gaining permission to ride at once to Vreta.

Abducting a maiden from a convent, and that was what it would be called no matter now willingly Helena came running, would provoke all of the bishops. And such internal strife was not something that the fragile new realm could tolerate. As long as Sverker, the former king, was still alive, he was the only one who could give her hand in marriage; that was a right that no one could take from him. And as long as that was so, taking Helena in such a fashion would be considered stealing her from the cloister. It didn't matter how much the two young lovers wished to think otherwise.

Arn could see only one possibility for Sune, and that would be a great misfortune for others at the same time. If Sverker came back with another Danish army, if King Valdemar the Victor truly hadn't had enough of seeing his men obliterated, then taking Helena from the cloister would be a different matter. Because then King Sverker would be dead.

Even Cecilia, who felt great sympathy for the love of these young people, could do nothing but dread what her husband had just described. Stealing a maiden from a cloister was a heinous deed and, in addition to upsetting all the bishops, it was an unforgivable sin.

Hence there was only one man in the realm who hoped for another big war, and that was the dejected Sir Sune, who now set off for Älgarås to start his life as a teacher of warriors on his own estate. Arn sent with him all the Saracen builders who still remained in order to build stone walls where the wooden walls, now burned, had once stood.

✠

On the mild spring day when Alde Arnsdotter turned seventeen, a feast bigger than any in a long time was held at Forsvik. Since there were fewer young noblemen in training than in previous years, there was room for all the Christians and even people of other faiths in the great hall. A joyous mood spread, as if everyone at Forsvik were of the same clan, even though they might not all speak the same tongue. Forsvik was not only the biggest weapons manufacturer in the realm but also a place where much wealth was created, and all the Forsvikers contributed to this endeavor. Smiths, glassmasters and coppersmiths, feltmakers and saddlemakers, hunters and millers all considered themselves just as much Forsvikers as the young noblemen or their teachers. Alde was also much loved by everyone because of her merry laugh and the interest that she showed in everyone's particular skill.

Both she and young Birger Magnusson had now spent seven years studying with Brother Joseph; they had learned everything they could from him, and he had now started over with a small group of Christian children. Alde would one day inherit Forsvik, and the skills that she would need then could not be taught by Brother Joseph. Instead, Cecilia had started teaching her daughter the secrets of keeping account books, which were both the heart and soul of all the wealth that was created with one's own hands and through the work of others. So that Alde might better understand what this accounting could reveal, she accompanied her mother to speak with all the workers and tried to find out about even the smallest details of every task.

For Birger Magnusson, his time with Brother Joseph was also over, and he was now in his third year of training with the young noblemen, with Sigurd in command. Since he was Arn's grandson, Birger was favored with something not bestowed on ordinary young noblemen. Arn's *lectionis* in the knights' hall regarding battlefield logistics was really only intended for the Forsvikers who had been knighted or who commanded a squadron. But from now on, Birger was invited to join these sessions.

Arn had more time for both the young people than ever before at Forsvik. His brother Gure took care of everything that had to do with the workshops and construction; Cecilia supervised all the trade by ship; and the young knights and commanders trained the new Folkung youths with regard to sword, lance, and horse. Arn had gained more time in his daily life, or at least a new vision of how he could devote more hours to something that he had neglected for too long. Part of this had to do with his own daughter Alde and her cousin, Birger.

Arn had no doubt that Brother Joseph had taught them well the two most important languages of Latin and Frankish, for he was able to speak with them as easily in either of those tongues as in their own language. Nor did he doubt that Brother Joseph had pounded into their heads philosophy and logic, grammar and the Holy Scriptures.

But there was something else that a Cistercian, no matter how God-fearing and learned, could not know, something that was not found in books and could only be learned on the battlefield or at royal council meetings and from the mightiest men of the church. There was no word to describe this type of knowledge, but Arn called it learning about power. He began giving private *lectionis* for Alde and Birger on this topic.

According to Arn, the most important thing to learn about power was to understand that it could be both evil and good, and that only a well-trained eye could distinguish one from the other. Power could rot or wither just like the roses that grew in great abundance around the house where he and Cecilia lived, as well as in the gardens down by the lake. Cecilia's gentle hands tended to these beloved roses from Varnhem, making use of both shears and water.

And it was not difficult to understand what the water of life was: it was God's Word, the pure and unselfish belief that could make power grow as a force for good.

Strength was power, of course; many iron-clad knights represented strength, and hence power. But a God-fearing person had to use strength correctly, for as Paul said in the epistle to the Romans:

"We who are strong are obliged to help the weak with their burdens, and should not think of ourselves. Each of us must think of his neighbor, of what is good and edifying."

These words of God were of course about the water of life,

and it was in accordance with these words that they tried to live and build at Forsvik.

The most difficult thing to understand was how much the clear water of faith could muddy the minds of people, which was what had happened in the Holy Land. Yet it was necessary to try to see the direction in which this folly of faith was headed before it was too late. And that was only possible by using reason. No bishop's miter was greater than reason.

Arn admitted that if he had said such things during the time that he was a knight in the Templar Order of God and the Holy Virgin, his mantle would have been torn from him, and he would have been sentenced to a lengthy penance. For many of the faith's highest guardians, there was no difference between faith and reason, since faith was everything, great and indivisible, while reason was merely the vanity or conceit of a single person. But God must have wished for human beings, His children, to learn a great and important lesson from the loss of His Grave and the Holy Land. What other intention could there be in such a harsh punishment?

And what they had learned was that conscience was power's bridle. Power without conscience was doomed to lapse into evil.

But power was also trivial and as exhausting and monotonous as the daily toil of a farmer in his field. On several occasions Arn took Alde and Birger along to the king's council meetings at Näs. There they were allowed to sit as quiet as mice behind Arn and Eskil, who had now reclaimed his seat on the council. Everything that they saw and heard was then discussed for days back home at Forsvik. Power was also the ability to unite the conflicting wishes of various individuals, which was an especially important trait in a king. King Erik often found that the council's worldly members had an entirely different view of how to manage the realm than the bishops did, who were less interested in building fortresses, the cost of new cavalry, or Danish taxes. They preferred to talk about gold and silver for the church or possibly about new crusades to the lands of the east that were still being plundered. The king's power was not to speak in a loud voice, slam his fist on the table, and turn red in the face. It was to coax all the council members, worldly as well as ecclesiastical, to reach a mutual decision; perhaps no one would be entirely satisfied with it, but neither would anyone be completely dissatisfied. When King Erik used this method to accomplish what he had intended, though never at the cost of discord in the council, he showed that there was another side to power. Blessed Birger Brosa had been the strongest advocate of this type of power among all the Folkungs.

Yet another side of power was that used most effectively by Eskil, Alde's paternal uncle and the brother of Birger's paternal grandfather, Arn. Power as strong as that of the sword could be found in trading transactions between various countries and in the flow of wealth that such trade set in motion.

Pure faith guided by conscience, the sword, and gold were the three pillars upon which power rested. Many men felt themselves called to serve one of these aspects of the trinity of power, but few were able to master all three. Yet kings had to possess great knowledge of everything pertaining to this trinity of power, otherwise they would be deposed like King Sverker.

Cecilia was not convinced that these types of conversations were what her daughter needed most, and deep in her heart she thought that it was a great risk, at a place like Forsvik, for a young woman to be raised like a man. The manner in which Alde rode could not described as befitting a fair maiden's hand, even though she'd been given one of the most gentle of the Arabian fillies on her twelfth birthday. But it had proved impossible to keep her away from the horses.

Since Cecilia was herself an excellent rider, she had at first tried to keep Arn and the young noblemen away from Alde's horseback lessons, choosing to teach her daughter on her own. But she couldn't be everywhere at once, and the accounts took much of her time each day. Soon she saw Alde racing with Birger and other young men. It did little good for Cecilia to fret or worry about the matter.

And when the great game drive of the autumn arrived with the first snow for tracking, Alde was one of the hunters positioned at the pass while all of Forsvik's riders set off in a long horseshoe-shaped loop to drive in the wild game. Already during her second year, Alde shot her first wild boar.

Yet this time was like the harvest of her life, Cecilia realized. Her hair had turned gray, as had Arn's, and now they were both closer to death than to birth. But it was glorious to be alive when everything was going so well for them, and no evil or danger was in sight, even far in the distance where the heaven and the earth met.

She would remember even the last Christmas before the war as a time of calm and confidence.

They had celebrated the Christmas ale at Arnäs in the big, warm stone hall with log fires; never had life seemed so good. At the dawn church service on Christmas Day at Forshem, Arn could now without embarrassment show his pride at what he had commissioned to be built, even the fact that his own image was depicted above the church door as the one handing the keys of the church to God. Since it had become easier to talk with the bishops after the victory at Lena, many of them had assured Arn that such an image represented neither a sin nor pride. On the contrary, it offered a good example to everyone. For what better deed than to pay for such a beautiful church and please God by consecrating it to His Grave?

The image of the grave was located in the center aisle, in front of the altar, and it had been adorned with Master Marcellus's best work. At this last Christmas service before the war, Arn and

Cecilia sang the hymns for the mass alone, she providing the first voice, he the second. Their voices may not have been as pure as before, but everyone thought that they could see God's angels standing before them when they heard their song.

✠

The Danes came in the middle of summer in 1210, two and a half peaceful years after the victory at Lena. Sverker Karlsson was determined to take back his crown, and unfortunately he had persuaded King Valdemar the Victor to give him a new army, which was almost as big as the one wiped out during the winter war.

At first word of the enemy's arrival in the realm, Arn headed south from Forsvik with three squadrons of light riders to procure information; at the same time requests for help were sent to both Svealand and Norway.

This time it would not go as easily, Arn realized on the second day as he and his horsemen rode along the length of the Danish army. And when he came to the middle where Sverker Karlsson and his bishop Valerius were riding, his heart clenched in pure, cold terror; he hadn't had that feeling since his first years in the Holy Land. Around Sverker Karlsson rode almost a hundred men in the uniform of the Hospitallers, their red shields and surcoats marked with the white cross.

What would have induced the Hospitallers to ally themselves with Sverker Karlsson or with King Valdemar the Victor? It was not easy to understand, but one thing was sure: a hundred Hospitaller knights was almost the equivalent of a hundred Templar knights, and such a force would have been feared by Saladin himself. No one in the North would be able to defeat it.

Like a Templar knight, each Hospitaller knight would be comparable to ten Danes or five Forsvikers. What astonished Arn the most, once he'd reconciled himself to having to fight against the best knights in the world, was that they were not riding at the head as they normally did. That was how it had always been in the Holy Land. The Hospitallers rode in the vanguard and the Templars took the rear, because these two locations were the most exposed for an army on the march. But here the Hospitallers were riding in the middle, leaving both the supply train in the rear and the Danish knights furthest forward in danger of attack by light cavalry. Arn guessed that the Danes had decided that the protection of Sverker Karlsson's life was most important in this war. Hence they would rather take losses in the front and rear than risk the life of their pretender to the crown.

This time the Danish army was headed for Falköping, as if they intended to return to Lena to avenge their previous defeat. Because it was the middle of summer and the harvest had not yet been brought in, it was not grain but meat and draft animals that the enemy could plunder for their own provision. And even though the Danish army was least protected at the rear, where all the ox-carts with the supplies were traveling, it would not be wise to attack there until the enemy had passed Falköping.

More important would be to ride back and warn the inhabitants of Falköping and try to get them to hide all the oxen and livestock that otherwise would end up in the maws of the Danes. It took two days to get this done, but when the Danish army arrived, Falköping was emptied of everything that the enemy most would have wanted to plunder.

Arn was more cautious in his command than he had ever been before, and it was almost a week before he did anything but ride back and forth along the enemy's serpentine column of foot-soldiers and riders. He was awaiting reinforcements from both Bengt Elinsson and Sune Folkesson; when they arrived he not only had more light cavalry but also a squadron of heavy riders. Then he could not afford to wait any longer.

Together with Sir Bengt and Sir Sune he had quickly decided

on how the first attack should proceed. But it had to be launched at the right place so they could carry it out at high speed. It was a few more days before the Forsvikers found a high hill with sparse leafy forest where the Danish army would have to pass. There they took up position and waited.

By this time the Danes had become accustomed to seeing constantly in the distance the blue-clad light riders who never seemed to venture into battle. So the first attack did not come merely like lightning from a clear blue sky, but surprised them even more because of its great force. Three squadrons of light cavalry suddenly thundered down from a beech forest to the side and front of the head of the Danish army. As they approached the riders fanned out into a long row and rode in close, each man firing his crossbow and leaving behind a tumult of shrieking horses and Danes howling in pain. If they got close enough they aimed at the enemy's legs. If they struck home the enemy had one knight less and one more wounded man to drag along. If they missed then they usually killed a horse.

When the last of the light Forsvikers rushed by, the heavy cavalry came in from the side at high speed. Their own horsemen scarcely got away before the knight squadron with lances lowered crashed into the already heavily mangled Danish group in the forefront. Just as quickly as the Forsvikers attacked they were gone, and more than a hundred enemy lay dead or severely wounded.

Two days in a row they repeated essentially the same attack. When the Danes then moved up infantry with shields and bows to protect the front, nothing more happened up there. Instead the Forsvikers assaulted the rear of the army, killing almost all the draft animals and setting fire to large parts of the provisions. Then they dashed away before the knights wearing the white cross on the red field came to the rescue. Arn had strictly ordered his men to avoid any battle with these knights.

When the Danes improved their protection with infantry and archers both in front and in the rear, the attack came instead a third of the way along, where most of the infantry marched in close formation. Arn led the heavy cavalry straight through the Danish army and left a wide swath of fallen and wounded behind, wherever the light Forsvikers rode in with swords drawn.

The war continued in this manner for a week as the Danes slowly advanced toward the same region to the west of Lake Vättern as the previous time. It was hard to know what they now had in mind. In the winter they had the opportunity to cross the ice to Näs, but in the middle of summer? Arn guessed that they intended to entrench themselves at the fortress of Lena, or first take it and then wait for the winter and ice while they were already in place, instead of trudging all the way up from Denmark in the snow. So there was plenty of time, and the important thing was to take action wisely and with patience and not venture too early into a great battle.

Arn left the command of his cavalry forces to Bengt Elinsson and Sune Folkesson and rode up to Bjälbo, where the Swedes and the rest of the Folkungs and Eriks would gather. This time the Eriks had not been trapped in the south, but were able to travel north along the eastern shore of Lake Vättern. King Erik was with his kinsmen.

The war council that was held ended unhappily in Arn's opinion. Folke jarl, the leader of the Swedes and Folkungs in Eastern Götaland, wanted to engage the Danes as soon as possible; he wanted to have the war over before the harvest. King Erik made a protracted attempt to force through the decision that Arn wanted. He said they should wait as long as possible and let the Forsvikers keep hammering at the Danish army in the meantime. The invading force had already been reduced by a couple of hundred riders and was seriously delayed by the loss of so many draft animals and horses. The Danes were the ones in enemy territory, yet they were the ones who had the stronger army for the time being. And they had the most to gain from a pitched battle fought as early as before harvest time.

But the leader of the Swedes, Yngve the Judge, thought that this was the prattle of weak women and hardly worthy of a king from the clan of Saint Erik. Waiting a long time before a battle would enervate every strong man; better to show vigor and courage when the desire to fight was still fresh.

To Arn's disappointment, Folke jarl and Magnus Månesköld were both in favor of going to battle as soon as possible in order to save the harvest. Perhaps they had been struck by pride after the fortunate victory at Lena two and a half years before.

Not even Arn's objection that they should wait for reinforcements from the Norwegians—who this time had sent a message with a promise to come in force to help—would make the thick-headed Swedes show patience. As usual, they would rather die at once.

It was decided that the entire army would be shipped across Lake Vättern as soon as possible so they could head south and meet the Danes near the same blessed place as last time.

With a heavy heart Arn rode to Forsvik to summon every man who could sit on a horse with a weapon, or load carts with meat, weapons, and shields, or send messages that they should all gather near Lena.

To Cecilia's dismay he took with him the sixteen-year-old Birger Magnusson as his *confanonier*, the one who would ride next to Arn with their new emblem, a blue banner with the Folkung lion on one half and the three Erik crowns on the other. On his own shield Arn had ordered a red Templar cross to be painted next to the gold Folkung lion, just as Birger Brosa had had a Frankish lily and his son Magnus Månesköld had a half moon. To Cecilia he said that young Birger would be safer as his flag-bearer than anywhere else, for Arn's obligation this time was not to fight without fear, but to keep himself alive until the battle was won. There were far too many in the kingdom who were eager to die quickly.

For eight days Arn and his Forsvikers succeeded in delaying the final battle by constantly attacking the Danish army. But when there was less than a day's ride left before reaching the place south of Lena called Gestilren, where Swedes, Folkungs, and Eriks and the newly arrived Norwegians under Harald Øysteinsson awaited, Arn decided that there was no point in being cautious any longer. Now the Forsvikers needed to start attacking the group of Hospitaller knights in the center of the enemy army; they had assiduously avoided doing so until now. It could not be done without significant losses on their part, but the Forsvikers were the only ones who had the slightest chance against the Hospitallers. Now that the final battle was approaching, although foolishly early, every Forsviker had to do his part.

Arn had put himself at risk by issuing this command. Because how could he keep himself in safety when they were going into battle? He changed over to heavy armor with a new horse and decided that he would lead two squadrons straight in among the red surcoats after the light cavalry had attacked with their crossbows.

The Forsvikers were in a good position inside a forest on a hill, and they prayed as they waited. It was tense and quiet among them; the only sound was an occasional snort of a horse or clinking of a stirrup. Down below, looking through the beech trunks, they could see the Danish army struggling forward with the sun in their eyes, unconcerned and chatting as though they had gratefully relaxed after being left in peace for two whole days. For Arn had been very precise about selecting the right place and angle of sunlight for the attack.

He prayed to God for forgiveness because he was now going into battle against his own brothers the Hospitallers. He tried to excuse himself by saying that there was no other choice when they came as foes to seize his kingdom and kill those near and dear to him. For once Arn did not pray for his own life, since he found it presumptuous just before an attack on his dear Christian brothers. Then he sent off Sir Bengt and Sir Sune in a wide arc down the hill so that they would come in at an angle with the sun at their backs. He hoped they would kick up so much dust from the dry ground that the enemy would not know before it was too late what was happening on the other side as fast blue-clad riders descended upon the army.

Deus vult, he thought involuntarily as he raised his arm and ordered all the men forward at an easy trot. When they emerged from the woods they took up formation so that they rode close together without leaving the slightest gap, riding knee to knee. Then they sped up to a brisk trot.

Arn kept his eye on the last of the light Forsvikers riding down below who were causing an astonishing commotion and great fear among the Hospitallers. They did not even change formation into their normal defense.

Then he yelled his signal to charge, which was repeated by all those near him, and in the next moment they were all thundering forward with lances lowered straight in among the red-and-white-clad knights, who fell without resisting, hardly managing to defend themselves at all. The Forsvikers came out on the other side without having lost a single man, and when Arn saw this he turned his entire force and charged back through the red knights at full force. After that the chaos was too great to perform a third attack.

They were missing only two men when they regrouped by the waiting light squadrons. Arn observed the great confusion that prevailed in that part of the army which had seemed to him invincible. Almost a hundred Hospitaller knights had now been killed or wounded. What he saw was impossible, and his mind stood still for a moment. If the Forsvikers with a single attack had vanquished so many Hospitaller knights, it was a miracle from God. But he didn't believe that God would smite His own most faithful fighters with such a punishment, nor did he believe that God was constantly intervening in the petty struggles of humanity here on earth.

The Danes had employed a stratagem of war, he realized. They had falsely dressed themselves in red surcoats with a white cross so they would look like Hospitallers and thus sent fear into the hearts of the enemy. And they had almost succeeded.

Without a word Arn left his bloody lance with the closest man, took his *confanonier* Birger Magnusson with him, and rode down toward the Danes. He stopped an arrow-shot away and held up both hands in the sign that he wanted to parley. At once six men dressed in red and white rode up to him.

At first he addressed them politely in Frankish, of which they understood not a word. Then he switched to their own language and asked that the two bodies they had left behind be delivered to them, since they were dear kinsmen who had fallen. The Danes replied that this could not be done without something in return. Arn said that for his part he considered that honor demanded that both sides conduct such business without gain. Then the Danes relented. He asked them about their clothing, and they explained that it had been given to them by God during a crusade in the east, and that the white cross on the red field was now the emblem of the kingdom of Denmark.

⳨

At Gestilren there were several high hills, and there Arn had positioned both his heavy cavalry and his longbowmen, since he didn't believe it would work again to keep all his longbows at the same place; few Danes would ride into that trap for a second time. Down on the plain stood the entire Folkung heavy cavalry under the leadership of Folke jarl and Magnus Månesköld, and behind them all the crossbowmen, who in turn blocked the way of the already impatient Swedes. Farthest back stood five hundred Norwegian archers that Harald Øysteinsson had brought from his home region.

It was an absurd arrangement with everyone standing in everyone else's way. But as if by God's Providence it was now close to dusk, and the battle would have to wait until the next day. They had the night before them to alter things, in the event it was possible to make the Swedes and the stubborn highborn kinsmen understand that the positioning of the troops in the new type of warfare was more important than courage in the breast.

It was a long night with much argument and troublesome moving about in the dark. But the next morning at dawn, as the Danish army began to be visible through the mist, they were at least better arrayed than the night before.

Arn sat on his horse next to King Erik atop the highest hill along with the entire heavy section of the Forsviker cavalry and two squadrons of light cavalry to protect the king or remove him from danger. For Arn and his heavy riders there was only one task. They had to kill Sverker Karlsson.

Sune Folkesson, who was the one person in the world who most wanted to take the life of the former King Sverker, had requested to ride heavy and next to Arn, who was his master and teacher. Arn could not refuse him this request; he had attempted to put together this group containing only the best and the eldest of the Forsvikers.

From up on their hill they could look out over the entire battlefield. If the Danes sent off their cavalry toward the Eastern Goths and the Swedish foot-soldiers, this time they would have the black clouds of arrows from the longbows falling on them from each side. The Eastern Goths themselves would not attack before they saw a blue flag raised from the king's position. That was what they had finally agreed on.

The battle looked to be starting well. The Danes had discovered that this time too they were superior in the number of heavy horsemen. If they could break through the lines of the Eastern Goths, they would have a clear field to mow down all the foot-soldiers from Svealand.

The temptation was too much for them, and they made ready to attack in just that manner. Arn bowed his head and thanked God.

But when the Danes came in their attack, Folke jarl and Magnus Månesköld did not wait for the blue signal from up on the king's hill, but went on the attack themselves. So the first wave of Folkungs rode into the same rain of arrows as the enemy. The middle of the battlefield was transformed in a few moments to a mass of the dying and wounded. Then the Swedes could hold back no longer but began running toward the battle so that they arrived gasping and worn out. From up on his hill Arn and King Erik watched powerlessly as everything was about to slip out of their hands. There was a moment of salvation from Harald Øysteinsson and his Norwegians, who on the other side of the valley began to run up the line of battle to get into position so that they would be sure that their arrows fell only among the Danes.

The entire Forsviker light cavalry stood outside the battle, because the plan had been for them to attack to the rear of the Danes. But there they had a much too large and concerted force against them, since the Danish army had not advanced far enough into the trap. Arn sent riders to bring the Forsvikers as quickly as possible to the middle of the battle with the command to attack at will.

Everything was about to be lost. For in a protracted, unorganized battle, the side with the most men would win. Arn said farewell to King Erik, left Birger Magnusson with the double

Folkung and Erik flag on the hill with the king, and led all his heavy cavalry in a wide arc upward and back.

They reached a position where they could see where Sverker Karlsson and his massed standards were located, at a safe distance from the battle itself. There was no longer any reason to wait, and any hesitation would only serve to allow the enemy more time to prepare.

They rode out of the woods in disarray, but quickly fell into formation in a line as they trotted forward toward the heart of the enemy. They sped up to a full gallop and lowered their lances when they had only a few breaths left before they engaged. Next to Arn rode Sune Folkesson; they had both spied Sverker Karlsson's emblem, the black griffin with the golden crown, and headed straight for it.

The Forsvikers smashed straight through the first lines of Sverker's defenders, but by then most had lost both their speed and their lance, or had broken it and had to draw their swords or war hammers and start hacking their way toward Sverker. They made slower and slower progress, and several of them fell on the way.

But it was too late to turn back. Arn fought his way forward in a frenzy, discovering that his sword had grown heavier in recent years. Then he flung away his shield, shifted his sword to his left hand, and pulled out his long war hammer with his right. He killed four men with his war hammer and two with his sword before he reached Sverker. At the same time Sverker was parrying blows from Sune Folkesson, thus exposing the back of his neck to Arn, who swiftly slew him with his war hammer.

As Sverker fell from his horse there was a sudden silence among the Danes and Sverkers who were still in the saddle. The battle ceased, and everyone looked around. Half of all the Forsvikers had fallen, but still they were more numerous than the Danes, who were slowly rallying around Archbishop Valerius and his emblem.

Only now did Arn discover that he was bleeding in several places, and that he had a broken lance-tip sticking into his waist on the left side. He felt no pain but pulled out the lance and tossed it to the ground. Then he lowered his head for a moment to catch his breath. He calmly got down from his horse, went over to the dead Sverker and hacked off his head. Picking up a lance he slipped Sverker's head and shield with the royal emblem onto it, before with some effort remounting his horse. Sir Sune fetched Arn's shield and handed it to him. The Danes around Archbishop Valerius had stopped fighting, nor did Arn have any intention of continuing the battle with them.

With the remainder of his heavy Forsvikers he then rode slowly back to the battle itself, with Sverker's head and shield raised up before him on the lance. He stopped a short distance from the fighting and waited until the first shouts of victorious intoxication mixed with cries of horror began to stream toward him. The battle stopped at once.

During the stillness and silence that descended on the battlefield, Harald Øysteinsson's Norwegian archers were able to come closer, as did all the crossbowmen from the Folkung side who had not yet accomplished much. The light Forsviker cavalry which seemed to have suffered few losses quickly gathered into new battle groups of four or by squadron.

If the battle were now to continue, it would be just as bloody as the last time.

Then King Erik rode down from his hill, surrounded by Forsviker riders, and headed out to the middle of the battlefield. There he proclaimed in a loud voice that he would pardon all those who now surrendered.

It took only a few hours to reach an agreement. Some of

Sverker's kinsmen, those among his standard-bearers who were still alive, were given a royal letter of safe passage to take his body for burial to the Sverker clan's church at Alvastra cloister. The Danish army was permitted to stay long enough to bury their dead before they returned home. It was late July, and the heat made it essential to take care of all such tasks quickly.

The victory was great but very costly. Among the Folkungs who could not hold themselves back from attacking too early, almost all were dead, and half of them had fallen to arrows that came from their own side. Many Folkungs died at Gestilren, including Magnus Månesköld and Folke jarl. Only half of the Swedes who had come to the battle returned home.

But King Erik's realm was saved, and he decided that the new kingdom's emblem for all time and eternity would be the three Erik crowns and the Folkung lion.

⁎

Vreta cloister had been built on a hill out on the plain of Eastern Götaland, with an unobstructed view in all directions. Everyone at the cloister, including Abbess Cecilia Blanca, who was King Sverker's sister, the nuns, the lay sisters, the novices, and the twenty Sverker retainers who were sent as protection, knew that the war would be decided soon. More than one of the cloister's residents sought a reason to go up in the bell tower or onto the walls to gaze out over the wide plain where the grain which would soon be ripe was waving as far as the eye could see. Helena Sverkersdotter was the most anxious of them all, and she was the one who saw them first.

In the distance a group of riders was approaching with the blue mantles fluttering behind them like sails. There were sixteen men and they rode faster than anyone was used to seeing, despite coming from far away. For Vreta was truly no Folkung region.

The twenty Sverker retainers did what they had sworn to do, riding in full armor toward the sixteen Folkungs, and they were slain to the last man.

When the brief battle was over the Folkungs walked their horses toward the cloister, where all the gates had been closed and where many terrified eyes watched them from the walls.

A small side door was opened and out ran the maiden Helena toward the foremost of the Folkungs, whose horse stood a few paces in front of the others. Sir Sune was bleeding from several wounds, because he had come straight from Gestilren. But he felt absolutely no pain.

When the maiden Helena, gasping and stumbling, reached Sir Sune, he unfurled a blue mantle to wrap around her.

Then he lifted her up in the saddle before him and all the Folkungs rode off without haste, for it was a long way to Sir Sune's fortress of Älgarås.

There she bore him four daughters, and the song of Sune and Helena and the cloister abduction at Vreta lived on forever.

✚

Arn Magnusson's wound in the side which he had received from the lance of an unknown warrior was the death of him. If his physician friends Ibrahim and Yussuf had still been at Forsvik, where he was taken, he might have lived.

He died slowly, and Cecilia sat with him during the days and nights as his life ebbed away. Alde sat at his bedside almost as often.

What troubled him about death was not the pain, because he'd had much worse pain from other wounds. But he said that he would miss all the days of peace and quiet that now awaited everyone. He could have sat under Cecilia's apple trees and among her red and white roses with her hand in his and watched

Alde find her happiness, which she herself would be allowed to determine.

No Swedish judge's son would be chosen for her unless she wanted him. On that her mother and father were agreed without even needing to discuss the matter, since they were both unusual people who believed strongly in love.

Young Birger Magnusson came to say farewell to his grandfather who had taught him everything about war and power. His face was red with weeping at losing within such a short time both his father and grandfather, but there was more talk about the future than about sorrow. Arn made Birger promise never to rule the land from such a remote location as Näs, but to build a new city where Lake Mälaren ran out into the Eastern Sea. That would require most of all the support of the Swedes, and if no one else offered to help, then they could simply call the new kingdom Svea Rige, or Sweden.

Birger swore to do as his grandfather willed, and on his deathbed Arn handed him his sword and told him its secret and what the foreign symbols meant.

A thousand people followed the esteemed marshal to his grave at Varnhem. Only one of them had the right to wear a sword inside the church at the funeral mass, and that was the young Birger Magnusson. For his sword had been blessed, and it was the sword of a Templar knight.

In the cloister church at Varnhem, Birger swore before God to live as he had been taught by his beloved grandfather. He would build the new city and call the kingdom of the three lands by one name: Sverige.

History remembers him by the name of Birger jarl.

About the Author

Swedish-born journalist Jan Guillou is the creator of the two most successful Swedish works of fiction of all time—the Hamilton series and the Crusades Trilogy. His books have been translated into over twenty languages.